T0339072

Skookum Summer

SKOOKUM SUMMER

A Novel of the Pacific Northwest

Jack Hart

UNIVERSITY OF WASHINGTON PRESS

Seattle & London

University of Washington Press
PO Box 50096, Seattle, WA 98145, USA
www.washington.edu/uwpress

Library of Congress Control Number: 2013958277
ISBN 978-0-295-99347-8
The paper used in this publication is acid-free and meets the
minimum requirements of American National Standard for Information
Sciences—Permanence of Paper for Printed Library Materials,
ANSI Z39.48–1984.∞

Skookum Summer

1

The blacktop climbed and turned to gravel. The Takamak, running hard with spring runoff, hissed with whitewater. I turned onto South Fork Road, and the firs grew denser and taller, protected by the set-back rules that kept loggers two hundred feet from the banks. The canopy closed overhead, and the brush that choked second-growth timber disappeared. Open carpets of fir needles stretched back into an ancient forest where trees ran eight feet through the trunk.

A narrow dirt lane led to a small meadow next to the river. On the far side, the South Fork crashed against boulders, kicking spray into the morning sun. Below the rocks, a rainbow arced through the mist above a deep pool.

I popped the trunk and geared up. Stocking waders, cleated wading shoes, a canvas creel strapped over my shoulder, a fishing vest, and a long-billed hat. I assembled my grandfather's split-bamboo rod and plucked a no. 14 Adams out of my fly box.

My thoughts drifted back over the past few hellish weeks. My fingers stiffened, and I botched the cinch knot, which slipped free when I tugged on the tippet. The Adams fluttered to the ground, bringing me to my knees, cursing and searching.

I found the fly, shoved the tippet through the eye, and yanked the cinch knot home. Then I slammed the trunk and stalked across the clearing, simmering with quick, unthinking anger.

The Cable Hole, the locals called it, for the snarl of weathered logs and old logging cable that had somehow drifted downstream from a clear-cut and piled up against the opposite bank. I often thought of it, no matter where I was, and it was almost always part of my Klahowya County itinerary on visits home. I loved the way the pool caught the morning light and the way the spray drifted down from the rapids above. I loved the sound of the place, too, the roar of the rapids pushing back into the silence of the big trees. And the smell—fir and water, vine maple and wet sand. It never occurred to me then, but the Cable Hole was a restorative for me, a way of shaking off pressure, paranoia, and ambition, of getting back in touch with who I really was. And it probably had something to do with the way the rest of my life was destined to spool out.

I stepped off the bank and onto the gravel bar below the pool. The cold penetrated the thick neoprene of the waders, and I felt myself relax. I stood silently, lightly holding my rod parallel to the river's surface. A water ouzel ran between stones along the upper end of the pool, disappearing beneath the surface as it dashed along the bottom. A cloud of mayflies rose off the surface into the dappled sunbeams streaming through the trees. Two swallows dipped and turned through the cloud, snatching their breakfast from the air and driving the insects back down toward the surface, where dimpled water signaled waiting trout. For the mayflies, it was death above and death below.

"My God, Tommy boy," I whispered, "will you look at this!"

I raised the rod with my right hand and pulled line off the clicking reel with my left. The bamboo swooshed through the cool air while I stripped off more and more line, feeding the loops that cascaded through the air over my head. The Adams settled onto the water at the head of the pool, turning and spinning as the current caught it. A thirteen-inch rainbow trout broke the surface violently and snatched the fly. It felt the hook and streaked toward the far bank, stripping line off the whining reel.

*   *   *

The *Big Skookum Echo* rolled off an old Hoe rotary press every Thursday morning, just as it had fifteen years earlier when, as an eager high school freshman, I'd hunted-and-pecked my way through my first *Echo* baseball brief on an old Royal typewriter. Harris, the crusty printer who kept the ancient machine turning, stood at the folder and pulled out occasional copies, scanning the ink levels. The headline read "Summer Leagues Set for Busy Season." Harris looked up from the broadsheet spread between his two big hands, smirked, and shouted over the roar of the press. "You got yourself some real news on this one, kid."

"That's what passes for news in Bent Fir," I said, grabbing a copy out of the folder and turning away from the Hoe. "And it's not exactly my ticket to the *Washington Post*."

In hindsight, I can guess what Harris was thinking as I sauntered toward the front office, reading my story with a Marlboro dangling from the corner of my mouth. But when that long-ago summer began, I was oblivious to everything but the turmoil that erupted when everything I always thought I wanted to be collided with who I was. All I could see was that Tom Dawson, hotshot investigative reporter from journalism's big leagues, was back at the little country weekly where he'd started. Back in the boonies where women's softball rated as a page-one story.

The door to the front office swung shut behind me, dampening the *ca-chunk-ca-chunk-ca-chunk* of the press. The Regulator clock ticked placidly on the wall, its brass pendulum swaying. Dust motes drifted in the morning sun slanting through the venetian blinds. At her rolltop desk against the far wall, Marion Mayfield twisted her head and watched me stroll into the room. More than thirty years have passed, and women pretty much ignore me these days. But in 1981 I was a broad-shouldered six-footer with big baby blues and lots of sandy-blond hair that curled over my ears.

The hair is mostly memory now, and so is the misplaced ambition that carried me right out of Bent Fir the autumn after my high school graduation. Never a moment's hesitation, not a quiver of doubt. Look out, baby. I was out to conquer. And I still carried some of the old teenage hubris that day when Marion Mayfield turned to look me over in the *Echo*'s office. She must have smiled inwardly at how silly I looked in my Hawaiian shirt, baggy tan slacks, and sandals over socks. I was all SoCal, a lone palm tree lost in a million Douglas firs.

But outwardly, Marion ignored my Sunset Boulevard uniform, just as she had when I'd come crawling back to the *Echo* after my humiliation in L.A., desperate for a job where I could be close while my mom struggled through chemo. Not that Marion didn't need the help. She was an editor without a staff, a one-woman newsroom in a one-horse town. And even a country weekly is an ever-hungry maw that sucks up a constant flow of copy, photographs, meeting notices, engagement and birth announcements, police runs, and school-lunch menus.

Marion Mayfield had been a year ahead of me at Big Skookum High, a pert brunette with a head-hugging pageboy that bounced down halls filled with big-hair blondes. More than her hairstyle made her different. There was the cultured, slightly stilted speech

5

passed down from her mother, the high school's aloof mistress of American literature. The scholarship in the English Department at Lindley, the pretentious little liberal arts college north of Seattle. And the big dreams about a literary life, editing maybe, for a New York publisher.

But for some reason that eluded me then, she'd cast all that aside and come back here to Bent Fir. Instead of nuanced novels, she edited stories about county-commissioner meetings and Rotary Club luncheons. And instead of evenings in literary salons, she sat at the Mayfield dinner table, listening to her husband argue with her father-in-law about the best way to bid a Forest Service timber sale or to gut a black-tailed deer.

The black rotary-dial phone on Marion's desk jangled, and she picked it up before it could ring twice. As she listened, she leaned forward and pressed the phone deeper into her ear. "Say again," she said, pulling a half sheet of copy paper across the desk and grabbing an editing pencil. She scribbled on the newsprint, hung up, and pushed away from the desk, spinning her scarred oak chair around on its rollers. "A log truck's off the road up on Forest Service 2103," she said, holding out the half sheet. "You'd better get yourself up there."

* * *

I veered off the Forest Service road and parked next to the yarder, its steel boom towering over the patch of level ground the Mayfield Logging cat had carved out of the hillside. The main line stretched from the top of the tower. I climbed out, lit a Marlboro, and glanced down. The cable ran down the denuded slope and disappeared in the mountain mist that haunted these ridges. A couple of chokers dangled to the scarred ground.

I left the old Dodge at the landing and walked back down the gravel road to where I'd passed the sheriff's big Chevrolet cruiser, its red-and-white emergency lights flashing.

Walt Hasslebring and the half dozen men standing around him peered into the ravine. A logger in a hardhat tugged a quarter-inch cable off the winch on the front bumper of a pickup. The winch whined, spooling out. The logger gripped it with two gloved hands, stepped off the shoulder, and disappeared down the slope.

"Hi, Sheriff," I said as I walked up to the gaggle of men. Hasslebring turned.

The sheriff looked to be in his mid-fifties. He moved slowly. He spoke slowly. He lumbered around in his old Eisenhower jacket and rumpled tan slacks and never seemed excited about much of anything. He'd liked me during my high school glory days. He thought I was a little full of myself, maybe, in my button-down shirts and chinos, but playing quarterback for the Big Skookum Loggers made up for a lot of pretentious big-city ways.

"How ya doin', Tommy?" he asked. "Heard you was back in town. Workin' at the *Echo* again, eh?"

I shook off the embarrassment and bored ahead. "How's it look?" I asked.

"Not good. But Stubby's headed down for a close-up."

"You know how it is," Hasslebring added. "Nobody lives through one of these. Skid off the road and head down the gulch. The cab hits a stump or a rock, and the logs just keep on goin'. They shear the top right off the cab and the man inside right along with it."

The sheriff stepped aside, opening a view down the furrowed earth that led through the huckleberries and salal. Near the bottom, where the mist hung heavy, lay a jumble of logs, tires, and twisted metal.

"Hal knew what was gonna happen the instant he went over," Hasslebring said, chewing on a fat White Owl. "He had six seconds to think about it before the truck hit whatever it hit."

"Hal?"

"Yep. Hal Mayfield. Last guy you'd expect to lose it on one of these turns"

"Hal Mayfield? Oh Christ!"

* * *

The blue Ford pickup appeared on a curve high above Cougar Reservoir, dust boiling up behind it and all four wheels skidding sideways in the gravel. The driver laid on the horn, and I jerked the wheel toward the outer shoulder. I fishtailed along the edge of empty space, pumping the brake and cursing. To my left, a grim-faced Lars Mayfield blew past in the pickup, rushing to his father's corpse. Then the Dodge straightened out, angled back to the center of the road, and plunged into the dust.

7

The Mayfields went back as long as anybody in Klahowya County could remember. Always woodsmen. Always independent operators who somehow stayed afloat while the big timber companies sank the other gyppo loggers one by one. Hal Mayfield, the barflies along Front Street liked to say, had one helluva sharp pencil.

I hit the main highway, thinking about the Mayfields and the stories I'd be writing about Hal's death. Say what you wanted about him, Hal was a calculating bull of the woods who could hold a finger to the wind and bid a federal timber sale just right, undercutting the big boys while still leaving just enough margin to pay the rigging crew, service the skidders, and keep the family in beans.

Lars was something else. He'd somehow mustered the good sense to marry Marion, but beyond that he was a redneck cipher, volatile and unpredictable. He'd been my half back in high school. He ran the plays I called without question, but he never hesitated to blindside me during a scrimmage. Hard as he was to figure, one thing was for sure: He was a hothead, especially when he got a few beers in his belly. Cross him, and he'd take a chain saw to your ass.

I cruised into Bent Fir and turned into the *Echo*'s gravel lot. As I pushed through the big oak door, Chesty Arnold, the owner and ad salesman, looked up from his desk. Marion rose and looked at me with a stricken expression. She'd obviously heard the news but seemed to be holding out some hope that her world hadn't just shifted under her feet.

"Is it true?" she asked.

2

After leaving the *Echo* that June afternoon, I climbed back into my car and headed east on Front. The Big Skookum Inlet, the arm of Puget Sound that gave the whole region its name, heaved quietly on my left, the wake of a purse seiner undulating along the bank. On my right was Benny Brill's Hardware and Sporting Goods, where I'd found the dirt-cheap upstairs apartment I'd moved into three weeks before. Then I cruised past the Washington State liquor store, my father's post office, Big Skookum High School, and a few houses flanked by fenced pastures. Two stolid chestnut mares stood at the barbed wire, their tails lazily brushing flies off their flanks.

The ridges on both sides of the Big Skookum fell away, and the horizon opened. I punched in a Seattle oldies station midway through "Tears on My Pillow."

"You don't remember me," Little Anthony crooned, "but I remember you."

The Dodge accelerated, salt air streaming in the open window. Then the burgundy relic, a well-worn '65 I'd found in a lot on Sepulveda Boulevard, coughed, sputtered, and died. I punched the clutch in, coasted, downshifted, and popped the clutch out again. The car shuddered and the engine caught. I slammed my hand on the dash. What a goddamned comedown from the BMW I'd been wheeling out of my Marina del Rey garage every morning just a month before.

The car crested a slight rise, and Oyster Bay popped into view. Beyond it, Puget Sound stretched to the east and Mount Rainier reddened in the rays of the setting sun. Olympia, the state capital, lay hidden along the next inlet, which, like the Skookum, snaked to a dead end at the Sound's southern end. Out of sight to the north were Tacoma and Seattle and the city bustle that seemed a thousand miles from the sleepy solitude of Bent Fir, the tiny town I once again called home.

The car hit sixty and quit missing. I drove south along the beach, the two-lane blacktop humming by. The Imperials moaned, and Little Anthony wallowed in regret. "If we could start anew," he pleaded, "I wouldn't hesitate."

A mailbox marked "Dawson" stood by a narrow driveway leading up the hill. At the top, Mount Rainier's reflection shimmered in the windows of my folks' brick rambler. Below them, in white window boxes, the buds on Mom's geraniums had opened enough to show hints of red. I felt some of my foul mood drain away.

I stepped into the front hall, and my mother appeared in the arched doorway leading to the kitchen. She looked gaunt, and her hand trembled as she reached out to steady herself against the door-jamb. "Hi, sweetheart," she said, before turning back to the kitchen. I hurried after her and caught up just as she reached the counter, steadied herself, and reached for a well-blackened Dutch oven.

"Mom! Take it easy, would you? I'll help with that." I grabbed the big iron pot, dropped a heavy lid on it, and slid it into the oven. "C'mon," I said, taking my mother's hand. "A pot roast takes— what?—forty minutes? Sit with Dad and me for a while."

"Go on, Tommy. I'm not completely useless, and I can manage the salad. You and your father talk. I'll be out in a bit."

I left her at the kitchen table and headed back into the living room. Dad looked me in the eye and shook his head. "Best just let her do her thing," he said. "She feels even worse when she has to just sit around with everybody fussing over her."

"How's she doing?"

"Every treatment gets tougher. I only hope she can handle the last two."

He rose and padded through the arch, returning with two bottles of Heidelberg beer. "Here," he said, extending one of the rounded little keg bottles. "Have one of Tacoma's finest."

He dropped into his recliner, put his feet up, and said, "Hear about Hal Mayfield?"

One more reminder that I was back in the sticks. From his listening station at the post office, Dad was the main interchange for the Bent Fir gossip network. The first customer who walked up to his window in the morning usually had a tidbit. Dad passed that along to the next customer and collected more news in return. And so it went . . . at every meeting place in town. The Bent Fir Telegraph, the locals called it. On big stories, the town didn't even need a newspaper.

I dropped onto the chintz couch. "Yeah," I said. "I was up there. At the logging show. I didn't go right down to Hal's rig—it was way down in a ravine. But Stubby Lancaster did. And from the look on his face, it wasn't anything you'd want to see."

We talked until Mom lowered a platter onto the table. "C'mon, boys," she said. "You must be starved."

At the table, the talk turned to fishing, just like the old days. I reported on my trip to the Takamak. Dad said spring chinook were still showing at the mouth of Cutthroat Creek, and trollers were doing okay on dodgers and plugged herring. He'd seen a twenty-eight-pounder hanging on the marina's scale two days before. "A bea-u-ti-ful fish," he said, lingering over each syllable.

And what was I reading? my mother asked. Her fellow teachers at the high school were raving about *Nobel House*, she said, although she considered it mass-market pandering. But I should try *Mornings on Horseback*, the new Teddy Roosevelt biography. She was just about to finish, and I could have her copy. I smiled. "I'd like that."

What I was thinking, of course, was quite different. My mother was a sweet old gal, and she deserved indulging. Especially now that she was dealing with chemo. But I was still burning with righteous journalistic fervor. It was 1981, after all. The Israelis were bombing Iraqi nuclear plants, trying to start World War III. Al Haig was in China, selling weapons to the commies. And Mom was still riding up San Juan Hill.

We finished with a pie made from the huckleberries Mom and Dad had picked on Shotgun Ridge the previous September, a dozen quarts that crowded Dad's venison in the basement chest freezer. We rose from the table, Dad poured two neat shots of Jack Daniel's, and we settled back into the living room while Mom cleared dishes.

"You hear anything about the funeral?"

"It's Saturday. It'll be big. We'll front-page it, and I suppose I'll write the whole thing. Marion won't be in any shape to deal with it. Her name shouldn't be on it anyway."

"Doesn't make much sense," Dad said. "Hal's been driving those roads since we were kids."

* * *

The Dodge rumbled down the long driveway. A full moon hung in the blue-black sky, just above Mount Rainier. The dark ridge of the Cascades, the mountain barrier that trapped winter rains and summer fogs over Western Oregon and Washington, stretched off into the blackness, north and south. I pulled off the road, rolled my window down, and lit a cigarette. A ribbon of moonlight ran across the bay and ended on the Oyster Bay beach. Waves lapped sand. A bat jerked back and forth across the glow of sky and mountain.

I leaned forward and crossed my arms on top of the steering wheel, blind to the scenery, lost in thought.

Reagan's man Al Haig in China. Jesus. Selling weapons? No way. Had to be some kind of deal cooking. What was the trade? What did the Chinese have to offer anyway? Back at the Times, *I'd at least have a shot at the story. Talk it up with the boys on the international desk. Look for some kind of local angle. Shit. In L.A., there was always a local angle. The airplane plants and the Skunk Works. Hughes. The missile guys.*

Not to mention the kind of women the Beach Boys sang about. A cool fifty grand a year. And crossing the street after work to drink at the Redwood with some of the best reporters on the planet, veterans who'd throw back a few bourbons and tell stories that just wouldn't quit. The Redwood. Geez. An editor picked up a red phone on the city desk at the Times, *and it rang on the bar at the Redwood.*

Local. Well, you have local now. You have local at $298 in your paycheck every Friday and news that ends at the county line. Log-truck accidents and county-commissioner meetings. With stories like that, how do you even get enough decent clips together to climb back out, to somehow put the mess in L.A. behind you?

I gave myself another kick in the butt. My life story had been held, I told myself, but not spiked.

Find a couple of good stories. Get on at one of the regional papers. Land a book contract. It could happen.

People forget.

What was I reading? my mother had asked. And I'd been embarrassed to admit it was *All the President's Men.* For the third time. Woodward and Bernstein and the *Washington Post.* Bringing down Nixon.

Now THAT *was journalism.*

I slumped back in the bench seat and turned the ignition key. Nothing happened. One more time. Nothing again. I clenched my fist, pounded the steering wheel, and fumed, cursing the fates that had thrown me back in time and stolen everything I'd worked for. I climbed out, pushed the car onto the highway, and got it rolling forward. I jumped in and engaged the clutch, and the big V-8 caught.

The two mares still stood at the fence outside town, frozen in the moonlight. I wheeled into the parking lot behind Brill's and climbed the two flights of rickety wooden steps that rose up the wall of the old brick building. The flimsy door hesitated when I pushed on it and then popped open.

Benny Brill had turned the attic into eighty dollars of extra monthly income by enclosing a toilet in one front corner and tucking a kitchenette into the other. Dishes teetered on the drain board, my boyhood fly-tying vise rose from one side of the old chrome-and-Formica kitchen table, and water dripped from the spigot into a rusting sink. I pulled the string dangling from the overhead light. On the end table, a pinpoint of red glowed on my Radio Shack answering machine.

When I punched "play," Walt Hasslebring's gravelly voice filled the room. "Listen, Tommy," he said. "I guess you're the local press on this story, and you should be the first to know. Better get down to see me first thing tomorrow.

"There's a reason Hal Mayfield lost it on that turn."

3

I turned out of bed early on Friday morning, downed a cup of coffee, and walked up the street to the county courthouse, thinking about what the sheriff had told me the night before. Which wasn't much. Somebody had tampered with Hal Mayfield's truck. The brakes failed on the first turn below the landing, and a routine drive down the mountain turned into Hal's last load. When I pressed him, Hasslebring fell back on what I eventually came to realize was his signature line. "All in good time," he said.

The sheriff's office was tucked into the ground level on the left side of the building, facing the parking lot. Bold black letters spelled out "SHERIFF" on a frosted-glass globe hanging over the door. I pushed on in. Walt Hasslebring leaned over a mug of coffee at the front counter, chatting with a deputy. He straightened and looked at me. "Mornin', Tommy. You ready for a little ride?"

He steered his big Chevy west on Front. It was still a few minutes before seven, but Bent Fir was a working town. Well-worn pickups and battered sedans generated a steady hum along the main drag, barely slowing when the drivers spotted the sheriff's cruiser.

Hasslebring pulled into the Shell station that sat at the head of Front Street, just past the *Echo*, and rolled down his window. A lanky, unshaven attendant slid his creeper out from under the big Freightliner parked against the fence behind the station, tossed a cigarette onto the pavement, and stood up. He ambled up to the cruiser, and I recognized Arnie Dykes, the one kid who'd dropped out of my class at Big Skookum High.

"Mornin', sheriff," Arnie said in a sleepy, bored voice. "Fill?"

Hasslebring grunted, and Arnie dipped his head so that he could look past the sheriff at me. He gave a little wave. "Mornin', Tommy. Heard you was back in town."

I'd been hearing the same thing every time I turned a Bent Fir corner, and it put me on the defensive regardless of the source. But hearing it from the class screw-up riled me more than usual. Arnie seemed smug, taking some kind of perverse pleasure in my return to his world of failure.

Hasslebring signed for the gas, pulled back onto Front, and headed up the Longmont Grade. I steered the conversation back to Hal Mayfield.

"So who figured this out anyway?"

"Marvin. First thing he looked at when we winched the truck outta the gulch was the brake lines. The man thinks like the mechanic he is."

"So how do you rig a brake line to fail at just the right time? Why didn't Hal notice right away when he pulled off the landing?"

Hasslebring held up his big right hand, palm out like a traffic cop's. "All in good time, son. You'll see soon enough."

He turned into the gravel fronting Marvin Dervish's wrecking yard. Behind the weathered wooden fence, we found Marvin and a deputy bent over the twisted remains of the Mayfield Logging truck I'd seen in the ravine. The deputy was brushing fingerprint powder along the cab's undercarriage. He heard us approach and turned to look up at Hasslebring. "Dunno, Sheriff. Nuthin' but mud down here for the most part. Don't look like we're gonna find anything that'll hold a latent."

"Got to look, Steve. Give it your best shot. Then get everything in the cab. And get the engine cover, too."

I peered over the deputy's shoulder.

"What you see here, Tommy, stays here," the sheriff said. "I understand that you gotta tell the folks why we're treating this as more than an accident. So you can tell 'em the truck was tampered with. But that's it, at least for now. Got that?"

In L.A., cops were the enemy, the other side in an endless battle to find and publish something that somebody wanted to hide. There, I would have bristled at the demand that I suppress news. But in the face of Walt Hasslebring, a father figure right out of my small-town childhood, I slipped easily into an entirely different ethic.

"Yessir," I said. "And I appreciate the head start on the story. You can trust me."

"Okay, Marvin. Show him what you showed me."

Marvin Dervish, a short, plump man with thinning hair and thick horn-rimmed glasses, stepped up and pointed to the truck's undercarriage. "Look there," he said. "Just below the master cylinder."

Aluminum foil and duct tape dangled from the brake line. Hydraulic fluid had stained the mud-covered steering gear below that. The line itself was shiny where the tape had pulled away, the only clean metal in the entire engine compartment.

"Wasn't really rocket science," Marvin said, hooking his thumbs behind the straps of his greasy overalls. "They cleaned off that little stretch of line and scored it with a hacksaw or something like that. Cut it about halfway through. Then they wrapped the foil around it and taped that on before much fluid could escape. A light tap or two wouldn't break it open, but some heavy footin' would."

Hasslebring broke in. "Hal headed down the hill and rode the brakes hard at that first turn. The pressure blew the tape off, fluid sprayed out, and the pedal went right to the floor.

"He probably tried the air brakes. But that line was cut clear through. Jesus. Imagine what the man was thinking right about then. Christ almighty! That was really pucker time."

* * *

The Saturday-afternoon funeral crowd at the Baptist church spilled out into the parking lot. Old men wore the double-breasted gray suits they'd bought when they came home from World War II. Their sons made do with tight Harris Tweed sports coats their mothers had picked out at Penney's for high school graduation. The women had helped both generations knot their ties.

I sat in the front pew, where I could hear the preacher and the testimonials. Hal had been tough, they all said, but fair. He came back from the Pacific after the war, bought a primitive chain saw and an old truck, and started one of the most successful gyppo outfits in the South Sound. He paid a living wage, and he ran a safe show. If a man was stove up, Mayfield Logging paid the bills and Hal Mayfield visited regular.

Lars spoke last. The old man was everything he and his brothers had ever hoped to be, he said. Hal never overbid a Forest Service sale, and he always got his elk. Now the outfit was in his hands, Lars said, his eyes darting around the pews and the mourners standing against the back wall of the sanctuary. A lot of folks depended on Mayfield Logging. He'd do his best.

I glanced across the aisle at the family. Marion sat in the front pew, next to the spot Lars had just vacated. She wore a pillbox hat I'd never seen before and stared blankly at the pulpit. She probably was wondering what would happen next. Hal had been a steady deck that everybody could stand on, but Lars was a loose cannon. Marion's world could come completely undone.

Lars finished. I slipped out the back door and made my way toward the front of the church. The crowd flowed out and down the steps. Knots of men stood among the rows of cars, smoking and pulling at their collars. Never would've expected Hal to lose it on a turn, they said. Some green kid, sure. But Hal?

I nodded to classmates and family friends, scribbling quotes into my notebook and snapping pictures with the *Echo*'s Rolleiflex. The old double-lens reflex camera was nothing like the sleek Nikons photogs used at the *Times*. The Roly was shaped like a small shoebox, and to frame a photo, you held it vertically at belly height and stared down into the viewfinder. I felt like a doofus with the damned thing hanging from my neck.

I was standing on the edge of the parking lot, jotting down scenic details, when Walt Hasslebring strolled over to me. "Quite a turnout," he said, his voice flat.

"Yeah. I don't remember anything quite like it."

"Oh, there were a couple during the war."

Hasslebring lit a White Owl and scanned the crowd. I pulled a Marlboro out of my pocket. "Anything new on the truck?" I asked, keeping my voice low and my eye on the mourners to make sure nobody got close enough to hear. I snapped the lid of my Zippo open with one hand—I was proud of that move—and bent over the flame to light the cigarette.

"Nah," Hasslebring said. "No prints other than what you'd expect. Hal, Lars, Stubby, couple of other guys who drove the rig once in a while. No tool marks on the brake line—it coulda been cut with any ten-cent hacksaw blade. And the tape our man used to seal the line was garden-variety duct tape, the kind you get at Brill's, or the Thriftway, or just about any goddamned place."

"Pretty calculating. It's not like somebody suddenly blew up and brained the man with a tire iron. Who had it in for Hal Mayfield enough to plan something like that?"

"Hard to figure," Hasslebring said. "Hal could be a hard man, but the woods are full of hard men. Don't know of anybody who really carried any kind of grudge against him. And angry husbands usually use a gun, not that Hal chased a whole lot of skirts.

"Fact is, we haven't got a clue."

*   *   *

I spent Sunday morning at my folks', celebrating Father's Day with a brunch I whipped up in Mom's kitchen. After the omelets and hash browns, I'd presented Dad with a new Penn saltwater reel, a big salmon rig with a stainless-steel star drag. Benny Brill gave me a good price on the reel, but it just about wiped me out. Still, Dad seemed genuinely touched. And I had enough cash left to gas up in town that afternoon before heading out on U.S. 101 and then winding up FS 2103 to Mayfield Logging's operation. The Bull of the Woods sale, they called it, for the nearby Forest Service fire lookout on top of Bull of the Woods Mountain.

It looked like every other timber cut in the Western Washington woods, what loggers called a "show." The hub of the operation was a patch of level ground alongside a Forest Service road—a landing— where trucks loaded the freshly harvested timber. On flatter ground, skidders—sturdy tractors equipped with grappling arms and cable winches—wrenched the fallen trees out of the woods. But on steep ground, heel-boom loaders—shovels—moved timber around the landing. The shovel driver positioned logs for the bucker, who cut them to length. Then the driver either loaded the logs on a truck or stacked them for temporary storage.

Steep slopes like the Mayfield show called for a highlead rigging system. A metal boom—the business end of a yarder—rose vertically from the back of a hefty vehicle and anchored the rigging used to yank logs off the slope. Once upon a time, a rigging crew trimmed a big fir—a spar tree—to fit with pulleys and cables. They powered the rig with a steam engine called a "donkey" and used the system to denude a slope. Old-timers persisted in calling a yarder a "steel tree."

A long cable—the main line—ran from the yarder boom to the bottom of the show. A carriage controlled by another cable, the haul-back, moved up and down the main line. And from the carriage dangled the chokers, shorter cables that choker setters hooked to the logs left in a jumble by the falling crew. A series of coded whistles announced the system's relentless stops and starts, signaling the crew to move clear of danger.

My first job in the woods followed my junior year in high school. I was in prime shape then, a three-sport athlete with a country boy's legs. But setting chokers just about broke me. Up and down the steep slopes, over downed logs and through brush, brutal hour after hour. The chokers fought back, the cables snagging on stumps and twisting fiercely. Gasping, I looped them around the fallen firs, securing the hook and stumbling back at the sound of the whistle, my quivering legs driven by fear fueled by tales of crushed skulls and broken backs. Then the second whistle, the yarder's roar, the haulback grinding through the pulleys, and the logs, leashed by the chokers, bounding up toward the landing, bouncing and heaving through the stumps in a lurching dance of death.

That's when I realized Dad had been right. Logging roads all started in some crummy bar in some crummy Northwest mill town, and they all led to dead ends somewhere in the mountains. College, the old man had said, that was the ticket. The city. A future that stretched beyond the inevitable end of the old-growth timber.

An old GMC pickup clattered through the rutted landing and parked next to my Dodge. Stubby Lancaster climbed out, all five and a half feet of him, and strolled toward me in full logger's gear—a worn shirt of heavy denim, wide suspenders with "Stihl" printed vertically on each strap, and canvas pants trimmed short above heavy boots. Technically, the spiked boots were "caulked." But lots of loggers corrupted the term and called them "corks."

"What's up kid?" Stubby asked. "What's so damned important we gotta be out here on a Sunday?"

Stubby hunted with my dad, which is why I'd called him. He was probably the only Mayfield logger who'd give me the time of day. Not that he didn't have his own suspicions about any son of Bent Fir who'd gone off to college and tried to find a life somewhere other than in the woods. But in the Skookum, a hunting buddy's kid deserved a little slack, regardless. It was Stubby who'd found me that high school job setting chokers, not for Mayfield but for another one of the independent family operations known in timber country as gyppos.

"Nothing much, really. Just wanted to see the show. What with the Hal thing and all."

"What's to see?" Stubby asked, scanning the yarder and the logs piled on the landing. "Looks like every other show there ever was."

"Yeah. I know. Just thought I might see something that'd get me thinking."

"You know your business, I guess," Stubby said. He walked to the edge of the landing and sent a cheekful of tobacco juice arcing down the slope. Then he stepped over the edge.

This wasn't a place for sandals and Hawaiian shirts. I had no corks, but I'd dug an old denim shirt, jeans, and a pair of Timberland boots out of a box I'd left in my parents' basement. So I was able to follow Stubby down through the torn ground under the high line. "Nuthin' much to see," he said, strolling around the stumps and through the broken brush as if he were on a city sidewalk. "You seen it all before."

True enough. But I'd been straight with Stubby. Partly straight anyway. When you're on a story, you *do* want to see every scene connected to it. At least you do if you think you're a writer, and not just a legman. This was where Hal Mayfield spent his last day on Earth, and seeing it as he'd seen it was important because, someday soon, I'd want to describe it that way on newsprint. But what was really important was talking to Stubby. On a Sunday, the Mayfield show was good place to have a private conversation. And in my experience, sources opened up on familiar ground.

Stubby reached the bottom of the cut. He propped a foot on a gnarled root, bent over, and let fly with another spurt of tobacco juice. "What kind of show was this?" I asked.

"Whadda ya mean?"

"I mean how'd everybody get along? How was the job going? Any fights? Any threats? Anybody fired? Anybody just really pissed off?"

"You mean, anybody have it in for Hal?"

"Yeah, I suppose. But more than that, too. Anything out of the ordinary?"

"Why you askin'? Hal killed hisself. Missed a turn. Skidded over the bank. That's all."

"Yeah . . . I know. But when somebody dies in any way that's out of the ordinary, they do an autopsy. Same thing with newspaper guys.

We poke around. So I'm poking. Anybody have it in for Hal?"

"Nah. Not really. This Mayfield bunch, they been together a long time. Lars and the old man, they squabbled some. Like always. But nuthin' new about that."

"Squabbled how?"

The usual family stuff, Stubby said. "Old bull, young bull . . . that kind of thing."

"What kind of thing?"

"Nuthin' much. Just a kid and his dad, arguing. My kids argue with me. Your kids . . . they'll argue with you. Lars pushed. Hal pushed back. That's all."

The subject clearly was one to save for later. Maybe when Stubby had a few beers in him. I changed the topic.

"What about outsiders?"

"Hal didn't take no shit from nobody. Didn't have no use for hippie tree-sitters. They come around, and he run 'em right off the show. Had some run-ins with that crowd down on Rush Creek. And old Hal, he had a sharp pencil, y'know. Beat out a lot of gyppos on a lot of sales. But them bids was just business. Guys be pissed for a week or two. Then it was back to 'Hey, Hal! How ya doin'?'"

I'd learned a lot about interviewing from an investigative veteran at the *Times*, and I tried one of his simplest tricks on Stubby. "When they hit you with bullshit generalities," the old reporter said, "just keep your goddamn mouth shut. People hate silence in the middle of a conversation. If you don't talk, they will."

I looked at Stubby quizzically. He looked up at the trees still standing on the edge of the show. He spat. He reached into his pocket, pulled out his pouch, and pushed another pinch of tobacco into his cheek.

Then, without a word, he turned and headed back up the hill.

4

The sun came out Monday morning, and the King Alfred daffodils that filled the beds lining the *Echo*'s front walk glowed a brilliant yellow. I climbed the stairs and stepped into the little lobby.

Marion flinched at the sound of the screen door slamming behind me and looked up from her desk. She wore a faded cotton print dress, blue Keds, and a pair of dark circles under her eyes. I felt an unfamiliar stab of guilt. Hal Mayfield's death was the biggest story to hit Bent Fir in years, and I couldn't help thinking that, with luck, it might even be my ticket back to a real newspaper. After the time I'd spent in the big leagues, I thought like the hyper-competitive newsmen who saw personal profit in the misfortunes of others. They were my models, the cynical outsiders who served only their own take-no-prisoners, independence-at-any-cost ethic. But I couldn't help but realize how hard this situation was on Marion.

I pushed through the swinging wooden gate in the center of the counter that ran across the *Echo*'s lobby, separating the public area from the workspace I shared with Marion and Chesty. "How's Lars?"

"Hard to say. He's still drunk."

"How about you?"

"Oh. I'm all right. Truth be known, Hal was a crude, rude old man. And a bully. I hated it when the family got together and he got into a bottle."

I dropped into my chair. "He kept the outfit running for a lot of years."

"Yeah. You can say that about him. Hal had a sharp pencil." She stood and took the three steps to my desk. She leaned forward, both hands on the worn oak. "So what's this about Hal's rig?"

"Walt says somebody screwed with the brake lines. He called the state troopers, and they sent a crime-lab guy over from Olympia yesterday."

"And?"

"Dunno. Walt's announced a press conference this afternoon at three. Not that anybody important will be there. In Seattle, it'll be a brief. Three inches tops."

"Well, it's important here. Let's talk to Chesty. If he's ever going to go for an extra, now's the time. We have the funeral for downpage A1 and a murder investigation for the top. We'll be out at the same time as Shelton and Olympia."

She straightened. "Let's take a look at the funeral art."

"Sure. But I don't promise much. That Roly is an antique, and I'm no photographer."

"If you work at a weekly," she said, "you're a photographer. And you process your own stuff. So follow me."

She turned and walked toward the darkroom. I grabbed the Rolleiflex off the counter where I'd dumped it and followed. She disappeared through the black revolving door. Then I joined her in the darkroom's red glow, spinning the door shut behind me.

She turned to face me and held out her hand for the camera, smelling of shampoo and White Shoulders. "A Roly's pretty foolproof," she said as she rewound the film and snapped the back of the camera open. "Lots of weeklies still use them."

"I feel like some old fart in *The Front Page* with the damn thing around my neck."

"Those were Speed Graphics."

Marion picked up a wire spool and started coiling the 35mm film onto it. She held the spool in front of my face where I could see what she was doing in the dim light. "Here," she said, and handed it to me. "You finish. The important thing is to make sure the film never touches itself."

I coiled the rest of the roll onto the spool, and she introduced me to the chemicals. The pungent smell of the developer and fixer made me lightheaded, but I felt a surprising burst of satisfaction at the black-and-white images that appeared when Marion threaded the finished film into the printer and exposed the photo paper. She guided my hand to the knobs that adjusted the image's size and focus.

When we finally got to prints on paper, Marion allowed as how the shots I'd taken at the funeral were adequate. There wasn't anything from inside the church. A *Times* photographer might have risked angering the Mayfields by snapping away during the service, but I

23

still carried enough small-town sense to know better. Besides, the photos of the crowd out front showed the magnitude of the thing. And a couple of them were even in focus.

I followed Marion out through the darkroom door and headed for my desk. Then I sat and stared at the wall, thinking about Hal Mayfield frantically downshifting his big Kenworth, his foot pumping the slack brake pedal as the truck barreled toward a curve he knew he'd never make.

* * *

Walt Hasslebring sat on the edge of his battered oak desk. A grizzled reporter from the *Olympian* slouched on the couch along the opposite wall in a shapeless tweed sports coat. A young radio reporter wearing corduroy and a ponytail sat next to him, his cassette recorder primed to capture something for the little AM station in Shelton. A stocky young woman with wire-rimmed glasses had come over from the Associated Press capitol bureau in Olympia and was perched primly on a wooden chair. The dailies in Seattle and Tacoma would use her stuff, if they used anything at all.

I grabbed a seat, scooted up to the conference table in the corner, and pulled out my notebook.

"Here's the deal," Hasslebring said, leaning forward and glancing at the fistful of notes clutched in his right hand.

"Hal Mayfield died at approximately 5 a.m. on Thursday, June 18, 1981, according to John Hodges, the Klahowya County coroner. John lists the cause of death as massive trauma sustained when the truck Hal was driving left Forest Service Road 2103 near a Mayfield Logging show in the upper Cougar Creek drainage, on the Olympic National Forest."

Hasslebring laid his notes on the desk. "All that stuff's on the poop sheet," he said, waving his hand at a stack of mimeographed paper. "What's not on the sheet is why this is a murder case."

Every pair of eyes in the room locked on Hasslebring, who told the tale in the homespun way that kept getting him reelected and had eventually fixed him in one of the warmest corners of my memory. He told the reporters how the Mayfield crew had winched the twisted remains of Hal's rig back up onto FS 2103 and hauled it down to Marvin Dervish's wrecking yard. "That's when we discovered," the sheriff said, "that somebody had tampered with the truck's brakes. Both the hydraulics and the air brakes. Nothing accidental about that. And when truck brakes fail on one of those mountain roads, the result is almost always fatal. That's why we're saying that this was murder."

The print reporters scribbled in their notebooks. The radio guy perched on the edge of the couch, holding his microphone out in front of him. The veteran from the *Olympian* pressed Hasslebring for details on the mechanics of the brake failure. The sheriff dodged the question, citing the ongoing investigation. The reporter tried a couple of times more, finally gave up, and shifted his line of questioning.

Why, he asked, was a fully loaded truck left on the landing the previous night?

Because Hal and Lars did all the Mayfield driving and Lars headed down with his last load Wednesday afternoon. Hal left early, too, because his wife wanted him home to take her shopping in Shelton. He hitched a ride with one of the choker setters while the rest of the crew bucked and loaded the last logs on his Kenworth.

So somebody had to know the rig was sitting on the landing all night, unattended?

Yep. It looked that way.

What other evidence turned up on the truck or on the landing?

No comment.

What was next with the investigation?

The usual stuff, the sheriff said. Interviews with everybody on the crew and anybody else who did business with the Mayfields. Picking through the company records. Police work, that's all.

The AP woman raised her hand and asked why anybody would want to harm Hal Mayfield. "Dunno," the sheriff said. "Hal was a pretty popular man around here. He filled a lot a lunch buckets. He generally played by the rules. And having him dead sure doesn't seem to benefit anybody. It's not like there's a lot of big timber left to fight about."

Nope. The old growth was nearly gone. And I didn't see how killing Hal Mayfield would help anybody get what was left. I pondered other possibilities, but none seemed serious enough to motivate a murder.

"That all?" the sheriff asked. When nobody answered, he slid off the desk and picked up the leftover press releases. The reporters closed their notebooks and filed out.

* * *

The "hippie tree-sitters" Stubby Lancaster had mentioned lived up Rush Creek, a stream that tumbled off the east slope of the mountains north of town. Like most loggers, Stubby considered anybody with long hair a hippie, but the Rush Creek crew qualified in only the loosest sense of the word. They had the long hair, all right. And the Rush Creek Commune started out in the early seventies as a true peace-and-love, back-to-the-land enclave of naïveté. But the little gathering of beards, beads, and bongs eventually morphed into something quite different.

The day after Walt Hasslebring's press conference I steered left off the state highway onto Scatter Road, the two-lane strip of county asphalt that rose toward FS 2103 and the Mayfield Logging show. The car rattled over the Rush Creek bridge about two miles in, and I turned north on rough gravel. A mile of lurching through potholes and ruts brought me to a clearing scented with wood smoke. Ramshackle cabins roofed with mossy cedar shakes rimmed a meadow. The scene would have been idyllic if it hadn't been tainted by hulks of old cars, heaps of household trash, and thickets of blackberry vines.

I drove onto the hard-packed dirt that fronted the circle of cabins and killed the engine. The door to the first cabin swung open, and a man wearing bib overalls and a ZZ Top beard stepped out onto the sagging porch. In his right hand was a twelve-gauge shotgun.

Hard-core environmental activism swept into the commune in the mid-seventies. I was already gone, off to the university and then to my police-beat job in Bend. But when I came home to spend holidays with my folks, I heard the stories.

While the rest of the country celebrated a benign succession of Earth Days, commune members pursued an escalating strategy of confrontation with the timber companies. They showed up at Forest Service auctions and drowned out the bidding for timber allotments with chants and drums. Even before Earth First! started pulling in national publicity with tree sits in Oregon, they perched in old-growth firs on federal timber sales and dared loggers to cut the trees out from under them. Then a band saw at Skookum Wood Products exploded into metal fragments midway through a cut, showering the mill with shrapnel and sending two mill hands to the hospital. Someone had driven a heavy steel spike deep into a fir scheduled for harvest. When the tree reached the mill, the saw hit the hidden steel and went off like a grenade.

Another spiked tree tore up a saw at a Shelton mill. Then a mill worker lost an eye when a band saw came apart in Tacoma. The simmering hostility between New Age environmentalists and old-school timber culture broke into open warfare. Loggers thrashed two Rush Creekers who made the mistake of wandering into the Grizzly on a Saturday night. Somebody—everybody assumed commune members—shot up the equipment on a Simpson logging operation west of Shelton. Then a half dozen Rush Creekers climbed into an old-growth fir on a gyppo show just up the road from the commune, daring the fallers to cut. The loggers cursed. A skidder driver rolled right over the two rattletrap sedans the protesters had left on the landing. Then a big man walked onto the scene, grabbed a chain saw, and fired it up, staring up at the six longhairs perched on the giant fir's lower branches. He walked to the tree and commenced cutting. As the wood chips flew, the protesters hurriedly dropped lines to the ground and shimmied down. Loggers kicked and shoved, running them off the show and down the road.

Hal Mayfield, the chain saw still idling in his hand, stood laughing at the base of the fir. Then he turned back to the tree and resumed the cut.

I stepped out of my car. A couple of men in bib overalls and a woman in a long cotton dress had gathered on one of the other porches, watching. The man with the shotgun stood by his front door, immobile. "That you, Maxy?" I asked, trying to peer past the beard.

"Tommy?" the man said, leaning forward. "Tommy Dawson?" He propped the shotgun against the railing and stepped off the porch, holding out his hand.

Max Stewart came from an old Klahowya County logging family, and his betrayal rankled locals even more than the arrival of the city kids who founded the Rush Creek Commune. He'd been a year behind me at Big Skookum High, a shy boy who drew abuse for his liberal politics and bookish ways. I was the only jock who ever took his side in an argument, and one time I'd stepped in when three of my teammates cornered him in the back of the lunchroom and threatened to take him apart. I had no particular sympathy for Maxy, but I didn't like the odds.

Max remembered, apparently. In any event, I was soon sitting at his greasy kitchen table, sipping on an impossibly strong cup of coffee that must have been simmering on the woodstove all morning. We talked a little about old times. I asked about his family. He wondered about my mother—he'd heard she was sick.

"Yeah. Lymphoma. But they caught it pretty early. It had spread some, though, and she's going through chemo now."

"Damn! She's a skookum old gal. How's she doin'?"

"Feeling pretty punk, truth be told. But she's only got two treatments to go."

I changed the subject. "You hear about Hal Mayfield?"

"Hell, yes. He bought it just up the road from here, on 2103. And Rush Creek musta been the first place old Walt Hasslebring stopped after he left the scene. Can't say as I blame him. Shit! No love lost between us here and that asshole Mayfield."

"So I've heard. Had quite a run-in with him a couple of years back, didn't you?"

"Yeah. He called our bluff all right. Got the best of us on that one."

"So . . . anybody around here maybe thinking about settling the score?"

"Nah. Can't see it. Only a few of us left. Don't do much direct action anymore anyhow. Besides, those of us who grew up around here know Hal and his kind. Loggers. Shit! Can't see beyond the next tree. Why expect 'em to do any different than Hal did?"

"How many left?"

"A dozen or so, depending. Mostly guys. This way of living wears on the women more than the men. They start feeling penned in. And the guys that are left . . . they ain't the greenies they once were. Still don't like seeing the big trees go. But they're mostly gone anyway, you know."

We drank the rest of our coffee, gossiping about classmates and

Klahowya County families. I took my leave and shook Max's hand on the creaking porch.

At the intersection with the main highway, I sat at the stop sign, thinking about Maxy Stewart. I'd noticed the look when he first walked out of his cabin. The skin drawn tight across the scrawny neck and sunken cheeks. The nervous eyes, jitterbugging around their sockets. The receding gums and bad teeth. I'd seen it all before in backwoods Oregon.

Max was tweaking—snorting methamphetamine that he'd probably cooked up from cold tablets. The poor man's heroin had reached plague proportions across the rural Northwest, fueling a crime wave and a social disaster. Tweakers dropped out of the job market. They burglarized to support their habits. They neglected their kids to the point of starvation and abandonment. They destroyed houses with the poisons the meth-cooking process created. And they gradually lost their minds in a maelstrom of paranoia, desperation, and violence.

5

The June grass rustled against the undercarriage of the Dodge as I eased down the overgrown driveway. I pulled out into a bare-earth yard, parked next to a moss-covered house, and stepped out into the stench of chicken coops. At a small-town weekly, you may get an occasional crime story with a little juice in it. In the right place, you might even get an occasional murder. But the next day, you were back to the endless round of dull meetings and sappy features. I don't remember the specifics now, of course. But as I stood there in that reeking farmyard, I must have heard the big-city cynics in the *Times* newsroom seizing on the obvious metaphor. This was chicken-shit journalism in all senses of the phrase.

"Logan," I yelled. "Henry Logan. You here?"

A wizened head poked out the door of the nearest coop. "Now where in the fuck else would I be?" The old man disappeared back inside, and the spring-loaded door snapped shut. I walked across the yard and yanked it open again.

A miasma of chicken manure rolled out like a fog. Logan, grunting in filthy overalls, shoveled methodically from the catch boards under the cages into a rusty wheelbarrow. He looked up when I stepped in but kept shoveling.

"I'm Tom Dawson. Jess Dawson's son."

"Yeah. The postman. I know him. And I know'd you. Played some football, din't cha?"

Logan leaned the shovel against the wall. In the far corner, his birds milled around, an oddball collection with nary a true Rhode Island Red or Plymouth Rock among them. The old man and his mongrel chickens were remnants of the Skookum I remembered from my childhood.

"Ain't you gone off somewhere?" Logan asked.

"Bend. Down in Oregon. Then Los Angeles. But I'm home. Been here a couple of weeks now, working down at the *Echo*."

In my mind's eye, I saw the reporters who sat around me in the *Times* newsroom turn and look as though I'd just confessed to shoplifting. And the old man kept asking questions that embarrassed me even more.

"The *Echo*? You got a degree from the U-Dub, and you're back in this piece-a-shit excuse for a town? Talkin' pretty fast, too, ain't cha. Somebody wind ya up, down there in the city?"

"I'm working at the *Big Skookum Echo* now," I said, trying to slow down to a pace more suited to the Washington woods. "My mom's sick, and I came home for the summer."

"The *Echo*? Agin? Din't cha write sports for the *Echo* way back when? Like when ya was in school?"

I took a deep breath. "I heard you had a little trouble with the Navy."

"Fuckin' Navy," said the old man, putting his shovel aside. "C'mon in," he added, brushing past me and pushing through the door. "I'll get ya a Co-Cola."

Logan cleared dirty dishes off the kitchen table, reached into the old Frigidaire, and grabbed a Coke. He popped the top with an opener hanging from a dirty string and set the bottle on the table. I pulled up a chair. The Coke fizzed faintly.

"Fuckin' Navy," Logan said, sliding into the opposite chair. "Maybe you kin nail 'em, city boy. More power to ya then. But I called 'em lots of times and got nuthin' but the bum's rush. I kinda doubt you're gonna find out one goddamn thing."

* * *

The two-lane county asphalt snaked through the Douglas firs like a river through a canyon. I lit a Marlboro, oblivious to the rushing walls of green, and tried to ignore the lingering stink of the chicken ranch. Henry Logan's story had an oddball quality that gave it some legs. Logan was nothing if not colorful, and he took no guff from anybody—not even the United States Navy. You had to admire the crusty old guy.

Who knew where Logan's little tale might lead. A lot of scoops started small. Dig a little, I'd been taught, and you just might turn up something that smelled bad enough to turn heads.

And this Logan story . . . Well, it just went to show you. The ugly boot of the federal government even stepped into a countrified stream of Rotary Club meetings, church fund-raisers, and women's softball games. Sure, Logan's yarn started in a chicken coop, I told myself. But it reached beyond the old man's little universe.

The car crested the ridge, broke out of the second-growth timber, and started down the Longmont Grade. Below, the Big Skookum arced through town, its banks clogged with logs for the mill.

The Dodge hit level ground and coughed. I lurched onto Front Street and passed peeling frame houses, a Thriftway grocery, and the *Echo*'s square wooden facade. I slowed. The town's two taverns, the Grizzly and the Spar, drifted by the driver-side window, a scattering of pickups nosed up against the log barriers that separated the angle-in parking from the sidewalk. The doors stood open on this unseasonably warm spring morning, and I could see silhouettes of early drinkers hunched over both bars.

"Fuckin' Navy," the old man had said. And in those days, with the country so fresh out of Vietnam and Watergate and all the rest of it, I had no problem seizing on that angle for my story. Navy pilots fly strafing runs over their own citizens. No thought for the little guys. Arrogance. Entitlement. More high-and-mighty government bullshit. Yeah. Good outrage factor. And in the early eighties, at the big-city newspapers and national networks, outrage was the coin of the journalistic realm.

I passed the courthouse and crept onto the steel bridge that intersected Front in the center of town. The incoming tide swirled into the Big Skookum and around the log boom protecting the marina. Two streaked purse seiners, the last of Bent Fir's salmon fleet, rocked against the floats. A few well-worn sailboats and runabouts bobbed in the remaining slips.

The Dodge bounced down the incline on the far side of the bridge. I goosed the throaty V-8, and the 318 missed twice before winding out and shooting the battered sedan up the grade. At the top, it intersected with U.S. 101, where I headed north, keeping my fingers crossed as I covered the twenty miles to Cedar Springs Naval Air Station.

Logan, I figured, was probably right—the Navy wouldn't say a goddamn thing. But the old man knew nothing about the well-lubricated flight mechanic whose lips had flapped a little too much at the Spar the previous night. And what the mechanic had said was just the sort of leverage that might pry more out of the wet-behind-the-ears Navy flack who'd taken my phone call about Logan's little antiaircraft action.

The Marine guard at the main gate glanced at my press pass and stepped back into his booth to dial the public affairs officer. Lt. JG Harper said the magic words, and the Marine waved me through with a military flourish.

* * *

The lieutenant rose from her gunmetal-gray desk in the PAO's tiny office and walked around to shake my hand. "Sandy Harper," she said, smiling. "Welcome to Cedar Springs."

"Thanks. I grew up in Bent Fir. So I've been on the station a bit."

She stepped back behind her desk. I watched her turn and sat when she did.

Mid-twenties. Trim in her Navy blues. No wedding ring. Sandy Harper would have turned the head of about any young male in L.A. And some not so young.

A bit more chitchat. Then the lieutenant got down to it. "So," she said. "What can I tell you?"

I popped the reporter's notebook out of my hip pocket. "How many A-6s were involved in this thing anyway?"

The question sent her sliding into the weasel world where public affairs officers lived. "Well," she said. "There were three Intruders in the air. I'm not sure what you mean by 'involved.'"

Her little dodge snapped me into L.A. reporting mode—cynical, doubting, confrontational. "C'mon, lieutenant. Henry Logan emptied a Model 94 Winchester. They were a hundred feet over his chicken coops. No way he missed."

She retreated into passive voice. "Yes, there was damage sustained."

"Damned right," I said, leaning forward. "All three A-6s have holes in them. All three are grounded. Three $30 million fighter-bombers grounded by an old man tired of night exercises that scare the shit out of his birds. Grounded by an old man with a nineteenth-century rifle who's pissed off because his hens won't lay."

Lt. JG Harper leaned forward and put her elbows on the desk. "What are *you* doing at a little country weekly like the *Echo*?" she asked, smiling with enough warmth to revive a spawned-out salmon.

33

6

The *Echo*'s morgue stretched across the office's back wall. At the *Times*, the paper's archives consisted of clippings—millions of them—that librarians had painstakingly cut out of the paper with scissors and filed by subject in thousands of Manila envelopes. But the *Echo* had no librarian. On Thursdays, Marion tied that week's entire issue into a large binder and copied the headlines into a ledger that sat next to it. Ninety-two fat binders, each holding a year's worth of *Echo*s, filled a bank of cubbyholes below the back counter. Together, the binders held most of Klahowya County's recorded history, the cultural heritage of just about everything that had happened in the Skookum since the first white settlers arrived.

I started with the 1973 ledger, skimming the entire year for some mention of Rush Creek. Nothing. I finally found what I was looking for in the ledger for the following year, and I cracked open the big 1974 binder to the issue we'd published on August 8. I found the story inside, on page 6:

> The Terrance Johnson property, 80 acres on Rush Creek just west of U.S. 101, has sold to a Seattle corporation, according to the Klahowya County Assessor's Office. The parcel had been in the Johnson family since it was homesteaded in the 1870s.
>
> The private corporation, Rush Creek Collective, paid $165,000 for the property. One of RCC's directors, Roger Bachman of Seattle, said the company was formed to "fulfill the vision of a benefactor who wanted to leave a legacy that reflects the Northwest tradition of peaceful cooperation." He declined to specify what that meant for the future of the Johnson parcel.
>
> Terry Johnson, reached at his law office in San Francisco, said, "That land's been in our family for generations, and it breaks my heart to sell. But the second growth is gone, and the next timber harvest is decades away. We just can't afford to keep it any longer."

I leafed through the rest of 1974. One story noted that the planning office had issued permits for two small frame buildings on the property. Another reported on a vague, inconclusive interview with a new resident about the Rush Creek Collective and its plans. The first real news took the form of a major page-one feature in June of 1975. The collective was a commune incorporated in the peace-and-love spirit of the Home Colony, an anarchist outpost that rose just across the Klahowya County line on a little Puget Sound cove seventy-five years earlier. The anarchists had a going concern for decades, with the likes of Emma Goldman stopping by to celebrate the revolution. The anarchists eventually died out, the only remnant of their dream a sleepy little town called "Home." But Rush Creek's benefactor, an aging Seattle restaurateur smitten by the New Age bug, had picked up the torch. His will left money to buy land for the Home Colony's spiritual successors.

And they had come. Three cabins already stood on a creekside meadow, and the *Echo*'s photograph showed two dozen or more longhairs, barefoot, bare-chested, and bell-bottomed, at work on three more. The Rush Creek Commune was in business.

But that part of it was old news to me. What really mattered was the date I'd dug up on my first hit: August 8, 1974.

* * *

Friday morning dawned clear, with a light morning breeze that snapped the flag flying from the weathered pole in front of the *Echo*'s porch. I bounded up the steps and yanked the screen door open. Chesty looked up from a pile of ad proofs and smiled. I pushed through the swinging gate and stood over his shoulder. "We gonna stay in business another month?" I said, leaning down to scrutinize the proofs.

"Yeah, maybe. Thriftway's planning to put beefsteaks on sale for $2.68 a pound. They could hardly go bust with something that big comin' up."

I turned toward my own desk. "But I'll tell ya," Chesty continued, "things are getting a little tight over at the old T-way. Mitch always moans about how bad things are, but he's starting to sound serious about it."

The wooden swivel chair creaked as I settled into it. My eyes flicked across the piles of pictures stacked on the desk. The high school graduation photos. The junior high photos. The grade school photos. All published in the past two weeks. Chesty's words, intoned when I first set foot in the *Echo*, flitted through my mind. "Every name in town," the older man had said, lifting his arm through a wide arc that indicated the whole universe of Bent Fir, "at least once a year."

Not a bad motto for a country weekly. But not exactly Watergate or the Iranian hostage crisis either. I sighed, reached forward, and started sorting the photos into piles I could take back to the schools. Some of the grade school faces had familiar features smiling out over names I recognized. Several of my classmates had a head start on families of their own.

The screen door creaked open, and I looked up. "Hi, Marion," I said. "What you up to today?"

She wore snug black slacks that showed off her full hips, sensible shoes, and a crisp white blouse with a high collar. "I'm not sure," she said, smiling for what must have been the first time since the funeral. "How about you?" She pushed through the gate and gave Chesty a brisk pat on the shoulder as she passed. He grunted in acknowledgment. She leaned against the back of her desk, facing me. Gold pendant earrings swayed below her close-cropped hair.

"Thought I might drive by the schools," I said. "Drop these off." I swept my arm past the piles of photos on my desk. "Then maybe stop by the mill. See how they're doing."

"Mind if I come along?" she asked, tilting her head. "I need a story."

I gathered the photos and pushed through the gate. Marion followed. Chesty grunted again.

In the car, Marion made a quarter turn and lifted her left knee onto the bench seat, facing me. She asked about my folks, my latest fishing trip, my school friends. I talked absentmindedly, happy that she seemed to have Hal Mayfield's death off her mind.

The classroom wing of the grade school was a glassy, one-story structure built in the late fifties. The winter rain had corroded the aluminum window frames, and the summer sun had faded the colored plastic panels that lined the breezeway. Marion waited in the car while I strolled into the office, exchanged pleasantries with the school secretary, and delivered the photos.

We repeated the process a few blocks farther down Front at the old two-story brick building that housed both the high school and the junior high. Then I pointed the Dodge toward the mill. "What's next for you, Tom Dawson?" Marion asked. "Where will you go, once your mom gets better and you're ready to move on?"

"*If* she gets better."

"Oh, she will. And you will."

"I hope you're right on the first part. On the second part, I'm not so sure."

Marion's voice dropped in pitch and took on an almost-scolding tone. "Look, Mr. Dawson," she said, "you have no reason to mope around feeling sorry for yourself. You can dig. You can write. You're young. What got you to the *Times* can get you pretty much wherever you want to go."

"My name's on the great big journalism shit list in the sky. Who's going to hire me?"

"That L.A. stink will blow over. You know how this business works. A couple of good stories will wipe the slate clean. Besides, you don't have to work for a newspaper."

"What else am I gonna do? Ink for blood, you know. Newsprint for skin."

"Books. Magazines. High-priced private eye. C'mon, Tom. You can do lots of things. And in Seattle or Portland. New York. You name it. You can go anywhere if you want."

"Fishing's no good in New York."

Marion never did buy the smart-ass side of my humor. "Fishing wasn't any good in L.A. either," she said sharply.

"What about you?" I asked.

"Me?" she said, as though the thought of leaving had never occurred to her. "I'm married to a logger. Besides, I kind of fit here."

I didn't really know her then, and my first thought was that she didn't fit at all. She spoke good English, drank wine out of corked bottles, and bought her clothes in Seattle. And she was a looker who'd turn heads on Rodeo Drive. Marion Mayfield, I foolishly figured, was wasted on Bent Fir.

I turned into the parking lot at Skookum Wood Products. The old wigwam burner rusted next to the driveway, its fires snuffed out a dozen years before by new environmental regulations. I still remembered the school-day smell of burning fir scraps that had wafted through recess when a west wind blew. But even if the Clean Air Act hadn't, economics would have extinguished the big metal teepees that rose in the yard of every Northwest mill. Scrap was too valuable to burn by then, and Skookum Wood shipped truckloads of the stuff to the chipping plant in Shelton.

"You'd think somebody would salvage that thing for the steel," I said, nodding at the wigwam.

"You'd think," said Marion. "But that would take some initiative."

* * *

Steam billowed up into the blue sky from a stack on the two-story building that housed Skookum Wood Products' main plant. Inside, a band saw whined, and the little pusher tug's engine revved on the log pond out back. Marion and I walked into the office, and Marty Brantly looked up from his desk behind the cluttered counter. "Ah," he said. "The press is out in force. What's the deal? Smell some bad news?"

"Should we?" Marion asked.

"Jesus," Marty said. "Interest rates are 12 percent. Who's gonna be buying our two-by-fours to build a new house? We got nuthin' but bad news.

"C'mon," he continued, rising from his chair. "I gotta make my rounds."

Marty walked us into the plant, where the noise shut down conversation. Second-growth logs, just a couple of feet through at the butt, bounced up the conveyor from the pond and into the saw room. Sawyers eyeballed the logs, rotated them to minimize waste, and sent them through the humming band saws. With every cut, a whine rose in pitch, hit a deafening plateau, and then abruptly stopped as the blade popped through the last bit of wood and into empty air.

Marty, a University of Washington forestry major who'd finished at the UW a decade ahead of me, shouted between cuts. "A computer should be figuring out how to break down the logs," he said. "And the new ones run the saws, too. A couple of guys in a glass box can operate the whole shebang."

"All we need," I said with a wry smile. "This town's got too many jobs, and it's always good news when we get rid of a few more."

We stepped out onto a metal catwalk that ran along the green chain, where the freshly cut lumber spilled out on a long, wide line of steel rollers for sorting. Young men new to the mill reached out into the passing jumble of fresh-cut lumber and pulled their assigned dimensions into stacks. They lifted their heads as we passed, staring impassively at their college-educated boss and the two college-educated journalists who strolled past their purgatory. We walked on by, with our clean hands and clean clothes. They went back to their endless bending and pulling and lifting.

"Now the green chain is something you should computerize," I said.

Marty grinned. "Ain't so bad these kids gotta work the chain," he said. "We all did."

The catwalk led down to the floor. We strolled out the big freight doors at the end of the building and into the yard. A jitney buzzed past, on its way to the green chain to pick up another stack of two-by-sixes.

Marty stopped and turned to us. "Look," he said, "I might as well tell you. You don't print for a week, and we're gonna tell the men tomorrow anyway."

He paused and looked down, his shoulders slumping. He inhaled and looked up again. "We're shuttin' down the graveyard," he said. "Lumber's stackin' up, and it just don't make sense to keep on cuttin'."

Around us, in the yard, piles of cut and cured lumber covered the asphalt. A half dozen flatbed trucks sat idle next to the pond. The pusher tug tooted as it maneuvered another raft up to the conveyor, where two men with pike poles waited to steer logs onto the lift. "The youngest men work the graveyard shift," Marty said, looking directly at Marion. "Some don't have families yet."

We pulled out our notebooks and asked questions. How many men on the shift? Sixty-two. How long a layoff? Dunno. Will the men get unemployment? Sure—for twenty-six weeks. What about the swing shift? Dunno about that either. And, said Marion, looking intently up at Marty's face, what about the loggers who supply the mill?

"Shit outta luck," Marty said. "We ain't buying nuthin' until we cut the log inventory back. Waaay back."

7

I rolled out of bed early on what was supposed to be a day off, fired up the Dodge, and headed for Olympia. The highway passed through Shelton and wound along the muddy bays of Puget Sound's southernmost reaches. The huge neoclassical capitol dome appeared across Budd Inlet long before I reached the city.

I found the office I wanted in a staid stone building that fronted Capitol Lake. The place was busy—in those days the secretary of state's office stayed open on Saturday mornings for anybody who wanted to incorporate a company, check a trademark, file for office, or register a charity. And the good citizens of Washington State were taking advantage of the opportunity.

Armed with the Rush Creek Collective's date of incorporation, I stepped up to the counter in the corporations division and smiled my best smile at the perky young brunette who walked over when she saw me. In a couple of minutes I had the complete file in front of me. I pulled out my notebook and got to work.

The articles of incorporation included a complete list of the Rush Creek Collective's board of directors. In the old egalitarian spirit of the Home Colony, it contained a dozen names—apparently every one of the original commune members. All you had to do to have a legal say in how Rush Creek operated was to live there.

The state also required an annual report—"FILING FEE $1.00"— for all nonprofit corporations. Each listed the corporate officers and members of the board, and the Rush Creekers had stuck with their practice of including everybody living on the property. The paper trail revealed the name of each hopeful new arrival and each disillusioned departure. Max Stewart's name was there, and so were three or four others that I recognized. One was a head-scratcher—I never figured Arnie Dykes for the peace-and-love type.

I jotted the names down in my notebook, figuring I could follow up with county criminal records. But any progress on that particular paper trail would have to wait. I handed the file back to the perky brunette, pointed the Dodge toward Bent Fir, and let the V-8 unwind. I had a date.

*   *   *

"Lieutenant Harper," I said. The Marine guard snapped a salute and waved me forward, all in the same motion. I drove onto the base and followed the directions Sandy Harper had given me Thursday night when she'd called and invited me to an Officers' Club dinner dance. The route wound through curves lined with cedars to a two-story brick building with a flat roof and open stairwells that flanked it like bookends. A sign read "Bachelor Officer's Quarters, Building 7."

I squinted at the list of occupants next to the building's metal door and pushed the button next to "Lt. JG Harper." A metallic voice chirped "Be right down" through the speaker grill.

Sandy Harper pushed through the door looking even better than I remembered her. Blond hair against clear skin glowing with color I didn't remember from her official presence in the PAO office. The jacket of her blues squeezed her waist and flared at her hips. She wore her skirt well above her knees, and her thighs were tanned. "You're right on time," she said through a wide smile.

"Some things are worth being on time for," I said, pushing the front door open and following her through into the balmy spring evening. I opened the passenger-side door.

"A gentleman," she said as she slid onto the bench seat.

"But not an officer," I said, satisfied with my own wit as I slammed the door and jogged back to the driver's side.

She directed me through the twisting lanes and down a long grade toward the harbor. The Officers' Club, a long, low building with a swimming pool at one end and tennis courts at the other, hugged a sandy beach piled with driftwood. Six identical fourteen-foot sailboats lined a floating dock running straight out into the bay.

The open door led to a buzz of conversation, the acoustic bass downbeat of a jazz trio, and a thicket of blue and white uniforms. I felt instantly self-conscious in my blazer and chinos.

Sandy took me by the arm and guided me through the crowd and into a bar overlooking the bay. We collected gin and tonics and settled onto stools along a counter that spanned the picture window.

I lit a Marlboro. "So," Sandy said, over her first sip, "what are you doing in a place like Bent Fir?"

"I'm from here. My folks are here. I like salt water."

"I'm from a small town, too. Dallas, Oregon, a little burg down in the Willamette Valley. Pretty place. But I spent three summers working at the vegetable-packing plant, and that was enough small-town life for me. Rows and rows of dumpy women shucking peas and peeling carrots. Their idea of excitement is when the line switches from beets to beans."

"So what kind of excitement are you looking for?"

"Who knows? That's why I signed up for NROTC at Oregon State. You know: Join the Navy; see the world. I figured I'd know the right kind of excitement when I saw it."

"You're surrounded by hotshot Navy fighter jocks," I said. "Isn't that enough excitement for you?"

"Hey! I may be a flack, but I majored in journalism, too. I like men who can read. Besides, dating one of these hotshot fighter jocks makes my job way too complicated."

Two dozen round tables covered with blue tablecloths filled the dining room. We found our name tags and settled in to crab cocktails and a decent salmon dinner. I quizzed the lieutenant commander next to me about base cutbacks imposed after the Vietnam War ended and Jimmy Carter butchered the defense budget. Nothing new on that front, the officer said. And the Reagan administration didn't look all that much better. At least not yet. He wouldn't be surprised to lose another squadron of Neptunes or Intruders before the end of the year. The supermarkets and bars and sporting-goods stores in the neighboring towns would feel one more pinch.

"Watch out," Sandy said. "You're talking to the press."

The lieutenant commander gave me a long look. "You're the reporter from the local weekly," he said, "the one who did the story on our A-6s."

"Guilty," I said.

"And you," he said to Sandy, "are the PAO who let him get away with it." She smiled. I smiled. The lieutenant commander smiled.

"And he got all the facts right," Sandy said. "Sometimes the brass doesn't realize that's what public affairs is all about. We're not here to suppress the news."

"Of course not," the officer said, holding his hands in front of him as if trying to push the abhorrent thought away. "And I'm happy to see you're working overtime on the fact-checking angle of this particular story."

We all laughed, and I watched Sandy's cheeks flush. She looked beautiful, her hair shimmering in the rosy light, her eyes sparkling with enjoyment of the moment.

"And I have to admit," the lieutenant commander added, "that your story is the talk of Cedar Springs. It's been hard to find a copy of your paper to pass around."

"It's the talk of Bent Fir, too," I said. "But it doesn't take much to get us locals yapping."

"Oh, I don't know. Your old man and his Model 94 make for quite a talc. And he convinced me of one thing."

"What's that?" Sandy asked.

"I'm not flying an A-6 anywhere near anybody's chicken coop."

* * *

The trio shifted into dance mode with "A Summer Place." We asked the lieutenant commander to excuse us, and I steered Sandy to the polished wooden floor. To the east, across the bay, a few scattered clouds picked up pink from the sun, setting out of sight behind the ridgeline above the base.

I ordered bourbon, neat, and was surprised when Sandy did, too. We talked and danced, danced and talked. The trio stuck to ballads, and she settled into my shoulder. I leaned down into her and savored each breath of perfume. After a half dozen dances, she kept holding my hand as we worked our way back to the table. "It's a pretty night," she said.

"Should we leave?"

"You can't come into the BOQ."

"We could go for a drive."

"Let's."

We rolled the windows down, and I steered back up the hill and out toward the main gate. The guard nodded as we passed.

I turned south on the highway. Sandy slid across the seat and lowered her head onto my shoulder. I slowed and turned left at a viewpoint. The road wound up a slight grade and out onto a headland. From the parking lot, the lights of Angel Harbor twinkled to the north. In the distance, I could see the blinking navigation light that marked the entrance to the Big Skookum.

At that point, Sandy seemed like just what I was looking for—single, self-sufficient, and on a course out into the big, broad world I was so eager to conquer. I turned to her, and she leaned into me, raising her face, her eyes half closed.

8

On Monday, I took a midmorning break, stepped out onto the *Echo*'s porch, lit a Marlboro, and headed down the street to the courthouse. The assessor's office filled a third of the first floor with oak filing cabinets. I stepped up to the counter, and birdlike Ethel Prescott, one of my mother's oldest friends, skittered toward me like an excited wren. "Tommy!" she twittered. "You're home!"

I was hearing those kinds of greetings every time I turned a corner that June. They had a strange way of comforting and annoying me at the same time.

I chatted with Ethel, mostly about my mother's health, and finally asked for the tax-lot numbers for the Rush Creek Collective. Once she found those, Ethel quick-stepped over to a file cabinet and returned with a big cardboard binder clasped to her chest. She dropped it on the counter, and I carried it over to a reading table.

I hadn't expected much from the tax records, but in the early stages of an investigation you check everything. Sometimes some odd fact pops up that actually leads somewhere.

Mostly, the paperwork told me what I already knew. The land's selling price—$165,000—had automatically become its assessed value after the deal closed. The assessor's tax notices also listed every member of the collective as an owner, and the names matched those in the corporations division records. Terry Johnson hadn't lied about the value of the land's timber. The half dozen cabins the Rush Creekers had built on the property bumped the valuation up a few thousand bucks, but after that it barely moved. Which brought me to the one curious fact that lay inertly among the numbers. For the first few years, the commune had struggled with the annual $800 property-tax payment. The members never paid more than the half-year minimum, and most of the time they were late with that. Then, in the late seventies, the Rush Creekers suddenly turned into responsible citizens. They made full-year payments at their first opportunity every year, and they made every payment on time.

* * *

Monday afternoon's Forest Service press conference in Shelton drew the usual suspects. The reporter for the *Shelton Pioneer* was there, of course. I had met the rumpled, middle-aged glad-hander with the beer belly a couple of times on stories just like this one—government handouts gave some agency information officer something to do. The Shelton guy seemed to know every bureaucrat and always asked after the kids, by name. Just doing what he had to do to serve his readers, I suppose. But, young buck that I was back then, the thought of a lifetime doing the same thing made me cringe.

The Olympia paper was there, too, along with three or four weeklies, a couple of radio stations, and a half dozen kids from a journalism class at the community college. The only outside face belonged to a serious young woman from the *Tacoma News Tribune*. Odd, I thought. The *Trib* didn't usually stray this far. But Tacoma had several big lumber mills, and the paper did take an interest in logging stories.

The public information officer stepped to the front of the room and sat on a gray Formica counter that ran below a row of aluminum windows. The windows hinged outward at the bottom, and somebody had pushed a couple of them open. The little bit of air that floated in did nothing to dispel the stuffy government-issue atmosphere. A gnomish man in Forest Service green stepped to the PIO's side, looking as uncomfortable as a kid dressed for church.

"This is Charlie Adams," the PIO said. "He's been down here working out of Shelton for the past few weeks, running an investigation with the help of the fine officers here in our own station."

"Howdy," said Adams, with something between a wave and a salute.

"I'll let Charlie tell you what's going on," the PIO continued. He stood, grabbed a stack of handouts off the counter beside him, and circulated through the room, handing one to each reporter.

Adams pushed his round little stomach against the table and launched into a dry recitation that echoed the handout's facts on the Forest Service and the Olympic National Forest. He was out of the Seattle office, where criminal investigations for the entire Pacific Northwest were headquartered. A dozen Forest Service investigators worked out of the office. Local police agencies handled state criminal-code violations. The Forest Service handled anything to do with public resources. Mostly, around here, that meant logging.

The reporters stared out the windows. On the parking strip outside, a flock of juncos frolicked in a hawthorn tree, still blooming. Finally, the Tacoma reporter broke in. "Mr. Adams," she said, "what, specifically, brought you down here?"

"Well," he said. "The state police stopped two logging trucks on U.S. 101 this past month. Both were traveling at night. Both had full loads. Neither load was branded, and the drivers had nuthin' to show they'd ever been through a Forest Service scaling station."

"In short," he said, "they was log rustling. Them two loads was worth nearly $12,000. An illegal cut and an illegal transport. The service didn't get a dime for them loads. They was stolen from the taxpayers, and we busted the drivers."

"Charlie," the Shelton reporter said, "mills are closing all over the South Sound. There's no market for the timber. Why would anybody be trying to steal what they can't sell?"

"This was clear fir," Adams said. "You can always sell old growth."

The experienced reporters stirred, and the students looked at one another, figuring there was something they should be getting but weren't.

"Where'd it come from?" I asked.

"Dunno. The trucks were stopped near the Takamak River, headed south on 101. The drivers won't talk."

The PIO was moving through the room again, handing out another poop sheet. It provided the bare-bones public-record information on the two arrests. Dates, names, places, charges. I recognized neither name.

"Just between us," Adams continued, "these two boys was out-of-work loggers. There's more and more of 'em every day. They got to feed their families, and this is one way to do it. But these here trees was from a protected watershed. Enviros is gonna raise hell if much of this goes on, and rightly so.

"The perps won't talk—they probably got family and friends involved, and they ain't looking at a whole lotta time anyway. We're searchin' in the woods to find out where these logs come from. But the Olympic is one big forest. And right up the road we got the national park. Plenty of big trees up there. Park Service is lookin', too, to see if maybe some might be missin'.

"What we're hopin' is that you folks will get the word out. The people up there in the woods, they know what's goin' on. We're hopin' somebody will come forward. Put a stop to this now, before it gets a whole lot worse."

A few more questions followed. Adams and the information officer left, and the students headed out the door. I buttonholed the Tacoma reporter, whose name turned out to be Heather McKenzie, and peppered her with questions. Where'd she go to school? Where'd she work before the *News Tribune*? Who was her editor? Was the paper doing any hiring?

* * *

The unseasonable June sun was gone, and a spring cloud cover filtered the morning light. I threaded my way along the trail that ran through the woods behind my apartment. I've always enjoyed gray summer mornings in Puget Sound country. No, not gray—pearly. At least that's what my mother called cloud-covered summer skies. And the high fogs that so often roll in from the ocean eighty miles to the west do have a translucent quality different from the sodden winter overcast that oozes steady drizzle on Western Washington.

My crepe-soled shoes moved soundlessly over the bed of evergreen needles that padded the overgrown trail. I pushed some Oregon grape aside and stepped into the gravel lot behind the *Echo*.

The clatter of the little flatbed job press filled the back shop. Harris looked up from the machine, where posters for the Klahowya County Fair rose in a neat stack as they popped off the press, one by one. "How ya doin', kid," Harris hollered, grinning. "How's fishin'?"

"Killer. Those rainbows are dying to meet me."

I strolled up the aisle between the big rotary press and the two Linotype machines and paused for a minute by the flatbed. The old printer and I traded the currency of Klahowya County men. Harris had been out trolling the mouth of the Big Skookum for spring chinook. No luck. I had been back to the Takamak for an afternoon of fly-fishing above Mitchell Falls. Pretty good.

"Oughta take some big ol' night crawlers in there with ya, kid," Harris said with a hoot. "You'd clean them suckers right outta there."

I smiled, shook my head, and moved on past. "You're missing the whole point, old man," I said over my shoulder.

I pushed through the swinging gate and stepped into the front office. "Mornin', Tommy," Chesty said, looking up from his desk behind the front counter.

"Good morning, Tom," Marion said, without turning away from her typewriter.

Monday morning. No mail yet. I shuffled through some old press releases on my desk. Most were public-service blurbs for government programs, sent out to a mailing list that included not only the dailies but also every shopper and country weekly in the state. About the only thing with any relevance to Bent Fir, I figured, was the release about expanded hours at the state unemployment office in Shelton. I wedged the notice into my Selectric and pushed back from my desk. "Maybe I'll go see Jimmy Winthrop about his grand plans for the marina," I said. Chesty grunted, dismissive of Jimmy's hubris.

"Good idea," Marion said. "We could use something for the front page. Something with a picture."

I grabbed a notebook and the Rolleiflex on my way out. I passed Marion's yellow Volkswagen Bug, the only car in the *Echo*'s lot, then strolled past Brill's and the churches. The Spar was still closed. But a couple of pickups were parked in front of the Grizzly, their drivers, I figured, making a quick stop for their morning beer and tomato juice. Or maybe they had been laid off the mill's graveyard shift and would sit at the bar all morning, staring into red beers and bitching about the government and the goddamned environmentalists.

I angled across the street toward the ramshackle building that teetered on the bank just past the bridge. The sign—"Big Skookum Marina: Moorage, Storage, Repairs"—hung crookedly from a post, faded to near illegibility.

I walked through the vacant office and followed the clanging and cursing that floated through the dusty air. In the shop, Jimmy Winthrop stood behind an old sixteen-foot Larson runabout. Gull droppings splattered the bow decking and the roof of the half-cabin. Barnacles encrusted the bottom. Jimmy held a long-handled spark-plug wrench with one hand and took another swing at it with a three-pound hammer. The twenty-five-horsepower Evinrude hanging on the Larson's transom shuddered, but the corroded plug held fast.

"Watch it. You'll bust the block."

Jimmy turned and squinted. "No great loss," he said, laying the hammer on the transom and putting his hands on his hips. "So what's the press up to this fine morning?"

"Thought I'd see how your plans for the marina are coming."

Jimmy smiled, took a step toward the office, and motioned for me to follow. "C'mon," he said. "Got something to show you."

At the cluttered desk behind the parts counter, he unrolled a tube of paper and weighted its four corners with boat hardware. An architectural drawing showed Big Skookum Marina as it might be. A new office building and shop. A paved parking lot ringed with shrubbery. Expanded moorage with sleek sailboats and pricey powerboats filling forty-foot slips. The Big Skookum Bridge, gleaming in new paint, arching across the water in the background.

"Got these last week," Jimmy said proudly, his hand gesturing toward more paper tubes that, presumably, contained blueprints and elevations. "Been saving up to hire the architect for a year. Now I've got what I need to get the loan."

Fat chance, I thought. The architect's little paper tubes were headed into the same big tube that was sucking down the rest of the town. "That's great," I said. "The town could use some good news. But the mill just laid off the graveyard. Who's going to buy all those big boats?"

"Got it all figured," Jimmy said. "Get the right loan and we can offer moorage rates half those in Seattle. Hell, we can beat Olympia and even Shelton. And the South Sound's great cruisin'. We'll fill those slips with high rollers from the cities. And they'll bring their money with 'em. Buy beer from the Thriftway. Gear from the hardware store. Holy cow, they might even buy a copy of your paper."

"That's great, Jimmy," I said, feeling that guilty twinge I always get when I'm playing the nonjudgmental reporter. "What's next?"

"I'm not screwing around with these piddly little banks around here. Got an appointment with a loan officer at Washington Mutual, up in Seattle."

Sorry Jimmy, I thought. *But nobody in Seattle is going to think any business, even a marina, has much of a shot in a town like Bent Fir.*

Back at the *Echo,* I checked in with Marion at her desk, and she said the marina story would carry the top of page one, with a line shot of the plans for the new marina and my picture of Jimmy out examining his old boat slips. "C'mon," I said, hearing myself echo the voice of every city editor I'd ever known. "Jimmy's little scheme doesn't have a prayer. Why give it the kind of play that gives it real credibility. That's a lie. You know it, and I know it."

Marion answered from another journalistic planet. "I might know it. And I might not. But I do know one thing. This town deserves a little hope."

She stood, took a step forward, and stared up into my face, stern and unblinking. The Forest Service press-conference story, she said, would run across the page below the fold, with the head shot I'd snapped of Charlie Adams. It would jump to an open page inside, which would carry a package of related stories.

"So," she added, "we'd better get to work."

9

I spent Tuesday afternoon doing the best I could to pump a little of Marion's feel-good rah rah into my story on Jimmy's marina plans. I dropped the draft on her desk about five, and the two of us roughed out a plan for the log-rustling package. Then I headed over to the Spar, where I nabbed my favorite seat, the center booth along the row of windows that looked out over the Big Skookum. I nursed a beer and stared out across the water toward Mount Rainier while I waited for fish and chips and stewed over the Forest Service press conference.

A loud greeting snapped me out of my reverie. "Hey, Tommy!" bellowed a deep voice. "That you?"

I turned and saw the familiar shape of a huge Indian silhouetted in the light flooding in through the Spar's front door. "Little Jim!" I said, rising from the booth. The two of us met midfloor and gave each other high fives, the big man towering over me.

Little Jim Littlefoot had been a terror on the front line of the Big Skookum Loggers, opening gaping holes for Lars Mayfield and the rest of my backfield. And he was a rarity, a Takamak Indian who saw fishing as something more than gill-netting for salmon. All through high school Little Jim and I made a late-summer and fall ritual of casting for sea-run cutthroat trout at the mouth of the Takamak.

"C'mon," I said, "join me. You still blocking and tackling?"

"Nah. Got no cause since you quit fartin' around in the backfield. Geez. Some days we figured we had time to go down to the Griz for a beer before you got around to throwin' the damned football."

We sat in the booth downing Rainier until alpenglow appeared on the mountain of the same name. Eventually, the talk turned to Hal Mayfield. "This is a weird one," I said. "You don't expect somebody around here to grease a guy by screwing with the brakes on his truck. Klahowya County guys are a lot more direct than that."

"Don' cha know. Put a .30-.30 slug in your chest. Split your head with an ax. That's the way we settle scores around here."

"And who'd want to settle a score with Hal Mayfield anyway? Everything I hear, he was a stand-up guy."

Little Jim held his glass up close to his right eye, closed his left, and watched the bubbles rise through his beer. "Well . . . Hal was pretty much what you get in a Klahowya County bull of the woods, all right. But just because a guy's straight from the shoulder doesn't mean he's Mr. Popularity, you know."

"Yeah. I heard the Rush Creekers had a few bones to pick with him."

"Damn straight. You and I know what a hothead Lars is, too. What I hear, he and the old man had bad blood from time to time. Lars is a man full-growed. Musta been tough toeing the line for an old tight-ass like Hal."

"Cutting brake lines doesn't seem like Lars's style."

"No. It don't," Little Jim said, draining his glass. "But it sure was somebody's."

*　　*　　*

When I got back to my place, I picked up Mom's Teddy Roosevelt book, but the writing marathon I faced the next morning kept distracting me. I lay on the couch, *Mornings on Horseback* propped open on my chest, while I stared at the cracked ceiling and pictured the opening words to the log-rustling mainbar.

I'd landed a telephone interview with one of the state cops who'd stopped the two loggers hauling illegal old growth, and I had enough descriptive detail from the midnight bust to lead with a scene-setter. Then I figured I'd move to a nut graf outlining the scope of the problem and its implications, introduce Charlie Adams, and work my way through the press conference material chronologically, which would give me a chance to use Charlie's good quotes. I could wrap up with some additional context I'd picked up with several phone calls after the press conference—total public and private land left in old growth, the environmental protests, some history of old-growth logging in the Northwest. I'd do a sidebar on the continuing demand for old growth at specialty mills. Marion would kick in a sidebar on the logging recession and how that factored into the problem.

As I always did when I had a big story brewing, I popped awake a couple of times in the night and pondered the topic some more while I stood at the toilet, processing the evening's beer.

I bounded up the *Echo*'s front steps at 7:15 Wednesday morning, anxious to get cracking on the mainbar. Marion was in before eight. I looked up from my Royal as she pushed through the swinging gate with the kind of enthusiasm I hadn't seen since Hal Mayfield died. "Good for you," she said. "We'll need the whole day and then some." She headed for her own typewriter, rubbing her hands together in anticipation of the day's work.

Marion had her sidebar written by noon. While I tried to conjure up a snappy ending to my mainbar, she walked down to the Thriftway for a couple of the tasteless deli sandwiches Mitch made up each morning and stored in the beer cooler. "Got your kicker yet?" she asked when she got back to the office.

"I decided to let the Forest Service investigator have the last word. He put it pretty well."

"How so?"

"Guy's name is Charlie Adams. Seems to be a straight shooter. He wrapped things up by saying, 'We're hoping somebody will come forward. Put a stop to this now, before it gets a whole lot worse.'"

"Not terribly zippy," she said, "but it does sum things up."

She held out her hands, a sandwich in each. "Ham or turkey?"

"Wonder Bread?"

"What else?"

"That thin-sliced meat that looks like somebody peeled it off a legal pad?"

"The very same."

"All bound in Saran Wrap so tight that the whole thing's turned to mush."

"Prepared as only Mitch can make 'em."

"Then it really doesn't matter which one I choose, does it?"

She smiled and tossed me the turkey. We proofed each other's work while absently munching gummy white bread and dry lunchmeat. Marion took the finished copy back to Harris for typesetting while I banged out my sidebar. When I stepped back into the newsroom after handing that off to Harris, she rose from her chair. "C'mon," she said, cocking her head toward the front door. "We've been cranking for hours. Let's take a walk."

We headed down Front. As we passed the courthouse, she gestured toward the sheriff's office. "Have you heard any more from Walt?" she asked.

I said I'd called Walt Hasslebring late Monday, just before leaving the *Echo*. Nope. Nothing new. Hasslebring and his deputies had interviewed just about everybody working the Mayfield Logging show up on FS 2103. The sheriff had been through all the paperwork on the Bull of the Woods sale, too. Nothing there either.

"You already know most of what he told me," I said. That Hal had underbid a lot of guys on a lot of jobs. But that was business. Hal was liked. Respected. Feared a little. The top guy in a tough little society that operated pretty much on its own out there in the trees, beholden to nobody.

"What's Lars say?" I asked. "If anybody had it in for Hal, Lars would have known. Wouldn't he?"

"Lars is complicated. He keeps a lot inside, and he's been saying even less since Hal died. He snaps at me and his mother. He disappears for hours. He stares off into space. And, mostly, he drinks."

We walked slowly east on Front, past Benny Brill's. "That's where you're living, isn't it?" Marion asked. "Upstairs?"

"Yeah. It's okay. I can walk to work when I don't need the car. There's even a path through the woods if I want to stay off the main road."

We passed the taverns. Marion glanced left and scanned the parking lot in front of the Grizzly. "Well," she said, "Lars is working this morning. Or at least he's somewhere other than his favorite bar stool."

"What's up, Marion?" I asked. "What's wrong?"

"Oh, I don't know," she said with a sigh. "I guess I was hoping things would change a little now that Hal's gone. That Lars would take things a little more seriously."

I seized the opportunity to ask the question that distracted me almost every time I saw her. "Why Lars? How did you two end up together anyway?"

"Doesn't seem like much of a fit, does it? The college girl and the redneck."

She fell silent, and I waited.

"I was home from Lindley. Christmas, my sophomore year. A couple of local girls and I went to a holiday dance. Lars was there with

55

two of his buddies. He was a handsome guy. He still is.

"We danced some. Then we started taking little breaks in the parking lot, passing a bottle around. Eventually, the other two guys took off with my pals. So it was just me and Lars, and by that time I was pretty drunk."

After the music ended, Lars and Marion wound up in his pickup on a logging road. "Don't get me wrong," she said. "I wanted to be there. Lars has never forced me to do anything. If anything, he's been too deferential. To me. To his dad. He holds himself way down inside, way beyond anything I can reach."

After that first night with Lars, she woke up in her own bed, hung over and embarrassed. She was well into spring term when she discovered she was pregnant. Out-of-wedlock births weren't uncommon in Klahowya County, then or now. But then they ended only one way; so Marion and her mother didn't even consider any alternative but marriage. Marion dropped out of Lindley, came home, and married Lars in the Baptist church. The new couple moved in with Hal and Dottie Mayfield in the family's big log place north of town.

"You got pregnant; you got married," Marion said. "It was what you did. But I *wanted* to marry Lars. There was something about him, about the way he was always just out of reach. That aroused my competitive instincts, I guess. But he was tender with me, too, loving. And he was 100 percent Klahowya County, the living flesh of what I thought of as home. Lindley . . . it was so far away, not in miles, just in the whole feel of the place. The other girls . . . They knew nothing about the kind of life I'd lived. And, God knows, I wanted that baby."

She miscarried within a month, before most of the townspeople even realized she was pregnant.

We walked on, silently. Marion finally spoke. "We'd better get back," she said. "Harris will want us to read galleys."

We crossed the street and headed toward the paper. "You're something special in this town," Marion said softly. "Everybody knows it. Bent Fir doesn't keep boys like you."

"I'm twenty-nine," I said.

"Okay," she said. "Men like you."

"You're pretty special yourself."

"I'm a logger's wife," she said again. "Bent Fir's full of them."

"Bent Fir's full of women married to loggers. But you're the only one I've seen who takes responsibility for the whole town."

She stopped, and I turned to face her. "You know, Tom," she said, "you never get a place like this out of your system. It's still your town, too."

A log truck's air horn pierced the moment. Marion and I turned toward the street. A massive Kenworth, diesel smoke pouring out its stack and its engine winding through downshifts, rumbled toward us on Front. We stared up at the cab as it passed. Lars Mayfield glared back at us.

10

On Thursday morning, I was up early, shoveling down cold cereal and listening intently to my tinny clock radio. The Israeli air force had finally done it, swooping in to destroy an Iraqi nuclear reactor capable of churning out weapons-grade uranium. Tel Aviv was making sure only one Middle Eastern country had the bomb, but Saddam was a crazy man, and God knew what might happen next. In L.A., the *Times* newsroom was no doubt buzzing, the foreign desk vibrating with excitement while cityside desk editors dashed around, working up local angles and deploying platoons of reporters. And here I sat, staring into a bowl of corn flakes and prepping for an interview with a small-town sheriff.

Well, as a wise editor once told me, the story you have is the story you get. So I was out the door just after seven, hoping to catch Walt Hasslebring before he left the sheriff's office. I hoofed it over to the county courthouse, the deputy at the sheriff's office front counter waved me through, and I found Hasslebring in his office, hunched over paperwork with his fist wrapped around the handle of a white ceramic mug. He looked up and raised the mug. "Mornin', Tommy. Want some joe?"

At my nod, Hasslebring lumbered out to the front counter and returned with an identical mug. I tried not to grimace at the first taste of the thick, acrid brew.

"Siddown," Hasslebring said, gesturing at the beat-up oak chair in front of his desk. Then he dropped into his own chair, blocking the view of the Big Skookum flowing placidly by outside his window.

I warmed up by asking about a fireworks call. Local kids always jumped the gun on the Fourth of July, and that year one of them had screwed up badly enough to draw a reckless-endangerment charge. What, I asked, was all that about?

"Clancy Howard got a little too excited, I'm afraid." Hasslebring paused, considering what he'd just said before adding, "But don't quote me on that."

"I won't ever screw you with chicken-shit stuff like that," I said.

"And if I have any doubts about whether or not you're talking for the record, I'll ask."

The sheriff raised his cup and made a toasting motion. "Son," he said, "I'll hold you to that."

I returned the toast and managed another swallow of the vile brew in my cup. The stuff was even worse than what passed for coffee in newsrooms.

"Anyway," Hasslebring continued, "the good deputy Howard was maybe swayed by the fact that those boys out Angel Harbor way not only had a shitload of illegal star shells and Army M-80s but managed to burn Dick Reynolds's tool shed to the ground."

He grinned, and I knew the conversation was off to a good start. "So Clancy, he hauls the kids in and writes 'em up for arson and reckless endangerment. Locks 'em up, too, 'tho their daddy came in a bailed 'em out the next day."

"But what happened? I saw the charge on the court docket Monday. But when I checked again yesterday, it was gone. No arraignment. No nothing. "

"Ahhhh," Hasslebring said, his drawl thickening the way it did when he got especially folksy. "Boys gonna be boys, especially when it comes to firecrackers and such. I went out to Angel Harbor Tuesday evening and saw their daddy. Took him over to the Reynolds place. Dragged the kids along. They said they were real sorry, and their dad promised to build Dick a new shed. Problem solved. I pulled the charges before the DA even considered 'em."

That conversation put another nail in the coffin holding the opinion of the sheriff I'd had growing up. As I'd finally figure out that summer, Walt Hasslebring was a savvy country lawman. He could talk to storekeepers, loggers, stump farmers, and Indians. When it came to conducting a major investigation, he was nobody's fool. On the small stuff, he threw the book away. Loggers who brawled spent the night in jail and walked in the morning. A stump farmer who bounced a check had a week to scrounge up some work so that he could pay up. After a few years, half of Klahowya County's citizens owed him something, one way or the other. So, naturally, they kept voting him back into office, year after year.

I moved the conversation onto more sensitive ground.

"Anything new on Hal Mayfield?"

"Well, y'know, we're not just sittin' on our cans. This is a murder investigation, for Christ's sake. We've talked to everybody in the family, some of them two or three times. We've gone through every scrap of paperwork in Hal's office. But I figure Marion's already told you most of that. We been up in the woods, poking around. Hell, I figure we've talked to every welfare bum, dope dealer, and squatter within twenty miles of the Mayfield show."

He leaned back in his chair, rocked a couple of times, and looked me hard in the eyes.

"And while we was at it, I heard you and I have a mutual interest up on Rush Creek."

The comment startled me. Hasslebring had been to the commune even before me. It must have been one of the first places he went after Hal Mayfield's death. But that wasn't surprising. The commune wasn't that far from the Mayfield show, after all, and its members had an old grudge against Hal. But I was surprised that the sheriff had found out about my visit. The man had a way of tapping into all the scuttlebutt in the Skookum.

"I was up there, all right," I conceded. "Last week. Talked to Maxy Stewart. He and I went to high school together."

The sheriff took a slow sip of coffee.

"Yeah," he said. "Year behind you, wasn't he?"

"That's right. We weren't best buddies or anything, but we knew each other."

"So what'd you think?"

"About what?"

The sheriff put his cup down on the desk and leaned forward.

"Look Tom . . . If we're gonna get along, you can't be playing dumb with me. What I know, you'll know, in good time. But that's gotta go both ways.

"Now what did you think about Max Stewart? And about that goddamn commune, or whatever they call it?"

I sat for a second, looking past the sheriff. His bulk still blocked my view of the water, but I could see the mast of a sailboat moving slowly down the Big Skookum. It passed behind Hasslebring's head and then disappeared behind the right-hand edge of the window. I wondered if the Iraqis had responded to the air strike yet.

I forced myself back to the matter at hand. And the sheriff was right, of course. If I wanted to get anywhere on this story, I'd need his cooperation. And if I wanted information from him, I'd have to give something in return.

"Maxy's tweaking," I said. "He's all methed out. I could see it in his face, in his teeth. And the whole place looks like hell. The women are mostly gone. There's trash everywhere. Nobody's taking care of business. They're probably all meth heads."

"Got that right. That fuckin' commune has become problem numero uno around here. Half my burglaries and car clouts got to be coming from those clowns. And theft on construction sites. Hell, you can't build anything in the county anymore without fencing the site and taking every loose tool home with you every night. Logging shows, too."

"Logging shows?"

"Yeah . . . logging shows. Now what in the hell would you take from a logging show? Well, it turns out tweakers will take just about anything. Pulleys. Peaveys. Anything they can unbolt from a skidder or a Cat. They suck diesel right out of the tanks. No wonder Hal Mayfield went after 'em the way he did."

"I heard about that . . . the business with the tree sit."

"The tree sit? Oh that. Nah. That was a long time ago. I'm talking about what Hal did last month."

Hasslebring saw the blank look on my face.

"Oh ho! You missed that one, eh?"

I sat silently, waiting for the rest of it.

"This is strictly off the record," the sheriff said. "The last thing I need right now is a lotta lips flapping. Actually, I'm surprised it isn't all over town anyway. But I guess nobody involved saw much percentage in talking about it."

"Off the record," I said, raising my hand as though I were taking a courtroom oath.

"The Rush Creek boys were cooking meth up there. Not just little batches from cold pills they boosted from drugstores. Some serious quantities made from bulk chemicals. They had a cook shack up in the woods behind the commune. Sold some to a couple of choker setters on the Mayfield crew. Those boys showed up on the Bull of the Woods show stoned, and Hal Mayfield called them out on it. They blabbed. Next thing you know, Hal and Lars turned up at Rush

Creek, hauling a Cat on a lowboy and both of them packin'. A couple of the Rush Creekers come out, but they backed off when they saw the artillery. Hal fired up the Cat and headed up the road into the woods with Lars riding shotgun. And I do mean shotgun. He was carrying a twelve-gauge Remington pump."

"How'd you find out about all this?"

"All in good time," the sheriff said again. The line, I'd figured out, was a full stop, a signal that I wasn't going to get anywhere on that line of inquiry.

"Did Hal and Lars do what I'm thinking they did?"

"Yep. Drove the D8 right into the woods and flattened the cook shack. Drove over it a few times, just to make sure they'd done the job right. Broke every beaker, smashed every cooker, and ground all the chemicals into the ground. Then they ran the Cat back up onto the lowboy and drove off."

"Just like that?"

"Just like that."

*   *   *

Marion took Friday off, and Chesty spent most of the day out on calls. In the back shop, the Hoe press lay silent while Harris punched out lead slugs on the Linotype and arranged them in page forms on the composing counter. In the almost silent newsroom, the Regulator ticked away like a comatose patient's heartbeat.

I called the funeral home in Shelton to fill in some details on a couple of obituaries and then wrote them. I pulled together the previous day's police runs—a domestic disturbance, a noise complaint on a loud party, and two more calls on illegal fireworks. Then I spent two hours trying not to doze off as I went through a stack of building-code variance requests, tax liens, calls for road-construction contract bids, and other detritus generated by the Klahowya County bureaucracy. I pulled a dozen or so of the least trivial into a local government roundup and called it a day, more than ready for the cold one I'd planned with Little Jim Littlefoot when we'd signed off Tuesday night at the Spar. Jim suggested we get together again Friday night at the Grizzly, and I didn't object. The Griz wasn't really my style, but it served Heidelberg, my favorite.

The door stood ajar, and clouds of cigarette smoke drifted out. I stepped in and stopped to let my eyes adjust. Green light from plastic Heidelberg Beer chandeliers, done up to look like stained glass, cut through the smoke and illuminated the ragged green felt of the two pool tables. More beer signs—Rainier, Olympia, Pabst—glowed on the plywood paneling. Mill workers, stump farmers, and fishermen filled the booths lining the walls. Merle Haggard played on the jukebox. A couple of loggers, fresh from the woods in high-cut pants and wide suspenders, hunched over the bar. One of them, the older brother of a high school classmate, turned on his stool, smirked at me, and said, "Well, lookee here. College boy's come home on summer vacation. How ya doing, college boy?" I was suddenly very conscious of my Hawaiian shirt.

I gave the logger an empty smile and headed down the sticky black path worn in the linoleum. Little Jim sat at the far end of the bar, and I slid onto the wobbly stool next to him. Jim, oblivious, stared dreamily into the back-bar mirror. I dropped my right shoulder, leaned into him, and jerked upward, delivering a solid thump to his beefy upper arm.

Jim snapped to his left, released his beer, and clenched his right fist.

"Hey! Whadda ya . . . Tommy!"

He unclenched his fist and slapped me on the shoulder. "What ya drinkin', bro?" he asked, signaling for the barmaid.

A large woman in a shapeless gray muumuu waddled toward us, trailing cigarette smoke. "What'll it be?" she rasped.

I ordered a Heidelberg draft and turned back to Jim. "Hey!" I said. "You sandbagged me."

"Happy to oblige. But how, exactly, did I do that?"

"When I said the Rush Creekers had some bones to pick with Hal Mayfield, I was talking about the tree-sitting business. I felt like an idiot when Walt Hasslebring told me about Lars and Hal and the D8. How could a reporter working on the Mayfield story not know about that?"

Little Jim sputtered, blowing beer onto the bar and laughing loudly enough to turn heads all over the joint. "Shit," he said, "you flap your lips about Rush Creekers having bones to pick with Mayfields, I figure you be talking about that goddamned armored assault on the meth lab. How in the hell am I supposed to know you're sag-ass ignorant of something everybody in the county knows?"

The woman in the muumuu returned and banged a schooner of Heidelberg down on the bar, slopping beer over the rim.

"I've been gone a while," I said. "Probably a lot I don't know."

"Ahhh," Little Jim said, laughing again. "Recognizing your own ignorance is the beginning of wisdom."

"Geez. I got a fucking philosopher when all I really need is a friend who'll clue me in about shit going on in the woods."

"You buy," Little Jim said, gesturing at the row of taps behind the bar, "and I'll talk."

I quizzed him about Rush Creek. We talked about Maxy Stewart and the other classmates who'd ended up at the commune. Jim complained about them dealing meth to young Takamaks. "Bad shit," he said. "I'd known about the Mayfield raid, I'da gone along myself."

He drained his glass and motioned for another. "Not that you wanna mess with those idiots," he added. "God knows what a tweaker will do. You go snooping around that bunch, you watch yourself."

I ordered another Heidelberg and changed the subject, asking about some of the other Indian kids we'd known at Big Skookum High. Billy Bangs, who played halfback opposite Lars Mayfield, was dead, killed when, in a drunken stupor, he'd driven his pickup off Forest Service 2102. Billy's older brother, Freddie, on the other hand, was back from U-Dub fisheries school and had some deal going with the Washington Fish and Wildlife folks. The tribe was going to kick in some, Fish and Wildlife was going to kick in some, and together they were going to maybe build a salmon hatchery on the Takamak. A dozen jobs for the tribe. More white fishermen coming around to spend city cash. If the tribe could get its act together, that is. And F&W could get some kind of federal grant.

"Geez," I said. "That's a pretty big deal. For around here anyway. It's an *Echo* story for sure, even if it doesn't work out. Where's Freddie Bangs living?"

I glanced over Little Jim's shoulder and, through the haze, saw Lars Mayfield holding court in one of the back booths. He was tall, like all the Mayfields, with a long, gaunt face, a shock of blond hair, and big hands. Three other men were crammed in the booth, and one of them was Stubby Lancaster. The other two were unfamiliar, but they resembled each other in their ragged haircuts, three-day beards, and dirty denim. One of them glanced at me, caught me looking at him, and turned back to his table, saying something to Lars and tossing his head toward Jim and me.

"Hey," I said to Jim. "Who's that over there with Lars Mayfield?"

Jim peered into the back-bar mirror, trying to make out faces through the smoke. "Well, one of 'em's Stubby Lancaster, Mayfield's lead faller."

"Yeah. I know him. Who're the other two?"

"Ahhh," said Jim, raising his glass for a long draft of Pabst. "Them be the Dykes twins, Eddie and Terry."

"Moochie's brothers? Arnie?"

"Yeah. Arnie's the youngest, and Moochie's the kid sister. Guess Eddie and Terry never cared much about Moochie's honor, being as how they never came around school to keep the whole team from diddling her."

"That was just the linemen," I said, laughing. "The backfield had better taste."

"That's not what Billie Bangs used to say," said Jim, lowering his head and looking hard at me with an impish grin.

"So what's Lars doing with the Dykes boys?"

"Dunno. They're nothin' but a bunch of stump farmers. Grow a little pot. Rustle a few logs. Hard to imagine any of 'em would work hard enough to put in time on a Mayfield show. They're up there on Cutthroat Creek Road, not so far from where the Mayfields been cuttin' on 2103. But I can't imagine Hal woulda had anything to do with 'em."

A ruckus behind him cut off my next question. I turned back toward the bar and snuck a look in the mirror. An old man with a full beard hunched forward on the stool next to me, his nose pointed down into his beer. A burly woman sat on the next stool, her face red and her sausage-sized fingers wrapped around the handle of a half-full pitcher. "You fuckin' sumbitch," she suddenly shouted, her fingers whitening and her right bicep flexing.

I ducked toward Little Jim as the woman swept the heavy glass pitcher off the bar with a slashing backhand that cut through the smoky air, smashed into the bearded face next to her, and finished its arc with an admirable follow-through. The force of the blow snapped the old man back on his bar stool, nearly horizontal at the waist, and carried him a couple of feet back into empty space. He crashed to the floor, flat on his back, blood spurting from a flattened nose and a web of nasty cuts.

Beer rained down on Little Jim and me. The big woman slowly rose from her stool and strolled toward the bar's open door, the handle and a shard of glass from the pitcher still gripped in her right hand.

Little Jim turned to me, wiped beer off his face, and grinned. "Meet Donald and Maybell Dykes," he said. "Moochie's mom and dad."

11

Sandy Harper sat dead center on the BOQ steps, her eyes closed, her face turned up to absorb the summer sun. She wore jeans, tennies, and a pink T-shirt. A flowered cloth beach bag sat next to her.

I killed the engine and pushed the door open. At the sound, Sandy opened her eyes and grinned. She grabbed the bag, stood, and stepped off the porch.

"Mornin', lieutenant," I said, meeting her halfway up the walk.

"Good morning, Mr. Newspaperman," Sandy replied, tilting her head.

I took her by the hand, walked her to the passenger side of the car, and opened the door. "Still a gentleman, I see."

"Don't count on it."

"Ooohhh," she said, as I opened the driver-side door and slid into the seat. "Does that mean I can expect some fireworks today?"

"Hey. It's Independence Day. You better bet there will be fireworks."

We cruised out the main gate and headed down the state highway. "You know," Sandy said as we passed the turnoff to Angel Harbor, "I could have driven myself down."

"I know. You're a modern girl. But I'm an old-fashioned guy. I drive this old heap. And I pick up my dates in it."

"You have a lot of dates?"

"Only one when it counts . . . on the Fourth of July."

"You're a smooth devil."

"I'll buy the devil part."

She laughed and rolled her window down. "I don't think they make 'em like you anymore."

The day was cloudless, the blue sky echoed in the stretches of Puget Sound spreading out to the east and south. Angel Harbor lay below us, a thicket of sailboat masts rising from the marina.

At the mouth of Cutthroat Creek, I slowed and pulled off the highway at the Takamak fireworks stand. Sandy and I walked up to the counter, and I slapped a ten-dollar bill on it.

Little Jim Littlefoot strolled up and bent over the bill, squinting as though he were peering at a bug. "What kinda bang-bang do you think this piss-ant little piece a paper gonna buy you?" he asked. Then he looked up at me, deadpan. "This is the goddamned Fourth of July," he said sternly. "Ain't you got no pride in your country?"

Then he turned to Sandy and looked her up and down. "I was with a looker like this," he said, "I'd be showin' her some real bang-bang. I'd be buying every honking cherry bomb on the shelf."

I laughed at the double entendres, reached into my hip pocket, pulled out my wallet, and put another ten on the counter. "OK, big guy, bring 'em on."

"That's more like it," Little Jim said. "And who might this beauty be?"

"Jim Littlefoot, this is Lieutenant Harper," I said, turning toward Sandy. "She's up at Cedar Springs."

"Where you two headed for the Fourth?" Jim asked.

"Down to Oyster Bay beach," I said. "Roast some dogs. Drink some beer. Watch the bonfire."

"Damn," said Jim. "I'm stuck here. Today we make beer money for a whole summer at the beach."

"So pick us out some good bang-bang. We'll make some noise for you."

Jim moved along the back wall of the stand, pulling fireworks off the shelves. Zebra firecrackers and cherry bombs, illegal anywhere off the reservation. Pop-bottle rockets. Roman candles. Way more than twenty dollars' worth. "That enough fireworks for you?" I asked Sandy as we climbed back into the car.

"I have a feeling," Sandy said, leaning forward and putting her hand on my thigh, "that you have more fireworks than I can handle."

I twisted in my seat, waved at Jim, and turned the key. The engine cranked weakly twice and then quit responding altogether.

Nothing. I slumped in exasperation. Sandy laughed.

Little Jim appeared at the window, grinning. "No way to impress a girl," he said, slapping the roof of the Dodge. "Need some help?" I nodded, humiliated.

Single-handedly, Jim pushed the full-sized sedan across the gravel. When he reached a fast walk, I popped the clutch, and the engine coughed into life. "Better take that pile of junk in to Marvin Dervish," Jim hollered as we pulled back onto the highway.

Fifteen minutes later, we dropped down to the Big Skookum and onto the bridge. Sandy pointed to the sign posted at the bridge approach. "What's 'skookum' mean anyway? What language is it?"

"Chinook jargon," I said. "The trade language Northwest Indians used. They all spoke different dialects of their own languages, so they patched this jargon together. Eventually, it even included a bunch of bastardized English words. We're in Klahowya County. That's a corrupted form of 'how are ya?' It sort of means 'welcome.' But it's really just a friendly greeting, like 'aloha.'"

"So what's 'skookum'?"

"It doesn't translate exactly. It's 'magic,' I guess. Or 'spirit.' Or just 'big.' But it's more than that. A man can have skookum. So can a place. It's strength, a sort of mysterious power. 'Skookum tumtum' means 'big heart,' literally, but really it means 'brave heart,' or 'good-hearted.'

"Around here," I added, "we use the word pretty loosely. But when I tell Mom that her dinner was skookum, she knows just what I mean."

I turned right on the other side of the bridge, rolled a couple of blocks up Front Street, and turned into the Thriftway for picnic supplies. In a few minutes, we were back on the highway.

"What's going on with Henry Logan?" I asked.

"The old man who shot up the A-6s?"

"One and the same."

"The admiral had a meeting with his JAG officers. They're thinking about bringing federal charges. Destruction of government property. Assault on a federal officer. But they haven't brought the U.S. attorney in on it. Yet."

"Geez. That's heavy stuff. Henry could do some serious time."

"He could have killed one of those pilots."

"C'mon. Henry's a decent enough old codger. He was just really pissed off."

The bay came into sight a couple of miles outside of town. Mount Rainier glittered against the blue sky. "Besides," I added, "going after Henry that way would be a public-relations disaster. It would make the Navy look like a bully, a thug beating up on a salt-of-the-earth old guy who was just defending his homestead."

Sandy looked over at me, considering the point. "I understand what you're saying," she said. "I'm from a small town, too. I get the culture, the way folks pull together when outsiders threaten one of them."

"Well, you're the PAO. Give the admiral some public-relations advice. Tell him that going after Henry will backfire."

Sandy said nothing, and I backed off, uncomfortable with the way I was mixing up journalistic objectivity, government business, and a personal relationship. To my way of thinking back then, the conflicts of interest in this situation ran about six different directions. At Oyster Bay, I steered onto the gravel shoulder and stopped behind Mark Judd's Ford pickup. I grabbed the Styrofoam cooler I'd stashed in the trunk. Sandy slung her flowered bag over her shoulder and followed me over the jumble of logs.

Forty or fifty locals were already scattered around the beach. Several young men teamed up on twenty- and thirty-foot logs, dragging them through the gravel and sand toward the makings for a huge bonfire, a Bent Fir tradition. Others tended the boats beached on the gravel, setting stern anchors or readying water-ski ropes. Knots of older men stood around talking, each with a crooked elbow and a beer bottle in his fist. Cedar smoke rose from cooking fires, scenting the salt air. An unexpected surge of excitement and belonging ran though me. I hadn't realized how much I'd been missing the rituals I'd grown up with.

I set the cooler down in the shade under a huge table made from a row of sawhorses and three sheets of plywood. I spotted Mark kicked back against a big log, took Sandy by the hand, and headed toward him.

Mark started calling me "Little Brother" in high school when, at a hefty six two, he was a hard-blocking tackle who covered my butt in the pocket and cleared my route to the goal line. When we graduated and I headed to college, he joined the nightshift green chain at Skookum Wood Products. His grammar was right out of Bent Fir, and his profanity managed to top the standard set by local loggers. But he was bright, well read, and made better conversation than most of my college classmates. Besides, he was a fly-fisherman.

I introduced Sandy.

"If I'd knowed you was Navy," Mark said, "I mighta signed up myself."

Mark offered an Olympia beer, the thin brew favored by young loggers and mill hands. I'd always figured that its motto—"It's the water"—was reason enough to drink Heidelberg. I waved the aluminum can off.

"Too snooty for Oly, eh?" Mark said. "How about the lady?"

"Sure," Sandy said. She grabbed the can, downed a long slug, and smiled. "Now that's a drink for a hot summer day."

Down the beach, a four-wheel-drive pickup roared, the chain between it and the butt end of a thirty-foot log tightened, a squadron of young men hauling on Manila lines heaved, and the log slid into a pit, where it rose to the vertical. Sandy stared at the process as I explained how the log would serve as center pole for the bonfire.

"Hey, Little Bro. What's with the Hal Mayfield thing?"

"Not much, nearly as I can figure. Walt's got to be about done with the routine interviews. Guys from the state crime lab came down and went over the truck. Walt kinda hinted that they didn't turn up anything he hadn't already figured."

"Pretty weird for these parts. Somebody beans somebody in the Griz and kills 'em, that I can savvy. Somebody with a grudge nails somebody with a thirty-ought-six, even. But this shit is a little heavy for Bent Fir."

"Yeah. And a little heavy for a country-fried good ol' boy like Walt Hasslebring, don't you think?"

"I dunno, city cynic. Don't sell old Walt short. Folks just keep on electing him, and I suppose you can hold that against him. He does slap a lot of backs. But that old boy is one sly son of a gun. I reckon he's foxed more than one fast-talking city cop.

"Speaking of which," Mark said, grinning at me, "when you gonna slow down to Klahowya County speed? You still sound like a 33 rpm record running at 45."

"So what do you think?" Sandy asked. "Who could have done such a thing?"

"Dunno, really," Mark said. "Any a them in the outfit, I figure we woulda heard about the bad blood. The family, too. But Hal was a stand-up guy, at least by local standards."

"So what's that leave?" I asked.

"Not sure," Mark said. "Hal knew what was goin' on in the woods like nobody else around here, though. Maybe he knew *too* much."

"Maybe," I said, "we oughta take a little drive up Cutthroat Creek, to the Mayfield show. Sniff around a little bit."

Mark grinned. "Sure. Might even take some fly rods along. How's next Saturday look?"

* * *

Mark and I pulled on swimsuits and took several slalom runs behind the powerboats that pulled water skiers all afternoon. Sandy even managed a shaky first ride on double skis. We cooked hotdogs on sticks and ate them with potluck potato salad from the big trestle table. The beer coolers emptied.

The young bucks torched the bonfire at nine. I fetched the old Army blanket from my trunk and spread it on the beach gravel in front of a driftwood log. Sandy snuggled next to me on the blanket, and we watched as the fire licked up through the brush and lumber packed into the base of the bonfire. Then flames erupted around the logs leaning wigwam-style against the thirty-foot center pole. Sparks billowed out the top of the burning tower, bright against the darkening sky. Fifty feet back, Sandy and I felt the heat on our faces.

By ten, the bonfire was a white-hot heap of coals, twenty feet across. The moon had risen above Mount Rainier, and the eastern sky had darkened. I joined the young men igniting rockets and mortars. The crowd around the bonfire applauded and hooted for the best explosions. I sent a dozen or so projectiles into the sky, gave the rest of my fireworks to one of the younger guys, and rejoined Sandy on the blanket. "That the best you can do?" she asked, draping herself on my shoulder.

"Hey!" I responded, in mock indignation. "That's good stuff. Not one thing legal in the bunch."

She slid her hand across my thigh. "What should be illegal," she said, "is for you to spend your time way down there with me alone way up here."

We watched the fire burn lower. The reports of firecrackers and mortar shells stretched further and further apart. The hum of conversation slowed, and the moon moved south, leaving the mountain behind to hover over the faint glow of city light from Olympia.

"Let's go to my place," I said.

Back at the car, we dumped the gear into the trunk. I pulled her to me, and she lifted her face into a long, hungry kiss, our tongues flickering against each other, our faces twisting side to side. Even after more than three decades, an old man remembers moments like that.

"Yo!" shouted Mark Judd, striding by on the road with a bottle of beer in his hand, laughing. "Get a room!"

We broke the kiss and twisted to look at him. "Not a bad idea," Sandy whispered.

I steered back toward town, the midnight air—still warm—streaming through the open windows. When I slowed on Front Street, the Dodge coughed and died. I groaned inwardly. *Shit! Not now!*

I punched the clutch, and the old burgundy beast rolled silently forward. Sandy giggled; I downshifted, said a little prayer, and popped the clutch out. The engine caught and roared. *Thank God!*

I hung a left at Benny's and swung around back. Sandy and I kissed again on the seat. She pulled me back toward the passenger-side door.

"C'mon," I said, pulling back. "Or I won't be able to get up the stairs."

The old wooden steps creaked under us. We stopped on the landing for another long, wet kiss and then hurried up the second flight. I twisted the knob and pushed, but the flimsy wooden door stuck against the jamb.

"Damn!"

"Hey!" she said. "Every misfortune is an opportunity."

We kissed again, and I leaned back against the door, forcing it open. We duck-walked through, still locked in each other's arms, and I kicked the door shut behind us.

12

When I left the *Echo* at the end of the day Monday, I spotted Lars Mayfield's pickup angled into the log barrier in front of the Grizzly. What
the hell, I figured. The guy had been my halfback. No reason not to
have a civil conversation with him. So I ambled across the street and
strolled into the smoke and gloom. My eyes gradually adjusted, and I
spotted him at the far end of the bar, staring down into his beer and
oblivious to the after-work hubbub growing around him. I slipped
onto the stool next to him and ordered a Heidelberg. This time, the
barmaid's muumuu was a dirty blue flower print.

At the sound of my voice, Lars slowly turned to look at me. "What
you doin' here, Tommy?"

I lit a Marlboro. "I like the beer here," I said, turning toward him
with an open smile.

"This here's a logger bar. Place can be a little sketchy for someone
don't belong."

"We Dawsons go back a ways in this town. It's hard to imagine
anyplace we don't belong."

Lars raised his glass and took a hefty draft. "You left," he said
simply.

"Look, Lars . . . we've known each other for a long time. We made
a pretty good team once. No need to start treating me like I'm some
sort of tourist.

"And," I added, "I'm sorry about what happened to your dad."

"Hear you been digging around into that."

"It's my job to dig around. That's what I do."

"Thought your job was to tell us what Walt Hasslebring digs up."

"That, too. But sometimes reporters can get to things the cops
can't. Folks can tell us stuff, without worrying that it's going to come
back at them. There's a shield law in this state. Somebody tells me
something on the Q.T., and nobody can force me to reveal where I
got it. Tell something to a cop, and you get dragged right into the
whole mess."

Lars turned back to his beer, silent. I tried to wait him out, but he drifted to some place inside himself. I watched his dead eyes in the back-bar mirror. Nothing. So I finally made another run.

"Maybe I can turn up something that will help you find out who messed with your truck."

His lips tightened. "Don't need no help," he said. "Mayfields take care of their own business."

I persisted: "What about your dad?" I asked.

"What about him?"

"Anybody have it in for him? Anybody who would have wanted to give him a good scare? Or even want him dead?"

"Christ," Lars said sullenly. "Times I wanted him dead. He was a hard case, y'know. But he was one fuckin' bull of the woods. Lotta folks mighta wanted to mess with him. But nobody dared. And if they had, they'd had to come through me."

"What about the Rush Creekers? After you went down there with the D8, they had a pretty big bone to pick."

"Buncha pussies. No way they was gonna take on me or my dad. We run 'em off before. Woulda run 'em off again."

"Whoever took out your dad didn't exactly come straight at him. Kind of sounds like something a bunch of pussies might have dreamed up."

"You don't know what you're talking about," Lars said. He drained his glass, stood, and turned toward the door. I rotated on my bar stool to face him. He stared me hard in the face. "A little friendly advice, Tommy," he said, his voice low and even. "Keep poking your reporter's nose into places it don't belong, and you're likely to get it cut off."

* * *

Mom arched her neck, looked at the ceiling, and flinched as the chemo nurse slid the IV needle into her arm. "Does it hurt?" I asked.

She let out her breath. "Only for a minute. It burns a little when it starts to flow. But if it does what it's supposed to, that's a small price to pay."

"Good attitude," the nurse said, adjusting the IV stand as Mom tilted the big recliner back. "Just push the button if you need me." And with that, the nurse headed down the long row of identical chairs, each one holding a cancer patient connected to an IV bag hanging from a stand just like my mom's. Men, women. Young, old. Some looking strong and healthy. Some bald, gaunt, emaciated. I watched the nurse retreat and felt emotion well up in me. I turned to my mother with wet eyes, wishing I could do something to get her out of this sad corridor of the condemned.

Dad had been bringing her to this chemo-infusion room in Olympia every three weeks. She tanked up on poison, and he drove her home to days of vomiting, sleeplessness, exhaustion. As soon as she started perking up, it was time to do it again. After today, she'd be four months into it, with five infusions down and one to go. The last needle was just three weeks away.

In the meantime, the portly, flaccid woman reclining in the chair on the far side of Mom's aimed to make things as tough as possible. Apparently asleep, she suddenly popped her eyes open, sat up, and rasped, "You know what that stuff they're pumping into you now is, don' cha? They call it 'the red death.' Because of the color." She cackled. "The red death! Ha! That stuff can stop your heart."

Mom turned away from me to face her neighbor. She lifted her hand to her mouth, appalled, as the woman went on, one of those busybodies who takes perverse pleasure in misfortune, her own or anybody else's. "Another one," she added, cackling again, "is so nasty that it burns your skin if the nurse drips it on you. Just turns it black. Yes it does!"

I put my hand on my mother's shoulder and gently turned her back toward me.

"You're tough, Mom," I said. "And you want them to use the strong stuff. You're going to beat this. One more treatment, and you can start getting better."

The big woman behind her huffed. "That may be true," she said, and flopped back in her chair, closing her eyes again.

Mom smiled at me and patted my hand. "It *is* true," she said. "Absolutely. And I'm so happy you could bring me today. Your poor father has missed way too much work, what with hauling me in for all the treatments and doctor's appointments. And staying home with me on the bad days, too."

"I should have been here earlier, Mom. Dad needed somebody to share the load. And I could have helped around the house."

She dropped her head back on the recliner. The big dose of Benadryl that the nurse administered just before every treatment was taking effect, and her eyelids were drooping.

"Tommy," she said, clenching my hand, "you had your job. Los Angeles is a thousand miles away. The phone calls were plenty."

I squeezed her hand but said nothing. The phone calls were pro forma, I thought. And the flight from LAX to Sea-Tac was a couple of hours. I had no excuse for not being at her side within a day of her diagnosis. And I had no excuse for not making a trip every time I could talk the city editor into a three-day weekend. For the first time, the thought occurred to me that I'd been selfish, so wrapped up in my obsession with breaking the next big story that I'd lost sight of things that mattered more.

"The world's different now," Mom said, her eyes closed and her voice slowing. "When I was a girl, the whole family was within a few miles. Now the kids with get-up-and-go, they . . . well . . . they get up and go. To college. Off to a big city somewhere. And that's the way it should be. They should be what they can be."

Her voice trailed off, and her breathing settled into a sleepy rhythm. The chemo session had another two hours to run, and I sat silently, holding her hand and staring out the window into the July sunshine. Thinking.

Our family was scattered across the continent. Aunts, uncles, cousins—they were isolated in little pockets that stretched from coast to coast. My dad's and mom's great-grandparents settled in Klahowya County as homesteaders. They and my grandparents raised big families. Now only my folks were left in the Skookum. Except for me. Parked in the boonies. Dreams on hold. Being not what I could be, but what I'd left behind.

* * *

Marion turned in her chair and stared at me where I stood at the newsroom's little morgue, flipping pages in the 1976 volume of back issues. The Hoe thumped away in the pressroom, grinding out the Thursday run. "There's an index, you know," she said.

"Police runs don't show in the index. Not the individual runs anyway. The index just says, 'Police Runs, page so and so.' I have to find each week's list if I want to get the dope on where they went and who they busted."

"*Whom* they busted," Marion said. She smiled, but the comment wasn't entirely tongue-in-cheek. The woman has always taken language seriously.

I turned back to the counter, put the '76 volume away, and grabbed the '77.

If you want a Washington State rap sheet today, you go to the state patrol website, enter a name, and pay your ten bucks. No muss. No fuss. And you get every conviction anywhere in the state. Thirty years ago, thing weren't so simple. The state had a new public records law, but having a right to a record and actually getting one were two different things. Cops or court clerks didn't necessarily know the letter of the law, and they might deny access to records out of ignorance. Or out of general antagonism toward the press. Or just for the hell of it. Besides, the records weren't centralized. If you wanted a complete rap sheet, you had to show up at every agency that kept the records on some miscreant and request them. And without a friend with access to the FBI's master database, you had no way of knowing where all those agencies might be.

But Marion's small-town experience hadn't taught her all that. If I wanted police records, she asked, why didn't I just walk down to the sheriff's office and ask for them? Walt Hasslebring would probably hand over whatever I wanted, and if he didn't, I could file a formal request.

I still carried too much big-city, investigative-reporter attitude to accept any approach that simple. The police, in my L.A. experience, were secretive, defensive, and often corrupt. They wouldn't help you, even if you asked. So you came at them from the outside, or you cultivated secret inside sources itching to sabotage political enemies. True, Walt Hasslebring had been friendly enough. But I wasn't quite ready to throw my L.A. baggage aside and tip him to the line my investigation was taking. Hell, I didn't know where it was going anyway.

"I'd rather dig it out myself," I told Marion.

"So why are you looking at ancient police runs?" she asked. "What's that have to do with getting out Thursday's paper."

"Not a whole lot," I conceded. "But bear with me—I'm not wasting company time. This may get us somewhere on Hal's murder."

"Like what?"

"All in good time," I said, smiling inwardly.

Marion showed no sign that she recognized the Walt Hasslebring parody. She sighed, and turned back to her desk.

I flipped through the pages of old newsprint, scanning each set of police runs as I found it and copying anything having to do with Rush Creek into my notebook. The mid-seventies yielded a few arrests that apparently had to do with tree-sitting incidents. The reports also showed an occasional "welfare check" at the commune, a phrase usually used for courtesy police runs typically initiated by somebody like an absentee daughter who wanted the cops to look in on an elderly mother who wasn't returning calls. Maybe the parents of commune members actually were asking the sheriff's office to check on their wayward hippie kids. But I knew the phrase could also serve as code for an unannounced inspection, a casual drop-by to keep track of suspicious characters.

The welfare-check items did me no good because they yielded no names. But as I worked my way into the late seventies, the occasional Rush Creek mentions got more frequent—and more interesting. The run reports mentioned search warrants and arrests for petty theft. The name "Arnie Dykes" showed up twice, but that was no surprise. Arnie collected misdemeanor charges like log trucks collected dents.

The real mother lode was a report on what appeared to be a full-scale raid. Four carloads of deputies had shown up on a weekday morning in 1979 and arrested six Rush Creekers.

Armed with those names, I headed for the courthouse and climbed the stairs to the county clerk's office. Klahowya County voters had elected the current clerk long after I'd left Bent Fir, and I didn't recognize the name on the door. But the office held all the local court records, and I'd often been sent over to check one thing or another during my high school days at the *Echo*. In Bend and L.A., I'd spent hundreds of hours chasing down records. So I knew the drill. Within minutes, I was sitting at a table with heaps of superior court records generated by the 1979 arrests.

As I'd suspected, the raid was a meth bust, with more than a kilo confiscated from a lab hidden in the woods behind the commune's main meadow. Five sets of records petered out quickly. Initially charged with class C felonies, the defendants walked within weeks. Four had been diverted into a treatment program for first-time offenders. The DA simply dropped charges against the fifth. It was the classic scenario for a deal struck with an informant.

What was far more interesting to me was the paper trail generated by the object of this probable betrayal.

His name was Roy Hammer, and as I leafed through transcripts of hearings, paperwork from other jurisdictions, and depositions, an impressive biography of crime emerged. He was a Tacoma boy who'd somehow survived the gang wars, drug overdoses, and domestic violence of the notorious Hilltop neighborhood, the state's most crime-ridden patch of real estate. Not only had he survived, but he'd also turned what appeared to be a sharp-edged intellect into a scholarship across town at the University of Puget Sound. He'd majored in chemistry about the time Owsley Stanley started cooking up those famous purple LSD tabs for his buddies in the Grateful Dead. When Owsley purple double-domes flooded the market, they ushered in the psychedelic era.

The records didn't say whether Owsley acid inspired Roy Hammer, but the Hilltop chemist recorded his first drug bust in 1967, right after the Summer of Love. The LSD he produced in a North Tacoma bungalow was, according to police reports, of exceptional purity. It also, thanks to recent federal legislation, was a Schedule I drug, and Hammer's sophisticated North End laboratory earned him a two-year prison term.

His stretch in the Walla Walla state pen probably served as a kind of grad school for the young chemist. In any event, his release launched a paper trail of drug busts for creative chemistry. The Hammer, as he was known by then, piled up police paperwork as he was arrested and charged with manufacturing LSD, DMT, PCP, and most of the other acronyms that fueled the psychedelic seventies. The reams of records generated by endless arraignments and hearings carried the names of Seattle's top criminal-defense firms. The Hammer had plenty of money, apparently, and he spent it on the best legal advice it could buy. He was arrested and charged repeatedly but never convicted.

Methamphetamine started turning up in police reports with Hammer's name on them in the mid-seventies. Like the era's other meth cookers, the Hammer apparently operated by buying cold pills that squads of shoplifters—known as "smurfers" in the trade—

boosted from drugstores. Relatively simple chemistry converted the pills into crude crystal meth. But any biker-gang thug could crush and cook a few ephedrine capsules. In 1977, Whatcom County sheriff's deputies reported the first real meth operation in the state, a true laboratory with sophisticated equipment and fifty-five-gallon drums of precursor chemicals. The only thing that tipped the cops to the location of the lab, which was squirreled away in the woods near the Canadian border, was a noisy firefight that left three bodies on the floor amid broken beakers and smashed hot plates. The cook, one survivor told the deputies, was known only as the Hammer. And he was long gone.

He was long gone in Klahowya County, too. He posted a $100,000 bond after his arraignment following the Rush Creek raid. The huge bond was, apparently, simply one more cost of doing business in a lucrative trade. Because, after that, the Hammer simply disappeared, leaving his money behind.

13

The force of the turn slammed me against the pickup's passenger-side window. I snapped awake, frantically grabbed the dash, and swiveled to look at Mark, my eyes wide with temporary terror. Mark grinned and manhandled the Ford out of a screeching four-wheel drift. The F150 straightened out on the ragged blacktop of Scatter Road, and I glanced in the mirror to see the intersection with U.S. 101 falling behind.

"Time to wake up, Little Brother. Them cutthroat is waitin' for us, right up the road."

I relaxed and slumped back into the seat. Every Labor Day, Mark drove a heap in Shelton's annual dirt-track demolition derby, and he didn't drive much differently the rest of the year. But when he pushed his luck with me along, I was usually awake and braced for whatever came next.

Stump ranches appeared in clearings on either side of the winding blacktop. The state's rural poor collected in wooded mountain valleys like this, attracted by the dirt-cheap land. The deer, elk, salmon, and berries that once fattened Indians had been supplemented by diets of Pop-Tarts, frozen pizza, and generic beer. Ramshackle houses sagged in fields of stumps left when the owners' ancestors had stripped the old-growth Douglas fir off the land. You could count—and I had—hundreds of growth rings on the stumps. The trees had been old when Captain Cook sailed up the coast two centuries before.

We passed the handsome wooden sign marking the entrance to the Olympic National Forest. The pavement ended, and a cloud of dust billowed up behind the Ford as it streamed through the second-growth fir that closed in on both sides of the road. Forest Service 2102 climbed up ridgelines and snaked along open bluffs that looked out over valleys where the checkerboard pattern of clear-cuts marched over the ridges like a brown-and-green quilt. The wide gravel road, designed for big logging rigs, occasionally broke out into a cut and arced through acres of graying second-growth stumps.

Tansy ragwort swayed in the July breeze, its poisonous yellow flowers death to any stray cows stupid enough to wander up this far and lucky enough to escape the cougars.

Mark slowed where the road divided, the right branch heading up FS 2103 toward Bull of the Woods and the left, 2102, continuing up Scatter Creek Canyon. We started up 2102, pulled onto a shoulder, stepped out, and stared down at the creek. It tumbled through boulders thirty feet below, pausing occasionally in deep pools. The mountain snowmelt had already slowed. The creek, I thought, looked quite civilized, its roar subdued and the whitewater down to an acceptable level. "Not bad," I said. "Let's fish here for a while. Then we can head up 2103 and check out the Mayfield show. Maybe fish Cougar Creek if we have the time."

We climbed back in the pickup, and Mark drove another mile or so before pulling onto a siding. We rigged our fly rods and headed down a gravel spur that dropped toward the creek.

Mark pushed through the grass standing waist high in the old road, and I followed. Alder seedlings had sprouted from the mound between the tracks left years before by logging equipment. But something had been through much more recently. The supple little alders carried bark scars on both uphill and downhill sides. A vehicle undercarriage had scraped them as it passed through, coming and going.

"Shit," Mark said, glancing back at me. "Somebody been down here. I'll be pissed if some asshole meat fisherman already cleaned out this chicken-shit little creek."

At the bottom of the canyon, the road turned upstream. Mark barely broke stride, and I hurried along behind him, glancing at the pocket water formed as the creek bounced around rocks and piled up behind downed logs. A perfect stretch of water for mountain cutthroat trout.

The canyon widened out, and the brush gave way to a towering grove of old firs, the darkest of greens where they stood there in shadows. I stumbled and looked down. Braided tire tracks crisscrossed the heavy clay soil. The ground had been broken by heavy equipment, a big-tired skidder maybe, to load logs. And a truck to carry them. Plus one smaller vehicle for sure. Maybe more.

Mark plunged into the grove, stepping over and through a tangle of fresh logging slash. Huge branches had been stripped off logs and pushed to the side to clear a vehicle path, with no effort to salvage any of the wood or to pile the remaining debris for burning. I followed Mark through the mess.

The grove opened in the center, and Mark stood in the middle of the cleared space, his hands on his hips. "Take a gander," he said, nodding toward the ground in front of him. I hurried up and looked at the three giant old-growth stumps in the center of the clearing, each eight or nine feet across. Fresh sawdust was heaped around them. "Ain't this what you were just scribblin' about?"

"Jesus," I said. "You got it. The Forest Service says rustlers are snatching old growth all over the Olympic. But nobody said anything about Scatter Creek."

We leaned our fly rods against a pile of slash, fishing forgotten. Mark walked up to the closest stump and ran a hand over the close-packed growth rings. "They musta been gorgeous," he said. "Four hundred years old if they were a day."

*　*　*

At the first phone booth we found on U.S. 101, I phoned the sheriff's office with a report of what we'd discovered on Scatter Creek. I called the Forest Service, too, but nobody was in the office on a Saturday afternoon. I left phone numbers for my apartment and the *Echo* on the answering-machine tape.

"Wanna beer?" Mark asked as we descended the Longmont grade into town.

"Natch, but I've got a date. Better just get me home."

"Sandy Harper?"

"Better'n spending Saturday night with you."

"Watch out, brother. Them pussy-whip scars is already showing on your back."

"Hey. I asked *her*. And *she's* driving. That sound like a guy who's being led around by the nose?"

Mark breezed past the taverns and turned into the gravel lot behind Benny's. "Besides," I added, "I kind of think you'd make the same choice, given the chance."

I unloaded my gear from the pickup bed. Mark leaned out the window and looked back as the truck rolled forward. "So what you got planned for this hot night out? Just gonna go upstairs and roll around on that rickety bunk of yours?"

"We're headed into Shelton," I said, laughing. "Dinner at Momma's and a movie at the Roxy. *Raiders of the Lost Ark*."

"That Harrison Ford guy's a lot better lookin' than you. That should git her hot."

Mark gunned the F150, gravel kicked out from the spinning wheels, and he squealed onto Front. I climbed the wooden stairway to the second floor, popped the sticky back door open, and headed for the shower.

I was sitting on the top landing nursing a Heidelberg and enjoying the early-evening sun when Sandy's red Mustang pulled into the lot. She had the top down, and she looked up at me, the engine still running. "Don't move," I said. "I'll be right down."

The rent was paid, I had a double sawbuck in my billfold, and my date looked great. I felt better than I had since L.A.

When we hit the highway, she opened up the Mustang's V-8 and her blond hair streamed out behind her headrest. While I told her about the old-growth cut, she reached over and put her hand on my knee. "That'll make a good story," she said. "What's next?"

"I'll probably get a call-back from the Forest Service Monday. With any luck I can visit the site with Charlie Adams—that's the name of the Forest Service guy who's down here on the log-rustling thing. Maybe somebody from the SO, too."

"The SO?"

"Yeah. The sheriff's office. Sorry. Rein me in if I slip into cop-speak. Anyway, getting back out there with somebody official will give me a scene-setter. That's good enough to lead a story for next week's *Echo*. I can flesh out the rest of it with an update on the investigation. Probably not much new, but it will have to do."

Sandy kept glancing over to look at me. The highway was empty, but the Mustang was pushing eighty, and I found myself tensing up every time she took her eyes off the road. "You know," I said, "this is the time of day the deer start wandering around. A big old buck could step right out into the highway anytime."

She grinned. "Not an elk?"

"Nah. Elk have enough sense to look both ways when they come to a road. They stop and let the traffic go by. Deer just step out and get themselves killed. Take a lot of drivers with them."

"Point taken," Sandy said, backing off the accelerator and squeezing my knee.

We had steaks at Momma's and gazed out at the view from the bluff just south of downtown Shelton. Washington State raspberries were in, and we both ordered a slice of pie for dessert. Berry pie was one of the best parts of summer in these parts, and raspberry was my favorite.

The big Simpson mill stretched along the entire waterfront, a hodgepodge of weathered buildings, smokestacks, lumber, and docks that jutted into Oakland Bay. "Y'know," Sandy said, pointing out the window with her fork, "this would be a pretty view if most of it weren't filled with that godawful ugly thing."

"When it's feeding your family," I said, "a lumber mill is a beautiful thing. In boom times that mill would be humming, even now. But yesterday, the feds announced that unemployment was at nearly 9 percent. Car sales have fallen through the floor, and nobody's building houses. Simpson has shut down two shifts, and it probably won't be long before Big Skookum shuts down another one, too. This is turning into a monster recession."

"You picked a great time to come home."

"I didn't pick it. My mom was sick, and I was sideways with my editors in L.A. So I'm back here doing stories on log rustling, truck wrecks, and pissed-off chicken farmers."

"Those are pretty good stories, for a weekly."

I put my napkin on the table and pushed my chair back.

"For a weekly," I said. "Thing is, I was working at the goddamned *L.A. Times.* I was really on my way."

I walked around behind her and pulled out her chair as she stood. She turned and looked into my eyes without a trace of a smile. She reached up and lightly touched my cheek.

"Dammit, Sandy," I said. "I want to *do* something. I want to *be* somebody."

* * *

It was past nine, but a rosy glow still colored the sky when we left the Roxy, holding hands as we strolled to the Mustang. Harrison Ford had vanquished the Nazis. The lost ark was lost again, buried in some nameless government warehouse. And I was still thinking about the way I'd botched my L.A. opportunity and feeling like the ark must have felt.

Sandy turned to me at the car. "C'mon," she said, "buck up. It's too beautiful a night to be down in the dumps. I'm going to drive you home, and you're going to invite me up those scary stairs of yours."

She drove along the bay. Mount Rainier rose on the dark skyline, showing a faint shade of pink.

"You know, I only owe the Navy another two years and three months."

"But who's counting?"

"Actually, I'm not. I kind of like the service. I'm good at my job. My bosses seem to appreciate me. And a lot of cute young guys are around all the time. They appreciate me, too."

The surge of jealousy I felt surprised me and gave me the first hint that I was thinking about Sandy as more than just another Saturday-night date. Maybe she sensed my reaction. She giggled to show me she was kidding and squeezed my knee again.

"I'd even think about re-upping if I don't find anything better on the civilian side." She turned her head and gave me a look long enough to make me nervous about the road ahead.

"Those deer are still out wandering around, you know."

"They'll just have to look out for themselves," she said. But she turned her gaze back to the highway.

"So what might better look like?"

"I'm not so sure right now," she said. "I have a journalism degree, just like you. Maybe a newspaper job. Maybe a PR job. Maybe back to school for a master's degree. I could teach at a junior college someday."

I sensed that she was sending me a message. Her options were open, she was saying, and they might include somebody like me. I doubt I gave the thought much conscious consideration, but it must have threatened my independence. I backed away from the subject by saying nothing.

Sandy backed away, too. "In the meantime," she said, "I'm a sailor. This is the time to see the world. And have fun while I'm in port." She grinned and let the Mustang coast down the Longmont Grade. We pulled into Bent Fir and passed the taverns, the only signs of life on Front Street. She killed the engine behind Benny's, ran across the lot, and scampered up the staircase. I was right behind her.

On the top landing, she turned and faced me. I expected a kiss, but she looked serious and put both hands on my chest, holding me back before speaking.

"Understand one thing, Tom Dawson. You're not the only one who wants to *do* something. I want to *be* somebody, too."

14

Dad waved me off and hooked his right hand over the bow of the aluminum skiff. He dug his heels into the Oyster Bay beach, jerked the boat around, and dragged it toward the water's edge, raising a clatter as the gravel crunched under the metal keel. I followed, oars in one hand and fishing rods in the other. I admired my father's brisk scramble down the beach with the skiff in tow. The old man was still in good trim.

He splashed into the bay in his gumboots and climbed into the boat. I gave the stern a shove and stepped in with one continuous motion. My father took his first stroke with the oars. The entire operation was wordless and perfectly timed, the product of lives lived on water.

"It's a fine Sunday morning," said Dad, raising his face to the glowing gray sky and scanning the hillside receding behind him. Our brick house showed near the ridgeline. A pair of cormorants powered past between the skiff and the beach, just off the water. "Your mom and I built that house thirty years ago," he continued. "Just in time to give you a room of your own." He seemed to marvel at the thought. "Never had much money," he said, "working for the post office. But it's been steady. All in all, a good life."

We sat quietly, facing each other. Rasping crows squabbled up on the ridge. Dad's long, smooth strokes with the oars settled into a quiet rhythm. I took in the morning view and thought about the vast expanse of the *Times* city room. The grimy clutter of the place. Coffee cups that never saw the inside of a dishwasher. The stale smell of cigarette smoke.

Yeah. The Skookum was pretty. But it was a helluva long way from the action. And Bent Fir was dying on the vine. "The way things are going, Dad," I said glumly, "you'll be the last man standing around here."

"Oh, I won't be standing for long, son. Retirement's just around the corner. Get your mom well and we'll beat some pavement, see some country."

He rested the oars, coasted a bit, and backed the stern of the skiff up to our sixteen-foot Tollycraft. We climbed aboard, tied the skiff to the buoy, and released the Tolly. Dad choked the engine, turned the key, and the old thirty-five-horsepower Evinrude roared, billowing two-cycle oil smoke.

The run to Cutthroat Creek took us past the mouth of the Big Skookum and north along the shoreline for another ten minutes. The Evinrude droned, and the Tollycraft skimmed over the chop, the waves thrumming against the boat's plywood bottom.

I told my father about the trip Mark and I had taken up Scatter Creek. "That pretty grove of old growth was all torn up. Slash piled right in the road. Skidder tracks everywhere."

"Yeah," he said. "Guys around here have a hard time accepting the fact that the big trees are nearly gone. Time was, they stretched clear up to the head of about every drainage along the whole peninsula. Thank God we got the national park. Kids can still see what a fir that's all grown up looks like."

He throttled back, and the Tolly settled into the water near two boats already trolling a tidal rip two hundred yards off the mouth of the creek. Dad recognized one of them—Bill Henderson's fiberglass Bayliner—and waved. Henderson looked up, nodded, and shook his head. No action yet.

The sun broke through as we rigged our rods. "I'll start with two ounces," Dad said. "You go a little deeper."

I snapped a four-ounce weight onto my line and followed that with a metal dodger that would give the bait some action and two tandem hooks on six feet of leader. I reached into the cooler, grabbed a whole herring, and attached it to the hooks with a midbody kink that would cause it to dodge and twist as it trolled behind the boat. I dropped the whole rig over the side, spooled out a hundred feet of line, and settled into my seat. My father did the same. The Evinrude putted along with a hypnotic rhythm, pacing a Puget Sound ritual that tied generations of fathers and sons together. I considered the thing. What served the same function in Southern California? Surfing? Washing the car on Saturday morning? A Dodgers game? Maybe. But somehow not quite the same.

Dad started cranking on his new Penn reel, hauling in to check for seaweed on his rig.

"What's up on the Mayfield thing?" he asked.

"Not much," I said, "near as I can figure. Walt's gotta be done with his interviews by now. The truck was clean—no prints or anything like that."

"He must be stumped or he'd have arrested somebody by now."

I paused, considering what I'd just learned from Walt Hasslebring. The sheriff hadn't arrested anybody, but he wasn't exactly stumped. Still, I hadn't gotten as far as I had in the news business by violating confidences. Off the record was off the record, even when it came to sharing confidences with my own father.

"Well," I said, "if he knows anything, he's not talking publicly about it. But there's got to be a pretty powerful motive. Somebody doesn't just happen on a truck in the woods and cut the brake lines."

Dad nudged the wheel to bring the boat around. The two lines angled across the stern, swinging through the rip in a broad arc. "Not with a whole scheme to hold the brake juice in like that anyway," he said.

"What do you think, Dad? Why would anybody have it in for Hal Mayfield?"

"Dunno. Hal could be a tough old bastard. But he said what he meant, and he came at you straight ahead. I never knew him to sneak around behind anybody's back."

"Yeah. And Mayfield Logging wasn't the kind of operation anybody would kill for. Just another gyppo outfit sliding from one timber sale to the next."

"Yeah," Dad agreed. "Once old growth gets rare enough to be worth stealing, you gotta figure the real gold rush in the woods is over. The big outfits start growing trees on farms, just like any other crop. And the little guys scramble for what's left."

"You think Hal was above stealing an occasional big tree?"

"Way above. I've never heard of a Mayfield truck that wasn't strictly kosher when it came to branding its logs and checking in at the scaling stations. If anything, Hal would have gone after anybody breaking the rules. He was a man who demanded a level playing field.

"Why?" Dad added. "You find some connection to the log rustling?"

"Nah, nothing solid. I've been digging around a little bit on my own, though. Too much investigative history to leave it alone, I guess. Been digging around in the country records some."

"And . . . ?"

"Kinda some interesting doings up Rush Creek."

"Yep. Those hippies had a run-in or two with Hal, years ago. Just that chickenshit tree-sittin' nonsense, though. Nothing to get too bent out of shape about."

"And," I pointed out, "that meth bust."

"Yeah," Dad said. "No secret about that. Those kids got themselves into some bad shit. But Walt shut 'em down, and that was that. The city boys flew the coop, and now all we have is some ragged-ass hippies in the woods. Can't see that it has anything to do with Hal."

The sheriff had, apparently, been straight with me. The lid was still on the news of Hal and Lars Mayfield's little raid on the rejuvenated Rush Creek cook shack. Little Jim knew about the raid, but if my dad hadn't heard about it from his post at Klahowya County gossip central, hardly anybody else had.

"Hey!" Dad said. "Bill's got a fish on."

Fifty yards down the rip, Henderson stood at the stern of his Bayliner, his fiberglass rod bent deeply. He hauled up and dropped the rod tip, cranking furiously. Then he hauled up again.

"Pretty good story for you," Dad said, turning back to me, "this Mayfield business. Just your cup of tea."

"Yeah," I said, staring vacantly as Bill Henderson played his fish. "Your boy, the wunderkind investigative reporter."

"What happened down there, son?"

I sat silently, thinking. Dad waited patiently.

How could I have been such a fool? Smoking out an inside source with a phony leak was Dirty Cops 101. I knew perfectly well how it worked: If you're an LAPD detective privy to an internal investigation and the department's dirty laundry starts showing up in the press, what do you do? Well—duh!— you develop a short list of possible leaks, inside sources who might play department politics by slipping the latest news to a reporter. Maybe the turncoat wants to sabotage the chief or some other cop who stands in his way. Maybe he just wants to build up some credit with the press, a pocketful of favors that he can call in when the time comes. Whatever. If you want to nail your leaker, you invent a phony development in the investigation, something with enough juice to make the next day's front page. Then you spill that to your suspected

Benedict Arnold. The story appears, and bingo!—you have your two-timer, naked and shivering with the spotlight shining right on him. And given the value cops place on us-against-them loyalty to the department, your leaker is finished. One way or the other, he's on the way out.

And so, of course, is the dumb-shit reporter who fell for the whole scam.

"I just got snookered, Dad," I finally said. "Forgot everything I'd learned and let the L.A. cops feed me bad information. I should have checked it out. But my source had always been good. So I went with it. And I embarrassed my bosses at the *Times*. They had to run a front-page retraction, for God's sake. It was a black mark for the whole paper, for everybody who worked there."

"And they fired you?" Dad asked.

"No. They took me off the investigative team, though, and that was bad enough. I was just humiliated, Dad. I couldn't bear to walk in the newsroom every morning. I had to leave."

"Strike!" Dad hollered, rearing back and setting his hooks. He reached behind him and twisted the ignition key. The Evinrude sputtered and went silent as I reeled in, hurrying to get my tackle out of the water before it could foul my father's. I yanked the dodger and herring aboard and reached for the big landing net lying on the bow decking. As I turned, I saw Bill Henderson struggling to hold his rod in one hand while he maneuvered his own landing net in the other.

Dad stood, spread his legs, bent his knees, and braced his thighs against the starboard gunwale. He hauled and reeled, hauled and reeled, but the salmon still had the strength to run, stripping monofilament off the Penn with a frantic whine. Then, somewhere down in the green water, the fish turned and charged back toward the boat. Dad reeled frantically, desperate to keep the line taut and the hooks anchored in the chinook's black mouth. "Jesus." he said under his breath. "A big 'un."

The rod tip plunged rhythmically as the chinook shook its head, trying to throw the hook. The fish ran again and again. I leaned against the port gunwale and propped the landing net against the stern. Ten minutes. Twenty. Sweat ran down the back of Dad's neck in the cool morning air.

I looked up and saw Bill Henderson boat his fish, a fine fifteen-pounder that flopped and writhed in the net as he lifted it aboard.

Then Bill sat on the Bayliner's transom, watching as Dad pulled and cranked.

"Attaboy, Jess!" he hollered. "Don't horse the sumbitch. Take your time."

"Much more time," Dad muttered, "and this old boy will be having a heart attack."

I saw a flash deep in the green water. I grabbed the net and stepped forward. The fish turned again, eight or nine feet below the surface.

"Hot damn, Dad. You got yourself a derby winner."

Dad grinned. "Yeah," he grunted. "But where's a good derby when you need one?"

The chinook broke water, rolling slowly, exhausted. I leaned over the stern and dropped the net into the water, hiding it behind the Tollycraft's stern. Dad eased the salmon toward the boat, raising its snout. I slipped the net around and under the fish. But the sight of the aluminum handle spooked it. It thrashed, turned, and ran again, stripping more line off the Penn.

Local fishermen always referred to chinook as king salmon, a phrase that passed through my mind while I watched my father stand helplessly as the big fish ran with strength that seemed undiminished. They were the biggest salmon species in the Sound, the strongest and the best tasting. A king could top fifty pounds, dwarfing the cohos, chum, and pinks that also spawned in Northwest rivers.

Dad patiently worked the chinook back to the boat. I waited, the net in the water, immobile. When the big fish glided over the aluminum hoop and green nylon mesh, I reared back, gripping the handle with both hands.

"Yes!" Dad hollered, raising the rod as I lifted the net with a grunt and a whoosh of water and lowered it to the deck. Dad squatted and eyed his prize, thrashing on the plywood. "Thirty-five pounds," he said, "if it's an ounce."

I handed him the priest. He swung the club with sharp snaps of his wrist, striking the salmon three times on the top of its big black head. The fish shuddered and lay still. A trickle of blood ran across the deck.

Dad looked up at me.

"Son," he said, "one thing I've learned is that you can't live life without making mistakes. God knows, I've made 'em. And you'll make more. Sometimes they're big mistakes; they send your whole life veering off in an entirely new direction. But you know what?"

I looked at him, tilting my head slightly.

"When you look back from way down the years," he continued, "you see how things turned out. Not so bad, usually. Downright good, most of the time. My mistakes . . . well, I'm kinda glad I made most of 'em. I kinda suspect you will be, too."

I doubt I bought that bit of buck-up-boy philosophy when I heard it. But I've never forgotten it. And, looking back over the decades since, I've come to believe it more each year.

But Dad wasn't finished. He was a practical man who—true to form—quickly descended from life lessons to the matters at hand. "Y'know," he said, "I been thinking about your log-rustling story. Those big tires on a skidder get banged up something fierce. After a while, they're just like a logger's old boots. Every one's got a different pattern of cuts and gouges. And every one leaves its mirror image behind in the mud."

* * *

Mark slumped on the bench seat, ragging me about the Dodge. "This fucking old heap is a granny car, Little Brother. Bent Fir boys drive Fords. And them that has balls drive pickups."

I dropped the column shift into second and screamed around an S-turn. Mark bounced off the door and then pitched across the seat against my shoulder. He straightened and held his hands up in surrender. "Okay! Okay! I get it!"

I rounded a bend and spotted the sheriff's cruiser squatted on the shoulder above the spur road. We found Hasslebring himself standing in the old-growth grove, puffing a White Owl and watching Charlie Adams clamber over one of the big stumps with a tape measure. Adams, surprisingly agile despite his bulging belly, trailed smoke from his own stogie. He stood on the stump, took the cigar from his mouth, and grinned. "Hello, boys. Hope you don't mind. We got here first and just let ourselves in."

Hasslebring turned and motioned us forward. As we walked ahead, my eyes fell to the tracks crisscrossing the clearing. The largest probably belonged to a skidder. And Dad was right. Patterns repeated themselves every dozen feet or so, about the circumference of a skidder tire. The most distinctive must have been formed when mud squished into a deep gouge in the tire. It was shaped like a penguin.

Charlie and the sheriff took notes as they quizzed us on our Saturday expedition. I snapped Charlie's photo by the stumps, and then we wandered through the piles of slash. Hasslebring scooped up a couple of cigarette butts with a piece of bark, being careful not to get his fingerprints on them. He dropped them in a Ziploc bag as Adams wandered over to one of the remaining old-growth trees, staring up, his hands on his hips. He raised an old box camera and snapped a couple of pictures.

"Watcha got there, Charlie?" the sheriff asked, wandering over to stand next to Adams.

"Hooked a block up there, Walt," Adams said. "Looks like just the one. Must have used a guy-line rig."

Mark and I walked over next to them. "What are you two talking about?" I asked.

Hasslebring turned to face me. "Well," he said. "You take a log that's eight feet through the butt . . . something like that might weigh twenty, twenty-five thousand pounds. You ever think about how you get something like that off the ground and onto a truck?"

"Shovel?"

"Nah. No shovel's gonna handle that kinda load. Latch onto the log and lift, and all you'd do is pick up the shovel's back wheels. Log's just gonna lay there. Besides, equipment these days can handle about twenty-six inches. That's it. And with an eight-footer, you're talking ninety-six inches."

"I saw lots of trucks carrying three-log loads when I was a kid," Mark said. "There must have been some way to get that timber aboard."

"Sure," Charlie Adams said. "Old-time loggers figured out lots of ways, even with steam donkey engines. Mostly, they did it with blocks and tackle. Hitch a block to a tree, run a guy line down to the ground, move another block up the line with a loading jack, grab your big tree with loading tongs. Then move the block up the line, lift the log, and drive underneath. Really big log, use a couple of guy lines."

I knew enough woods lingo to puzzle out the system of pulleys, cables, and winches that he was talking about. And what he had been staring up at was the scarred bark where somebody had attached just such a rig to the trunk of the big tree.

"Or use a gin pole," Adams added. "Or a spreader-bar rig."

Mark nodded, but I had to ask. A gin pole, as it turned out, was just a portable log that could be used to hold the loading rig. A spreader bar worked by suspending cable between two sturdy trees and rigging it with pulleys and grapples to lift logs for loading.

"You don't see that kind of rigging around here anymore," Walt Hasslebring said. "Find it, and you'll find your rustlers."

I walked back into the center of the clearing and pointed to the pattern in the skidder tracks. "Find this on a skidder tire," I said, "and you'll find your rustlers, too."

The two older men walked to where I was standing and bent over, smoke rising from their cigars as they squinted into the mud. Adams snapped more photos. "When you develop those, Charlie," Hasslebring said, "I'd be beholden if you'd send a set my way."

15

Max Stewart met me in the Woodsman's Café, a ramshackle mom-and-pop burger bar on the Angel Harbor Highway. I figured he'd talk more easily if he didn't have to worry about eavesdropping Rush Creekers back at the commune. And besides, it's always better if you can conduct a sensitive interview on neutral ground. I offered to buy, and he suggested the Woodsman. We were the only two customers

Maxy picked at a greasy cheeseburger and jittered around in his ladder-back wooden chair, obviously cranked. Beyond him, through a dirty window, I could see Angel Harbor and its thicket of sailboat masts. I asked Maxy about his family. He asked about my mother. I went at my cheeseburger with a lot more enthusiasm than Maxy was showing toward his. Meth doesn't do a lot for the appetite.

"Look, Maxy," I finally said. "I know about the Mayfield raid on the meth lab."

He quit chewing, stopped squirming, and gave me a hangdog look.

"Why didn't you say anything about that when I saw you the last time," I continued, "up at the Creek?"

Maxy resumed chewing. He stared at the ceiling somewhere above my head.

"I'm sorry, Tommy," he finally said. "I'm not exactly proud of the way things have gone, y'know. I never thought Rush Creek would end up like this, or me neither." He dropped his eyes to his food. "We started out so fresh and green," he continued. "In the early days . . . well, I've never been so happy. Surrounded by brothers and sisters up there at the Creek. We were gonna change the fuckin' world, y'know. But now . . . Jesus."

"Things don't always work out," I said. "For any of us."

"You're a good guy," Max said, "and I owe you. You were asking about Hal Mayfield, and I shoulda been straight with you. Shit. That business with the cook shack put us right in the middle of the whole thing. Looks pretty obvious, don't it? We hated Mayfield. We live right down the road from his show. And we had one big bone to pick with him. Christ. Walt Hasslebring is watching every move we make.

And who can blame him?"

"How long you been cooking up there, Maxy? The real thing, I mean. The big stuff."

Maxy finally looked me in the eyes. His brow furrowed a little, and I knew he knew I knew about the big bust in '79. "Not so long," he said. "Couple of years."

"C'mon, Maxy," I said. "This is serious stuff."

He looked back down at his cold burger and limp french fries.

"Tell me about Roy Hammer," I said.

He looked up again, gripping the edge of the table with both hands. "You don't want to know about the Hammer," he said, his voice barely above a whisper. "You start fucking with that dude, and you'll wish you never had."

He paused. Pans rattled somewhere off in the kitchen before silence settled over the empty dining room. Maxy stood, wiped his mouth with his paper napkin, and walked away from the table.

At the door, he turned and looked back. "It'll be your last wish," he said, and walked on out.

*   *   *

"Pretty good paper," Marion said, dropping a fresh copy onto my desk. The Hoe press clanked away behind the closed door to the back shop, grinding through another of its Thursday-morning runs. I picked up the broadsheet and scanned the expanse of newsprint with a sense of wonder. The Hoe still ran on a web almost a foot wider than the modern presses used at nearly every daily. So the *Echo*'s folded pages were just over five inches wider. And the *Echo* still ran nine columns of type across the page, an undesigned jumble of words that formed no particular pattern of wheat and chaff. It looked, I thought, like something found in an attic.

My black-and-white photo of Charlie Adams, looking pensive as he surveyed the giant stumps along Scatter Creek, ran as a five-column halftone print across the top of the page. On the bottom of the page, the story on Jimmy Winthrop's plans for the marina butted up against a clutter of news briefs. Donald Dykes, one of them noted, was recovering from a severe concussion and had been released from the hospital. Another reported that the Navy had decided against legal action in the Henry Logan case.

I felt a twinge of guilt. Sandy, apparently, had taken my advice and lobbied the brass to drop the Logan prosecution. I'd butted in where, according to the rules of my profession, I had no business being. But I was already feeling the pull of different rules, a countrified code that placed compassion and community above objectivity. I liked the old chicken farmer, damn it. In a way, I even approved of what he'd done. So screw the rules they followed in L.A. and Seattle and every place where the editors wore ties.

Marion cleared her throat with an exaggerated call to attention that snapped me out of my Henry Logan reverie. She picked the *Echo* up off my desk, dropped it again, and repeated herself. "Pretty good paper!"

"Yeah," I said. "Great. They're talking about it in the big city rooms right now. 'That weekly sure is onto something down there in the boonies,' they're saying. 'Log rustling. Wow! Fancy that. And we thought the air-traffic controllers' strike was a big story.'"

"We'll send you to London," Marion said. "The prince is getting hitched."

"And his little blond princess-to-be ain't bad either," I said, looking up with a leer.

"Check the phone," she said with a disapproving edge in her voice. "The Forest Service has planned your Thursday for you."

I sat at my desk, punched the message button on the big black phone, and recognized the official voice of the Shelton PIO droning through one of the recorded alerts he occasionally phoned out to local media.

"First fire of the season on the Olympic," he said. "Up the Scatter Creek drainage on FS 2102, about four miles past the junction with 2103. We've got two crews on scene, but it doesn't amount to much at this point. Mostly we're just keeping an eye on things. I'll be there by nine if anybody wants to take a look."

I hung up. "A little fire up Scatter Creek," I told Marion. "What's going on? I haven't been up there in years. All of a sudden, I'm practically commuting to the place."

"Well," Marion said, swinging around to face me, "we don't have much of anything else going. And, like the man says, it's the first of the season."

I cruised north on 101 and crossed the bridge at Cutthroat Creek. The gray clouds still hung over the east slope of the Olympics, but they had the feel of a morning fog. I guessed they'd lift by early afternoon.

A couple of miles farther on, I hung a left on Scatter Road, started to climb, and smelled smoke after the first couple of turns. Two miles farther in and the haze was thick enough to be a bother, a dry, acrid pall that hung in the firs and mixed with the dust kicking up behind the car.

I crossed the creek and passed the spur where Mark and I had discovered the ravaged old growth. A couple of miles farther on, I came across the PIO, standing next to a green Forest Service panel truck parked above a bluff that looked out over the canyon. A half dozen other green vehicles shared the shoulder. A pumper truck, a supervisor's sedan, a couple of pickups, and two crummies, the squared-off little buses used to haul logging crews to a show. Just past the crummies an overgrown logging road headed down into the trees.

"Mornin'," said the PIO, nodding as I climbed out of the car.

"Mornin'," I said. "Tom Dawson, from the *Big Skookum Echo*. Am I the only press?"

"You're it," the information officer said. "This isn't that big a deal, and I guess you're closest."

I looked out past the PIO. Smoke choked the canyon, but I could see no flames. Chain saws whined somewhere below. "It started upstream, maybe half a mile, on the far side," the PIO said. "Damned if we can figure why. No lightning. No logging. That we know of anyway."

I glanced at the crummies. "So you have two crews on it?"

"Yeah. They both walked in at daybreak. But they're not doing much. The second growth is damned thick in there, and there's some old growth along the creek inside the setback. The only break is this here old logging road, which drops on down and runs along this side of the creek. And it's pretty overgrown. The fire's still on the other side, so they're cleaning up the old road, hoping to stop anything that gets across the water. It'll probably just burn out over there."

"You sure about that?" I asked.

"Young man," the PIO said, "you're never sure about anything in this business. But it's mid-July, and these woods are still damp. This fire probably isn't going anyplace. So it makes no sense to spend a lot of Uncle Sam's money to put it out."

"What if the weather changes?" I asked.

"Just got to sex this story up, don't you?" The PIO smiled.

"Well," he continued, "if the sun comes out and the wind picks up, the burn could get out of the understory and into the crowns. Then it would jump right over that road. And then we'll have to get some serious shit in here to fight it."

I pulled a reporter's pad out of my hip pocket and scratched some notes. "Don't quote me on the 'serious shit' part," the PIO said, laughing.

I collected an acreage estimate, the identities of the two crews, and a few more quotes. I pulled the Rolleiflex out of the car and snapped four or five frames. Then I headed back down the gravel, anxious to be out of the smoke. A quarter mile from U.S. 101, the Dodge coughed twice, backfired, and died. I downshifted and engaged the clutch. The transmission whined and the car slowed, but nothing happened. I steered onto the shoulder and sat there, listening to the engine tick as it cooled. I climbed out of the car and slogged toward the main highway. When I reached the four-lane blacktop, I stuck out my thumb.

* * *

I retrieved my car from Marvin Dervish's shop after he overhauled the electrical system. New points, plugs, and distributor. A new timing belt. The repair completely cleaned me out—I had ten dollars in my billfold and nothing else to last until next Friday's paycheck. But the car purred as I drove to Washington State Patrol headquarters in Olympia.

The state cops had bagged the two log rustlers on their midnight run down U.S. 101. The arrest records showed that Luke Johnson and Joseph Carbone both owned their own rigs, and both worked out of Hoodsport, a little town up Hood Canal, a few miles past the mouth of the Takamak. They'd already been arraigned, had entered guilty pleas, and were scheduled for sentencing the next week. In the meantime, they were parked in the Thurston County jail.

I flagged the date and time for the court appearance on my pocket calendar, gave the clerk who'd fetched the records for me a big smile, and headed back to Bent Fir. Marion was hunched over her Selectric when I got there, writing up a story on the speech some anti-fluoride crusader had given to the Rotary Club. I peeked over her shoulder. The guy claimed to be a biologist with a PhD from the University of Wisconsin. The fluoride in our city drinking water, he said, might prevent tooth decay. But it would take ten points off the IQ of Bent Fir's sons and daughters.

"Geez," I said. "How come an out-of-the-way little town like this attracts crackpots like that?"

"He sounded as if he knew what he was talking about. He even cited some studies. The Rotary guys were buzzing after he left."

"Did you check him out?"

"How so?"

"Well, that PhD sounds bogus to me. Call the Wisconsin registrar and see if he really has a degree."

"You're the investigative reporter. You do it."

I headed back to my desk and dialed information in Madison, Wisconsin. Then I called the university registrar. I gave the clerk who answered the Rotary speaker's name, and she put me on hold. A couple of minutes later, she was back. Yes, she said, the man in question had earned his biology doctorate in 1974. I thanked her, sheepishly, hung up, and reported my finding to Marion.

"You're such a cynic," she said with a smile. "You know, sometimes people are exactly who they appear to be."

The porch creaked, and we both looked toward the front door. It swung open, and Walt Hasslebring stepped in, filling the space before the counter.

"C'mon, Tommy," he said. "I'll take you for a little ride."

16

The sheriff steered his green-and-black Chevrolet sedan up U.S. 101. July sunshine streamed through the tall firs on the east side of the highway, glowing in long patterns of light and shadow intensified by the haze hanging in the air.

"That fire up 2102 just keeps on keepin' on," Hasslebring said, gesturing toward the smoky sky.

"Sheriff," I said, turning a little in the passenger seat, "it's been more than a month since Hal dropped into that gulch. This is the biggest story to come along in Klahowya County that I can remember. And we haven't printed anything that's really new since the press conference."

"That's why I asked you along," the sheriff said. "The ride'll give us some time to talk. At least I can tell you what we been up to. And I owe you something after that business with the skidder tracks."

I pulled my notebook out of my hip pocket.

"Put that away," the sheriff said. "Most of what I'm gonna tell you will have to be off the record. When we're done, I'll tell you what you can use for next week's paper."

The Chevy hummed over the Cutthroat Creek bridge, and I glanced down at the churning water. Jesus. Hasslebring was a piece of work. The feudal baron in his barony. I tried to imagine an LAPD cop telling the *Times* what could and couldn't be printed.

On the other hand, I'd known Walt Hasslebring since I was a kid. And no LAPD cop ran his county the way the sheriff ran his. So I kept my mouth shut and waited.

The sheriff slowed and cranked the steering wheel with the heel of his hand. The Chevy nosed down into a left-hand turn and leveled out on Scatter Road. Hasslebring throttled back up, and the big V-8 murmured lazily. "We talked to all these folks," he said, waving a hand at the stump ranches that streamed by on either side of the road. "Most of 'em don't have much truck with cops, and we didn't get a whole lot outta them. I can tell you this, though," he continued. "A lot of shit goes on up here that isn't what you'd call strictly kosher."

"Like at Rush Creek."

"You got it. Like at Rush Creek. And those boys are pretty logical suspects, aren't they? They're right here in the neighborhood. They had one big-ass grudge against Hal. And they're meth heads, which means they're half crazy. But they ain't dumb, most of 'em. And they sure could figure out how to wrap some duct tape around a brake line."

"So what do they have to say for themselves?"

"There are eleven men and two women still living on the creek," Hasslebring said. "Naturally, we've talked to them all. Separately. Usually, with that many folks, you're going to get something. Not everybody's equally guilty, and somebody's going to grab a deal if it's offered. Or somebody's got it in for somebody else. Whatever it is, somebody's going to break ranks."

The big Chevy whooshed across the Rush Creek Bridge as we talked. We both looked up the narrow lane that wound up the stream bank on our right.

"So what did you get?" I asked.

"Nuthin'. Not a goddamn thing. You'd at least expect some inconsistencies in the stories, that many folks involved. But nuthin'.

"Besides," he added, "get right down to it, these folks are old hippies. Peace and love and that sort of crap. They've gotten themselves into some heavy-duty shit, what with the crank and all. But deep down, they just don't seem like the kind of people who're gonna commit murder over something like that business with the cook shack.

"In any event, we don't have one certifiable piece of evidence that we could take to a DA. So we just gotta keep lookin'."

The cruiser crossed the national forest boundary, and the crunch of gravel replaced the hum of tires on pavement. Hasslebring barely slowed. Behind the car, dust choked the passage through the trees, settling on the firs like dirty snow.

"Don't forget now," the sheriff said softly, "off the record."

The Mayfield crew, he said, hadn't offered much. The only bad blood involving Hal, it seemed, was between him and Lars. Hal was a conservative old woodsman, the sheriff said, a cheapskate when it came to equipment. He hated risk, and he hated debt. Mayfield trucks and skidders were paid for, patched together long past the time one of the big outfits would have scrapped them. Lars strained at the tight reins. We ought to bid some of the big sales, he'd mutter to the rigging crew. On flatter land. Go up against the hotshot corporates. Go to the goddamn bank and get some loans. Buy some decent equipment. Show 'em all what loggin's really about.

"But by all accounts," the sheriff said, "that was just family stuff. Old bull, young bull . . . that kind of thing."

He chuckled as he angled the Chevy right and onto FS 2103, contemplating the story he was about to tell. A dusty sign pointed up the hill toward Bull of the Woods.

"Stubby Lancaster told me about one set-to they had," he said, smiling. "Right up here on the landing. That antique skidder of theirs broke down, and Lars blew up. He started screaming at Hal. 'You'd still be loggin' with goddamn horses,' he hollered, 'if you knew how to feed the fuckin' things.'"

The trees opened up to the left, the bank dropped away, and the expanse of Cougar Reservoir came into view. The sheriff looked across the seat at me. "And you know what Hal said?" he asked. I returned the glance.

"He said," the sheriff continued, "'I know how to feed you, dumb shit. And all the rest of these men, too. So shut the fuck up and fix that goddamned machine.'"

The sheriff snorted, taking obvious satisfaction in the older man's response. One more young punk put in his place.

"The other thing," he continued, "was that Hal played it absolutely straight. If the show bellied up to a creek, he took out a tape and marked the fifty-foot setback. I don't think he cared so much about muddying up the fish habitat as he did for the rule itself. 'That's the line, boys,' he would say. 'Nobody cuts beyond it.'

"Of course, Lars thought that only chumps followed the environmental rules to the letter. If a good saw-log was standing just inside the setback, you can bet he'd take it."

The car slowed, and Hasslebring pulled onto the shoulder. Yellow crime-scene tape surrounded the landing, fluttering in the July breeze. We stepped out of the cruiser.

The Bull of the Woods logging show, the sheriff said, had begun in early May, before the spring rains let up. Naturally, the landing was ankle deep in mud, torn up by equipment tires and treads. When the June sun arrived, it dried the tracks in place.

"That conversation we had down on Scatter Creek got me to thinking," he said. "I called the state patrol crime lab, and they sent me a forensics guy with a kit for doing plaster casts of tire tracks. We came up here to the Mayfield show and poured casts in every track we could find." He walked around to the rear of the Chevy, inserted the key, and popped the trunk. "Seein' as how you gave me the idea, I figured you deserved to see the results."

The trunk lid rose on its springs. Sunlight flooded the big luggage compartment. A jumble of white-plaster tire-track casts lay on the rubber mat, their tread sides stained with Bull of the Woods mud. "They all checked out," Hasslebring said. "They all match up with Mayfield Logging vehicles or the trucks the guys on the crew drove up here themselves."

He leaned over the trunk and grabbed one of the smaller casts. "Except this one."

I trailed the sheriff over to the landing, a sense of begrudging admiration growing as I realized what Hasslebring was up to. He squatted and pointed. "Hal's Kenworth was parked over there," he said, indicating a spot on the edge of the landing, near where the ground suddenly dropped away down the steep slope the Mayfields had been logging. "And we took this cast right here."

Hasslebring held the piece of plaster alongside one of the ruts running through what once had been mud. The faint pattern of well-worn treads matched the reverse impression in the cast perfectly. And the rut, which overlaid most of the other tracks frozen into the dried ground, matched another depression a few feet away. The two ruts had been left by a vehicle that pulled in next to the big logging truck, stopped, and then backed out.

"An LT235," Hasslebring said. Too small for a skidder or a crummy. And the treads are a little too aggressive for a car. "It's the kinda tire you'd put on a half-ton or three-quarter-ton pickup," he said. "And it was worn down to within an inch of its life.

"C'mon. Got one more thing to show you."

We climbed back into the cruiser. Hasslebring started the Chevy, wheeled it around, and headed back down the gravel road.

"So," I said, "just what can we say?"

"Well, you can sure as hell say the investigation's making progress." I jotted the quote in my notebook, using the brief-hand

I'd been perfecting since I left school: + ivnst's mkng prgrs.

"And," Hasslebring continued, "you can tell 'em that we've interviewed more than sixty people and that we've followed up on more than a dozen tips."

I wrote the numbers down.

"You can tell 'em," the sheriff said, twisting in his seat and looking straight at me, "that their sheriff has devoted all available resources to this case, and that we *will* solve it."

"But sheriff," I said, "that's just another place marker on this story. Isn't there something specific we can say?"

Hasslebring drove silently for a full minute, his eyes focused on the road ahead. Cougar Reservoir streamed by on our right, and the narrow shoulder of the gravel road dropped off nearly three hundred feet to the rocky shoreline. "Tell 'em," he finally said, "that we've discovered physical evidence we think will lead to a break in the case."

My attention level leapt a full octave. That was a lead for a real story, a headline that actually meant something. I scribbled more quickly. "You mean," I asked as I wrote, "the tracks on the landing? Couldn't they be explained a lot of ways?"

"Yeah," conceded Hasslebring, "they could. But what I'm about to show you couldn't."

He slowed, switched on his right-turn signal, cranked the wheel, and steered the cruiser onto FS 2102. As we climbed into Scatter Creek Canyon, the smoke thickened. "Oughta get some crews in here," the sheriff said, "and put this damn thing out."

More yellow crime-scene tape appeared on the left, stretched across the brushy entrance to the logging spur where Mark and I had found the old-growth stumps. Hasslebring parked and walked around to the trunk. He opened it and grabbed the same plaster cast he'd matched to the tracks on the Mayfield Logging landing. Then he stepped around the yellow tape and headed down the spur. I followed.

The sheriff lumbered down the steep grade, his shoulders pumping methodically as he pushed through the tall grass and brush. The road flattened out, and the piles of old-growth logging slash appeared. He slowed, scanning the bare earth. Then he knelt, held the plaster cast next to one of the ruts, and looked up at me. I stepped closer.

The sheriff looked back down at the cast and the rut. The tread patterns matched again.

"Sonny boy," said the sheriff, smiling, "it looks like your log-rustlin' story just got a whole lot more interesting."

* * *

Joe Carbone sat across the visitors' table, his face blurred by the smudges and scratches on the Plexiglas that separated us. He leaned forward, and the lipstick imprint of the kiss an earlier visitor had planted on the plastic lined up with his mouth. Strange juxtaposition, that scarred woodsman's face in drag.

Carbone and his buddy Luke Johnson still hadn't entered a plea on the grand theft charges they'd drawn after the state cops stopped them during their midnight log run down U.S. 101. Carbone was older, a fifty-three-year-old veteran who was past the age of heroics on behalf of the chain-saw brotherhood. So when I called the Thurston County jail to request an interview, I asked for him, not Johnson, who was twenty years his junior. Carbone's curiosity got the best of him, I guess. Or maybe he was just bored. In any event, my experience is that almost everybody will agree to a jailhouse interview.

I tried to turn on the charm. "Bad break, a guy like you getting nailed for just doing his business."

"Yeah? What business is that?"

"Logging. Isn't that what you do? Cut trees so that folks can build houses?"

Carbone wasn't buying it. He leaned back, crossed his arms, and grunted. "I don't cut 'em anymore. I just haul 'em. What's it to you anyway?"

"Like the man told you. I work for the *Big Skookum Echo*. Bent Fir lives or dies depending on what happens to the mill. So our readers care about what goes on in the woods. And some of them aren't too happy when guys like you get busted for doing what they're supposed to do."

"These days you get busted for cuttin' big trees. My daddy and granddaddy were big-tree loggers. Put beans on the Carbone table for two lifetimes. But that ain't the way it is anymore, is it?"

"Times change. But folks still need to eat. The boys working in our mill need to feed their families, too."

Carbone relaxed a little, leaning forward on his elbows. "Big Skookum Wood Products retooled a long time ago. In case you don't know it, sonny, your mill's rigged for second growth. Couldn't cut a big tree if it fell on it."

That's the point, I thought. Most of the Northwest mills retooled as the old growth ran out. Damned few could still mill logs like the honkers Carbone and Johnson were ferrying down the highway, whooshing by darkened log-scaling stations without a sideways glance. So where were they headed anyway? I put it to him.

"Look," he said. "Luke and I are facing two years for this little caper. We're sitting in the slammer; we're not making payments on our trucks. We both have families to feed. Luke's still got little ones at home. If we want a break, we got to trade something for it. And all we got to trade is information. So what kinda fool would I be to give it to you for free? What've you got to trade anyway?"

He had me there. In point of fact, anything I wrote was likely to make things worse for him by amping up the public pressure on law enforcement to do something about old-growth rustling. But I hadn't expected a gyppo log-truck driver to grasp the fine points of negotiating with the district attorney's office and the downside of talking to a small-town reporter.

I gave it one last shot: "I'm just trying to find the mill that's taking logs out of our woods. We like to do our own thing in Bent Fir."

"I couldn't help you with that anyway," Carbone said as he stood and motioned to the jailer. "Don't know nothing about any big-tree mills. Haven't done any business with one in a long time."

17

I throttled back at the Big Skookum entrance buoy. My father's Tolly-craft settled into the water and purred along at trolling speed. I felt the morning sun on my back and admired the mist rising off the waterway. I had to admit that it beat rush hour on the smog-choked Santa Monica Freeway.

Mill workers' houses teetered on the bank to my left, their weath-ered, unpainted siding blending into the shadows. Rickety steps descended the bank to decrepit wooden floats, tethered to pilings and bobbing in the boat's wake. Old fishing skiffs bounced at a dif-ferent frequency, setting up a waterfront syncopation.

I turned deeper into the waterway, and the Big Skookum Marina hove into view, the bridge rising beyond it. Sandy Harper, her flow-ered cloth bag at her side, sat on the marina's outer float in a red-and-black striped T-shirt and white capri pants, right where I'd asked her to meet me. I motored up, briefly hit reverse, and snugged the boat right up against the float.

"Mornin', sailor," she said, taking my hand and jumping aboard.

"I thought you were the sailor."

"Nah. The uniform fooled you. I'm from a little ol' farm town, ya know. And now I spend my days pushing paper around an office, on land."

I pulled away from the float and waved to Jimmy Winthrop, who was watching the operation from the rail that ran alongside his park-ing lot. Jimmy, who didn't often see beautiful women pull into his place and plop themselves down on his dock, waved back with a grin.

Sandy settled into the passenger seat, I slid the throttle forward, and the old Evinrude cleared its throat. The Tolly pushed slowly through the brine, throwing bow wakes to either side instead of ris-ing to skim across the surface. We cruised past a weathered white sign on a buoy, and the wake set it to lurching from side to side. "SLOW!" the sign said. "NO WAKE!"

"We'll go to the beach for our picnic," I said. "But I thought you might want to see the Big Skookum first."

We passed under the bridge, and Sandy craned her neck. Pigeons scuttled back and forth on the rusted green girders, nervously cooing. Once we'd passed the bridge, the water calmed to featureless flatness, mirroring the old brick of the courthouse on the south bank. Rotting pilings leaned at varied angles along the trash-strewn bank below the town's two taverns. On the right, along the north bank, ramshackle houseboats floated in greenish water.

"Bent Fir isn't anybody's idea of a classy waterfront resort," I said, grinning and gesturing at both banks. "But it's got its own brand of moldy charm."

We cruised past the mill. Log rafts lined both shores, chained to the massive dolphins built by driving a half-dozen or more pilings into the muddy bottom and lashing them together with steel cable. Loose logs filled the pond, and decks of logs stood stacked beyond the top of the twelve-foot bank that ran along the edge of the yard. "Geez," I said. "Look at all the damned inventory. With only two shifts running, Marty Brantly could saw all summer without buying any more logs."

The mill fell behind, the Big Skookum narrowed, and I slowed even more. The sun rose above the ridgeline ahead of us, and the wisps of mist still on the water disappeared. I reached into a cooler, pulled out two Heidelbergs, handed one to Sandy, and tipped the other back. Then we cruised into the Skookum as it once had been, the magic place where, I imagined, young Indian braves brought their sweethearts in cedar dugout canoes.

Settlers had logged the easy-to-reach old growth here first, more than a century before. Now the second-growth trees, nearly as big as their predecessors, towered more than eighty feet over the quiet waterway. Snags left from toppled alders and firs jutted into the channel, forming quiet eddies at the water's edge, the vegetation dampening the noise of the Evinrude. Mallards, surprised when the Tollycraft suddenly appeared around a bend, scooted for cover, ducklings paddling frantically behind them.

The Big Skookum twisted and turned, winding deeper into the woods. A narrow opening appeared in the bank, and I turned the Tollycraft into it. We slipped through the passage into a large circular pool, nearly two hundred feet across. "Old log pond," I said, twisting the ignition key and killing the engine. The boat glided to a stop in the sunlit center of the pool. Sandy sat silently, listening to the squawks of distant crows and the hum of insects in the shadows. Then she raised her keg bottle, tipped it back, took three deep gulps, and stood.

"I get it," she said, smiling at me and unfastening the top button of her blouse with her free hand. "Now I understand what 'skookum' is. This place oozes skookum.

"And so do you."

She released the last button, set her bottle on the Tolly's dash, and reached behind to unsnap her bra. She dropped it on the deck and leaned forward for a long, wet kiss that forced my head back onto the gunwale.

She finally broke the kiss. "But I've got some skookum, too," she said, laughing and unzipping her capri pants. She kicked off her shoes, pulled the pants down, and dropped her panties on the deck. Then she stepped up onto the transom, raised her arms over her head, and launched herself into a dive that barely raised a splash as she slipped through the water's surface. I rose from my seat and watched her naked form glide away from the boat under the clear water. She twisted as she went and turned onto her back. Bubbles streamed past her trim breasts, flat stomach, and the blond patch between her legs. Then she surfaced, looking straight back at the boat, shook water out of her hair, and laughed.

"Get your ass in here, you coward," she shouted. "Take a plunge and see what it gets you."

I stripped off my clothes and dove off the transom, surfacing next to Sandy. We kissed, sidestroked back toward the boat, and climbed back into the cockpit. Then we lay on the deck, slowly making love while the Tolly rocked in the quiet water.

Afterward, we lay on our backs, staring up at the dark-green firs. I lit a Marlboro and retrieved two beers from the cooler. We dropped into the Tolly's swivel seats, still buck naked.

"Tom," Sandy said earnestly, "I've got orders."

"What do you mean, you've got orders?"

"I've got orders, dummy. Navy orders. You didn't think Uncle Sam was going to let me stay in this lovely little backwater forever, did you?"

I sat upright and leaned forward. "Orders to where?"

"Not far," she said, pulling her thighs together and resting her elbows on her knees, her bottle cupped in both hands. "Just Seattle. To Pier 91. I'm the new public affairs officer for the reserve center."

"When?"

"End of September. Just in time to get out of here before the rain. But it won't be far. We can still see each other."

"Yeah," I said. "A couple of weekends a month. Then you'll be off to Subic Bay or some goddamn place."

"Tom," Sandy said gently. "We're young. The world's out there. This is our chance."

She reached out and put a hand on my bare shoulder. "You could come with me," she said. "Seattle. Tacoma. Everett. The other side of the Sound has hundreds of jobs for guys like you. All those weeklies. The AP. The small dailies.

"A year or two in the boonies is okay. Get the L.A. business behind you and pick up some good clips. You can always say you had to come home to help take care of your mom. Around here, you can always say you just hated L.A. But if you stay in Bent Fir too long, it will get harder. Editors want hungry guys, guys who are moving up.

"We could get a little apartment," she said. "On the hill, looking out at Elliott Bay. We could go to clubs, restaurants."

I sighed and took a long pull on my Heidelberg. Then I rose and walked to the stern of the boat, where my clothes were piled in a heap.

"Let's get dressed," I said, "and go to the beach."

* * *

The balky door to the apartment bowed out, stuck against the frame. I cursed, worked the knob like a piston, and jumped, startled, as the weathered plywood suddenly snapped open. I stepped onto the landing and turned to let the morning sun fall on my face. A breeze roiled the line of deep-green firs that stretched across the back of Benny's lot, sending ripples through their branches. It was going to be hot. And it was going to be windy.

I quick-stepped down the two flights of stairs and onto the trail leading to the *Echo*. Fir needles filtered down from the tossing boughs overhead, flecking my head and shoulders. The evergreens generated a low hiss, rising and falling, that put me on edge.

In the office, Marion sat at her rolltop, and Chesty was at his usual perch behind the counter, hunched over a pile of invoices.

The Regulator ticked in the morning quiet.

Chesty looked up. "Hey, Bub," he said. "Good weekend?"

"You bet," I said, glancing at Marion's trim back. She swiveled around to face me, expressionless.

"What's up this morning, hotshot?" she asked. "We've got the top of the page filled. But there's a lot of blank real estate below the fold."

I pulled my chair out from the desk and slid into it. "Dunno. Been meaning to get out and see the new chicken farm everybody's talkin' about. I could do that this morning and write it this afternoon."

I phoned information, got the number for the farm, and called the manager to arrange a visit. Then I sorted Saturday's mail delivery into neat piles on my desk—press releases, letters to the editor, and two dispatches from country correspondents. Myrtle Johnson, as usual, had the best stuff. One of the Benson boys had ripped the bottom out of his dad's boat on the Wycoff Shoal. Nobody hurt, but the kid was spending the rest of the summer paying off the damage by tearing out the Bensons' old asphalt driveway and getting the bed ready for a concrete pour. The Smithfields were down from Seattle for the annual summer stay at their Angel Harbor cabin. Penny Williams was expecting in December.

I copyedited the dispatches and delivered them to Harris in the back shop. Then I walked through the woods to Benny's parking lot and fired up the Dodge. The wind was far stronger on the exposed hills at the top of the Longmont Grade. Bracken ferns whipped back and forth alongside the empty two-lane road.

I passed Henry Logan's driveway and smiled, thinking of the old man's tangle with the Navy's A-6s. Short of the Mayfield murder, that was still the summer's best story. The Navy's decision to drop charges deflated it some, from a news perspective. But I was still glad about that. For once, my feelings had trumped my hunger for a good story. Besides, the Logan tale had developed legs even without a legal brouhaha. The *Seattle Times* metro columnist had picked up the yarn from my story, and that brought calls from the *Post-Intelligencer* and the AP. Those hadn't led to anything, but at least a couple of desk editors knew my name. And, of course, the story had led me to Sandy.

In the meantime, though, I was still at the *Echo*. Still covering chicken-shit stories. Literally, I thought, my foot pressing harder on the accelerator.

The entrance to Farm Fresh Northwest appeared a half dozen miles past Logan's place. I pulled in next to a large, boxy building covered in pale-blue aluminum siding. I walked toward a shed clad in the same metal. The two structures were spotlessly new, the driveway gravel was fresh, and the land had the bare-earth-and-stumps look of recent clearing. There wasn't a house in sight.

This was, I realized, a place of business, not a family farm.

I took a couple of pictures and pulled the blue door to the shed open. A shorthaired eager beaver in his thirties looked up from a metal desk. "Hi," he said. "You must be the reporter."

The farm manager stood with me in front of the big building and proudly ticked off statistics. More than sixteen thousand square feet. An investment of nearly $600,000. State-of-the-art nutritional systems. And nearly twenty thousand poultry units. Honest to God— that's what he called those miserable hens.

We walked inside. The smell of chicken manure hung in the air, but at much more tolerable levels than I had experienced at Henry Logan's. My eyes slowly adjusted to the dim red light that suffused the cavernous open space, and at least a dozen long structures emerged from the gloom.

The manager walked forward and motioned for me to come along. As we neared the first structure, I saw that it stood on waist-high metal legs and was made of chicken wire hung on steel frames. The entire apparatus had been divided into cages, each two feet square, stacked four wide and four high. It extended at least a hundred feet off into the dark distance, and in each cage were four white hens.

The manager proudly explained the operation's automated features. The chicken manure fell through the wire mesh into the open space between the metal legs, where it landed on a conveyor that carried it to bins at the end of the row. Most of it did, anyway. Some invariably splattered birds in lower cages. They stood silently blinking in the soporific red light, which was controlled by timers programmed to maximize growth and egg production.

Water dribbled down long troughs that ran through the cages. Feed dosed with antibiotics and additives dropped into containers in each cage at precisely calculated intervals. Eggs rolled out of the cages and collected in handy gutters. Two women periodically collected the eggs, candled and graded them in booths at the back of the building, and loaded them onto pallets that were trucked off to wholesalers in the cities across the Sound. The chickens were butchered while they were still young enough to provide moist, tender meat.

"And how young is that?" I asked.

"A year," the manager said.

I stepped closer to the cages and stared at one blinking bird. "One year," I said glumly. "One goddamn year."

My funk worsened as I steered back past Logan's. How in God's name was the old man going to stay in business against outfits like Farm Fresh Northwest?

18

The *Echo*'s office was empty. I sat at my desk, cranked a sheet of copy paper into my Selectric, and poured thinly disguised distaste into my story. For generations, I wrote, chickens had wandered around the back porches of Klahowya County, contentedly scratching in the dirt. When the sun dropped in the sky, they scuttled into their coops for the night. When it rose in the morning, they crowed or laid eggs. They took their chances with foxes and coyotes.

But now nothing was left to chance. The modern chicken, I continued, never saw sun or sky. The length of the day never changed with the seasons. For that matter, Farm Fresh Northwest chickens never saw a season twice. Twelve months, and they were on your table. Fresh, unscarred, purified with antibiotics, and cheap.

The jarring sound of my old phone interrupted my furious assault on the Selectric. I picked up the receiver, and Sandy Harper's voice dampened my dudgeon. "Hey, Mr. Newspaperman," she said. "I'm headed to Shelton for a meeting. How about I stop in Bent Fir for a little lunch with you?"

"Sure. I'd love a break from this story. Where do you want to meet?"

"How about your place? I can be there in thirty minutes."

I turned back to the keyboard, trying in vain to focus. I finally gave up, stepped to the front door, and set the "We'll Be Back" cardboard clock in the window. As I stepped outside, a gust of wind whipped across the porch, caught the screen door, and slammed it against the wall. The firs behind the building heaved, creating a low roar as they moved. I looked at the sky, watched clouds scudding by like a fast-motion movie, and jogged up Front Street.

Dust swirled in the gravel parking lot behind Benny's. I climbed the steps and sat on the top landing. Sandy wheeled in and punched the button that raised the Mustang's ragtop. Halfway up, the wind backed around and caught it, punching it back on its struts. I double-timed down the steps and grabbed one side of the canvas while Sandy steadied the other. We pulled in unison and gave the little electric motor enough boost to bring the leading edge of the top to the windshield. Sandy reached inside, locked it down, and we both headed up the stairs. The thrashing branches of the firs sounded like surf. I slammed the door, and in the sudden silence she wrapped her arms around me, kissed me hungrily, and pulled me toward the bed.

We sat down on the mattress and kissed again, our hands roaming each other's bodies.

The phone rang. "Damn!" I said breathlessly. "Who in the hell would be calling me here?"

I picked up the receiver, and Chesty's excited voice boomed through the line. "Tommy. My God! Glad I found you. Marion's not here, and the Forest Service PIO just called.

"It's that fire that's been smolderin' up Scatter Creek. The wind has whipped the bastard up good. She's jumped the west ridge and is burnin' like hell. It's into the Bull of the Woods, and it looks like the whole thing might go."

*　　*　　*

The pale-green Forest Service pickup was parked at an angle across the road, the light on the roof flashing. I braked and climbed out to talk with the ranger leaning against the pickup's fender.

A steady wind blew past me and on up Scatter Creek Canyon. I could still smell smoke, but the thick haze that had hung in the canyon a couple of weeks earlier was gone. The fire, I figured, had sucked it right up the drainage.

"Got a pretty good fire on up the creek," the ranger said. "No civilians allowed."

I pulled out my wallet and thrust the plastic window containing my *Echo* identification card toward the ranger's face. "Press," I said.

The ranger studied the card. "You're the first reporter. Command post's about four miles up. Check in with the PIO."

A mile or so up the road, I heard a roar and leaned forward to peer up through the windshield. A two-rotor Chinook helicopter passed overhead, a massive bucket dangling below it on a steel cable. I felt a surge of excitement, the old chase-the-fire-engine kind of rush that drives every true newshound. They were throwing some bucks at this baby, and that meant the fire was on the move. The Bull of the Woods was prime second growth, and it looked as though the Forest Service meant to save it.

Lines of flashing lights flanked FS 2102. Two crews snapped heavy chain tie-downs loose and unfolded loading ramps as they prepared to drive massive D9 Caterpillar bulldozers off lowboys. Two empty crummies and a half dozen empty vans meant that several crews had already headed up to the fire. The command post operated off the back of a Forest Service pickup. Three men in green uniform jackets leaned over maps spread out on the tailgate, talking. I recognized one of them as the district PIO.

When I popped the Dodge's door, a gust of wind caught it and pulled it open with enough force to make the hinges groan. I strolled up to the little group at the pickup. The three men raised their heads, and the PIO smiled. "Gentlemen," he said, "this here's Tom Dawson, from the *Big Skookum Echo*. He gets his facts straighter than the city boys we're gonna be seeing shortly."

"Oh?" I said, raising my eyebrows. "This is going to attract that much attention?"

"Hoo boy!" said a gray-haired ranger who grinned, leaned forward, and extended a hand. "I'm Bill Porter, and this is my show for the time being.

"And what we got here," he added, "is big trouble."

Porter and the other man turned back to the maps, tracing routes with their fingers and talking about the crews and equipment they hoped to deploy. The PIO gave me a briefing.

The wind had whipped the fire across Scatter Creek and the narrow logging track that had held it back when it first flared up. It jumped across FS 2102 in three or four places, joined into a single fire on the far side, and headed up the hill. It was advancing up the Bull of the Woods ridge on a broad front, creating its own weather as it went. The rising heat of the fire drew dry air up through the mouth of the canyon, feeding oxygen to the flames and creating more heat, more rising air, more wind. The geography of the place produced a natural blowtorch.

The PIO turned and pointed to the ridge. A line of red flame ran along the steep hillside to near the head of the canyon. Thick smoke billowed up from the fire front to the ridgeline and then swirled on over the top. The fire already was nearly halfway up the ridge, and—as the PIO pointed out—burning cinders from the advancing front blew ahead of it, sparking spot fires in the unburned timber ahead. That would make it hard to create and hold fire lines.

Furthermore, the PIO said, this fire was out of the understory and into the upper branches of the dry firs. In the language of woodsmen, it had crowned; it was racing from treetop to treetop. And as anybody who lived in this country knew, a wind-driven crown fire could be almost impossible to stop.

I strolled past the parked equipment and headed up the road.

* * *

I hiked three-quarters of a mile before I reached the smoldering trail of the fire. Cinders whipped by me on the wind and swirled up the blackened hillside on gusts that carried the acrid stench of burned timber. Footprints in the ash and trampled brush just outside the charred area revealed where the wildfire crews had headed up to the hill in an effort to flank the burn. I figured they'd try to clear a fire line just along the back side of the ridge. If they failed there, the next logical line of defense was Cougar Reservoir and FS 2103, the road where Hal Mayfield had died. If the flames jumped FS 2103, I realized with a growing sense of dread, they could burn right down the Cougar Creek drainage. And Cougar Creek entered the Takamak River right above the Cable Hole.

I turned and headed back down the road, passing first one D9 and then the other. Both drivers apparently planned to churn up the ridge on the same route the first wave of firefighters had taken on foot. The ponderous machines would be working on a steep, unstable hillside, but Klahowya County Cat skinners are used to working rugged ground.

I neared the knot of men and equipment around the command post. Two more groups of firefighters, freshly arrived, had gathered around their crew bosses on the roadside, receiving instructions. The PIO stood near Bill Porter's pickup, briefing a scrum of reporters. One television cameraman, his heavy gear on the gravel beside him, stared up at the ridge, looking for the best visuals. I turned and looked back. The fire still burned on an even front, and it had closed the distance to the ridgeline by a third. A helicopter appeared in the smoke over the ridge, swooped down along the fire front, and released a bucketful of water.

I stepped up to the reporters and tuned in to the PIO's presentation. Two Chinooks were on the scene now, he said, and they were refilling their drop buckets at Cougar Reservoir, making for quick trips back and forth to the fire. Three crews of Hotshots—elite firefighters who operated with military discipline—were on their way from Oregon. A second command post was planned along FS 2103, and some equipment was already headed there. If crews didn't stop the fire at the ridgeline, that would become the center of operations.

A reporter standing at the front of the scrum turned to look back at the fire and saw me. He stared for a second and broke into a broad smile. "Hey! Tom Dawson! What's up?"

"Geez, Greg Grant," I said, recognizing the classmate who edited the University of Washington *Daily* when I was a freshman reporter. I stepped forward and extended a hand. "How are you? I heard you landed a job at the *P-I.*"

Grant, two years ahead of me at the U-Dub, had parlayed the editorship of the student paper into a just-out-of-school reporting slot at the Bellevue *Journal-American*, a small daily just across Lake Washington from Seattle. The job was a plum, with plenty of chances at big stories and a guarantee that he'd be noticed at the downtown dailies. "Yeah. Three years now," Greg said. "I'm on the regional desk. Heard you left L.A."

We walked away from the knot of reporters and paused on the shoulder, next to one of the lowboys that had hauled the D9s. "Yeah," I said noncommittally. "I'm spending the summer chasing country news for our little weekly."

"Yeah?"

"More excitement than you might expect," I said. "We've got a murder case going. And there've been a couple of good brights."

"Oh right," Greg said. "We ran a couple of briefs."

"And there's this fire," I continued, turning to look up the hillside.

"Which may just turn out to be something," Greg said. "It jumps the ridge and it'll make the metro front, maybe page one. Especially with the smoke blowing toward Seattle."

We sat on the lowboy, talking about classmates and business. "Things are getting tight in the big city, Tommy. Inflation out of control. Interest rates through the roof. Shit. Nobody's buying anything. Which means nobody's advertising anything. Our linage is down big time."

"I know," I said. "It's worse here."

"And I'll tell you something, buddy," Greg said, turning to look me directly in the eye. "It ain't never going to get better here. Timber is dead. Fishing is dead. Klahowya County is too far out for tourists."

"Interest rates will go back down."

"Maybe. But with the environmental rules we've got now, you'll never see timber cut the way it once was. And the goddamn fish are gone. Just gone. They're never coming back.

"And one more thing," Greg said, poking me in the chest with his index finger. "The economy is crashing, and we're looking down the throat of a recession, big time. Before you know it, there will be hiring freezes at all the dailies. Happens every time.

"You want to get back in the game, you better get in now."

19

I pushed through the glass door to my father's post office. Brass boxes with glass windows lined the left-hand wall of the long, narrow lobby. Freshly polished linoleum tiles shone in the sparkling light that reflected off Oyster Bay and poured in from the bank of windows on the right. At the far end I spotted Walt Hasslebring's broad back, his khaki uniform shirt stretched tight, his big hands braced against the counter. Beyond him, on the other side of the counter, my dad had assumed the same pose. They chatted in the laconic, measured style of Klahowya County men, their only body language an occasional nod.

My footsteps echoed off the linoleum. At the sound, the sheriff turned.

"Well, hello, young man," he said. "Got yourself a hot story up there on Scatter Creek, eh?"

I smiled politely at the pun. Dad was more generous. He laughed out loud.

"What brings you onto federal property?" Dad asked.

"Just taking a little break from the keyboard. Thought I'd stroll down here and offer to take Mom in for her next treatment."

"Thanks, son. But it's her last one. I'd kind of like to be there for that. You want to come along?"

"You boys go ahead and work that out," Hasslebring said. He tipped his hat and turned toward the door.

"Hang on," I said. "I'll walk back downtown with you, if you don't mind. There's something I wanted to ask you."

I told Dad I'd call to work out the arrangements for the Olympia trip. Then the sheriff and I ambled out into the sunlight and followed the sidewalk into the small park that filled the point at the mouth of the Big Skookum.

"I've been thinking about Rush Creek," I said. "You said all the commune members had consistent stories. That nobody seemed inclined to rat out anybody else."

"Yep."

"And what you seemed to be saying was that you were stuck on that angle. That you weren't getting anywhere, and that you'd run out of ideas."

"That's about right."

"So why all the secrecy? Why not run a story in this Thursday's *Echo* and spill the beans on the way Hal and Lars took out the meth cook shack?"

"And what would be the point of that, other than to wipe out the value of some inside information that might prove useful when we interrogate suspects?"

"What suspects? Get some more information out there, and you might actually smoke a suspect out. Who knows? Get the town talking. Maybe somebody will remember something. Maybe somebody will make some connection that hasn't occurred to any of us."

"And maybe," the sheriff said, pausing to light a White Owl, "you get yourself a good story that don't do me a damn bit of good."

I reached into my shirt pocket, pulled out a pack of Marlboros, and lit one, using my fancy Zippo move. "Folks do have a right to know," I said. "That's the way the system's supposed to work."

Hasslebring puffed on his cigar, looking out over the mouth of the Big Skookum. "All right," he said. "Go ahead. But keep Roy Hammer's name out of it."

He turned and ambled on toward city hall. I watched him go, once again puzzling over the man's hidden dimensions. Roy Hammer? How in the hell did Walt Hasslebring find out I knew anything about Roy Hammer?

* * *

Harris stood at his usual Thursday-morning post in front of the folder, checking ink levels as the *Echo* rolled off the press. With all the noise, I had no idea how he knew I'd come through the back door and was standing behind him, looking over his shoulder at the front page. But he turned around, grinned, and held the paper up for me to see.

Marion had stripped a 72-point headline across the entire nine columns, giving the *Echo* a big-city look that obliterated the usual clutter. "Mayfield Raid Preceded Murder," it read. True enough, although the inescapable implication that the two events were connected was a leap of the imagination. Harris didn't seem to mind. "Got yourself some real news on this one, Tommy," he said, shaking the paper. "Got the lady softball back in sports where it belongs."

I took the paper and headed for the front office. A sidebar provided background on the 1979 meth bust at Rush Creek and quoted the sheriff to the effect that nobody had suspected the meth-cooking operation was back in business. The mainbar was more or less a straight narrative of how the Mayfield raid had gone down.

Marion stood at the front counter, chatting with Myrtle Johnson. "Not Hal?" Myrtle asked, shaking her head. "Not Lars? Neither one of them said a thing about it?"

"Not to me," Marion said. "Not to anybody, as far as I know." She turned when she heard me walk into the office. "The first thing I heard about this little escapade was when Clark Kent here turned in this story yesterday." As she spoke, she pointed at the front page of the *Echo* lying on the counter in front of Myrtle.

"Keep on digging, Clark," Myrtle said to me, her lips compressed and frown lines creasing her forehead. "We got to get to the bottom of this. Something's gone wrong in this town. And we got to put it right again."

I gave a little mock salute. "I'm working on it, Myrtle," I said. "We'll figure things out."

Myrtle gave me a half smile and a slight nod, reached over the counter to pat Marion on the shoulder, and headed for the door.

"Quite a headline," I said to Marion as the screen door slammed behind Myrtle.

"Quite a story."

"Don't you think you're pushing it a little?" I asked.

"How so?"

"Linking the business with the D8 to the murder that directly? We don't know there's any connection. The story doesn't say there's any connection."

"The headline doesn't say there's any connection either."

"It sure suggests one."

Marion looked grim. It was easy enough to see why she was taking the story personally. It *was* personal, for God's sake. But on the big tablet of journalistic thou-shalt-nots I carried around in my head, the cardinal sin was bringing personal interests into a story. The whole situation made me uncomfortable.

"If the shoe fits . . ." Marion said as she grabbed the paper, turned her back on me, and stepped over to her desk.

* * *

The Dodge ran perfectly on the forty-minute drive to Key Center. Sandy snuggled next to me on the big bench seat, quiet and contented as we swept past the firs on the two-lane blacktop that rose and dipped along the shoreline. A half dozen commercial buildings clustered around the junction formed where the highway met the road that headed off down the Key Peninsula. We parked in front of a Mexican restaurant, found a table, and chatted about trivia over combination plates. Then we strolled across the road to the rowdy bar that offered the only regular live music—then and now—in those parts.

The music fired up at nine, a quartet of good old boys who pounded out garage-band rock 'n' roll that was crude, but danceable. We downed three pitchers, worked up a good sweat on the sawdust-covered dance floor, and left about midnight, filled with youthful exuberance brought on by the music and exercise. Sandy pulled close to me, nibbling wetly on my neck and ear, breathing heavily, and pulling her knee up over my thigh. "Find someplace to stop," she said urgently.

I turned onto a logging spur halfway to Cedar Springs. We pulled off everything below the waist and made frantic love, her astride me in the driver's seat. Then, sleepy and utterly relaxed, we cruised back to the base. I showed her to the door of the BOQ, kissed her, and headed for Bent Fir.

It was nearly two when I finally trudged up the rickety wooden steps behind Benny's, eager for sleep. I reached the top landing and pulled up short, a prickling sensation running down my back. My door hung from one hinge, the jamb shattered, leaving the dark entrance to the little apartment gaping. I reached in and switched on the light.

The place had been completely trashed. The kitchen table lay on its side, and the mattress had been yanked off the box springs. My Salvation Army dishes were shattered in the sink. The apple-crate nightstand lay on its side, the bedside lamp crushed beside it.

I took three steps toward the corner where I stored my outdoor gear. The fly-tying chest had been upended, leaving feathers, thread, and bits of fur scattered on the floor. My waders had been shredded by the kitchen knife that lay beside them. My grandfather's fly-rod case lay open on the old couch. "Oh no!" I gasped, slowly reaching down to pick up the rod itself.

Somebody had taken the burnished old three-piece beauty, held it in two hands, and smashed it over a knee. I picked up the six shattered pieces, their ends roughly splintered, and felt a wave a sadness wash over me. Then anger. Then resolution.

20

"For God's sake," Mark said, "you can't expect anybody in a logger bar to talk to you if you're dressed like a California doofus."

I stood on my landing, looking down at my Hawaiian shirt, chinos, and penny loafers. Mark grabbed my shoulder, turned me around, and pushed me back into my apartment. We rummaged through my clothes and finally came up with jeans, hiking boots, and a ragged denim shirt. We piled into Mark's pickup and pulled out of Benny's lot.

Twenty minutes later, Mark piloted the Ford over a wooded ridge, down to the floodplain of the Takamak, and along a causeway running through marsh. A few cars lined the shoulder, and when we drove onto the bridge, Mark craned his neck, trying to spot fishermen standing in the river.

"Look," I said, "Carbone said he had no dealings with a mill."

"What else was he supposed to say, Little Brother? He was puttin' you on."

"He was watching what he said, all right. But what if he was telling the truth on that one? What if he was dealing with somebody other than a mill? Now who would that be?"

"A wholesaler, I reckon. I mean it works that way some places, even if you're legit."

U.S. 101 straightened and wound north along the shoreline. Hood Canal shimmered in the late afternoon light. It was a fjord, of course, not a canal at all but a wide, deep saltwater inlet carved by glaciers and now lined with some of the world's best oyster beds. But the way it ran arrow-straight along the eastern slopes of the Olympics sure suggested a canal.

"So tell me about this joint," I said.

"The Crosscut? Typical beer parlor, I guess. Loggers, oyster pickers, and them such. They swill Oly and spit on the floor. Got free popcorn though."

"Think they'll spill anything? Other than beer, I mean."

"Get any of these good ol' boys loaded, and they'll give their

129

wives Christmas lists for their girlfriends. It just depends on how easy they're feelin', you know. So stifle yourself on the reporter bullshit. And can the highfalutin' talk, college boy. Act like a normal chain-saw jockey. Grunt, nod, and fart once in a while. That oughta do it."

The Crosscut Tavern perched on pilings just south of Hoodsport, a rickety pile of weathered lumber that looked as if it might pitch onto the beach during the first big blow. The door opened to a wall of noise and a room filled with loggers and oystermen. The woods-men, fresh off their shifts, wore suspenders and canvas pants sawed off at the ankles. The oystermen sloshed around in rubber boots.

We perched on stools at the end of the bar. I lit a Marlboro and ordered a pitcher. By the time we'd finished our first schooners, Mark had introduced himself as a mill hand from Port Angeles and struck up a conversation with the six loggers at the table next to us. Before we'd finished another, we were at the table, swapping lies about salmon and women. Three pitchers later, we got down to business.

Mark mentioned Luke Johnson and Joseph Carbone. "Are their families doing okay?" I asked.

They could be better, the big logger across from me said. But they had their unemployment, and the neighbors were pitching in.

"Those boys seem to have missed the scaling station," Mark said.

Yeah, said the big logger, a lot of that was going around.

Mark ordered two more pitchers for the table. "If a guy had some big trees to sell, how would he go about it?"

If a guy had some big trees to sell, said a logger wearing red suspenders with the Stihl logo printed on them, then he needed a middleman. No mills on the peninsula were rigged for old growth anymore. And no mills on the other side of the Sound would buy from some stranger who rolled up to the gate with unbranded tim-ber.

"Well," Mark told him, "let's say I got some big trees. So just where do I find this man in the middle?"

Three of his companions turned and glared at the loudmouth, who took a long drink of Oly and then sat silently.

The conversation returned to fishing. Once we'd drained the two pitchers Mark had ordered, I stood. As Mark rose from his seat, the loudmouth in the Stihl suspenders piped up again.

"The state bulls stopped Luke and Joe just north of Cutthroat Creek. I don't figure they was going much farther than that."

"Thanks," Mark said, pushing his chair back to the table. "Much obliged."

*   *   *

By eight, the sun had dropped behind the Olympics, but July days in the Northwest last forever, and we still had nearly two hours of daylight. Mark drifted across the U.S. 101 centerline and then snapped the pickup back as a deadheading log truck, its trailer piggybacked for the run home, roared by northbound. "You okay?" I asked, nervously.

"Don't get them panties of yours all in knots, Little Bro. A few pitchers is jus' enough to wake old Markie up."

I was plenty awake. And I had been since my jailhouse interview with Joe Carbone. This was starting to feel like real reporting, one development leading to another, a story taking shape from the raw material I was generating day by day. For the moment, I'd forgotten about county commissioners and women's softball. But I hadn't forgotten about the SOB—or SOBs—who'd trashed my apartment and broken Granddad's fly rod.

Old Markie wrenched the wheel to the right and screeched onto Cutthroat Creek Road, headed upstream. "So now what?" I asked. "We have miles of woods in front of us. You could hide the mother of all log dumps in them. We haven't got a prayer of finding anything. And none of these stump farmers are going to talk to us."

"Patience, Little Brother."

Cutthroat Road quickly turned to gravel, lined with brush-choked third growth. The unkempt thickets contrasted sharply with the well-groomed plantations maintained by the big timber companies or the national forest. This was small-owner private land, scrubby and unproductive. The hot July wind still blew, stirring the firs, but smoke from the Bull of the Woods fire, still burning in the next drainage north, hung in the trees.

We passed rust-stained single-wide trailers on cinderblock foundations and ramshackle cabins in small clearings, surrounded by junked cars and old logging equipment. This little valley was even more down at the heels than the Scatter Creek drainage.

About three miles in, we pulled onto a wide shoulder occupied by an old step van and two battered pickups. A hand-lettered sign advertised the services of the mushroom buyer who sat on a stool behind a folding table, waving his arms as he negotiated with small, dark men who clustered in front of the table. "Hmong," Mark said. "They come out here since you left. They prowl the backcountry looking for shrooms, and they sell to these guys who set up on the roads coming out of the woods. Then the buyers sell to the fancy-pants restaurants in Seattle. Even ship 'em overseas on air freight.

"Nobody," he added, "knows the woods like a shroomer."

"And nobody's less likely to talk about what he's finding and where he's finding it."

"True, when it comes to shrooms. But we're not looking for shrooms."

Mark pulled in next to one of the Hmong pickups and motioned toward the buyer. "I run across this guy three, four years ago," Mark said. "Was a topper for a gyppo outfit out on the coast. Saw this shroom thing comin' and got in early. Sets up wherever the Hmong is pickin'. These guys are strictly wholesale, but he'll sell to me. Good deals on morels, boletes, chanterelles, you name it . . ."

Mark strolled over to the table and greeted the buyer like a long-lost cousin. I joined them, and Mark introduced me. Then, while I dickered for a pound of morels, Mark chatted up the Hmong. The buyer dumped my morels into a wrinkled paper bag, and I headed for the truck. Mark climbed in, and we headed up the road. "Now what?" I asked.

"Look for a big cedar stump. Hollow. About two miles. On the left."

The stump stood next to a dirt track leading into the third growth. The pickup lurched and bounded over the ruts. Then we rolled into a clearing freshly scarred by heavy equipment that had torn up the Klahowya County clay. A skidder and the lowboy trailer used to haul it stood at the far end of the open space. "These boys," Mark said, gesturing at the piles of logs ringing the clearing, "been operating their own goddamned yard here."

He braked, and the two of us walked toward the nearest pile, a stack that held a dozen massive old-growth fir logs, the largest six feet in diameter. I looked down at the muscular tire tracks crisscrossing the dried mud in front of the deck, where the skidder had rolled back and forth as it piled up the logs. I squatted and eyeballed one track. "Lookee here," I said.

"At what?"

"It's clear as mud," I said, pointing. And there, in the track, was the unmistakable shape of a penguin.

21

Walt Hasslebring ambled out the side entrance to the courthouse and lit a White Owl. I smiled and picked up my pace across the asphalt, genuinely glad to see him. I guess he'd warmed a little more to me, too. In any event, he'd quit calling me "Tommy" or "sonny boy." Expressionless, he contemplated me as I approached.

"Mornin', Tom."

"Mornin', Sheriff. Did that state cop who dusted my place get anything?"

"Just your prints," the sheriff said. "And Benny's. And some off the bedstead that show up on the federal register as belonging to a young lady lieutenant from up at Cedar Springs." He leered. "You don't suppose she's the one turned your place upside down, do you?"

"As far as I know, she's happy," I said, smiling.

"But you didn't need to drag me out here to ask me about prints," the sheriff said. "So what's this all about?"

"This time," I said, gesturing toward my Dodge, "I thought I might take you for a little ride."

"Well, son, that's right generous of you. But I don't think the sheriff ought to be riding around his county in a relic like that. It's a matter of respect, you know."

We climbed into the Chevy cruiser and rumbled out of the parking lot. The sheriff turned to me. "So where we going?"

I directed him up the Longmont Grade and onto the U.S. 101 connector. He reached the highway, braked to a full halt at the stop sign most drivers ignored, and then accelerated north on the federal pavement.

"What's the word on Hal Mayfield?" I asked.

"Well," the sheriff said, "can I tell you this off the record?"

"Sure. So long as you let me get it on the record when the time comes."

"That's a deal," Hasslebring said, falling back into silence. "Like I told you, we got nothing real solid out of our interviews with the crew," he finally said. "But there was some hinting around that was kinda interesting."

"You mean about the arguments between Hal and Lars? I thought that was just the usual father-son stuff."

"Well, there was maybe a little more to it than that. Stubby Lancaster and two or three of the other boys kept sayin' that Hal was raggin' on Lars pretty regular. Giving him some shit about something that neither one of 'em would talk about directly."

"Like what?"

"Don't know. That's what I'm tellin' ya. But it's fair to say that Hal knew something was going on back in those woods. And Lars knew about it, too. And that Lars was maybe even involved somehow."

I contemplated the possibilities. Lars pushed the environmental regs—everybody knew that. And Hal was a stickler for the rules. But Lars idolized his father, despite the constant disagreements and occasional shouting matches. Surely he wouldn't do anything to harm the old man.

At Cutthroat Creek, I directed Hasslebring west into the firs. The gravel crackled as the cruiser negotiated a sharp jog in the road. As it straightened again, a Forest Service pickup appeared on the shoulder, parked with the light on top of its cab blinking. Charlie Adams sat on the tailgate, smoking a cigar, right where I'd asked him to meet us.

Hasslebring pulled in behind the pickup and popped his door. I climbed out the passenger side. "Well, Charlie," the sheriff said. "You of all people should know that you ought not be smoking in the woods when it's like this."

"Want a stogie, eh," Adams said, reaching for his breast pocket. He pulled out a cigar, slid off the tailgate, and stood. He handed Hasslebring the smoke, reached into his pants pocket, extracted a cigar clipper, and handed that over, too.

"What about you, young man?" he asked.

"No thanks, Mr. Adams," I said, pulling out a Marlboro. "But I'm glad you could meet us here."

Adams shifted his eyes to Hasslebring, who was positioning the clipper to nip the end off his cigar. "This here's the sheriff's bailiwick," Adams continued. "So thanks for inviting me along on your little show-and-tell."

Hasslebring looked up, slid the cigar into his mouth, and leaned forward to catch the flame from the lighter Adams held in front of him. He puffed silently, rotating the cigar to get an even light. Then he stood upright and turned to me. "Let's see what you've got," he said, waving in the direction of the woods.

I led them down the dirt track. Forty-foot third growth arched over the lane, closing off the sky. Thick understory stood eight feet tall on either side. "Look at the fuel in here," Adams said, taking a long draw on his cigar. "One spark and you'd have an inferno."

We walked into the clearing. Hasslebring and Adams stopped cold and puffed on their stogies, surveying the stacks of old growth. Hasslebring walked to the nearest pile, a big heap of logs known in the trade as a cold deck. "Jesus," he said. "Why'd they stash 'em here? Why not just truck 'em straight to the buyer?"

"I'm guessing they just want someplace to sort 'em out and store 'em while they find buyers," Adams said. "Plus they can haul 'em outta here at night when nobody's likely to see 'em. And they can find different guys to haul, maybe even mixing up the loads with legitimate timber."

"There's something more," I said, stepping up next to the sheriff. I pointed down to the tracks we were standing on. Hasslebring leaned over, puffing his cigar and rotating to scan the pattern dried in the mud. He spotted the penguin in seconds. "Looks like we got ourselves a damned interesting connection," he said.

He stood upright. His eyes darted around the clearing. "And everything in this piss-ant valley," he continued, "connects to one thing."

Charlie Adams walked up to us. "Yeah," he said. "What's that?"

"This is Dykes country," the sheriff said. "And I think it's high time we paid old Don Dykes a visit."

* * *

Charlie Adams had business in Shelton, but the sheriff and I headed for the Dykes place. Hasslebring drove silently until he steered his cruiser onto the dirt track that led into a cluttered clearing. He stopped and looked at me. "Well," he said, "let's see who's home."

We climbed out, and I looked around. A '49 Ford without wheels sat on blocks in one corner of the yard. An even older logging truck, decrepit and doorless but apparently still operable, was parked on the other. An ancient steam donkey engine on skids, once used to yard logs off hillsides, lay moldering against the wall of fir that marked the boundary of the clearing. Piles of rusted metal lay all over the yard.

I glanced at Hasslebring. His eyes were darting around the clearing, taking in the scene, as he lumbered toward the unpainted house that squatted in the middle of the mess. I hurried after him.

Hasslebring clomped onto the covered porch and raised his hand to knock. He spotted eyes staring out at him from the darkness behind the rusted screen and lowered his hand.

"Watcha want?" asked a gravelly voice.

"Mornin', Don," Hasslebring said. "Just stopped by to say hello."

The screen door creaked open, and the sheriff stepped back to give it room. Standing behind his right shoulder, I stepped back, too. Donald Dykes shuffled out onto the porch. Four new scars, still bright pink, zigzagged down from his forehead and across his cheeks. A dirty strip of tape ran across the bridge of his nose, holding the broken cartilage in place. "So what can I do ya for, Sheriff?" he asked, blinking in the bright light.

"Oh," Hasslebring said, "nuthin' in particular. Just wondering how things are going with you and yours."

Dykes looked down and shuffled his feet. "Okay, I guess," he said. "We're all okay."

A sound in the doorway behind him drew my eyes. Moochie Dykes stood silently behind her father, a hand clutching her ragged housedress to her throat. She was staring at me.

"Hi, Moochie," I said.

She beamed. "Hi, Tom Dawson," she drawled, lowering her eyes.

Donald Dykes snapped his head around. "G'wan back inside," he growled. Across her father's shoulder, Moochie smiled at me again with an exasperated shrug. She spun on her bare heel and disappeared into the darkness, her well-formed bottom swaying with exaggerated motion under the thin fabric of the old housedress.

Dykes watched me watch his daughter. A thin smile broke through his beard. "Tom Dawson, eh?" he asked. "You're the postmaster's kid, ain't cha?"

"That's right," I said, "Jess Dawson's my dad."

"How about your boys?" the sheriff asked. "Eddie and Terry, aren't they?"

"That be the twins, all right," Dykes said sullenly. "Can't say that I know where they are, though. Ain't seen 'em in a while now. My boy Arnie's working down at the Shell on Front Street. That is, if you don't have him locked up again."

"Nope," said the sheriff, smiling. "Arnie hasn't been in one of my guest rooms for a while. See him pretty regular down at the Shell, though. Good to see he's workin' steady."

Dykes grunted noncommittally.

"Well," the sheriff said, "we'd just as well be going. Say hi to the twins for me when you see 'em, and Maybell, too."

Hasslebring shook hands with Dykes, stepped back, and headed down the steps. I turned to follow, but Dykes brought me up short. "Tom Dawson," the old man said, "my Moochie's lonely out here. Why don't you c'mon by someday? Take her to a movie or some such."

*   *   *

The sheriff steered the Chevy back down Cutthroat Creek Road and chewed impassively on the dead butt of the cigar Charlie Adams had given him an hour earlier.

"Well?" I finally asked.

"Well what?"

"Well, what do you make of all that?"

"Well, I figure," Hasslebring said, sitting a little forward and breaking into a broad smile, "that Moochie Dykes would like you for dinner. And maybe lunch and breakfast, too."

I slumped back into my seat with exaggerated exasperation. "C'mon. What'd you make of Don Dykes? What's going on back there?"

"Aw . . . Ol' Don knows something, all right. 'Course ol' Don knows a lot of things, and he doesn't much like talking to the sheriff about any of them."

"But what about the log poaching?"

"Well, you gotta figure the Dykes boys have something to do with it. Don clearly wasn't interested in tellin' me anything about Eddie and Terry. That may not be much of a family, but they keep pretty close watch on each other. I figure he knows where they are. Or at least has a pretty good idea."

"And?"

"You take a good look at that yard?" Hasslebring asked.

"A bunch of rusty junk."

"Some of that junk would be pretty useful if a guy was moving old growth," Hasslebring said. "That old Reo had fresh chips on the bed and shiny metal on the stakes. Been used to cart logs recently."

"Reo?"

"Yeah. Reo. That old-timer truck is a Reo. Was a big name in trucks, back when trucks was new in these woods.

"More to the point, those big ol' pulleys stacked with them snarls of cable over by the donkey engine . . . they're the kind of block-and-tackle gear the old-timers used to load logs. Big logs. And that skinned log with the blocks attached on the top end . . ."

"Yeah?"

"That's what you call a gin pole, son. You use it for holdin' a block-and-tackle rig when you got no tree."

I sat silently, pondering my own inadequacies. Walt Hasslebring and I had spent the same amount of time walking through the same yard. But the sheriff had seen a whole world invisible to me. My respect for the older man went up yet another notch.

But he wasn't through.

"You know those LT235 tires that have been leaving ruts all over this county?" he asked.

"Yeah?"

"Well, if you'd just looked down once in a while, you'd have seen those same ruts all over Dykes's yard."

I was still digesting that when Hasslebring suddenly slowed. A pale green pickup was roaring up the road toward us. As it approached, I could make out two identically colored vans behind it.

Hasslebring reached to his dash, flipped on his overhead light, and stopped in the middle of the road. The pickup skidded to a stop ten feet from his bumper. The driver-side door popped open, and a twenty-something in logger-style pants stepped out. Hasslebring climbed out of his cruiser and threw the soggy cigar stub in the ditch. I climbed out, too.

"Where's the fire?" Hasslebring said.

"Bull of the Woods, sir," the pickup driver said in his politest tone. "We're the Pine Mountain Hotshots, from Pine Mountain, Oregon. And we're told they need us there real bad."

"Well, son," the sheriff said, "you'll get there a lot faster if you take the right road. This here's Cutthroat Creek. You want Scatter Creek, which becomes Forest Service 2102. It's the next drainage north."

"Oops," the pickup driver said. "I guess we'd better turn around. Okay if we go?"

"Sure, sure," Hasslebring said. "Get your Oregon asses up where you'll do some good."

"What's going on with that fire anyway?" I asked.

"We just heard from the crew boss on the radio," the pickup driver said. "The wind is whipping things up something awful. The fire jumped the first line, and now it's burning downhill like crazy. Everybody's pulling back to the second line. We're supposed to report in at a place called Cougar Reservoir."

22

A framed copy of the issue still hangs in the *Echo*'s front office. A huge headline—"Fire Ravages Forest"—streams across the top of page one in what old printers called "second-coming type." My photo, taken from the fire line southwest of Cougar Reservoir, shows dense smoke boiling off Bull of the Woods Ridge. The date under the nameplate reads "July 30, 1981."

On that very day, Marion had stood at her desk and held the paper at arm's length. "Not bad," she said.

"Yeah," I said from where I sat at my own desk, puffing on a Marlboro. "But it would have been great in color. Geez. You can't show flames in black and white. We must have the last black-and-white front page on the planet."

"Lots of papers still have black and white. Dailies. Big ones."

The screen door creaked, and we both looked over to see Myrtle Johnson striding into the lobby. Short, thick, and determined, she looked like a mill-pond tug huffing and puffing up to a log raft. She wore her gray hair in a bun, Keds on her feet, and a purple dress that hit her mid-calf. The screen door slammed shut behind her.

"Phew!" Myrtle said, slightly out of breath. "The smoke's even bad down here. And it's terrible in Angel Harbor. Just *terrible*."

"That's a good sign," I said. "The wind's down. The smoke's spreading instead of just blowing off in one direction."

"I just loved your story, Tom," Myrtle said, slapping her weekly Angel Harbor dispatch onto the counter. "You did such a good job of explaining what it's like to be on a fire line. I could almost feel the heat. And I sure as heck could smell the smoke. Didn't even have to imagine that.

"Your story," she continued, "will help the folks around here appreciate those terrific young firefighters. The risks they take, my goodness. And how hard they work. Letting everybody know, now that's a real public service."

"Thanks, Myrtle," I said. The praise felt comfortable, motherly. Especially coming from a local fixture like Myrtle Johnson.

"You know, Tom," Myrtle said, "we need young men like you in Klahowya County. Young men who care about something other than drinking beer and killing deer. I'm really pleased to see you home. I hope you're thinking about staying. I truly do."

Marion walked to the counter and picked up Myrtle's dispatch. Myrtle's neat typing, banged out on an ancient Underwood, covered two sheets.

"What's new in the Harbor?" Marion asked.

"Oh, you know," Myrtle said. "The usual. The Hendersons got a new car. One of those boxy little Japanese things. And the Benson boy wrecked his dad's boat again."

I laughed. "I thought Mr. Benson still had him breaking rocks after the last time."

"He did," Myrtle said with a gleeful little squeal. "But those Bensons. You know they never did take to education."

She turned on her heel and marched out. The screen door slammed again.

Marion turned from the counter and looked directly at me. "She's right, you know. We *do* need young men like you. The old ways are dying. We need to find something new. If all the talent leaves, this place will wither and die."

I looked down at the neatly arranged stacks of paper on my desk. "You could build a life here," Marion continued. "You could lead this town somewhere. And you'd be somewhere you belonged, not lost in some strange city."

I looked up. "Marion. I trained to be a newsman. I can be good. I can really accomplish something."

"You *are* accomplishing something. Don't you see how much what we do here matters?"

"Marion. I write about chicken farms and church potlucks. I make $298 a week."

"The *Echo* holds this county together. That's important, to a lot of people. All you seem to be thinking about is how much you make, and how much glory you get.

"And," she added, "chasing blondes in Navy-blue skirts."

Marion had never so much as mentioned Sandy before, and the comment took me by surprise. If I'd been a little more self-aware in those days, I might have tumbled to something I hadn't suspected. Instead, I felt of flash of unthinking resentment.

"Sandy Harper," I said. "Her name is Sandy Harper. And she's quite a bit more than a blonde in a Navy-blue skirt."

"She may very well be. But I'm not talking about her; I'm talking about you."

I stood there, looking puzzled, my cigarette smoldering unnoticed in my ashtray.

"Look, Tom," Marion said. "You don't seem to know what you want, where you want to go. But you're never going to figure any of that out until you deal with the big questions first."

"Like what?"

"Like what really matters to you. Like who you are."

* * *

The line of equipment stretched for a quarter mile down both sides of FS 2103, right to the south shore of Cougar Reservoir. Dense smoke rose from the fire but then settled into the valley, stagnant in dead-calm air. The high ocean fog that had been rolling in as I left Bent Fir completely covered the sky. I stepped out of my car and felt the moist coolness of it.

The command center had grown into something far more substantial than the tailgate of Bill Porter's pickup. A green canvas canopy covered several hundred square feet alongside the gravel road, protecting two dozen aluminum lawn chairs and three long plywood tables. Porter himself leaned over one of the tables, pointing at a large Forest Service map while a gaggle of reporters watched and listened. I stepped in behind them.

The fire still burned west of Cougar Reservoir, but wind no longer blew flaming cinders ahead of it, leapfrogging fire lines and outflanking firefighters. Local crews were holding at the road, which blocked the flames on the south and southwest. The firefighters had extended the line down Cougar Creek where it flowed out the north end of the reservoir, and the two Oregon Hotshot crews had scratched out another line west from the creek. Porter confidently predicted that they'd join up with FS 2102 by the end of the day, encircling the fire.

"We've got 'er 90 percent contained," he said, looking up from the map. "If this humidity holds, she's a goner."

The reporters scattered around the command post, jotting in their notebooks. Greg Grant looked up and saw me. "Hey, Tom! Looks like your big news is about to wimp out."

"We thought it was snuffed once before," I said, smiling. "Don't ever count a Klahowya County fire out."

"Read your story," Greg said. "Damn. You really nailed it. All the guys were passing it around. They're all writing straight news, and you got readers right out there with the crews. Great description. Man, you really made it sing."

I reddened. Greg turned to the two reporters sitting in lawn chairs behind him. "Hey, guys," he said. "This is Tom Dawson. He went to the U-Dub with me. He wrote that great piece in the local weekly."

The reporters stood, stepped forward, and extended their hands.

* * *

Mom bounced back from every chemo session more slowly than from the previous one. After I drove her home from her fifth infusion, she hardly recovered at all. She vomited for a week, and then an intestinal virus overwhelmed her almost-nonexistent immune system. She lost so much fluid that Dad had to take her in for an IV.

When the date for her sixth and final session rolled around, Dad and I each took an elbow and helped her from her bedroom to the car. "You can do it, Mom," I said as we crunched across the driveway. "Just keep thinking, 'It's the last one . . . ever.'"

Through it all, she'd never complained. But this time, her voice quavered as she said, "And that's a lucky thing, too. I honestly don't think I could manage another one. I think I'd have to quit."

"No quitting now," Dad said, helping her into the passenger seat. "We've nearly made it to retirement. We've got places to go, things to see. We've been waiting a long time for this."

We fell into silence on the drive to Olympia. At the hospital, Dad waited while I ran into the lobby for a wheelchair, and then we rolled my mother up to the infusion room. The three of us sat tensely, waiting to see if the preliminary blood test showed a white-cell count high enough to permit another treatment. She squeaked by, and we all managed faint smiles. My mother popped her Benadryl, the nurse hung the bag of caustic chemicals above her on the IV stand, and the slow-drip infusion began. Exhausted as she was, Mom succumbed to the Benadryl in minutes, her eyes closing and her chest settling into a gentle rhythm. Dad caught my eye. "Might as well go for a little walk," he said.

We found our way to the hospital courtyard, a quiet garden surrounding a fountain. The architect must have designed the place for Dad and me and the others of our kind, helpless loved ones waiting out treatments or surgeries or some doctor's report on a patient's prognosis. The two of us sat on a curved concrete bench.

"What's this I hear about your apartment?" Dad asked, catching me totally by surprise. I hadn't said a thing about the mess I'd discovered at my place a week earlier. But the Bent Fir Telegraph had apparently been clicking away, and Dad knew all about it anyway.

He quizzed me about the particulars, and I coughed up the bad news about my grandfather's fly rod. Dad's jaw clenched and his eyes narrowed. He wasn't a fly fisherman, but it had been his father's rod.

"You got any protection?" he asked.

"Protection?"

"Yes. *Protection.* You have any firearms over there?"

"Dad, I don't need a gun for God's sake. I'm a small-town newspaperman."

"Whoever broke into your place was damned serious about something. Or just crazy. Either way, you shouldn't just be sitting around naked. I want you to have some protection."

"Like what?"

"Like my old .38. It's a revolver—only takes six rounds. But it packs enough punch to stop somebody coming through the door. When we get your mother home and into bed, I'll get it for you. Don't have much ammo. But Benny can fix you up."

23

Sometimes I still think of that perfect trip across Puget Sound when I take the ferry from Bremerton to Seattle. Sandy's blond hair glowing in the sun and blowing in the wind. My jacket ballooning out around my back and snapping in the breeze. From the deck rail, we could see the Olympic Mountains rimming the horizon we were leaving behind and the city straight ahead. Fir-covered islands fell behind on either side. Whitecaps flecked the water.

Sandy slipped her arm around me and pulled close. I inhaled the salt air. "When you see it like this," I said, "you wonder why anybody would ever leave."

Sandy laughed. "Yeah. I'll give you that. But how often do you see it like this? This winter, I was beginning to think this water actually *was* gray."

The ferry passed Alki Point, entered Elliott Bay, and came into full view of downtown Seattle. The forty-minute crossing from Bremerton, where I'd left my car, ended right on Alaskan Way, smack-dab in the middle of the central waterfront.

We grabbed our overnight bags and joined the foot passengers streaming from the big boat. Cars rolled off the ferry, each producing a loud metallic *ka-lunk* as it crossed the steel docking ramp. Frenzied herring gulls ran up and down the dock's wooden railings, their wings spread and their heads extended as they squawked for food. The ferry's deep-throated whistle blew.

We walked hand in hand down the waterfront, passing curio shops and restaurants with fish-and-chips counters that opened onto the Alaskan Way sidewalk. I shifted my duffel and Sandy's suit bag from one shoulder to the other. The press of tourists crowding the sidewalk set me on edge. "I forget how tacky it can be along here," I said.

"Oh, c'mon," Sandy said, giving my hand a little yank. "You're out of Hicksville. Have a little fun with it."

We checked into the Edgewater Hotel. I had called days before, hoping to get a first-floor room hanging out over the water. And we'd scored. I opened the door to room 183, grabbed Sandy's hand, and moved directly to the big window. I slid it open, and we dropped to our knees, resting our forearms on the sill and staring out over Elliott Bay. Gulls keened. Tour boats pulled out of the Alaskan Way piers.

I sucked in the rank salt smell of a working waterfront, sighed contentedly, and rolled onto the carpet, pulling Sandy onto me. She straddled me, pulled up her knees, and rested her elbows on my chest. "Hey, country boy," she said, "don't you want to see the town?"

"I spent five years in L.A.," I said, fiddling with the top button on her blouse, "half of them stuck in freeway traffic. I'd say I qualify as a city boy. Besides. I spent four years here. I know this town up and down. And we have the whole weekend."

"Hmmm. And this is how we're going to spend the whole weekend?"

"Why not?" I struggled with the third button. She laughed, popped it open, quickly finished the rest, and pulled the blouse off. Then she reached behind her back, unhooked her bra, and shrugged out of it.

"Quite a show for the sailors," I said, looking up at her and nodding toward the open window.

She pulled my windbreaker open and started on the buttons of my shirt. "Well," she said, "let's give the lady sailors something to look at, too."

*　*　*

I lay on the bed, propped on an elbow, and watched Sandy dress. She sat on the edge of the mattress, pulled up her panty hose, stood, and wiggled the waistband up over her hips. She caught my gaze and giggled. "A reverse striptease," she said, slipping into her bra and grabbing her Navy blouse off a closet hanger. She stepped into her blue skirt and backed up to me so that I could pull the zipper up and snap the hook.

"Why should I be helping you cover up all this beautiful scenery?" I asked.

"The scenery's out the window. Besides, I'll only be a bit. A little courtesy call, that's all. Meet the captain, and I'm outta there." She moved to the vanity, put on some lipstick, and fiddled with her hair.

"I'll go for a walk. Meet me at the market at noon."

"Where at the market?"

"At the pig. Just inside the main entrance. You can't miss it."

She pulled her jacket on, stepped to the door, blew me a kiss, and vanished.

I lay on the bed a few more minutes, gazing out the window at all the activity in the harbor. A ferry leaving the downtown terminal, where we'd arrived an hour before, cut loose with a long whistle blast as it picked up speed and headed out through the pleasure boats. I picked out the name on its hull: Klahowya.

"I'm just fine," I said, throwing my legs over the side of the bed. "How are *you*?"

I dressed and was out the door, squinting in the early August sun. Traffic roared on the Alaskan Way Viaduct. When the two-deck roadway was built in the forties, nobody worried about the fact that it cut downtown Seattle off from its waterfront. And the viaduct was supposed to solve the city's traffic problems forever. But Seattle just kept growing. By 1980, the freeways were so jammed that they threatened to shut the city down altogether. It was a problem, I figured, that Bent Fir would never have.

I walked up Wall Street to Sixth Avenue and stood across the street from the Post-Intelligencer building, watching the giant *P-I* globe revolve above the front entrance. The *P-I* nameplate encircled the turning planet at the equator, an image that boasted of grand ambitions. I liked the Hearst paper, as much for its second-place pluck as for its quality. "Geez," I thought, watching the globe rotate. "That's what a *real* newspaper looks like."

Nine blocks east, the *Times* presented a much more sedate image. I sat on a bench in the little square out front for ten minutes, soaking up the view of a handsome building that looked like a bank, with a modest entrance and heavy stone features. The paper produced inside fit the town, though. Its buttoned-down, good-citizen approach to the news suited both Boeing engineers and Scandinavian fishermen. Every time the *P-I* sold two copies, the *Times* sold three.

But either one, I figured, would generate a lot more excitement than the *Echo*.

I walked a few blocks south and headed down Pike Street. Elliott Bay lay beyond tall buildings, sparkling.

Several singles stood around the big bronze pig inside the Pike Place Market's front entrance, a favorite Seattle meeting place, scanning the crowd for their mates. I leaned against a doorjamb and watched the Saturday-morning action. Shoppers streamed through the doors headed for the seafood shops and produce booths. A young father lifted his toddler astride the pig. Fishmongers put on a show, hollering out orders and pitching twenty-pound salmon through the air.

Sandy turned heads as she wandered out of the mob clogging the main row of produce booths. Her eyes danced, a hint of a smile brought out her dimples, and her crisp uniform popped out from a Seattle grunge background of ragged denim and wrinkled plaid. She spotted me, and the smile spread across her face. She walked past the pig and right into my arms.

"Hi, sailor. Hungry?"

"Hmmmm. What's on the menu?"

I took her by the hand and tugged her a few doors down to the Athenean, the well-worn market restaurant that had been shoveling out traditional Puget Sound seafood for generations. We squeezed into a cramped booth and stared out at the harbor and mountains. "I love the old-time feel of this place," I said. "They'd really screw it up if they changed it. And the view's even better up here than from our room."

"But," Sandy said, reaching across the scarred wooden table and taking my hand, "our room has its advantages."

We downed two bowls of steamer clams, garlic bread—"I'll eat some if you'll eat some"—and a couple of Rainier beers. Then we were down the market steps, across Alaskan Way, and back into the Edgewater. I shut the door to room 183 behind us, and we both had our clothes off before we made it to the bed.

24

Marion usually was at her desk by eight, but her bright-yellow VW Bug was missing from the lot and the *Echo*'s office was still dark when I rolled up in front Monday morning. I climbed the steps, fumbled for a key I hardly ever used, and unlocked the door, puzzled. The Regulator, ticking placidly away inside, read 8:30. I flipped on the lights, sat at my desk, and sorted through the mail. Marion showed ten minutes later, looking somber. "What's up?" I asked.

She pushed through the swinging gate and slumped back against the counter. "Sorry I'm late. But I stopped at the Spar for a cup of coffee and ran into Marty Brantly."

"And?"

"And the mill's shutting down the swing shift. Marty says the lumber market has completely tanked. And what with the fire restrictions, they can't get any logs anyway."

"Shit."

"I'll second that," she said. "You and I are well on our way to becoming Bent Fir's last salaried employees."

The screen door creaked, and Chesty Arnold stepped in. "Did you hear?" he asked.

Marion turned toward him. "I'm afraid we did. What's everybody saying?"

"Dunno about that," Chesty said. "But I heard it from Mitch. He says this may do it. The store's on the ragged edge anyway. He loses this many more customers, and the Thriftway people will just shut 'er down."

"People have to eat," I said. "And the men will get unemployment."

"Yeah," Chesty said. "For six months."

I tried to look on the bright side. "Maybe more if the feds pass an extension."

"Whatever," Chesty said. "It's just a matter of time."

We spent the day pulling mill stories together. Marion did the mainbar—the official announcement from Skookum Wood Products, pro forma reaction from local bigwigs, down-in-the-mouth comments from mill hands and their wives. I did sidebars on the general state of wood products, the county unemployment situation, and a time-line history of the Big Skookum mill. By the time I trudged up the steps to my apartment that evening, all I wanted was a beer, a book, and my bed.

I fell asleep with the book on my chest. It was still there when the phone woke me at 2 a.m.

*   *   *

The meadow glowed red, the light flickering off the surrounding wall of firs. Where each cabin had stood, heaps of hot coals glowed red and pumped sparks toward the star-speckled sky. Three sheriff's office patrol cars and a state police cruiser, warning lights flashing, sat at random angles along the gravel road like derailed train cars. The only thing familiar about the scene at Rush Creek Commune was the smell of wood smoke.

I stepped off the road to let an ambulance leave the scene. Then I resumed the walk that had started a mile back, where the deputy manning an SO roadblock on Scatter Creek Road had forced me to leave my car. Two men sat in the back of the first patrol car, handcuffed to the mesh that separated the front and back seats. Two more were handcuffed in the next car, and three more in the next. The man in the window seat next to the road twisted his head, recognized me, and nodded. I nodded back, and Stubby Lancaster broke into a grin.

Walt Hasslebring turned as I approached the knot of uniformed men standing next to the state police cruiser. "Well, well, the press finally arrives. You guys don't move so fast at 2 a.m. The last ambulance just left, and you missed all the blood."

He stepped away from the scrum of deputies and strolled with me as I continued up the road, stopping twice to take pictures with the Roly. "Thanks," I said, "for getting word to me."

He took a White Owl out of his mouth. "Now what makes you think I did that?" he asked.

"Well, somebody woke me out of a sound sleep, and I kinda figured that you'd radioed the desk deputy and asked him to call me."

"Coulda been me, I suppose. Not saying it was, of course."

"What happened here, Sheriff?"

It had all started at a table in the back of the Grizzly, where a half dozen Mayfield loggers traditionally held court. Usually, they stopped in after the show closed down on Friday, had a few pitchers, and headed home to their families. With logging shut down, they came early and stayed late, getting more bellicose with each schooner of Oly.

"From what they tell me," Hasslebring said, "they was yakking about that shenanigan Hal and Lars pulled with the D8. That got some laughs, naturally, but it also got 'em thinking."

Given who they were and where they lived, the Rush Creekers had motive, means, and opportunity to cut the brake line on Hal Mayfield's Kenworth, the Mayfield men figured. By midnight, they had a dozen men howling at the rafters. The constant hassles with environmental rules, the harassment from greenies like the Rush Creekers, the backbreaking work, the ups and downs of the timber economy . . . it all was enough frustration and resentment to fill Cougar Reservoir. The recession, the mill cutbacks, and Hal Mayfield's murder pushed all that resentment right over the dam and sent it rushing down the valley.

The vigilante loggers piled into pickups and headed north. They roared into the commune meadow, and Rush Creekers stumbled onto their cabin porches to see what the ruckus was about. Two women and two men fled in an old Microbus, unmolested. With fists and ax handles, the loggers tore into the men who remained. A few managed to escape into the woods. The vigilantes left the half dozen who didn't bloody and moaning on the ground while they rampaged through the cabins, swinging axes and shovels.

"Our boys was right on their tails," Hasslebring said. "The barmaid at the Griz called when things started to get out of control, and the night-patrol deputy followed these yahoos"—he gestured toward the patrol cars—"right outta town. He was sitting here watchin' when they started torchin' the cabins. But he didn't dare start bustin' heads until some backup got here."

By the time the sheriff, two carloads of deputies, and the staters were on the scene, every cabin was ablaze. The lawmen rounded up the loggers, who'd worked off their rage and dropped back into a beery stupor. "We did what we could to patch up the hippies while we waited for the medical techs. Should be okay, most of 'em. Couple of broken bones for sure. Lots of scrapes and bruises. Probably a concussion or two. But I've seen casualties just as bad from a good bar fight."

"What about Lars?" I asked. "Wasn't he with the Mayfield guys?"

"No sign of him," the sheriff said. "Kinda funny that. He's the worst of the hotheads."

"And Max? Maxy Stewart? Is he hurt bad?"

"No sign of him either. Maybe he run off into the woods. Whatever, he sure ain't here."

*　*　*

Even in good weather, the narrow lanes and oncoming traffic on the Tacoma Narrows Bridge tightened my grip on the steering wheel. Nowadays, we have a second bridge and plenty of room to maneuver. But back then, I never failed to cross the old suspension span without visions of Galloping Gertie's harrowing plunge into fierce tidal rips forty years earlier. Still, my route from Bent Fir to Tacoma led across the mile-wide narrows. And Maxy Stewart was in Tacoma.

Maxy's mother had been wary when she cracked the door open earlier that morning. But she recognized me and invited me in for a cup of bad percolator coffee at the kitchen table. Accumulated frustration furrowed her brow as she explained that her boy was cooling his heels in the Pierce County jail after a meth bust in the Hilltop. She and her husband had been over to see him Tuesday morning, she said, which explained where Maxy was when the loggers burned Rush Creek to the ground that night. And, yes, she and her husband had once again hired an attorney to show up for one of Maxy's arraignments, this time on charges of manufacturing with intent to distribute. Big-time felony charges.

So I'd headed out for the City of Destiny. I tried to enjoy the beautiful view from the midpoint of the bridge, the sun sparkling off the water two hundred feet below and Mount Rainier filling the horizon beyond the eastern towers. But I didn't really relax until the Dodge reached the Tacoma shore and started climbing the hill beyond. At the top, I pulled into a branch library and looked up the Hilltop meth bust in the *Tacoma News Tribune*. Armed with the address, I headed east on Sixth Avenue toward downtown and turned south when the street dipped toward Commencement Bay, opening up the view toward the docks and the tide flats, where mills belched smoke that obscured the mountains beyond.

The Hilltop had once been a respectable enclave of working-class frame houses clustered around K Street, a strip of family restaurants, grocery stores, and neighborhood taverns. But crack, gangs, and white flight left the Hilltop a battleground. At its lowest point, the neighborhood was the most crime-ridden piece of real estate in the Pacific Northwest, a place where a squad of Fort Lewis soldiers once brought automatic weapons and fought a Vietnam-style firefight with the locals, who'd done them wrong in some way that was never entirely clear.

I found the address I'd plucked out of the *Trib* and pulled up in front. Yellow crime-scene tape still surrounded the run-down bungalow that sat atop a knoll in the midst of a garbage-strewn yard. Windows had been crudely boarded up. The front door hung from its hinges.

I had no idea what I was looking for, but something had told me I should see the place, that I should get a feel for whatever had drawn Maxy all the way from Rush Creek. Not that I didn't have a pretty good idea of *who* was behind Max Stewart's little sojourn in the Pierce County jail. It didn't take Sherlock Holmes to figure out that the route from Rush Creek to the Hilltop was strewn with Roy Hammer's methamphetamine. This was, after all, the Hammer's old 'hood.

I climbed the front steps and peered through the open doorway into a hallway filled with trash. I made my way around the house into a backyard that looked even filthier than the front. The back door had been broken down, too, but I had no intention of stepping inside. Few things on Earth were more toxic than a meth cookhouse. I circled the house and climbed back into the Dodge.

Just a few blocks north, the old county-city building, a twelve-story aluminum-and-glass relic of the 1950s, stood on the edge of the decaying downtown. I took the elevator up to the county jail and told the front-desk deputy that I wanted to see Max Stewart. I sat in a seedy waiting area for twenty minutes before another deputy called my name. He led me to the visiting room, where I sat at a table and waited some more. A few minutes later, yet another deputy showed up, trailing Maxy, who slumped in the chair across the table from me.

"How you doing, Maxy?"

"What you think? Pretty shitty. This place is a real hellhole. Noise all night long. Breakfast at 4:30 in the morning. Christ—4:30! What's the point of that?"

Gaunt cheeks. Black half moons under his eyes. Greasy, unkempt hair. Maxy didn't look as though he'd slept in a couple of weeks. And given that he'd been busted in a meth lab, he probably hadn't.

"You're a long way from Rush Creek, Maxy. How'd you end up in the Hilltop?"

"Came to collect Arnie. Kinda just stayed."

"Arnie?"

"Yeah. Arnie. Arnie Dykes. You know Arnie. Lives at the Creek, sometimes."

That's when it all clicked for me. The arrest and disposition records for the 1979 busts at Rush Creek. Six arrests. One class A felony charge. Four class C felony diversions into a drug-treatment program. And one dropped charge.

The heavy-duty charge was, of course, against Roy Hammer. And the dropped charge was, most likely, the price the DA had paid to secure the witness needed to put the Hammer back in Walla Walla. I hadn't paid much attention to the name of the turncoat at the time, but when I thought about it this time, everything fell into place. Who else would cross Roy Hammer but Klahowya County's most persistent screwup, Arnie Dykes?

I played dumb and pushed ahead with Maxy. "So what's Arnie doing in T-Town?" I asked. "And why in the hell did you need to come get him?"

"He's kind of one of the brothers, y'know. Like I said—he lives at the Creek. Sometimes, anyway."

"Maxy, look. This is serious business. You're facing some hard time over this one. You have to let me know what's going on if I'm going to help you."

"How you gonna help me?"

"I haven't got a clue because I haven't got a clue about what's going on. Look, you can talk to me. Washington has a shield law. Nobody can make me talk about what you tell me. Level with me, and maybe I'll think of something."

Maxy stared at the scarred tabletop, managing to slump and fidget at the same time. I tried again.

"Max. Why did you need to come and get Arnie?"

"Wasn't a good place for him to be."

"No meth lab is. What was so special about this one?"

"Guy who ran it."

"You mean Roy Hammer?"

Maxy looked around furtively, as though he was afraid somebody at a nearby table might hear. "Whatever," he said, half under his breath.

"Look, Maxy," I said, leaning forward and lowering my own voice, "I've seen the records. I know Arnie ratted out Hammer after the big bust at your place. So what in the hell was Arnie doing on the Hilltop, in a place where Hammer was cooking?"

Maxy sat silently, staring down. I waited. He finally looked past my shoulder, out a dirty window that opened onto a gorgeous view of the bay, Brown's Point, and the open reaches of the Sound beyond. "Arnie ain't the brightest bulb on the tree, y'know," he said. "He was the lab rat for the Hammer at our place. Got all the crank he wanted. Even some to peddle. So when Arnie finds out about this T-Town cook, he comes up here and signs on, seeing as how he already knows how the whole thing works. The Hammer needs somebody who knows the score to kinda watch things when he ain't around."

"And?"

"And that's what happens. Roy leaves Arnie at the Hilltop while he comes back to the Skookum to do a little business. Good place for peddling crank, Klahowya County. And the Hammer, he already knows all the peddlers. So while he's there, the Hammer reads your story in the *Echo*, and he's royally pissed that you're stirring all that up again. Plus he starts askin' questions, like how'd the DA make a case on him anyway? Roy can't just walk into city hall and read the case files, him being a fugitive and all. But he sends somebody down to the courthouse anyway, to check the records."

"Who'd he send?"

Maxy seemed to slide a foot farther into his seat. He closed his eyes. Then he barely whispered.

"He sent me."

We sat there, saying nothing. Then I asked, "So you told him about the dropped charges against Arnie?"

"Yeah, I told him. But, shit, I didn't want Arnie greased. The dumb bastard is a Rush Creeker. Sometimes, anyway. I hightailed it right over here and told him he needed to get the hell out of Dodge, fast. So he clears out, pronto. On foot. I wait a few minutes, get in my car, and head out of town, too. The T-Town cops pull me over three blocks away, cuff me, and take me back to the lab. They been watchin' it, I guess. By the time we get there, they're all over the place. Next thing I know, I'm gettin' up at 4:30 in the fuckin' morning for breakfast."

The deputy leaning against the wall behind Maxy glanced at his watch and started toward us.

"So where," I asked, "is Roy Hammer?"

"Time's up," the deputy said, reaching down to take Maxy by the elbow.

Maxy started to rise. He looked back over his shoulder as the deputy led him away.

"Far as I know," he said, "he's still in the Skookum. Right in your goddamn backyard."

25

Most of the loggers who'd attacked Rush Creek were out on bail by the time I'd finished my story and made a final check with the jail. Theoretically, they faced serious assault and arson charges. In fact, Klahowya County justice wasn't going to come down terribly hard on some local boys who got carried away with a bunch of long-haired meth dealers. Like small-town journalism, small-town justice didn't necessarily operate with cold impartiality.

The phone on my desk rang just as I was handing my copy off to Marion for editing. The sound of Mark Judd's voice reminded me that he was out of work, too. "Sorry," I said. "This is a rough break."

"What? The layoff? Fuck that. Twenty-six weeks of unemployment ain't bad. Trout season's long gone by the time that runs out anyway. In the meantime, I fish every day until the rains come, and then I'm off somewhere with some goddamn sunshine."

"I'm glad you're putting on a brave face. But the whole town's practically in mourning. This sucks."

"Yeah, maybe. But I didn't call so that you could hold my hand while I blubber into my hanky. Drop your cock and grab your socks. I'll be over in ten minutes."

One of the Hmong he'd talked to on Cutthroat Creek road had tracked him down through the mushroom buyer and called him. The shroomer was excited, Mark said. Talking fast. Barely understandable through his accent. But he made one thing clear. He'd been shrooming up the Scatter Creek drainage and found something other than morels and boletes. "You go!" he'd said. "You go right now!"

"If it's so damned important, why didn't he call the cops?"

"These guys don't truck with cops. Shit, back where they come from, everybody was shootin' at 'em. Vietcong. NVA. Cambodians. Everybody. Think about the shit you're in when your only friend is some guy from the CIA. And you ain't sure about him. These be hill people, Little Brother. Don't read. Don't write. Don't trust nobody."

It was five minutes, not ten, when he pulled up in front of the *Echo* and honked. I ran out, climbed into the Ford, and Mark stomped on the accelerator, throwing gravel before the wheels bit into the Front Street asphalt, squealing.

"So how was the big weekend with Sandy?"

"A guy could get used to that big-city stuff. We hit three clubs Saturday night. Every one packed. And rockin'. We got back to the hotel at 2:30."

Mark turned up the Longmont Grade. "I'd been in Seattle with Sandy Harper, I'd a been back to the hotel a whole lot earlier than that." He laughed loudly as he crested the hill and turned out toward the federal highway.

"How'd you feel the next mornin'?" Mark asked.

"Like sleeping in," I said. "But we got up, dressed to the nines, and went for brunch at the Olympic. Geez. You should have seen the food. And not a pair of corked boots in the place."

"Yeah? No corks? That's goin' a little too far. Them fancy hotel people afraid the spikes gonna tear up their pretty floors? What then? Back to bed?"

"Nah," I said. "Woodland Park Zoo. Saw a gorilla looked just like you."

"That weren't no gorilla," Mark said. "You was in the john, you hung-over son of a bitch. And you was lookin' in the fuckin' mirror."

Mark stepped on the gas, and the Ford rumbled up U.S. 101. Twenty minutes later, the sign announcing Scatter Road appeared on the shoulder. We drove by stump ranches and Scotch broom, entered the national forest, crossed the creek, and took a left onto FS 2102. I spotted the turnout where I'd met the Forest Service PIO on the first day of the fire. Beyond it, the blackened hillside rose to Bull of the Woods Ridge. A sour smell hung in the air. But no smoke rose from the charred stumps and heaps of cinders. The fire was out.

Mark drove on. We passed the spur road the first crews had taken to tackle the fire. Then Mark slowed at the track leading down to the butchered old-growth grove we'd discovered the month before. "Here?" I said.

"That's what the man said. He talked funny as hell, but I finally figured the place he was gibbering about."

Unburned second-growth fir and brush still lined the road halfway to the bottom of the canyon. Then it suddenly gave way to sooty ruin. Black snags and stumps stuck out of a six-inch layer of ash. Toppled logs lay helter-skelter. "Chanterelles love a fresh burn," Mark said. "This place gonna sprout shrooms like nobody's business after the first rains. Maybe that's why our man was up here. Gettin' the lay of the land."

I knelt by the creek while Mark wandered on upstream. It hadn't rained since this hillside had burned, and the creek water was still fairly clear. But a dusting of ash floated downstream on the surface, and a scattering of dead trout lined the bank. The heat, I figured, had killed them.

Mark's voice, pitched an octave too high, broke the stillness. "Holy shit!" he shouted. "Look at this!"

I jogged upstream through the wasteland of ash. Mark stood on a charred log, looking down into the creek. I stepped up alongside him.

The first man lay facedown on the bank. His back was blackened, his clothes and hair incinerated. Heavy cork boots still covered his feet, and a black band encircled his waist. I realized it was his belt, an odd survivor of the intense heat that had swept over the body.

The other man was lower, spread-eagled on his back with his head in the creek. His jeans had burned below the knees, but the rest of his body extended into what must have been a cooler zone created by the flowing water. His plaid shirt was intact. His hair streamed downstream off his head, which moved slightly with the push and pull of the creek. His pale face stared up at us, lids open and eyes rolled back.

"My God," I whispered. "That's Eddie Dykes."

*   *   *

Walt Hasslebring perched on the edge of his desk, just as he had for the press conference after Hal Mayfield's murder. I was in the same straight-backed chair at the sheriff's conference table. But the cast of characters had expanded. The radio guy with the ponytail was there again. So was the old print reporter from Shelton and the stocky wire-service woman. But this time the rest of the state had taken notice, too. The room was jammed with reporters from Olympia, Tacoma, and Seattle.

"Okay," Hasslebring said. "Let's get this show on the road." The buzz of conversation died. The radio reporter switched his recorder on and shoved the microphone forward. "You all know," the sheriff continued, "that we have two more murders on the Olympic National Forest. The particulars are right here in the poop sheet," he said, sweeping his hand past the stack of mimeographed handouts next to him. "The victims were Eddie and Terry Dykes. Both thirty-four years of age. Both unemployed. Both lifelong residents of the Cutthroat Creek Valley.

"The key finding is the coroner's. Both victims died from gunshot wounds to the back of the head." Hasslebring paused, picked up one of the handouts, and scanned it to make sure he wasn't missing anything he'd meant to mention. Then he surprised the city reporters by skipping right over any mention of his office's extensive investigation, the number of hours devoted to solving the crime, or the certainty that the killers would be brought to justice. Instead, with typical terseness, he simply announced, "Now I think I'll just avoid wasting anybody's time by jumping right ahead to the questions."

Reporters, surprised by the abrupt surrender of the floor, leafed through their notebooks. The *Times* regional reporter recovered first. "Would you call these execution-style killings, Sheriff?" he asked.

"Sure would," Hasslebring said. "A bullet to the back of the head qualifies as an execution in my book. It looks as though somebody made these two boys kneel in the dirt and then popped 'em, first one and then the other."

A half dozen copy desks had their knee-jerk headline: "Two Dead in Execution-Style Slayings."

The *P-I* reporter spoke next, apparently seizing some prerogative that granted the big-city papers the right to go first. "Sheriff," he asked, "what makes you think the murders are connected to the Mayfield killing?"

"Did I say that?" Hasslebring countered, with a little smile.

"No," the reporter said. "I suppose not. Not in so many words. But you've sure dropped them in the same kettle."

"So I have," the sheriff said. "But this here kettle's fairly circumstantial. All three killings were in the same general area. The Dykes boys worked in loggin'—when they worked—and so did Hal Mayfield. The three men were acquainted, although most men in that neck of the woods are acquainted. And we've had quite a bit of other crime reported on the forest."

What kind of crime?

"Log rustling. Moonshining. Meth cooking. Petty theft. Stuff like that."

Any other evidence connecting the three?

"Nope."

When had the men actually died?

"Impossible to tell exactly. Before the fire, obviously—the bodies were badly burned. But the heat made any further determination impossible."

Who found the bodies?

I stiffened. I knew the question was coming, but it was still awkward. I was supposed to be a reporter, not a witness. And the blurred roles put me on the spot. This was my story. I wouldn't ordinarily be sharing much of what I knew with other reporters, regardless of whether they were direct competitors or not.

"Why, that would be your colleague here," said the sheriff, gesturing toward the conference table. "Tom Dawson, of the *Big Skookum Echo*. Along with Mark Judd, who lives here in Bent Fir."

The reporters shifted their collective gaze to me. The AP reporter from Olympia started to speak, but I cut her off. "Let's finish with the sheriff. I'll take any questions you have outside, afterwards."

The assemblage turned back toward Hasslebring. "What about the gun?" the old reporter from Shelton asked.

"Now, Henry," the sheriff replied. "You been around long enough to know I'm not gonna talk about that. That's gun's probably at the bottom of Cutthroat Creek somewhere. But maybe not. And maybe the son of a bitch who used it hasn't watched enough TV to know that we can use the gun to tie him directly to the killings. So I'm not gonna go spooking the bastard if he's too stupid to get rid of the damned thing. So don't be putting nothin' about the gun in your stories, ladies and gentlemen. Please."

A few more questions. Then a long pause.

"That it?" asked the sheriff. "Well, here's the poop sheet. I'll be around if you need me."

The reporters rose and shuffled forward to grab the handout. I slipped out the door and stepped onto the concrete porch. Reporters circled me, and my discomfort grew. I was supposed to be on the other side of this equation, facing down some reluctant news source on the steps of the courthouse.

"What about it, Tom?" the AP reporter asked.

"Look," I said. "I figure you guys deserve the basic facts that you'd get from anybody else who stumbled across two bodies in the woods. So I'll tell you exactly what Mark and I saw and where we saw it. Then I'm off to work on my own story. That fair?"

I fielded a dozen questions. No, not me—Mark Judd actually found the bodies. Yes, we had a tip. No, we couldn't talk about the identity of our source. No, we had no idea the men had been shot. We saw the bodies, returned to Mark's truck, and drove back down the road to the first house, where we used the phone to call the sheriff.

The *Times* reporter, silent to that point, finally spoke. "C'mon, Dawson," he said. "This is your story. Are you trying to tell us that you got a call out of the blue that just happened to produce two bodies in the woods?"

Exactly, I thought. *But you'll never believe that anyway. So think what you want.*

I looked the *Times* man hard in the face and smiled. Then I gave the group a little wave, turned on my heel, and headed down the steps.

26

I propped my feet on the desk and rocked in my oak chair, working my way through the scroll of yellow paper that had spooled off the Associated Press teletype over the weekend. At her own desk across the room, Marion hunched over one of the Seattle papers, a white ceramic mug of coffee steaming in her right hand. My chair creaked rhythmically. The Regulator ticked. "You know," I said, "these old teletypes are history. Another couple of years, all this stuff will be coming straight into computers, right in the newsroom."

"What's a computer?" Marion asked, looking up and smiling.

"Yeah, right," I said. "It'll be the next century before we see one around here. Geez. And that Hoe press of ours could go in a museum. Ever heard of offset?"

"You think Harris could learn to run an offset press?"

"They say the South Americans are buying all these old letter-press units. Harris could go to Panama."

"Do you think Harris could learn to speak Spanish? Besides, Panama is in *Central* America."

I paused on a Northwest Wire item out of Portland. "How about I go down and do something on these climbers they pulled off Mount Hood?"

"How many of them from Bent Fir?"

"Fat chance. Nobody from here ever does anything, let alone get stuck on a mountain. We gotta get out of this place."

She sang the rest of the line from the old Animals tune: "If it's the last thing we ever do."

"And at this rate," I said, "it will be."

"The ferry strike's still on. The good citizens of Bent Fir occasionally ride a ferry."

"No ferries around here," I grumbled, "except the ferry prisoners take from Tacoma to McNeil Island. How about I go to McNeil, see how the convicts are doing without a ferry?"

"That's a local ferry, and it leaves from Steilacoom, not Tacoma. But those crews aren't on strike. If you have to get out of here, go to Bremerton; go to Southworth. The state ferries to Seattle *are* on strike. And we rubes do sometimes go to Seattle." She raised an eyebrow and stared at me with an awkward little half grin on her face, waiting for me to say something. I ignored her.

I stopped scrolling and stabbed the yellow AP printout with my finger. "Now here's something," I said, pulling my feet off the desk, planting them on the floor, and sitting upright. "They're airlifting the goats out of the park, collecting 'em all at Hurricane Ridge, and taking them somewhere over in Eastern Oregon."

"Goats?"

"Yeah. *Mountain* goats. They're going crazy up there, making little goats and eating all the huckleberries . . . and everything else. I read about it. They're the ruination of Olympic National Park."

"Little goats are called 'kids,'" Marion said, smiling.

"C'mon. I'm serious," I said, slightly irritated at all the corrections, even if they were lighthearted. "They caught all these damned goats and they're choppering them out this afternoon. Great pictures. And it's an *ecological* story. They screwed up and introduced these critters to the park where there never were any goats. They started killing all the native vegetation, and now the feds have to undo what they did. It's a metaphor!

"Besides, the park starts just up the road. So it's a local story, right? And I can stop in Bremerton on the way back and get your boring ferry story. You happy?"

*   *   *

The Marine guard waved me through the gate, and I rolled slowly into Cedar Springs. Sandy sat on the steps of the BOQ in the sunshine, wearing a red-and-white striped T-shirt, jeans, and hiking boots. She saw me, sprinted down the walk, and jumped into my arms. I held her there, her feet off the ground, her head above mine. "Oooh," she said. "AWOL for a day. I'm risking my career for a herd of smelly old goats."

I let her slide to the ground. "These aren't smelly old goats. These are *mountain* goats. Clean as all outdoors."

"So," she said, pushing free and walking toward the car, "you've really moved up to the big time, goats and all."

"Hey! This is a good story. It's the kind of feature that could make page one at a city paper." I opened the passenger-side door, and she slid in. "Besides," I said, leaning over for a kiss, "we're headed to one of the most beautiful spots on the planet. You're lucky you could get away."

The route took us through Hoodsport and up the west shore of Hood Canal. The water sparkled in the late July sun. The far shore was dense with firs, not a house or cabin among them. Sandy scooted close on the bench seat, her right hand dropped onto my lap, and she stroked the inside of my thigh. "Easy does it," I said with a grin. "We have an appointment with some goats. And it's more than an hour to Hurricane Ridge. Besides, I have something to tell you."

"Tell me you have a job in Seattle and you're going to move with me."

"Not quite. But I'm working on it. I got a call from a Tacoma reporter I met at a press conference. The *News Tribune*'s cops reporter got a job in Portland. The Tacoma job hasn't even been posted yet, so I'll have a head start on my application. And I have lots of experience covering cops."

"Tacoma?"

"Aw . . . Tacoma's not so bad. The mills stink, and there isn't a decent restaurant in town. But it's only forty minutes to Seattle."

* * *

The road up to Hurricane Ridge led out of Port Angeles, the big mill town just west of where Hood Canal joined the Strait of Juan de Fuca. I flashed my press pass at the national park gate, and the uniformed woman in the booth said, "Better get moving. They're supposed to load 'em at noon."

The road climbed steeply. Soon we were into alpine meadows broken by groves of spruce. Sandy turned on the seat and stared back the way we'd come. Far below, the Strait of Juan de Fuca glistened past the smokestacks of Port Angeles, the shore of Vancouver Island a distant blue line near the horizon. Two big ferries passed a mile offshore, one headed toward the U.S. terminal, the other cruising toward Victoria, the oh-so-British city on the southeastern point of the island. "Oh, Tom," Sandy said. "It's a calendar picture."

The parking lot at the top bustled. A few tourists headed for the trail that led along the ridgeline, opening onto views of the mountains and the strait. But mostly the lot was filled with green Park Service pickups, television vans, and news cars. I pulled in next to one of the vans, slapped a white cardboard sign carrying the word "PRESS" onto the dash, and climbed out. Sandy sat for a moment, realized I wasn't coming around to open her door, and climbed out to scurry after me. She found me on the edge of the crowd, talking to another reporter. "Hey, Sandy," I said as she walked up. "This is Greg Grant, from the *Seattle P-I.* We went to school together."

Greg stepped forward and shook Sandy's hand. "This one's a hoot," he said. "Wish they were all like this."

He looked back at me. "And the *Times* isn't here. We'll have an exclusive."

"What's your angle?"

"We'll do a regional brief tomorrow. Then a big takeout for A1 the following Sunday. I'll peg it to the goats, but we'll use that to explore the whole issue of invasive species. Meddling with the natural order. That sort of thing."

A park official in a suit cleared his throat in front of a corral jury-rigged from wire fencing. Inside the corral, two dozen dazed mountain goats, their long, white hair matted and mud-stained, circled nervously. A couple of rams squared off for an instant, legs quivering. Then they dropped their heads and rejoined the milling herd. The suit started to yak and then droned on. After a few minutes, I turned to Sandy. "That blowhard may go on all day. And he won't say anything that's not in the handout. Great day for the National Park Service. New level of commitment to conservation. Blah, blah, blah."

"What about her?" Sandy said, nodding at a young woman leaning against one of the vans, her arms crossed and her face impassive. She wore a faded Park Service shirt, khaki hiking shorts, and heavy hiking boots. Her legs, tanned, scratched, and muscular, looked like a soccer player's.

I walked over and gave her my most fetching grin, dimple and all. "Hi. I'm Tom Dawson, from the *Echo,* down at the other end of the park."

"Hi," she said, her voice flat. "Melody Andrews. NPS." She extended a hand.

"You have anything to do with this circus?" I asked, cocking my head toward the corral.

"I guess so," she said. "I'm the field biologist who's been keeping an eye on these critters for the past three years."

"You mean you've been up in the mountains with them? Don't they stick to the really high country? Don't they climb like crazy?"

She nodded.

"So you're like the Jane Goodall of mountain goats," I said. "You probably know each animal. You probably even have names for them."

"They have numbers," she said, looking down. "But yeah, I have my own names for them. Most of them anyway."

"Look," I said, scanning the parking lot and spotting an empty picnic table on the far side, "can we sit over there and chat a bit?"

Once she started talking, it poured out. The solitude of summer nights in the high country, the sky a brocade of stars. The rams battling on the ridges far above the tree line. The kids frolicking in mountain meadows.

"Don't get me wrong," she said. "I'm happy they've succeeded so well. They just ate themselves out of house and home, that's all. They'll do fine in Oregon. That's where they were meant to be; that's where they always were. The stuff that grows there can handle goats."

"But you're a little sad, too, aren't you?" I asked. "Sad to see all this end?"

"I suppose so," she said. "It's been a special time in my life. And the goats, they're sort of like family, if you can understand that. I know them all. I know every little thing that's going on among them."

A helicopter rose above the ridgeline, rotors thrumming, and we turned to watch. A cargo net slung below it held three more wide-eyed goats, their legs thrust rigidly through the netting. Two rangers stood with arms up-stretched in the corral as the pilot maneuvered over them. The net descended, and the rangers guided it to earth. They unhooked it and freed the animals, which scampered to join the rest of the herd. The chopper rose, banked sharply, and dropped out of sight behind the ridge.

"That's the last of them," Melody Andrews said. "They'll go into crates. Then into that truck over there. Then they'll be gone."

I thanked her, closed my notebook, and found Sandy leaning on a cedar-rail fence alongside the ridge trail, looking blissfully out toward the strait. "Thanks for the tip," I said. "That was great. She's the only one who was really there. I mean right there with the goats. Up in the mountains. She saw it and heard it and felt it. The rest of those guys"—I looked toward the reporters by the corral—"they just have a bunch of pompous quotes. I've got a *story*."

"C'mon," she said. "You still need some pompous quotes of your own—from the ferry folks down in Bremerton. Get those fast, and maybe we can make a little stop on the way home."

We climbed back into the car and joined the line of traffic streaming down off the ridge. Sandy slid close to me again and laid her head on my shoulder. "Did you bring a blanket?" she whispered.

27

The blooms of my mother's red geraniums spilled out of the window boxes. And extending from the driveway, on the far side of the house, was a new concrete slab that measured a good forty feet long and fifteen wide—way bigger than anything Dad would need for a car or a boat. I pushed the door open. "Hey," I shouted, "it's me."

Dad appeared in the arched entrance to the kitchen, his right hand wrapped around a keg bottle. He broke into a smile. "Tom! 'Bout time you saw fit to visit your poor old folks."

Mom appeared next to him. She wore an apron festooned with little bears, which also wore aprons. She still looked pale, and her cheeks were sunken. She'd gone without the usual wig, and she had a scarf wrapped around her head. But, as always, she put up a brave front. "Not poor," she said, "and not old. How are you, son?"

"I'm great. But the important question is, 'How are you?' Did you get the latest scan results?"

"She sure did," Dad said. "Things are looking great. No sign of the Big C at all. Two weeks since the last treatment, your mother feels better every day, and we've got nothing ahead but clear sailing."

Mom managed a faint smile and turned back to the kitchen. Dad raised the Heidelberg. "Want one?"

"Sure. But what's with all the concrete?"

"Oh that. Figured I'd get me a big old yacht and sail it around the world."

"C'mon, Dad. What are you up to?"

"Well, I'm not pulling your leg that far—I'm serious about retirement. With your mother through treatment and all the tests looking so good, we thought we'd get ourselves a motor home and see some of the country. Put some money down on a nice one in Shelton a couple of weeks ago. Gonna need someplace to park it."

"You keep talking about retirement," I said, "but you never set a date. When's the big day?"

Dad turned back into the kitchen and emerged with another bottle of beer. We strolled into the living room, and he settled into his recliner. "Well," he said. "It all depends on the numbers." He reached up and switched his reading light on. "You know the government. Everything's a formula."

I dropped onto the couch and took a swig of beer. "So what does the formula say?"

"A few months, maybe. I have my thirty years in this October. I don't think it pays me much to hang on any longer." He raised his bottle. "Anyway. Your mom and I have been homebodies long enough. With the motor home, we can get away from the rain in winter. Hell, there're even some places I'd like to go in summer. Maybe even head up the Alcan to Alaska. Do some fishin'."

Mom appeared in the arched doorway to the kitchen. "Have you finished *Mornings on Horseback*?" she asked.

"Haven't wrapped up," I said. "Mark gave me a copy of *Nobel House*, and I can't put it down."

"Tom!" Mom said, her voice lowered and stretched into a mock scold. "We didn't raise you to read mass-market trash like that."

"What's for Sunday dinner?"

"You're staying?"

"Depends."

"How about pork chops, whipped potatoes, and green beans?"

"Sold."

Mom turned back into the kitchen, and I looked back to my father. "I took the Navy lieutenant I've been dating up to Hurricane Ridge yesterday," I said. "Got some good stuff."

"Pretty place."

"Yeah. And the Park Service was rounding up the last of the mountain goats that have been tearing up the high country. They're shipping them off to Eastern Oregon."

"Never should have introduced those animals in the first place," Dad said. "The country wasn't suited to them."

"But it was a good story. I found the field biologist who's been riding herd on the goats for the past couple of years."

"No pun intended," Dad said, laughing and raising his bottle again.

I smiled and continued. "She had great stuff. Details. Scenes. She could remember specific things. You don't get that very often."

"So have you written the story?"

"I started it last night. It's good, maybe better than my fire feature. I called the regional editor at the *Seattle Times* to see if she'd be interested. She said she'd take a look."

"But," Dad said, turning serious, "you work for the *Echo*."

"Yeah. But I picked up a story on the ferry strike on my way back from the ridge. That's enough for the *Echo*."

"Weren't you on *Echo* time? When you were up at the ridge, I mean?"

"I suppose so. But it's not like we punch a clock or anything. The *Echo* gets its pound of flesh. Nothing says I can't freelance now and then."

"You know your business, I guess," Dad said. "But I never delivered any private circulars when I was supposed to be working for Uncle Sam."

"This story will get a lot more attention in the *Times*. And Greg Grant was there. On the ridge. Covering the story for the *P-I*. They'll probably run it out next Sunday, as a special feature. So maybe the *Times* will buy freelance, just so they have something of their own."

"Kinda old news by next Sunday."

"Not if you spin it forward, use the goats as a way into some larger story. Greg's going to take on the whole business of moving species around into new environments, disrupting ecosystems, all that."

"He tell you that?"

"Sure. He and I go way back."

"You get your story in the *Times*, won't you be stealing from Greg?"

"No, Dad. I was there. I covered it, too. And I'm taking my own angle on the story. I got an exclusive interview with the naturalist who's been keeping an eye on the goats for an entire year."

"I don't know, son. Seems a little sneaky to me."

"Ah, Dad. If the story runs in the *Echo*, a few thousand people will see it. If it runs in the *Times*, tens of thousands of people will see it. And a bunch of editors, too."

"I guess you know your business," Dad said, his face expressionless.

* * *

Harold Froelich was the worst of them. A bull-necked logger who'd dropped out of school in the tenth grade, he talk-talk-talked his way through each meeting. After listening to Froelich drone on through three or four endless Tuesday-night sessions in the Klahowya County Courthouse, I decided the county commissioners were the worst part of my job. Froelich had no idea what he thought until he heard the words come out his own mouth. Even then, his diatribes followed no discernible pattern. He pursued unpredictable tangents, returned to the agenda item in front of him briefly, and then sailed out into the ether again, apparently set off by whatever random elements collided in his thick skull.

Tonight's subject was the Community Employment Training Act, a federal program Congress cooked up as its instant answer to the deepening recession. The program funneled money to local governments, where bureaucrats supposedly used it to hire the jobless into positions that would teach them new skills. Mostly, cities and counties used it to fill jobs for office functionaries and manual laborers. Klahowya County qualified for enough CETA money to hire a half dozen clerks or road-crew grunts, but first the three commissioners had to accept the federal grant. Froelich, leaning back in his chair behind the commissioners' table on a platform at the front of the room, was raving about his boyhood in the logging camps, about how hard he'd worked feeding cordwood to a donkey engine.

Residual heat from the early August day baked the nearly empty meeting room. I dozed in the press row. The only other reporter, a young woman who covered the county for the *Shelton Pioneer*, tried to stay awake next to me, her head slowly sagging forward and then suddenly jerking upright. The meeting crawled through its second hour. An elderly couple, the only other occupants of the wooden benches that filled the audience section of the room like church pews, waited patiently for a ruling on their property-tax appeal.

One of the other commissioners, Roald Hanson, finally sighed and broke in. "For Christ's sake, Harold," the old Norwegian fisherman said. "It's free money. It'll put six of our boys back to work. Two shifts are down at Big Skookum Lumber, and unemployment runs out after this winter. This goddamned grant will keep food on six tables."

The other reporter and I looked up, blinking. "It ain't free money," Froelich retorted. "It's the goddamn taxpayers' money, that's what it is. And this is goddamn make work, not real work. If the county needed these people, we'd tax ourselves and hire them."

"Now, Harold," said Larry Lutham, the Shelton grocer who served as the third commissioner. "If we don't take the money, somebody else will. It's not like you're saving anybody anything. You're just hurting six boys from right here in this county."

"But," Froelich sputtered, "they're telling us this here is a goddamn retraining program. What in the hell is some out-of-work mill hand gonna learn shoveling gravel on the goddamn road crew?"

"Not much," Lutham conceded. "But that's not what this is about, is it? The feds are handing out the money, and we're sure as hell going to take it. I'm voting with Rolly on this one. So you can save the logging-camp stories. I move the question."

I recorded the comments and the 2-1 vote in my notebook. The couple in the back pew pleaded their case, and the commissioners turned them down. They always turned down property-tax appeals. Hanson, the commission chairman, banged his gavel. "Meeting adjourned," he said.

I thought briefly about my story as I walked out of the courthouse. It was a no-brainer, pure formula:

The lead—*The Klahowya County Commissioners approved a federal retraining grant Wednesday night, opening the way for six additions to the county payroll.*

The nut—*The federal money will provide a few additional minimum-wage jobs in a county wracked by growing unemployment but will do little to relieve long-term unemployment in the area.*

The body—The brief flash between Harold and Rolly, followed by the outcome of the property-tax appeal.

The kicker—*"This grant," Commissioner Roald 'Rolly' Hanson said, "will keep food on six tables."*

If I landed another job on a daily, I might have to start out paying my dues on snores like the county commissioners. I'd done some of that in Bend, the Central Oregon town where I'd started out after college. But then I'd busted the Deschutes County sheriff, and I'd never looked back. The cubs covered the commissioners. Sharks like me cruised with an investigative team, sniffing for blood in the water.

At the *Echo*, though, there would be no cub to save me from Harold Froelich's rants, let alone an I-team. Chesty Arnold might hire a college kid to cover summer vacations, but that would be it. I imagined decades of listening to the commissioners and grinding out formulaic meeting stories. Looking back, I think I was starting to see some of the rewards that came with small-town journalism. But at that point, I probably didn't think the life would be worth the costs that came with it. Especially if one of them was Harold Froelich.

I drove straight to the office and banged the story out in thirty minutes. I dropped into the Spar on my way home to wash down the bad taste it left in my mouth with a cold Rainier. I was on my second when I felt someone slide onto the stool next to me. "I'll have what he's having," Chesty Arnold told Henry Anderson.

"Sure thing, Mr. Arnold," Henry said, turning toward the tap.

"Geez," I said, "you look like Harris dragged you through the press."

Chesty slumped forward, elbows on the bar. "Ah, Tom. At least the press might leave something printed on my backside. Which would leave me ahead of where I am now."

Henry came back with another schooner of Rainier. "You'd better buy," Chesty said. "Last week's paycheck may be the end of it."

"Oh, c'mon. You've been through tough times before. It can't be that bad."

"So you haven't heard the news," Chesty said with a sigh.

"What news?"

"About the mill."

"What about the mill?"

"Marty Brantly walked into the office to tell us himself," Chesty said. "They're shutting down the day shift. They're shutting down the whole shebang."

* * *

Moochie Dykes peered through the rusted screen, her eyes widening at the sight of me standing on her porch. "Gosh, Tommy," she said. "Hardly expected to see you here."

"Hi, Moochie. How you doing?"

She pushed on the door, and I took a step backward to let it swing wide. Moochie stepped out in a T-shirt and cutoffs and—from the look of their fit—nothing else.

"It's a little uptight around here," she said. "You know what I mean?"

"A little, I suppose," I said, leaning back against the porch railing.

"But no, I don't guess you ever can really understand what something like this feels like."

"Daddy's on a rampage. Drinking. Cursing. Kicking and hitting. Eddie and Terry, they were everything to him. Me and Arnie, we never counted for much."

"Want to go for a ride? Get away for a little while?"

"Sure," Moochie said, her voice rising and her face brightening. "Just let me get some shoes."

She disappeared into the darkness of the house. In a minute she was back, wearing a battered pair of Nikes. She yanked the passenger-side door open and jumped in before I had a chance to open it for her. I pulled out of the driveway.

"Where to?" I asked.

"Don't care," Moochie said, turning in her seat to face me. "You pick."

I drove to 101 and turned north.

"I'm surprised you're still around, Tom Dawson. Most of the smart ones, they up and leave first chance."

"Well, I didn't plan it this way. But it's growing on me. I'd forgotten some of the things I liked about this place. And the job at the *Echo*—it isn't bad. Maybe there's more of the country boy in me than I thought."

"Must be fun to get all around the county and talk to all kinds of folks?"

"Yeah," I said. "But a little discouraging, too, lately. Everything around here seems to be headed for permanent low tide."

I turned onto the Takamak River Road. The Scotch broom was still blooming along the roadside, bright splotches of yellow jumping out from the dark fir background. At a break in the trees, the river appeared alongside the pavement, and I glanced past Moochie to appraise it with a fisherman's eye. The boils of dark-green spring runoff had been replaced by a hissing ribbon of blue. Whitewater splattered around exposed rocks and sweeper logs jutting from the banks.

"Isn't this a beauty of a river?" I asked.

Moochie glanced out the window. "Yeah. I guess so." She returned her eyes to me and scooted a little closer on the bench seat. The road turned to gravel, and dust choked the view in the rearview mirror.

The drive along the Tak made me think of a story my father liked to tell. He'd drifted the river in his old World War II rubber raft and had taken out near the mouth. He'd stepped out onto the road to thumb a ride back to his car, six or eight miles upstream. A new Cadillac pulled up with a Takamak Indian at the wheel. He pulled the door open and slid in, making conversation as the Caddy accelerated up the road. He sniffed. Then sniffed again. Then he twisted around and looked in the back seat, which was filled to the armrests with the bloody, slimy carcasses of fresh-caught salmon.

The yarn never failed to get appreciative, knowing laughs. And, I thought, to serve as a litmus test for every prejudice the local whites carried about the natives. The Indians slaughtered whole runs of salmon by stretching nets bank to bank in the spawning streams. They squandered government money on fancy cars and drunken binges. They acted on impulse, trashed their possessions, and took nothing seriously.

"Where we goin'?" Moochie asked. "You know some place up here?"

"A beautiful place. And we're nearly there."

"I hope it's a nice quiet spot. You know what I mean?"

"Moochie," I said gently, "why would anybody want to kill Eddie and Terry?"

"I suppose a lot of guys might want to kill 'em. They sure did their share of fighting and such. And somebody mighta had it in for them because of that."

"But shooting somebody over a fight doesn't sound much like Klahowya County. Especially shooting them this way."

"I suppose not," Moochie said. She dropped her cheek onto the back of the seat and gazed at me through her eyelashes.

I turned onto the dirt lane that led to the Cable Hole. "This is a pretty spot," I said. "Want to get out and sit a while?"

"Sure," she said, brightening.

She jumped out of the car and scampered over to the water. By the time I reached the gravel beach, she had her sneakers off and was wading in the pool."Oooh," she said, smiling, her two dead brothers forgotten. "It's cold. Want to go for a swim?" She grabbed the hem of her T-shirt, pulled it up a couple of inches, and stopped, her head cocked, waiting for a reply.

"Better not," I said, settling onto the gravel and leaning back against a log. "Look, Moochie, I have a girlfriend. I just wanted to talk."

The hint of a pout flashed on her face. She heavy-footed it out of the water and dropped down next to me against the log. "So talk," she said.

"Tell me about Eddie and Terry. What they did. Who they did it with."

"Whadda ya mean? They was just the twins. They did what they always did."

"Like what?" I asked. "What have they been doing the last few months?"

"Oh, I don't know," she said. "Drinking. Sleeping. Fighting." She frowned, pulled her knees up, and wrapped her arms around them, staring out at the Tak. "And loggin'."

I pressed her. "Logging what? Where?"

She turned her head to face me and rested it on her knees.

"I dunno," she said. "I guess they logged whatever Lars told 'em to."

"Lars?"

"Sure. Lars Mayfield. He was always comin' around. He'd roust 'em out at Daddy's, and they'd go on up to the yard."

"The yard?"

She raised her head, looking exasperated. "Yeah," she said, "the yard. That place up the road where they dumped the logs. That's a yard, ain't it?"

"Sure is, Moochie," I said. "Sure is."

She smiled and extended her legs, rolling onto her hip and facing me full on. She reached across and laid her hand on my thigh, her fingers massaging gently. I took her hand and lifted it off my leg. "Come on, Moochie. We should go. Like I said, I've got a girlfriend."

"That's okay. I don't mind."

"C'mon," I said, rising and pulling her to her feet.

"Ahhh, Tom Dawson," she said, jerking her hand away and reaching for her Nikes. "I knew you didn't really like me."

28

The car's tires popped in the gravel that led off the state highway, past the shuttered fireworks stand, and into the grove of tall firs. The old frame houses scattered about in the deep shade wore thick cushions of moss on shake roofs. Despite the August sun pounding the highway asphalt, the previous winter's growth of green slime still tinted their unpainted siding.

A clutter of old cars and rusty machine parts lay scattered behind the third house. Two big black-and-white mongrels rushed around the corner of the building, hair on end and barking furiously. Little Jim Littlefoot followed. "Shut up!" he hollered. "Shut the shit up! Give the white boy a break." The dogs settled down, and the murmur of Cutthroat Creek filled the cool air.

Little Jim grinned broadly. "Hey!" he said, walking forward and planting his hands on his hips. "You're on time. Don' cha know it don't work that way around here?"

"Oh, I know," I said. "Your blocks were always about a second late."

"That's just because you were too fast," Little Jim said. "C'mon to the porch."

We rounded the corner and stepped up onto the deck that ran the width of the house. The floorboards creaked under the big Indian's weight. "You want some coffee?" he said, gesturing toward his own mug on the porch railing.

"Sure. Black."

Jim stepped into the house, and I turned toward the creek. It was wide here, maybe forty feet. And deep. A long chute ran straight past the front of the house, rounded one bend, and dumped into the Sound. Another couple of weeks and the sea-run cutthroat would be charging right by the place, bound for their spawning beds.

Little Jim stepped back onto the porch, the screen door slamming behind him. He set a steaming mug in front of me. "Any bluebacks yet?" I asked.

"Haven't seen any. But it's early. Come back in a couple of weeks, and we'll catch some right here off the porch."

We drank our coffee and talked. More about fish. The Bull of the Woods fire. The layoffs at the mill. Women.

"You still cattin' around with that perky blond sailor?" Little Jim asked. "She some kinda nice, that one."

"Sure. Sandy and I are still seeing each other. But she's been transferred. To Seattle. Pier 91."

"How you feel about that?"

"To be honest, I'm not sure. It's complicated. She's starting to act as though she has some sort of mortgage on me. I feel weird sometimes. Y'know, when she starts planning our future. Stuff like that. Besides, she's Navy. She could end up anywhere."

"Seattle ain't far."

"Nope. Seattle ain't far. And she usually has weekends off."

"My kinda weekend," Jim said, picking up his coffee cup and walking into the house. I did the same, happy for the distraction from the Sandy conversation. In the cluttered kitchen, I changed the subject by asking about the Dykes twins.

"Those boys ended up like most of us figured they would," Jim said.

"How so?"

"Oh, c'mon. Any bad shit around here, they was ear deep in it. Everybody knew that."

By then, I pretty much understood what he was talking about. But I decided to do a little fishing. "Yeah?" I said, bending the word into a question. "Like what?"

Jim put his coffee cup in the sink, already mounded with dirty dishes. "You're some kinda newsman. You don't know nuthin' about your own backyard."

"Like what?" I asked again.

"Like crystal meth. Everybody knew they was tweakers. Did some cookin', too. With them Rush Creekers. Bad shit, that crank. Fuck you up something awful."

"Yeah. Lots of crank back in these hills. What else?"

"Trees," Jim said.

"Trees?"

"Like I said. Trees. You know, the tall brown things with the green on top. Those two was moving more old growth out of the Olympic than any of the legit gyppos."

"Yeah, I kinda figured that. The Dykes boys weren't exactly cagey about covering their tracks. You ever see them actually moving any old growth?"

"Shit! They lived right up yonder. They ran their own goddamn yard up there. We'd see that beater rig of theirs rolling down the creek road all hours. Carryin' big trees. Skookum trees. Lotta three-log loads be comin' down that road in the dark."

We walked out of the house, climbed into Little Jim's old Chevy pickup, and bounded out the dirt driveway, arcing into the air at every high spot and bottoming out in the holes. "Ever think about some new shocks for this thing?" I asked. "You're going to bust your head open on the roof of the cab."

"Shocks! Shit! The Lone Ranger here would have a goddamn hissy fit if I lashed him down with new shocks."

"Or anything else new for that matter. Don't you want to keep this wreck running?"

"If he dies, he dies. It's fate, brother. The will of the Great Spirit."

The truck rattled to a stop in front of another moldering house, this one facing the road. Freddie Bangs heard the Chevy and appeared on the porch. He wore his black hair cut short, even shorter than mine. Trim jeans, a pair of light Timberland hiking boots, and a striped polo shirt completed the collegiate look. He bounded down the steps and yanked the pickup door open.

"How ya doin', bro?" Freddie said to me. "Good to meet you."

Little Jim broke in. "Hey, cuz. Easy on the charm-school shit. This here's my football buddy, and he don't need no glad-handing."

"I played with your brother, too," I said. "I was real sorry about what happened."

"He was drunk," Freddie said. "He drove that truck of his off the road. I miss him. But he didn't have to do what he did."

"I'm looking forward to this," I said, changing the subject. "The Takamak is my home water, and I'd love to see the tribe get some-thing going."

"Sheee-it!" Jim said. "The tribe. The tribe ain't never gonna get nuthin' goin'. Other tribes, they got their own mills, hatcheries. Shit. They got fuckin' tree farms. You think any Takamak gonna think far enough ahead to plant a tree and then sit around waitin' for it to fuckin' grow?"

"This Tak would," said Freddie. "It's about time we started getting our act together."

The Chevy rattled north along the state road, occasionally breaking out of the timber to cruise along above the cobbled beach, the Sound sparkling to the east. "Pretty day," Little Jim said. "Us chumps ought to be on the sand with some honeys and a ski boat, not wasting time talking to the goddamn federales."

"They're staters," Freddie said, the truck plunging back into the cool shadows under the firs. "Washington Fish and Wildlife. The money's federal, but the state spends it."

"Whatever," Jim said, smiling. "All the same anyway."

"The tribe has to match the federal grant," Freddie said, and I pulled my notebook out of my hip pocket. Pressure against the seat had curled it into the shape of a banana.

I wrote as Freddie talked. Lots of the river's original salmon and steelhead runs were gone, he said, wiped out by reckless harvesting that sometimes left nets stretched from bank to bank for two weeks at a time. Careful breeding could introduce new strains that would time their arrivals between the surviving runs. The Takamak would recover some of the steady progression of runs that had once made it one of the state's most productive salmon streams.

"Makes sense," I said. "Most hatcheries just dump fingerlings into the river that compete with the natives. Pretty soon, no natives."

The firs fell behind, the road twisted down a clay bank, and the estuary of the Takamak opened in front of us. Green brush carpeted the bottomland, divided by the sinuous curves of the main river.

Jim steered the pickup into a boat-ramp parking lot on the edge of the river and pulled in next to a Fish and Wildlife truck. We introduced themselves to two F&W officers standing on the water's edge. The Takamak hissed by.

I took notes hurriedly as Freddie Bangs and the two F&W men talked about the project. The grant applications were about ready to go. The tribal council had approved the scheme in principle and was looking for a line of credit to back up its financial commitment. The fish biologists had completed the design for hatching tanks and holding pens.

The five of us walked back up to the two pickups. One of the Fish and Wildlife men pulled the hatchery blueprints out from behind the seat of the state rig and unrolled them on the hood. He pointed out specific features, talked about the latest trends in fish science, and then handed the blueprints to Freddie to take back to the tribe.

Back in Little Jim's Chevy, we rode in silence. "You know," I finally said, "it just might work. And it could make a big difference around here. Bring in the sports. Whip up some business for guides, tackle shops, motels. Give people a little hope."

* * *

Mark Judd rose from my kitchen table and strolled over to the corner where I stashed my fishing gear. I had the little apartment above Benny's pretty much put back together. But I hadn't been able to do anything about the damage that mattered most to me. I couldn't bring myself to throw out what was left of my grandfather's fly rod, so I'd just propped the shattered pieces in the corner next to my waders. Mark leaned over and picked them up.

"Who in the fuck would do something like this?" he asked, holding the six pieces of bamboo out in front of him. "This is just plain evil. Way beyond sending a message or acting out on some kinda grudge. Jesus. This was a thing of beauty, like a goddamn Greek statue or something."

"Maybe whoever did it wasn't a fly fisherman. Maybe it was just something to grab and break."

Mark stepped back over to my kitchen table, sat, and picked his Heidelberg keg bottle up off the gray Formica. "Nah," he said. "This guy went to some trouble to break this rod. Took some strength, for Christ's sake. Three pieces of split bamboo all together . . . breaking that over your knee. Don't know that *I* could do it." He lifted the Heidelberg to his lips, tipped it back, and gulped, his Adam's apple bobbing.

"Yeah," I said. "So I grant you the malice-aforethought theory with the rod. What's that tell us?"

"Not much, I s'pose. Just that the guy's a bait fisherman."

I sputtered, blowing beer across the table. Mark ducked, wiped foam off his sleeve, and laughed along with me. Just about every male in Klahowya County was a bait fisherman, and few of them had much use for the citified airs and elegant gear of their fly-fishing counterparts.

"Nah, seriously," I said. "Why would anybody have this big a bone to pick with me? I'm just another son of the Skookum, doing his job."

"Well . . . not quite. You lit outta here soon as you got the chance. And you come back wearing that goddamn California clown suit. But you be right, Little Brother. That's not enough to explain the bile behind what happened to this place."

"So that leaves . . ." I said.

Mark interrupted: "Like you said—the job. Somebody don't like what you been writin' in the paper. The way you been snooping around."

"Which means somebody connected to the business with Hal's truck. Or the twins."

"Which means we be right back on that square one you hear so much about."

"Right. Hal's murder. And then the twins. All of which I've been over a thousand times in my head. Who wanted Hal dead? And what did the twins have to do with it?"

Mark drained his bottle and headed to the fridge for another. "Maybe nuthin'," he said. "Just 'cuz one thing follows another, don't mean the first thing caused the second."

"Yeah," I said. "The *post hoc, ergo propter hoc* fallacy."

"What the fuck's that mean, college boy?"

"What you just said. It's a logical fallacy to think that just because one thing follows another, the first thing caused the second. But how long since the last murder in Klahowya County?"

Mark dropped back into his seat at the table. "Dunno," he said, turning his eyes toward the ceiling and thinking. "That asshole beat his old lady to death up past Angel Harbor? Six, ten years ago? A coon's age."

"Exactly. Some lowlife goes off the deep end once a decade. That's the closest we come to a murder spree around here. Now we have three extremely purposeful, premeditated killings in six weeks. What's the chance they aren't connected?"

"Gotta point, Little Brother. But so what? Don't answer no questions."

I pushed back from the table and headed for the refrigerator myself. "Well," I said, "we know the twins were rustling logs, big time."

184

"Got that right. That dump a theirs was some kinda operation. Who'd a thought those yahoos woulda had it in 'em."

"They didn't," I said. "At least not on their own."

I told Mark about my little chat with Moochie, and what she'd told me about Lars Mayfield.

Mark banged his keg bottle on the table, and beer foamed out of the neck. "Shit! Did Hal know about that? Christ, Lars should be the one that's dead. Hal woulda whupped his ass."

I reached behind me, grabbed the dish rag hanging on the kitchen faucet, and tossed it onto the Formica, intercepting the beer running from Mark's bottle. "Maybe," I said. "Or maybe he would have whupped the twins' asses."

"That'd be Hal, all right. But he was in the ground by the time those boys got popped."

"Hard to beat that alibi," I said. "So who would've wanted both Hal and the twins dead? And me intimidated in the bargain?"

"You makin' one a those fallacies?" Mark asked. "Assuming one guy did it all?

"Or that it was a guy at all," I said. "But you're right. Nothing says we're dealing with one perp here. Or that the three incidents are even related. So let's go back to the beginning. Why would anybody mess with Hal's brake line?"

"You ask me, those fuckin' tweakers had something to do with it."

I took a long pull on my Heidelberg and thought about it. Again.

There had been bad blood between Hal Mayfield and the Rush Creekers since the days of the tree sits. And the business with the D8 and the meth lab only made things worse. Besides, the meth-cooking operation brought Roy Hammer into the picture. Lethal violence seemed out of character for the regular residents of the commune, but the Hammer was something else again.

On the other hand, Roy Hammer was a businessman with brains. Trashing my apartment seemed petty in his scheme of things. Why call attention to himself by messing with a newspaperman? And what did he have against the Dykes twins anyway? Every theory had as many arguments running one way as the other.

Mark stood and walked back to the refrigerator. He brought two keg bottles back to the table without asking if I wanted another one. "You don't even know if the asshole who messed with Hal's brakes wanted to grease him," he said. "Maybe he—or *she!*—just wanted to send a message. Besides, Lars usually drove the goddamn truck. Maybe the brake-line business was aimed at him."

We drank and talked, plodding through each scenario, setting up plausible chains of events, and then knocking them down. We drank some more. Mark finally stood, swayed a bit, and announced that he was headed home. "Got a headache from all this bullshit," he said.

"No wonder," I said, looking at the empty keg bottles that had accumulated on the kitchen counter until a whole half case stood there in neat rows.

"Ain't the beer," Mark said. "A six-pack of this pussy brew you drink ain't enough to get me up in the middle of the night for a piss."

"I know what you mean," I said. "The whole business gives me a headache, too."

"And you know what?" Mark asked as he pulled open the door and looked up at the hint of midsummer twilight that lingered in the sky. "All this blather may not have nuthin' to do with nuthin'. Shit! We don't know half of what goes on back in them woods. We could be bouncing around the edges of something we ain't never heard about, talked about, or even goddamned thought about."

29

I pulled open Walt Hasslebring's office door and found him sitting behind his oak desk, feet propped on an open drawer, looking out the windows at the Big Skookum. He looked around as I stepped in. "Well, well," he said. "What brings the Fourth Estate to calling on this fine summer day?"

"I had a couple of questions," I said.

"Then maybe you oughta sit yourself down and ask them."

I dropped into one of the two wooden armchairs in front of Hasslebring's desk. "About the gun . . ."

"Yeah, what about it?"

"Well . . . do you have it?"

"All in good time."

"If I ask you off the record?"

"Are you? Asking me off the record, I mean?"

"Absolutely. Nothing about the gun is going in the *Echo*, regardless of what you say."

Hasslebring lifted his feet off the open desk drawer, dropped them to the floor, and opened the drawer above his footrest. He pulled out a large Ziploc bag and dropped it on the desk with a heavy metallic thud.

"The gun," he said.

I leaned forward, staring at the rusty mass of metal inside the plastic. "I'll be damned. Where was it?"

"In the creek, as expected. In a pool about a mile downstream from the bodies. State patrol divers found it the day after you found Eddie and Terry. Shit. That water's so clear we hardly needed divers. You could see the damn thing down there. Somebody wanted to get rid of it real quick and wasn't thinkin' real straight."

I reached over the desk, grabbed the plastic bag by one corner, and lifted it. "It's a big one," I said. "An automatic, isn't it?"

"A semiautomatic. An automatic fires continuously when you pull the trigger. This one, you pull once for each shot."

"How do you know this is the gun that killed Eddie and Terry?"

"We found the slugs that come outta that weapon. And this was the weapon they come out of. The state crime lab says so."

"So what kind is it?"

"This, my boy, is your standard Army officer's sidearm. Model 1911 Colt .45. Not very accurate, but it packs a helluva wallop at short range."

* * *

The Marine stepped briskly out of his guard shack. He looked as though he'd been stamped out of the mold that produced the Cedar Springs guards, and I expected him to do the same thing they always did—give me a quick once-over and wave me through. But this Marine raised an open palm, demanding a full stop from the slowly rolling car. I hit the brakes, the tires gave a little screech, and the Dodge rocked on its old springs.

The guard, his face impassive, leaned down to the driver's window.

"What's your business, sir?"

"Press," I said, reaching for my wallet, flipping it open, and holding it up so the guard could see my press pass. The guard said nothing.

"I'm here for the Trident arrival," I said. I grabbed the news release on the seat beside him and held it up. "There's a press conference. At two o'clock."

The Marine walked back to the guard shack, grabbed a clipboard, and scanned it. He returned to my window and leaned down again. "Mr. Dawson," he said, "Bangor is a closed facility. Please drive directly to the public affairs officer's station and wait there." He handed me a map of the submarine base with the route to the PAO's office highlighted in yellow. Then he stepped back, extended his upper arm, and stiffly motioned the car ahead. I crested a slight rise and the view opened to the entire base. Battleship-gray buildings filled the gentle slope right down to the edge of the bay, where three sleek attack subs floated placidly in their pens.

The highlighter's trail across the map led me to a substantial concrete-block building on the waterfront. Somebody had used a Magic Marker to scrawl "press" on a sheet of butcher paper taped to the wall. An unsteady arrow pointed toward a door.

I parked next to a panel truck from one of the Seattle TV stations and walked inside. More signs led to a large room filled with a half dozen rows of metal folding chairs arranged to face a raised platform. Reporters, photographers, and camera operators milled around in the open space behind the chairs, helping themselves to the coffee, doughnuts, and cookies spread on a table against the back wall.

I spotted Greg Grant. "Yo," I said.

"Hey! Tom Dawson," Greg said, turning from the photographer he'd been chatting with. "Get your goat story written yet?"

He smiled, smugly triumphant. "Mine's on page one of the Sunday bulldog. If no big news breaks, it'll hold for the main."

I smiled, too. We didn't get the first edition—the bulldog—of the Sunday *Times* in Bent Fir on Saturdays. But the city desk had let me know my story was stripped across the bottom of page one. Like Greg's in the *Post-Intelligencer*, it would stay there unless World War III broke out and bumped it back to the regional section. I resisted the temptation to do a little gloating of my own. Greg would find out that I'd pulled the rug out from under his exclusive soon enough.

"Solved that murder yet?" he asked.

"I'm working on it. But today is all about submarines."

"Yeah. Ain't that the truth. I can't wait to see this mother. I'd love to take a ride."

"Not much chance of that. Nobody's going to see the inside of these buggers who doesn't have security clearances all the way down to the soles of his feet."

"For once," Greg said, "I can understand the secrecy. You sure as hell wouldn't want the bad guys to get their hands on one of these."

Somebody cleared his throat behind us, and we both turned. A Navy lieutenant in his blues stood on the platform at the front of the room, his hands clasped behind his back. Two enlisted men in whites had taken up positions behind him.

"Gentlemen," he said, scanning the room to confirm that no women were present, "welcome to Bangor. It's a red-letter day for us here, and we're glad you could join us." He gestured to the folding chairs. "Please take your seats."

He kept his presentation mercifully short. Ohio-class subs were the latest addition to the "arsenal of democracy," he said, prompting

Greg to lean close and whisper in my ear, "Jesus. Can you believe he said that?"

The submarines were huge—560 feet long and nearly 17,000 tons displacement. They dwarfed the attack subs stationed at Bangor, a fact the reporters would see for themselves when the Ohio herself arrived at 1100 hours. Sailors called them "boomers," a grossly understated nickname for a machine that could instantly unleash more firepower than all combatants had expended during all of World War II. "Each sub carries twenty-four Trident missiles," the lieutenant said, "each MIRVed."

Greg whispered in my ear again. "What's 'MIRVed'?"

I whispered back: "Multiple Independently Targeted Re-entry Vehicles."

"Jesus. And one goddamn Navy captain has the key to all that."

The reporter next to him glared in our direction, and we fell silent.

The lieutenant continued for another ten minutes, singing the praises of the Trident subs, the deadly armament they carried, and the Navy systems that would guard against the mistake that could bring on Armageddon. "The Trident is the ultimate deterrent," he concluded. "When the planned fleet of eighteen Trident subs is complete, it will carry half the strategic warheads in our arsenal. The subs will be able to stay submerged for as much as year, unseen and unheard, anywhere in Earth's oceans. Any despot, anywhere in the world, now knows that a decision to use nuclear weapons against the United States or its allies will result in his complete and immediate destruction."

He took questions. The city reporters pressed him on the precautions that would keep the missiles in their silos unless the president ordered them fired. I asked about the economic impact of the new operation on the peninsula.

The lieutenant jumped at the question. The six boomers that eventually would operate out of Bangor would carry crews of more than nine hundred officers and sailors. Another thousand Navy and civilian employees would provide onshore support. Building the Trident pens, which required more than two hundred local construction workers, would continue for another two years. Most of the officers and men crewing the boats would bring their families, buying homes in the area and supporting local supermarkets, clothing stores, and churches. "And these are the cream of the crop," the lieutenant said. "The best the Navy has to offer. They'll be a fine addition to your communities."

I whispered to Greg. "Yeah. They'll add a whole new dimension to the fights in the Bent Fir bars."

The lieutenant glanced at his watch. "It's 1055 hours," he said. "The Ohio should be in sight. What do you say we all go take a look?"

One of the enlisted men stepped forward. "All photographers— still and video—stick with me. You must observe security restrictions."

The lieutenant led them out the door and down to the waterfront. Greg and I walked together, chatting. "Did you hear about Jim Hensen over at the *Journal-American*?" Greg asked.

"The little guy with the wire-rims? A couple of classes ahead of me?"

"That's the one. And the son of a bitch just upped and quit, walked away from the Bellevue cops beat with a big ol' recession bearing right down on us."

"To do what?"

"Dunno. He'd been there three or four years, though. Probably figured he wasn't going anywhere. Maybe he's off to write the great American novel."

"Geez. Then the job's open?"

"Far as I know. You interested?"

"I sent clips to the *News Tribune*. But the *Journal-American*. Geez."

"It's a good place to get noticed, all right. The guys downtown can't help but see your stories. But do you think you're up for running cops? Three, four stories a day, and not much chance to ever do any takeouts. Not like a weekly."

"The *News Tribune* job is cops, too. But I gotta do something to get back in the game. You take the big stories out of your hide anyway. Nights. Weekends. Whatever it takes."

"You got that right, brother. I still know some of the guys there, including the city editor. Want me to put in a word for you?"

"Yeah. I guess so. But I suppose I'd better move fast."

"You got that right, too."

The group clumped to a stop atop a massive concrete bulkhead that ran along the shoreline. "There she is," the lieutenant said.

"Jesus," one of the reporters said. "Look at that bastard."

Out in the bay, a large dark shape approached, its massive black bulk growing by the second. Instead of cutting through the water, it created a huge bow wave that washed up and over the forward portion of the hull, as though the submarine was at that very moment beginning to dive.

"The Armageddon machine," Greg said flatly. "Every science-fiction writer's favorite nightmare."

"Yeah," I said. "Doom in a tin box. And here it is, cruising right into our forgotten little corner of the world like the prodigal son."

* * *

I banged out the Trident story in a marathon session Saturday afternoon, while the chilling sight of the big sub cruising into Puget Sound was still fresh in my mind. I finished just as the Regulator struck five times. After a quick edit with a soft lead copy-editor's pencil, I dropped the copy on Marion's desk and headed down Front Street to the Spar.

My usual booth was full, and I turned toward the bar. Henry Anderson had a Rainier in front of me before I'd settled onto my stool. I stared out the window toward the Sound, thinking about black shapes lurking below the tranquil blue water and mushroom clouds rising in front of Mount Rainier. Henry's voice jolted me out of my reverie.

"Want another one, Tommy?"

"Sure," I said, looking up and realizing that my glass was already empty. "Why not?" I watched absently and lit a Marlboro as Henry stepped to the tap and drew another schooner of Rainier. "Thought you were gonna quit smoking," Henry said.

"I'm working on it."

"What in God's name for?"

"Dunno. Guess I'd just like a little fresh air."

"Shit. Breathing fresh air is like drinking water."

"What do you know about guns, Henry?"

Anderson walked back down the bar with my beer. He set the glass on the pine counter and leaned forward, resting on his elbows. "The usual. What every guy knows."

"You own any guns?"

"Sure. Who doesn't?"

"What kind?"

"Shotgun. Deer rifle. Pistol. What everybody owns."

"What kind of pistol?"

"A fucking blunderbuss. An old .44 my dad give me. That sucker's in the nightstand. Break into my place, and kiss your ass good-bye."

"Is that a semiautomatic?"

"Nah. Revolver. Don't even know if a .44 comes in a semiauto."

"Yeah," I said, thinking of the pistol hidden away under the wooden crate next to my bed, the one I used as a nightstand. "My dad has a revolver, a .38."

"Police sidearm," Henry said. "Works fine in the right hands."

"What about a .45?" I asked. "That much different from your .44?"

"You mean a Colt .45? The gun that won the West? Not so different. Same basic design. A lot older though. Wouldn't carry a powder load like my daddy's .44."

"No. That's not the gun I mean. I'm talking a semiautomatic. The kind of gun Dick Tracy waves around."

"Oh yeah. An Army pistol. Lots of those around. They're real blunderbusses, too. Knock down an oak door. But you gotta be standing right in front of it to hit it."

*   *   *

The *Times*, I noticed, had used an Associated Press photograph, a big newspaper's last resort on a local story. But none of its staff photographers or regular freelancers had been on Hurricane Ridge, and my black-and-white Rolleiflex shots wouldn't do for a cover photo.

The AP guy had done pretty good work, I concluded, admiring the angle of the shot. A net full of goats filled the foreground, and the helicopter hovered against a mountain-blue sky. Goat legs protruded from the net, and wild, terror-filled goat eyes added some emotional wallop.

But the best thing on the page by far was my own byline. It carried a freelancer's credit—"special to the *Seattle Times*"—instead of the standard staff credit. But it was my name on page one of the state's biggest newspaper.

I tucked the *Times* under my arm, turned away from the news rack in front of the Thriftway, and stepped lightly toward the *Echo*'s offices next door. The brown remnants of daffodil blossoms drooped like wet newsprint along the front-porch border. Time for the star reporter to haul the gardening tools out of the back-shop closet. Reporters for the *Times*, I figured, probably weren't expected to tidy up around the paper's front entrance.

I pulled the screen door slowly open and stood in the doorway for a second so that I could ease it shut. Marion heard me anyway. "My, my," she said, looking up from her own copy of the *Times*, "if it isn't the big-city reporter. I'm surprised to see you here, seeing as how you've decided to take a job with the competition."

Chesty had a copy of the *Times* spread out on his desk, too. He looked up, scooted his chair back, and stared at me, expressionless.

"Ah, Marion," I said, pushing through the swinging gate and heading for my desk, "don't be like that. It's just a freelance piece. I wrote it on my own time."

"Really?" she asked, raising both eyebrows. "I could have sworn that I approved an assignment to cover a goat story for the *Echo*." She stood and walked across the room to stand in front of my desk, both hands on her hips.

"Marion," I said, my cheeks flushing with indignation, "the *Echo* gets a helluva lot more of my time than it pays for. And the *Times* isn't the competition, for Christ's sake. When was the last time you saw any Bent Fir news in it. Nobody stands in front of a news rack saying, 'Hmmmm. Should I buy the *Times* or the *Echo*?'"

"Listen, buddy," Marion said, her voice tight and her hands trembling. "You work for the *Big Skookum Echo*. You write for this town, for our people. You don't go peddling your cute little ass all over the goddamn state, looking for the highest bidder."

Chesty walked over and stood next to Marion. His voice was quieter than hers, but it was steady and hard. "I'm disappointed, Tom. You've been doing some good work for us. Your fire coverage has been first-rate. And we've sold some extra papers because of it. But *Echo* people don't double-dip. You were on my dime when you headed up to Hurricane Ridge. You had no business selling what you produced to somebody else."

He put both hands on the edge of my desk and leaned closer to me, looking me hard in the eyes. "Now clean out your desk and get the hell out of here," he said. "You're through at the *Echo*."

30

I walked back down Front Street in a daze, oblivious to the summer breeze and the scent of fir. I reached Benny's, headed around back, and stared up at my steep stairs. Then I turned on my heel, jumped into the Dodge, and steered for the Longmont Grade. When I crossed the county road at the top of the hill, I thought of Henry Logan and cranked the wheel to the left.

The overgrown gap in the trees that marked Logan's driveway looked strangely vacant. The old hand-lettered sign advertising eggs, I suddenly realized, was gone. I drove down the driveway and into the yard. The air was fresh. Like the egg sign out front, the reek of chicken manure had disappeared.

I spotted Henry Logan through his dirty kitchen window, sitting empty-eyed at his table with a white coffee mug in front of him. I poked my head through the open front door and announced myself. The old man started, looked around, and saw me. "Hey!" he croaked in a voice that sounded as though hadn't been used for a while. "Tommy Dawson come a-callin'."

Logan walked across the cracked linoleum to the door. "C'min and visit a spell. Ain't talked to nobody in days."

He walked to the Frigidaire and retrieved two cans of Olympia beer. I slid into one of the kitchen chairs. "How you doing, Mr. Logan?" I asked. "How come you took your egg sign down?"

"Ah, kid," Logan said, dropping into his seat and popping the pull tabs on the beers. "That sumbitch up the road is selling eggs for twenty cents a dozen. Can't buy feed for that. Can't figger how the bastard does it."

Logan pushed one of the beer cans across and took a long pull on his own. He hadn't shaved in days. One of his overall straps hung loose.

It was only eleven, and I eyed the Oly. *What the hell, it's not like I have anything to do.* I lifted the can to my lips.

"So what did you do with your chickens?" I asked. "You had dozens of them."

"Ahhh," Logan said. "My girls. Yep. Well, the girls is all gone to the packin' plant."

He paused, lost in the thought. Then he cackled. "Haven't had any particularly tough chicken dinners lately, have ya?" he asked.

"Geez," I said, taking another gulp of Olympia. "How about you? You getting along okay?"

"Got my guvmint check," Logan said, letting his shoulders sag a bit. "Not to worry."

I took another pull on my Oly. The beer went down like water, a quality that made it hugely popular with college kids. "Gotta admit, though," Logan added, "it's awful quiet around here without my girls. They kept me hoppin', all right."

"How about family?"

"My boys up and moved to Seattle. They still come down once in a while."

"What about moving up there?"

"I visit," Logan said. "Was up there just last year. Noise. Traffic. Bad air. Hate the place. "Nah," he continued, "this is my spot. Paid it off in '51. Reckon I'll hang around long as the checks keep comin'.

"Way things are goin'," he said, "that's all there's gonna be in Klahowya County. Old farts collectin' guvmint checks."

* * *

I dropped another empty back into the Heidelberg six-pack that sat next to me in the sand. Four down, two to go. I leaned back against a log and felt an I-sure-feel-sorry-for-myself drunk of monumental proportions coming on.

The tide was nearly high—waves lapped on the beach a dozen feet away. Across Oyster Bay and the open water beyond, an oddly shaped lenticular cloud hovered above Mount Rainier like a flying saucer. "Just come and take me away," I said to the saucer. "There's no damned reason for staying here. And there's no place else to go."

I'd reached the point where I was having trouble blaming everybody else for my troubles. Things hadn't quite come together yet, but plenty of pieces were floating around in my brain, bumping into each other and causing a commotion that was tough to ignore. Getting fired from the *L.A. Times* was one thing. Getting fired from the *Big Skookum Echo* was an entirely different deal. Office politics?

There weren't any. Pressures from advertisers, government agencies, and journalism reviews? None of those either. Getting blindsided by bureaucratic catch-22s and obscure, tight-ass rules? For God's sake, my own father had sent a clear message that I was out of line. And I sure as hell knew I was screwing over Greg Grant, who was going out of his way to give me a hand.

The bottom line was that the *Echo* was a small-time country weekly. If I couldn't keep a job there, it was hard to keep thinking of myself as God's gift to journalism.

I picked up the what was left of the six-pack, stumbled over the driftwood piled between the beach and the road, and staggered to the Dodge. The engine cranked weakly, barely turning over, and failed to catch. I pounded the wheel. "Marvin Dervish, you son of a bitch! I paid you my last nickel to fix this piece of shit."

I twisted the cap off beer number five, took a hefty swig, propped the bottle between my legs, and turned the ignition key. The engine turned slowly three times . . . and caught. I weaved down the highway toward town.

I'm not sure why I picked the Grizzly. Maybe the Spar just seemed too civilized for my black mood. Maybe I just didn't want to face anybody I'd be embarrassed to face. Maybe I just wanted to drink alone.

But it just wasn't a day when things went my way. As I hunched over the bar staring into my third or fourth bourbon, the door opened behind me and I heard a familiar voice. "Well, now, if it ain't the college boy."

Lars Mayfield stood there with two loggers I didn't recognize. "Hear you're fresh outta work," he snarled. "Guess you got no cause to be snooping around in the business of us miserable country hicks no more."

He stepped forward and hit me in the face with a roundhouse right. Through the fog left by that day's beer and the forty years since, I barely remember what happened after that. I dimly recall hitting the floor, and then the lights went out. Given the concussion and the loose teeth, somebody must have kicked me in the head. And given the cracked ribs, the footwork didn't stop with one shot to the temple. All I know for sure is that when I woke up in the Shelton hospital, I looked like I'd been run over by a skidder. And I had the worst hangover of my life.

* * *

When my eyes flickered open, I saw my mother sitting next to the bed. She reached forward and put a hand on my cheek. I winced.

She pulled her hand back as though she'd touched a hot burner. "Sorry, honey. Oh . . . Sorry, sorry, sorry."

My father stood sullenly behind her, his arms folded across his chest. When he saw that I was awake, he turned and left the room. My mother reached forward again, but this time she held my hand. No pain there—I hadn't thrown a punch.

Dad returned with a doctor carrying a clipboard. The doc pulled a penlight from the pocket of his white coat and shined it in my eyes. He checked my ears and put his stethoscope to my chest. He flipped the covers back and probed my heavily taped ribs, making me gasp in pain. Then he stepped back, scribbled on his clipboard, and cleared his throat.

"You'll live," he said. "But I don't guarantee the same prognosis if you keep fighting in logger bars."

"Amen," my father said.

"You've had a concussion, but your skull's intact."

"What's in it is a different matter," Dad added.

"You have scrapes, bruises, and contusions. And four cracked ribs, which we'll have to keep taped. But you're a lucky man—all that will heal.

"Any questions?"

Dad, Mom, and I looked at one another and said nothing. The doctor turned and left the room.

I held up both hands, palms out, and winced again. "Dad," I said, "I wasn't fighting in a logger bar. I was just sitting there when Lars Mayfield walked up and coldcocked me."

"Just like that? For no reason? What in the hell did you say to him?"

"Nothing, I . . ."

My mother broke in and mercifully turned the parental lecture in a less dangerous direction. "You shouldn't have been in the Grizzly Tavern anyway. Promise me you'll stay out of that place."

The door opened a crack, and Sandy stuck her head in. Dad turned, Mom rose from her chair, and I stumbled through an introduction. "Come in, dear," my mother said, walking forward to take

Sandy's hand and pull her into the room. "I'm glad you could come."

Mom turned her head toward me, still holding Sandy's hand. "What a lovely young woman. Why haven't we been introduced long before now?"

Sandy blushed. Dad awkwardly extended a hand. I asked Sandy how she knew where I was. "She telephoned us," Mom said, "looking for you."

"I called your house," Sandy explained. "When you didn't answer, I called the paper. Nobody there seemed to know where you were, so I called your folks."

After three or four minutes of small talk, Dad held up my key ring, which he'd apparently confiscated when I was in never-never land. "Your car's still in front of the Griz," he said. "I'll drop it over at your place."

"Good luck," I thought, remembering the last time I'd tried to start the Dodge.

"My God, you look terrible," Sandy said as soon as my folks left the room. She lightly caressed the bruises on my cheeks and forehead. "What in the world happened?"

"Aw, there's always been hard feelings between Lars Mayfield and me. And he's been giving me a bad time since I got back into town. I guess I had a little too much to drink. When he said something, I said something. You know how it goes."

She seemed satisfied with that. And, lord knows, even a little time in the Navy makes the occasional bar fight seem perfectly normal. In any event, she happily moved on to a subject that made me almost as uncomfortable. "I saw your story in the *Times*. It looked terrific. Did you get much reaction?"

My God, I thought. *Did I get much reaction?*

But I sure wasn't ready to get into all that. Sandy would find out about my joining the ranks of Klahowya County's unemployed soon enough. And I didn't want to think about *her* reaction.

"A little."

"Anything from any editors?"

"Nah. Newspapermen don't gush to other newspapermen about routine work. Still, it's hard to miss something stripped across page one of the *Times*."

"Hear anything from Tacoma?"

"No. But it's pretty early. My letter and clips just went out last week."

"You must feel terrible," she said. "I'll let you get some rest."

She'd just slipped out the door when Jimmy Winthrop pushed it halfway open and knocked softly. I gave him a weak wave and a smile, and he stepped into the room, holding an improbable bunch of summer flowers. He held the daisies and dahlias out to me, and I waved them toward the nightstand.

"I heard you had some trouble over at the paper."

"I had trouble everywhere yesterday."

"Geez, Tom. I'm sorry. I don't really understand what this is all about. But you wrote some good stuff about the marina. I'd hate to see you leave."

"Speaking of the marina, how'd it go with Washington Mutual? What's the deal on your loan?"

Jimmy turned his head and looked at his flowers. "Didn't get it."

"You didn't get it? Why not? What'd they say?"

"Said we were in a recession. Said money's tight. Said they didn't see timber coming back anytime soon. Said they had their doubts about the future of a town like Bent Fir."

* * *

After I'd been in the hospital for two days, my folks picked me up and settled me back into my old bedroom at their place. Mom brought me her Teddy Roosevelt book from my apartment, and I finally finished the damned thing. Not bad, actually. But it didn't do a thing to cheer me up.

Dad was at work, of course. Mom helped me through a couple of embarrassing episodes with the bedpan I'd brought home from the hospital that morning and went grocery shopping in midafternoon. I lay there in the silence for a few minutes after she left, and then managed to swing my feet off the bed and onto the floor. Grunting with pain, I shuffled to the bathroom down the hall. Then I lurched into the living room and slumped in the easy chair next to the phone. I still remember the damned thing—a bright-yellow rotary-dial number that sat there like some kind of poisonous toad. Eventually, I reached out and dialed the *News Tribune*'s newsroom. I asked for Heather McKenzie, the reporter I'd met at the Forest Service's log-rustling press conference in Shelton.

In those days, city newsrooms, virtually empty in the morning, started to fill in the afternoon as reporters returned from their leg-work and banged away on typewriters, churning out copy for the line editors and copy desk to shovel into the next morning's paper. Heather picked up on the first ring. I gave her the standard greeting journalists use to open phone calls with other journalists. "You on deadline?"

"Yes, but I have a little breathing room."

"Did my clips get to the city desk? I haven't heard a thing."

"They're here. I asked last week. The desk is swamped with clips. The recession, you know. Hardly any jobs are posted, and every one that is gets a blizzard of applications."

"Yeah. But not many can claim the kind of experience I've had."

"It's your experience that's the problem," she said.

I felt a sudden emptiness above my diaphragm, the hollow feeling you get in the instant between a slip and a fall.

Heather paused for a couple of beats and then broke the silence. "When I asked about your clips, the city editor seemed all excited about you. Then he called L.A., got stonewalled, and he came back to ask if I knew anything about what had happened there. I told him that I didn't, really, but that you seemed like a great guy, that I'd been following your log-rustling stories, and that they were top-notch."

"And?" I asked

"Nothing. He just left, and I didn't hear anything more until yesterday."

"Yesterday?"

"He stopped me in the hall when I was headed out on a story. 'About your friend Tom Dawson,' he said."

I knew what was coming.

The city editor had called three or four personal contacts at the *L.A. Times*. Nobody would give him a straight answer, but it was clear, he said, that there had been trouble and that I hadn't left on the best of terms. Then he'd called the *Echo*—last Tuesday. His timing couldn't have been worse.

"Tom," she said, "he told me that you'd been fired at the *Echo*. And that you'd been in a bar fight. And that you were in the hospital. Is all that true?"

"It's a long story, Heather. I'll tell you all about it sometime."

I hung up and struggled to get out of the easy chair's deep cushion, each move painful. Clearly, I wouldn't be interviewing in Tacoma. I doubt I'd even get a note acknowledging my application. Editors had enough stress in their lives without taking on troublemakers.

I wobbled into the kitchen, opened the cabinet where Dad kept his liquor, grabbed the big square bottle of Jack Daniel's, and poured myself a stiff shot.

The bourbon erased a little of the pain, and I fell back into bed, thinking it couldn't get much worse. I was wrong.

Sandy headed over right after her PAO shift that evening and showed up on my folks' porch in her blues. From my bedroom, I could hear Mom and Dad fussing over her in the front hall. Mom offered her tea, and Dad offered her something "a little stronger." I admired her diplomat's sensibilities when she said yes to the tea.

Mom showed her to my bedroom and headed toward the kitchen to put the kettle on. Sandy shut the door and came back to stand beside the bed. "Your Bangor story's in the *Echo* today."

The news surprised me, although it shouldn't have. I'd left the story on Marion's desk Saturday night, and—as Chesty had pointed out with the goat story—it had been reported and written on his dime. There was no reason not to use it.

"Tom," Sandy added, "a little editor's note was at the bottom of the story."

My eyebrows rose.

"It said," she continued, "that you'd left the *Echo* to pursue other opportunities. That any news calls should go to Marion Mayfield."

I must have looked the ultimate sad sack lying there, covered with bruises, bandages, and crusted scabs, listening to Sandy recite my professional obituary.

"Did you get the Tacoma job?" she asked. "What opportunities are they talking about?"

I lay there, staring in the direction of my toes. "None," I finally said. "I'm a twenty-nine-year-old guy living with my parents. There aren't any opportunities."

31

By Saturday, I was feeling well enough to spend most of the day rattling around the house. I finished Teddy Roosevelt and returned *Mornings on Horseback* to Mom. I helped Dad polish some salmon spinners. I sat on the porch and watched Mom garden and then turned on the TV and watched a Mariners–Red Sox game. I rooted for the Mariners. They lost 5-3.

Dad and Mom had a date for dinner and pinochle with friends across town. Dad noted that I seemed bored and probably would appreciate a chance to get out of the house. He and Mom could drop me at the Spar for dinner and pick me up on their way home. Was I interested?

I hesitated. At the Spar, I'd have to face folks who knew all about the business at the *Echo* and my run-in with Lars Mayfield. I'd probably have to face awkward questions, but I'd been stuck in my parents' house for three days. "Sure," I said. "I'd like that."

The Spar hummed with the chatter of a lively, Thursday-night fish-and-chips crowd. Marty Brantly slipped into my booth and asked, "Mind if I sit a spell?"

I looked up from my Rainier. "Take a load off," I said. "Buy you a beer?"

Henry Anderson lumbered up to the booth. "Watcha drinking, Marty?" he said.

"One of those," Marty said, nodding toward my schooner.

Henry turned back toward the bar without saying another word. "Heard about you leaving the *Echo*," Marty said. "What you planning on doing now?"

"Thanks for putting it so diplomatically. But I didn't exactly *leave* the *Echo*. Marion and Chesty gave me the old heave-ho. And I'm not quite sure what's next."

"Yeah. I heard all about it. And for what's it worth, I think it's bullshit. You're the best thing that ever happened to that rag."

"What's up with you?" I asked. "Any chance of opening the mill again?"

Henry came back and set a glass down in front of Marty, hard. Beer slopped onto the table. "Hey!" I said. "Take it easy. I'm paying for that stuff." Henry gave me a long look and turned on his heel.

"Dunno," Marty said. "Maybe. We've gone through this shit before. Sooner or later, things turn around. Folks start building houses again. So I dunno. Maybe." He took a long pull on the beer, put the glass down on the wet table, and sighed. He stared out the window. A sailboat rounded the point. Mount Rainier stood on the eastern horizon. "But I tell ya," he continued, "this time feels worse. It ain't the same around here. Things are changing. Some things ain't never comin' back."

"Aw," I said, "it's the timber economy. Up. Down. You know."

"Yeah, maybe. But not for me. I'm outta here."

"What do you mean?"

"I mean gone. Things ain't that bad in L.A. yet. I'm throwing all my shit in the Ford, and I'm hittin' I-5. Get away from the goddamn rain. Find me a job before the unemployment runs out."

"Geez, Marty," I said. "That's a damn shame. Us young guys all leave, and this place really will dry up."

"It may rot," Marty said. "But one thing's for sure about Bent Fir. It ain't never gonna be dry."

*   *   *

On Monday morning, Dad drove me to Marvin Dervish's yard and walked into the shop with me. He'd managed to start my Dodge when he went to retrieve it from the Grizzly while I was in the hospital. It had started, just barely, and he'd driven it straight to Marvin's.

The old mechanic headed off any complaints before I could even get started. "Just a starter," he said as he stepped up to the counter. "Gotta be expected on a rig this old. Didn't have nothing to do with that work I did last month."

Marvin ripped the carbon copy off of his bill and held it across the counter. Dad grabbed it, glanced at the bottom line, and pulled his checkbook out of his hip pocket. "This is a loan," he said. "You can pay me when you get back on your feet."

We walked back out front. Dad still had his checkbook in hand, and he laid it on the hood of the Dodge. "This is a loan, too," he said, bending over and scribbling. He ripped a check out of the book, straightened up, handed it to me, and walked off toward his car. I looked at the check. Five hundred bucks. If I was careful, it would keep a roof over my head and some cheap beer in the fridge for a month. Maybe six weeks. I looked up at my dad, who was climbing into his sedan. I was too humiliated to say thanks.

The Dodge cranked energetically and started instantly. I drove back down to my apartment and carefully picked my painful way up the steps. The cardboard box stuffed with my office gear still sat on the kitchen table. Taking care not to aggravate my ribs, I eased the box onto the floor. Then I grabbed a Heidelberg out of the fridge, sat down at the table, and lit a Marlboro. It was 10 a.m.

*　*　*

I spent the next week in a haze of beer, bourbon, and cigarette smoke. Each day began with a Heidelberg breakfast and ended when I closed down the Spar and dragged myself back up the steps behind Benny's. I vaguely remember several long afternoons at the Oyster Bay beach, leaning against a log with a beer cooler next to me. I took no food, books, magazines, or even a transistor radio. I simply stared up at the cloudless sky and drank, running things over in my mind. The fiasco in L.A. The stupid, arrogant way I botched my job at the *Echo*. My hesitancy with Sandy and the growing tension between us. And, most of all, the alien underside of Klahowya County, the dark world that lurked under the Skookum's bright-green carpet of firs.

On Thursday, I stopped by the Thriftway for more beer and grabbed a copy of the *Echo*. When I slid back into the front seat of the Dodge, I unfolded the paper and propped it on the steering wheel. The usual collection of Bent Fir trivia spread across the usual nine columns. A couple of local candidates had announced for the November election. The fire chief wanted to remind folks that the burn ban was still in effect. The price of school lunches would go up in the fall. And, below the fold under a modest 24-point head-line, a Marion Mayfield story on guilty pleas from the two Hood-sport loggers arrested for transporting unbranded old growth. Luke Johnson and Joseph Carbone both drew one-year terms, with all but three months suspended. With time served, that meant they'd both be back on the highway by the time the rains came. Those boys, I thought, cut themselves a damned good deal.

That fact hadn't been lost on Marion. After she'd summed up the news in the first couple of paragraphs and filled readers in with the background boilerplate that rehashed the original arrest, she closed out her story with four paragraphs on what obviously was a plea bargain. Yes, the assistant DA who'd prosecuted the case conceded, Johnson and Carbone had cooperated with investigators. Among other things, they'd revealed where they were headed when they were arrested and who was paying them for their illegal loads. The investigation was continuing, the DA said, and that information was confidential. But in due time, he'd bring charges against everybody involved, including the mill operators who bought illegal timber.

"Bullshit," I said out loud, banging the palm of my hand on the steering wheel. Was this brash young DA going to bring charges against two dead men? Did he plan on descending to hell to subpoena the Dykes twins?

And the twins were the go-betweens who shuttled illegal timber to the mills. With Eddie and Terry permanently silenced, finding the mill owners who turned the old-growth logs into finished timber was going to require some serious investigation. I doubted anybody would go to the trouble.

Of course, there was always Lars. Who knew how deep he had his hooks into the business? Moochie said he'd been helping the twins move old growth off Mayfield buffers. Maybe he'd been involved in the wholesale end of the operation, too.

I was still thinking about the possibilities when I pulled into the lot behind Benny's. I climbed the stairs and stood in my doorway, looking at the battered old fridge, and realized the half case of Heidelberg was still in the trunk of the Dodge. "Ah, screw it," I said to the refrigerator, and—for the first time in more than a week—I went to bed sober.

* * *

When I woke up that Friday morning, my head was clear and my stomach growled with a healthy hunger. I rolled on my side and stared at the sun knifing through my open window. A breeze floated into the room, carrying faint caws and screeches from the robins, jays, and crows flapping around in the firs out back. I climbed out of bed, walked onto the porch, and looked out into the front end of a perfect late-August day.

I showered and shaved, vowing to postpone the morning's first cigarette until I had a decent breakfast. The sparkling views along the Angel Harbor Highway helped keep the gnawing nicotine hunger at bay until I pulled into the lot in front of the Woodsman's Café, and the restaurant's copy of the *Post-Intelligencer* kept my mind off smokes while I wolfed down steak and eggs. The feds were hiring replacements for the striking air-traffic controllers. The Federal Reserve was refusing to back down on the killer interest rates that were crippling wood products. Sebastian Coe ran the mile in a world-record 3:47.

I'd made it to nearly nine, but I had a Marlboro in my mouth the minute I stepped out of the Woodsman's front door. A couple of deep drags, and I was behind the wheel of the Dodge, heading over toward U.S. 101. I turned right on the big highway, let the Dodge off the leash, and in minutes was watching the firs stream by on either side of Cutthroat Creek Road. Two more minutes and I was into the Dykes driveway.

As near as I could tell, nothing had changed. The '49 Ford still sat moldering on blocks. The ancient Reo log truck hadn't moved. The resident mongrel barked furiously as soon as the Dodge appeared in the yard.

Donald Dykes stepped out the front door to meet me as I climbed the steps. "Mornin'," he said.

"Good morning, Mr. Dykes."

"Watcha want?"

"I was sorry to hear about the twins, Mr. Dykes. I'm not with the *Echo* anymore, but I'd still like to know what happened. I hoped I could ask you some questions. Maybe I can help."

"My boys is dead. Any help you got is gonna come a little late."

"Whoever killed your boys is still out there, Mr. Dykes. That's not right."

"Lotta things ain't right. You gonna fix 'em all?"

"I have some experience with these kinds of things, Mr. Dykes. I worked at some good newspapers. Big newspapers. With big-city police. Maybe I can help find whoever killed your boys."

Dykes looked past me, staring silently out at the scraggly second growth at the edge of his bare-dirt yard. He sighed and looked back into my eyes. I doubt he'd ever been to Seattle, let alone Los Angeles. His ignorance of the world outside the Skookum probably gave him more confidence in my abilities than they deserved. In any event, my pitch connected.

"The name's 'Don,'" he said. "Want some coffee?"

"I'd like that . . . Don."

Dykes looked back through the screen door. "Moochie," he hollered. "Coffee. Black." He looked back at me, and I nodded. "Two of 'em," he added.

He slumped on the porch bench, a rickety affair lashed together from skinny alder trunks, the mottled bark still on them, and looked at my Hawaiian shirt. "Don't see many of those around here," he said, looking more puzzled than disapproving.

Moochie pushed the screen door open, handed off the coffee mugs, and disappeared back inside. "Long way to come for bad coffee," Dykes said. "So whadda ya want to know?"

I settled onto the porch railing and took a sip. Not bad, actually.

"What can you tell me about the logging your boys were doing, Don? Where were they cutting? Who were they working with?"

"Ain't much a secret," Dykes said. "They'd head up the peninsula and scrounge a couple of big logs. You know. Old-time logs. The big uns. And they'd take 'em to one of the little eastside gyppo mills. That little one-lunger over in Maple Valley maybe. There's a fair call for clear-fir beams. Put 'em in the fancy new houses goin' up in the city. Paid pretty good.

"Just Eddie and Terry, though," he added. "Arnie wouldn't have no truck with fallin' and buckin' logs. Too damned much work."

"What about around here? Where'd they cut around here?"

"Shit," Dykes said with a sign. "Hell if I know. I'm too damned old to be headin' out on shows and such.

"They did some cuttin' with Lars Mayfield, sure enough. He'd come around. Plenty. Tell the boys he'd blazed a couple of big trees on the edge of a Mayfield show. Tell 'em right where they were. All roaded out and everything. Easy."

Dykes looked down into his lap. I leaned back against the rail and waited, sipping my coffee. The silence grew uncomfortable.

There's more. Just wait him out.

Dykes finally looked up. "'Course all that come to a screechin' halt," he said, "once Hal Mayfield got onto 'em."

"Hal knew about this?"

"Shit yes. He was fit to be tied. Come out here. Bearded Eddie right here on this porch. Told 'em if he come around a Mayfield show he'd have his sorry ass. Said he'd fill his butt with buckshot and call the sheriff."

I kept my mouth shut, but I leaned forward and looked intensely interested, trying to coax more out of the old man.

"Didn't sit too well with Eddie," Dykes said. "Terry come along about then and told old Hal he oughta be minding his own. Said Lars was cruisin' the logs for 'em anyway, and the goddamn Mayfields oughta get their act straight."

"And?"

"That really set Hal to goin'. Red goddamn face—thought he was gonna have a fuckin' heart attack. Told 'em Lars was his business. Family business. Told 'em Lars was done with this shit. Wouldn't be seein' him no more."

"What'd your boys have to say to all this?"

"Not much. Hard to get a word in edgewise when Hal was on a toot. When he blew off enough steam, I kinda asked if he wouldn't mind movin' along off my property."

"Then what?"

"Then nuthin'. Hal got into his pickup and drove off. And I told my boys they ought not to be fuckin' with Hal Mayfield."

32

The Takamak had settled down into its leisurely, late-summer flow, the clear water swirling slowly around boulders and lying almost still in the deepest pools. The occasional pickup parked alongside the road signaled that other fishermen were out on this bright Saturday morning, and I crossed my fingers, hoping nobody had reached the Cable Hole before me.

I steered onto the South Fork and eased back on the gas pedal as the road wound its way through groves of old growth. The calm of big trees settled over me even before I turned down the familiar dirt lane leading back into the woods. When I pulled into the meadow and saw that I had my refuge to myself, I quietly exhaled and rolled to a stop. My mind was already wandering as I stood by the open trunk, pulling on my waders and assembling an old fiberglass rod my dad had given me in high school.

I drifted an elk-hair caddis across the bottom third of the pool and hooked a nice rainbow on the third cast. After releasing the fish, I worked upstream a few steps, casting toward the logs and twisted cable on the far side of the hole.

The previous day's trip out to the Dykes place had given me enough focus to break out of my fog of booze and self-pity. The Cable Hole's clear air and water were helping me to see through my anger and arrogance. For the first time in my life, I was starting to see that chains of cause and effect always led back to some decision I'd made. Or at least to understand that was the only useful way see the world. I could control only myself. So if I wanted to take control of my life, I'd have to start acting as though it all started—and ended—with me.

Another rainbow, this one a gorgeous fifteen-incher, took the caddis. The fish leaped twice, broke off the tippet, and streaked toward the bottom of the pool. I held up a fresh fly to thread the leader, and my eyes settled on the dusty burgundy relic sitting in the meadow. I'd spent the past three months cursing the dumb luck that put me in an embarrassing old wreck that started about half the time. But whose fault was it that I'd blown my gig at the *Times* anyway? If I'd just thought things through, if I'd been more honest with myself about my story and my evidence, I'd still be driving a nearly new BMW.

I looked up at the ancient firs towering overhead. And what, I asked myself, did a goddamned pile of tin matter anyway, whether it was built in Detroit or Munich? For that matter, what did the *Times* matter? Smog, traffic, and ten million strangers. Did I really want to spend my life in a Hawaiian shirt and Oakley sunglasses? Or here, in this cathedral?

I turned back to the pool, raised the rod to cast, lowered it, and stood motionless. Upstream, the resident ouzel stepped across the rocks in jerky steps. Against the far bank, real caddis flies dipped and darted. Overhead, swallows swooped down to feed.

*   *   *

Hank Potash leaned across his cluttered glass counter and squinted at me skeptically. Flies buzzed faintly against the office window.

"So whadda ya want with Arnie?" Potash asked. "Hardly anybody got any use for the little asshole. Why should you be any different?"

The shrunken man in the greasy overalls looked exactly the same as he had when I'd pulled into the Front Street Shell station on my sixteenth birthday, thrilled to be behind the wheel on my own car for the first time and eager to buy my first tank of gasoline. He was a fixture in downtown Bent Fir, on the end of a gas nozzle or staring out at Front Street through the station's dirty window. He knew his way around a log truck, too. Hank Potash would stay late to clean up a balky diesel injector or fix a brake line and save a driver a trip to one of the big repair shops in Shelton. That might mean two days in wages, which accounted for the fact that a big rig or two usually was parked along the station's back fence.

"Arnie had some trouble in Tacoma," I said. "Maxy Stewart ended up in the Pierce County jail, and I thought Arnie might answer some questions that would help Maxy out."

"That useless sumbitch run off more'n three weeks ago. Shit. He only showed for work about two days outta three as it was. I invested some goddamn time in that boy, too, I'm tellin' ya. Was teachin' him about the big rigs and all. I'm gettin' old, ya know. Need some help around here. But I picked the wrong kid. Arnie ain't dumb. But all the little bastard cares about is smokin' dope and runnin' with his sicko friends, you know what I mean?"

Potash eased himself onto the stool he kept at the end of the counter and sighed, looking past me out the window at the gray clouds moving in from the southwest. "How's your ma doin', Tommy? How's your ol' dad bearin' up?"

For once I could include some good news when I gave Potash the practiced update on Mom's health I had to recite just about every time I ran into someone from the Skookum. He nodded approvingly. "That's good, Tommy," he said. "That's real good."

I steered the conversation back on track. "Did Arnie say where he was going, Mr. Potash?"

"Never said where he was goin'," Potash said. "Not then. Not never. Just didn't show up. 'Course I'd dock his pay. But that didn't seem to matter none. Arnie, he'd work just long enough to buy hisself more dope, get high, and then not give a goddamn shit about nuthin'."

"Any idea where he might have gone?"

"Used to crash out there on Rush Creek, but didn't that Mayfield crew burn that mess to the ground? Goddamn hippies got just what they deserved, ask me."

"Thanks, Mr. Potash," I said, reaching into my hip pocket and pulling out my notebook. I ripped out a page and scribbled my name and number. "If Arnie comes back to town," I said, handing the piece of paper to the old mechanic, "please let me know." I turned toward the open door and headed out into the gathering gloom. Hank Potash pulled me up short.

"Oh, he's in town."

I turned back into the office. "How do you know? Have you seen him?"

"Sure. I seen him. No lack of brass in that boy. Waltzed in here two days ago demandin' cash for the work he did before he up and run off. If you can call it work."

"So what did you do?"

"Told him he'd only been here two, three days that last week, near as I could remember. Give him a hundred bucks outta the till and sent him on his goddamn way. Probably still stoned on that hundred bucks."

I turned to go again.

"But he's around," Hank Potash said. "You can bet cash money the little asshole isn't all that far."

*　*　*

The gray August overcast hung from horizon to horizon, and the air smelled moist. I walked past the Shell gas pumps, ambled down Front toward the Spar, and then broke into a run when a driving rain came pouring down. The cloudburst took my mind off Arnie Dykes and shifted it onto the image of a cold Rainier.

My usual booth by the window was open. I slid in gratefully, nodded to Henry Anderson, and stared out at the view while Henry filled a schooner and silently delivered it to the table. I was three deep draughts into the beer when the door opened and Jimmy Winthrop stepped in. His eyes adjusted to the light, and he spotted me in the booth.

Jimmy stepped over and slid in. "How ya doing, Jimmy? You feeling any better? After the news on the marina, I mean."

"Oh, I'm not giving up," Jimmy said, motioning to Henry for a beer.

"You're the only one who isn't. Every time I turn around, I hear another flushing sound."

"Not from me you won't. I'm gonna keep trying. And did you hear? There's a new bank in Hoodsport. Local guys started it. Business guys. They got to have more faith in us than those Seattle suits have."

"Well," said I, raising my glass, "here's to you. There's something to be said for hanging in there. If everybody gives up, the town really will go down the drain. That much is for sure."

"I'm headed up to Hoodsport Thursday. Got my pitch all figured out. The new subs are coming in. You know. From Bangor. Navy officers. Sailboats. It's a natural. There'll be plenty of call for a marina."

"You bet," I said, raising my glass again. "We'll have yachtsmen parading up and down the streets in little blue hats with gold braid on 'em, spending money with every step they take. Jimmy, my boy, you may just save the goddamn town."

33

A lone figure sifted through the first mound of ashes with a garden rake. When he heard me pull into the meadow, Maxy Stewart turned and walked toward me, holding up a piece of twisted metal. "My Little League trophy," he said before tossing the shapeless mass into a small pile of similarly unidentifiable artifacts. It landed with a clank.

"Thanks for coming," Maxy said, holding out a hand. We shook, and I noticed that he seemed stronger, healthier. His cheeks had filled out and showed a little color. He'd trimmed his beard, and his hair had some shine to it.

"You're looking good, Maxy. Something agrees with you."

"Been staying with my folks, and it's true what they say about a mom's home cooking. No crank either. None since I got busted in Tacoma."

We walked and talked, picking our way through the debris in the meadow. Maxy had made bail a couple of days after I'd seen him in the hoosegow and then had quietly settled in with his folks. He was, he said, just wrapping up a few loose ends before leaving for good. He was through with redneck country, headed for Taos, maybe, or Big Sur.

We strolled along the row of cabins, every one of them burned to the ground. Scorched woodstoves, doorknobs, lanterns, and other chunks of metal protruded from piles of white ash.

"So why'd you call?" I asked.

"Wanted to get a few things straight. Especially since those loggers walked. Shit. Most of them served less than a week. What a joke. Guess that tells you what the county thinks of folks like us."

"The Mayfield crew figured you had something to do with Hal's death. I can see why they got riled."

We reached a log on the downwind side of the meadow and sat on it. A smell that reminded me of dead campfires drifted past. "It's all a bunch of hooey," Maxy said. "Walt Hasslebring knew it was a bunch of hooey."

"How so?"

"Because when Hal Mayfield died, just about everybody in the commune was gone. They were at Seed Camp?"

"Seed Camp?"

"Yeah, Seed Camp. It happens that time every year. We always go. Get everything ready for the big camp. Clear over in Colville this year."

When Maxy said "Colville," everything clicked. The Rainbow Gathering, that's what he was talking about. First week of July. Even now. Old hippies, and young ones, too, I suppose. Thirty thousand of them, descending on some national forest somewhere for a seven-day bacchanalia of peace and love. This summer, it had been in Colville, way over in the far reaches of Eastern Washington. Dope galore. Lots of nudity and, naturally, plenty of press attention.

"At the Rainbow Gathering? You were all at the Rainbow Gathering?"

"Most of us. At Seed Camp. We've been going since '74. We show up a couple of weeks early and set up. We stake out the campsite, dig latrines, get everything straight with the rangers . . . that kind of stuff. We've been all over. Montana. Arizona. Last year we went to West Virginia."

"And Walt Hasslebring knew you were gone?"

"He checked it out good. Tracked down a dozen witnesses who knew Rush Creek was there. And, damn it, he could have let folks know. He could have told you, put it in the paper. That would have kept those damned drunks from coming out here last month. We were all here then, back in plenty of time to get the living daylights kicked out of us."

I thought back to my conversation with Hasslebring, the one in his office just after I'd been to Rush Creek. Don't play dumb with me, the sheriff had said. A good relationship between a reporter and his source has to go both ways. Yeah. Right. Turns out I wasn't playing dumb; I *was* dumb. And Walt Hasslebring was one cagey son of a gun.

I processed all that and thought back to my own Rush Creek visit. It had been only a week or two after Hal Mayfield died. Max Stewart was there. So were two men and a woman.

"Maxy, you didn't go to Colville, did you?

"Nope. A few of us stayed here. We always do, just to keep an eye on things."

"That doesn't make for much of an alibi."

"We got the world's best alibi."

"How so?"

"Look. I sure wasn't sayin' anything to you when you came out. You're a newsman, Tommy. Some things you just don't want in the paper. But the fact is, Sheriff Hasslebring came swooping in here soon as he heard about Hal and Lars and our cook shack. He busted Butch, Sundown, Summer, and me on the spot. When Hal Mayfield died, we were in the Klahowya County jail."

* * *

Sandy sat in her usual spot on the BOQ steps in white shorts, her legs tan, her flowered cloth bag next to her. When I pulled in, she rose and walked toward the car, her bag swinging. "Great day for baseball," she said, slipping into the seat.

"Softball. And you've never seen softball like this."

I headed for the main gate. The Marine on duty snapped a salute, and Sandy returned it.

"You might want to keep your officer side tucked away once we get there," I said. "The players probably wouldn't take to it."

"Oh," Sandy said. "Why's that?"

I smiled cryptically. "You'll see."

The car rounded a curve, bringing Angel Harbor into view. Sunlight glittered on the bay and painted the moored sailboats a sharp-edged white. We drove south to the outskirts of Bent Fir and pulled into the county park. I left the car next to a backstop flanked by bleachers, and we found seats in the top row above the third-base line.

Nine beefy women in purple T-shirts and cutoff jeans lumbered onto the field, the word "Dolphins" emblazoned across their ample breasts. The catcher squatted behind home plate and lobbed a ball to the pitcher. She spun to her left and threw a bullet to first base, where it arrived at a waiting glove with a *thwack*. The first baseman whipped the ball to second. Without pause, it ricocheted to the player on third and then to home. The catcher bobbled the throw, which bounced in the dirt before she snatched it up and lobbed it back to the pitcher. A bench full of women below us erupted with jeers, their yellow T-shirts rising as one, arms thrust upward with clenched fists. "You ham-handed pussy," one yelled. "You probably need help holding your old man's pecker."

I turned to Sandy and grinned. "These are the gals your petty officers and boatswain's mates go home to at night. They're the reason your enlisted men are so damned tough." Sandy, tight-lipped, said nothing.

A Dolphin with weightlifter's biceps stepped to the plate and hammered a pitch to the left fielder, who faded back and gathered it in without effort. When I signed on with the *Echo* and learned I'd be covering women's softball, I'd grimaced, thinking the assignment was more small-town tedium like the Rotary Club and county commissioners. But a couple of games had changed my mind. Covering the enlisted-wives league had been a hoot, one of the best things about my job. And the Barracudas had been the biggest hoot in the bunch.

The Dolphins trotted to their dugout behind the first-base line. The Barracudas took the field for their warm-ups. The ball whipped around the bases even faster.

A pickup truck pulled into the parking lot, and a grizzled walrus of a man stepped out. He lifted a canvas bag out of the truck bed and walked to the edge of the backstop. Tattoos covered the forearms bulging out of his blue shirt. The ump pulled on his chest guard and mask and had a brief conversation with the captains before the first Dolphin batter, a squat woman with huge, pendulous breasts, stepped up to the plate.

"Batta, batta, batta," yelled the shortstop.

"How ya gonna swing around those tits?" hollered the third baseman.

I glanced over at Sandy. She was sitting on her hands in stony silence. I put my hand on her knee. She ignored it.

The Barracuda pitcher cranked up her arm, took a huge step forward, and released an underarm bullet that whooshed by the batter and raised a puff of dust from the catcher's glove. The batter stepped back from the plate and shook her tight curls. Catcalls erupted from the Barracuda bench, and the center fielder waved both arms like the takeoff chief on a carrier deck. "Hit it to me, you wuss!" she shouted. "It's lonely out here."

The Dolphin batter watched another strike fly by her and then swung wildly at the next pitch. The next two batters managed two foul balls apiece before going down swinging. The Barracudas trotted in from the field and began a steady succession of base hits. By the time the Dolphin shortstop gathered in a pop fly and retired the side at the bottom of the third inning, the Barracudas led 6-0.

Sandy turned to me as the yellow shirts took the field. "What's going on, Tom? You can't spend the rest of your life watching foul-mouthed women insult one another. What are you doing about your future, for God's sake?"

I felt a wave of defensive resentment wash over me. I sat silently while it passed, took a deep breath, and told myself to relax. No point in blowing my relationship with Sandy, too.

"I figured I'd go on being a newspaperman," I said. "I've applied for a job running cops at the Bellevue *Journal-American*."

She brightened. "Oh, Tom . . . That's great. Have you heard anything back?"

"Yeah. I'd kind of given up on them. But a letter came yesterday."

"And?"

"They've invited me for an interview."

"When?"

"I don't know yet. I need to call tomorrow. Set something up."

"Oh, Tom. That's great. You'll wow them."

I could feel the pressure behind her enthusiasm. Sandy wanted out of the Skookum, and she wanted me with her.

The metallic thud of an aluminum bat put a period on the sentence, and I jerked my head back toward the field. The ball rose into the blue sky, peaked over the center fielder, and finally dropped behind the low cyclone fence that ringed the field. The Dolphin batter, a short, round woman in flowered shorts, waddled around the bases as her teammates jumped out of the dugout and danced in the dirt.

I smiled. Sandy scooted an inch or two away from me.

The Dolphins crawled back into the game. By the top of the fifth, when a pickup pulled in with an aluminum beer keg in the back, they had three runs and the Barracudas were stalled at six. The first Dolphin batter singled, the second walked, and the third—the rotund woman who had hit the fourth-inning home run—stepped to the plate. She cocked the bat, the butt well behind her ear and the shaft orbiting in a lazy oval above her shoulder.

Catcalls poured in from the Barracudas on the field. The two sailors who'd carried the keg to the sidelines tapped it and pumped. Foam spurted out the hose. The pitcher stood upright, clicked her heels together, and saluted by raising the ball to arm's length. "Hum-mmm," she bellowed. "We know what to do with that." The players cheered.

The batter stepped back to the plate, resumed her stance, and once again belted the first pitch over the center-field fence, driving in the two runs on base. She circled the diamond and touched home base with a flourish, tying the score. Both teams broke from their positions and milled around the keg, sloppily toasting with large plastic cups.

The players lined up at the keg every time the teams shifted position, and the foul-mouthed trash talk grew raunchier as the play grew sloppier. The first Dolphin staggered as she stepped up to the plate at the top of the seventh. "My God," Sandy said, "they'll never make it through nine innings."

"Don't have to. Softball's just seven."

The Dolphins loaded the bases and scored a run before a pop fly ended their last at bat. The first three Barracudas at the plate, most of them into their fifth or sixth beers, slashed wildly at the ball and went down swinging. The players swarmed onto the field, toasting one another in a collage of purple and yellow T-shirts.

Sandy was up and moving the minute the game ended. I trotted down the bleacher steps after her and caught up as she turned toward the parking lot. "Hey," I said, "let's have a couple of beers. Don't you want to join the fun?"

"I worked with women like this at the packing plant," Sandy said. "They're one of the things I wanted to put behind me."

34

I was headed for the Spar, a lunch of fish and chips on my mind, when I spotted Myrtle Johnson sitting with an unfamiliar middle-aged man in the booth next to my usual perch. I didn't relish the idea of an awkward conversation about everything that had happened at the *Echo*, and I thought about quietly leaving before Myrtle could spot me. But she looked up, saw me, and smiled. I walked up to her booth.

"Hi, Myrtle. What's the news from Angel Harbor?"

"Oh, just the usual comings and goings," she said, lowering her chin and looking up at me from under her eyelashes, her brow furrowed with concern. "How about you, Tom? I've been worried about you."

"Ah, thanks, Myrtle, but I'm doing okay."

"Oh, I'm so rude," Myrtle said, gesturing toward the man across from her. "I should have introduced you. This is my cousin Terry. Terry, this is Tom Dawson."

The table blocked the man opposite Myrtle in the booth from rising completely, but he managed a sort of crouch and stuck out his hand. "Terry Johnson," he said. "Pleased to meet you. You're the newspaperman, aren't you?"

"Well, I was," I said, embarrassed by the confession. But it was clear from Johnson's comment that Myrtle had filled him in on all the local gossip, making detailed explanations unnecessary.

Terry Johnson. The name rang a faint bell, and I pondered it as I reluctantly accepted Myrtle's invitation to join the two of them in the booth. I sat next to Myrtle and looked curiously across the table at the big man opposite, trying to place the receding hairline and walrus mustache.

"Terry was in Seattle on business," Myrtle said. "He decided to come on over for old times' sake. There's only a few of us Johnsons left around now, but once upon a time we were all over the Skookum."

"I miss this country," Terry Johnson said. "More than I ever thought I would. I wanted to get out and see the old family place one more time. Myrtle was kind enough to put me up."

Then it clicked. *Terry Johnson*. The name leaped up off a yellowed page of the *Echo*, circa 1974. Terry Johnson was the San Francisco lawyer who'd sold his longtime family property to the Rush Creek Collective. He looked just like the mug shot that had run with the story. "You owned the Rush Creek property!" I said. "You sold it in the mid-seventies. To some kind of collective."

"True enough," Johnson said. "And I always felt bad about that sale. I was sort of holding the property in trust for the rest of the family. Not legally, you understand, but it felt that way. To me, anyway. But the taxes kept going up, the family was drifting further and further apart, and nobody could get out here to enjoy the old place anyway . . . You understand?"

"Sure," I said, probably not truly understanding a bit of what he was saying at the age I was then. "But have you kept up with what's been going on out there since?"

"A little. You can't have Myrtle Johnson for a cousin and not have a pretty good idea of what's going on in the Skookum. And she tells me those hippies out on the creek have stirred up quite a fuss."

"Them and the loggers," Myrtle said, cackling. "Not sure which is worse."

"It must have made you sad to hear about everything burning down out there, Mr. Johnson," I said. "You having roots that go so deep on that land."

Johnson smiled wryly, shaking his head. "Oh, the cabins that burned . . . they didn't have anything to do with our family. The hippies built those. And the old homestead's still standing. I drove out there yesterday. The place is a little overgrown, but the house my great-grandfather built, the one we used for family reunions and such, it's still there. Looks pretty good, too."

I must have looked puzzled. Myrtle broke in and explained. "The Johnson place isn't anywhere near the hippie meadow, Tom," she said. "We were way over on the other side of the property, with a road that climbed up from the main highway. Big lawn. Great view of the Sound and Mount Rainier."

"A beautiful old place," Terry Johnson agreed. "Gramps built the original out of old growth harvested right there. Wish I could have seen the inside again. The fireplace is gorgeous, built of river stone taken right from Rush Creek."

"Didn't you at least peek in?" Myrtle asked.

"No," Johnson said. "That would have been a bit presumptuous. It was already late, and there was somebody there. Smoke was rolling out of that old river-stone chimney."

* * *

The Dodge purred as it rolled up U.S. 101, the afternoon sun sparkling off the calm Puget Sound waters spreading off to my right. Marvin Dervish had the old wreck running like a well-tuned chain saw. I resisted the urge to light a Marlboro and inhaled the fresh air rushing in the open windows.

I slowed when I passed the country store just north of Cutthroat Creek, just as Terry Johnson had told me to, and spotted the gravel drive leading into the woods on my left. I zigzagged up the hill, the Dodge kicking up a cloud of dust, and drove onto a cracked asphalt drive that curved across an expanse of long grass and daisies. The meadow must once have been the vast lawn that Terry and Myrtle described. On the far side stood a large log cabin—a lodge, really—with stone pillars and old-growth timbers enclosing an imposing porch. No smoke from the chimney, of course—the bright sun had pushed the temperature to nearly eighty.

I pulled in behind a rattletrap Ford pickup with rust spots on the fenders and a missing tailgate. The identification marks on the nearly bald left-rear tire were almost illegible, but I licked my thumb and rubbed it across faint patterns of raised rubber. The letters and numbers that emerged spoke volumes: Goodyear. Inflate to 35 pounds. LT235.

The door stood open, and tinny rock 'n' roll drifted out. I thought of my dad's .38, still hidden under the apple crate next to my bed, and wished it were tucked into the hip pocket of my jeans. Suddenly on high alert, I stepped up to the door and hollered into the gloom inside. "Yo! Anybody here?"

No answer.

I shouted again.

Still no answer.

I stepped inside and looked off to the right, where sunlight streamed through old sash windows into a living room dominated by the magnificent river-stone fireplace Terry Johnson remembered so fondly. The room was empty except for a broken-down couch propped up against one wall atop pieces of cordwood. Next to the couch sat an old boom box, the source of the driving heavy metal I'd heard from the porch. On the couch sprawled Arnie Dykes. Empty cans of Olympia lay scattered on the floor in front of him. In his hands was a pump-action twelve-gauge, its barrel pointed at my chest.

"Well, well, well," Arnie drawled. "If it ain't the asshole newspaperman. Still nosing around where he don't belong."

"Hello, Arnie. I kind of thought I might find you out here."

"What's it to ya, asshole? This here's Rush Creek land, and I got every right to be on it. You got none."

"Look, Arnie, you don't need to worry about me. I just wanted to ask you a few questions. How about you point the pump at the floor?"

"Don't want no questions from you, asshole," Arnie said, waving the barrel of the twelve-gauge in the direction of the front door. "Just haul your big-city bullshit right on outta here and leave me be."

"I've been looking into what happened to your brothers. I figure you must want whoever did that caught pretty bad. We're on the same side."

"We ain't never gonna be on the same side, asshole."

"Just take it easy," I said, holding up a hand with the palm out. "I'm from here. I knew your brothers."

"Fuckin' football star. College boy. Guys like me, they didn't exist for guys like you. So just save the old-buddies bullshit and beat it."

Arnie moved the barrel of the shotgun in a slow circle. Then he continued. "You ain't even workin' for that chickenshit rag in town no more," he said. "Got no cause to be askin' questions about nuthin'."

I tried the tactic I'd used on Don Dykes, explaining how useful my investigative skills might be. But Arnie cut me off. "Jesus! You just don't fuckin' get it, do ya? You just ain't wanted here. How fuckin' clear does the message got to be? Nobody says nuthin' to you. Your place gets trashed. That goddamn wuss fishing pole you use to wave bugs around in the air gets busted. Christ! What's it take?"

I stood there dumbfounded. It was Arnie Dykes who had vandalized my apartment. Burning with old resentments and feeling threatened by God knows what, this paranoid little tweaker had taken my grandfather's fly rod and viciously snapped it over his knee.

Arnie shook the shotgun. "Now git!"

I opened my mouth, but before a word could come out, the room shook with a deafening blast as Arnie put a load of birdshot into the ceiling. Dust and pieces of plaster rained down into the space in front of me. Arnie jacked another round into the chamber, and the ejected shell rolled across the floor.

Without saying another word, I turned and headed for the front door. Quickly.

*   *   *

It took three beers at the Spar to wind down from my encounter with Arnie, and the stairs in back of Benny's felt steeper than usual. I paused on the landing, lit a Marlboro, and leaned on the railing. It was nearly ten, but summer twilight still filled the sky. I took another deep drag. My plan to cut back on smoking gradually wasn't working—if I had smokes in my shirt pocket, I lit up whenever I felt stressed or out of sorts. I vowed to quit entirely . . . when the time was right.

I climbed the second flight of stairs, pushed through the balky door, and spotted the glowing red light on my answering machine. I twisted the knob to "playback," and Sandy's voice, pocked with static, filled the room. "Hi, baby," she said. "I felt bad about the way things went yesterday, and I thought we should talk about it. Call me. Please."

I wasn't exactly a fountain of self-awareness in those days. But looking back, I can see a little deeper into the resentment I felt when I heard the well-meaning message. Sandy's constant pressure to move up and move on grated on me. I was embarrassed about Tacoma, and I worried that the same thing would happen in Bellevue, derailing Sandy's plans. I wanted space to sort through my own conflicted feelings about Bent Fir, the *Echo*, and the ambition that had driven me so far from home.

I picked up the phone and dialed. Sandy answered on the second ring. "It's me," I said, my voice flat and noncommittal.

"God, it's good to hear your voice. When can I see you?"

"When were you thinking?"

"How about tonight?"

"It's a little late."

"The Officers' Club bar is open till two."

* * *

The Dodge hummed along the highway. By the time Angel Harbor appeared below me, the sky had turned a deep indigo, and the village lights carved a sparkling arc around the little bay. I slowed at the Cedar Springs guardhouse, told the Marine I was meeting Lieutenant Harper at the O-Club, and was waved on through.

She sat on a stool by the windows that looked out onto the bay, the place we'd perched on our first date. It was past eleven, and the small sailboats lined up with military precision on the dock marched one by one into the darkness. She looked up with a half smile as I slipped onto the stool next to her. "Hi," she said. "I'm glad you could come."

"Yeah, me, too," I said, not sounding much as though I meant it. I waved across the room at the bartender.

"Anything wrong?" she asked.

"Nah. Nuthin's wrong. What makes you say that?"

The bartender strolled up. "One of those," I said, waving a hand toward Sandy's glass, nearly empty.

"It's Jack," she said flatly. "And I'll have a refill."

We sat silently, looking at each other while I fidgeted on my stool.

"Tom, I'm sorry. I know I put a bad end to yesterday. You just wanted to do something fun, and I got way more uptight than I should have." She paused and looked into her empty glass. "I spent all day thinking about why I was that way, and I'm still not sure."

She swirled the ice cubes around in her glass. "I think it's just that those awful Barracudas reminded me of the women I worked with on the line at the packing plant," she said, a little frustration slipping into her voice. "So small-minded and ignorant. So small-town. Everything I've wanted to get away from since I woke up to the big world around me."

The bartender returned to the counter and set two glasses on the table, the ice tinkling. Sandy wrapped both hands around her glass and looked down into it. The bubbles and fractures in the ice cubes caught the amber light filtered through the bourbon.

I took a long pull on the Jack Daniel's. "C'mon, Sandy. Those women are good people. You don't need a damned college degree to give something to the world. The sailors, the chiefs . . . their families. There'd be no O-Club like this if it weren't for them. There'd be no country, for Christ's sake. And the Skookum's full of good people just like them. They work hard and take care of their families. We get to do what we do because they do what they do."

Sandy settled back on her stool and looked out the window. The moon had risen above the mouth of the bay, and a shimmering ribbon of pale light ran right up to the Officers' Club dock. "Well," Sandy said, "you'll make a small-town newsman yet. Next thing you know, you'll be going to Rotary and organizing the Fourth of July parade."

I stared into my drink. "Bent Fir doesn't have a Fourth of July parade."

Sandy drained her glass. "Maybe you could get one started. Write a letter to the editor or something."

I finished my bourbon, too. "Yeah, maybe," I said, rising.

"Don't go. Have another drink. Then maybe we could go for a ride." She gestured toward the bay. "Let's go back up to that place we parked that time. We can look at the moonlight."

"Some other time. I'm beat, and I need to get some sleep. I'll give you a call. We'll figure something out for the weekend."

I turned and walked toward the door, wanting a smoke.

35

I wheeled off Oyster Bay Road and pulled in behind a line of cars and pickups that filled half the length of the driveway. A shiny new Pac-West motor home stood on the concrete pad in the late-afternoon sunshine, balloons dangling from every piece of exterior hardware. Men clutching bottles of beer stepped in and out of the open door and poked around in the cab.

I walked into the buzz of voices in the living room. My father sat in his corner recliner, surrounded by old townies. My mother hovered over a table of hors d'oeuvres in the dining room. Dad looked up, saw me, and motioned toward the kitchen. "Cooler's on the counter. Get a beer and join us."

I worked my way through the gaggle of women in the dining room, greeting each one with the smiles and nods and personal updates that Klahowya County etiquette required. I stepped into the kitchen, headed for the cooler, and pulled up short. Marion Mayfield leaned against the counter, sipping from a highball glass and talking to Myrtle Johnson. I stopped and stood there stupidly. Myrtle turned, saw me, and excused herself.

I practically stammered. "I didn't expect to see you here," I said lamely.

"Why not? The editor of the *Echo* could hardly pass on a retirement party for the postmaster. Besides, I was invited."

She looked me in the eyes, saying nothing. Then Dad's voice boomed over the buzz in the living room. "Listen up, everybody," he said. "I've got a little announcement to make. C'mon out here, Phyllis."

Marion and I stepped out into the dining room and watched Mom hurry to Dad's side. She turned back to face us, looking a little embarrassed. Or maybe the color in her cheeks had simply been missing since I'd been home. Her face looked fuller. And she was beaming.

"It's been more than a month since my lovely bride went through her last chemo," Dad said. "Last week, she had a PET scan. Everything looks completely clean. The doc says she's in total remission."

Dad stepped back, turned to face Mom, and put a hand on each of her shoulders. "No two ways about it," he said, "this was damned tough. But my girl never complained once. You're the bravest person I know. And I love you."

He bent forward, kissed her on the lips, and gathered her up in a crushing hug. The room broke into cheers and applause.

Benny Brill leaned forward on a folding chair. "So," he said, grinning, "you're cashin' in our tax dollars and runnin' out on us, eh? Leavin' the Skookum."

"Not leaving," Dad said. "Just dodging a little Skookum rain, that's all. And after thirty years of lifting catalogs for fishing tackle and hardware on your account, you owe me the tax dollars."

Benny laughed and lifted his beer bottle. "You got that right, old man," he said. "Just don't forget where you came from."

"I'm still working for another month," Dad said. "Then we'll fire up the motor home and head down Arizona way for a spell. Back for Christmas. Then we'll see. Next summer, it's up to Alaska for salmon. We'll park 'er right on the Homer Spit."

Marvin Dervish harrumphed on the couch. "Everybody's leavin' the Skookum. Marty gone. Mitch is headin' down the road. Now you. Ain't gonna be nobody left."

"I'm left," said Jimmy Winthrop. "And I'm staying. I'll get my loan, and you'll all see how smart I was. The new marina's gonna do great. New folks coming in, what with the new subs and all. Seattle people, too. One of the old cabins south of Angel Harbor sold last week."

"The county's changing," Dad said. "That's for sure. We see it down at the PO. Lot more government checks coming in. Old families gone. The loggers. The fishermen. New names on all the routes. But you know, the volume of mail's actually up."

"With what?" asked Marvin Dervish. "Eviction notices?"

I looked at Marion, still standing next to me. "Like to go see Mom and Dad's new motor home?" I asked.

She took a sip of her highball. Paused. Then finally looked me in the eye. I thought she was about to tell me she'd already seen the PacWest or make some other excuse.

"Sure," she said.

* * *

With the party rolling inside, the motor home was empty. Marion and I glanced around and made insincerely polite comments on the EZ Boy decor. Then she dropped onto the plaid sofa, took another sip of her drink, and said, "So . . . you're sorry."

"I don't know what I was thinking. You had every right to can me."

"You've got that right," she said, nodding at the other end of the sofa and motioning me to sit. "And it was all so unnecessary. If you'd just asked me about freelancing a piece, we could have worked something out."

I settled onto the sofa. "I can see that now. But—I don't know—I was just feeling so cramped and frustrated. All I was thinking about was myself. The chance at some big-time ink. I couldn't see anything else."

Marion nodded, considering. She looked away from me, across the center aisle, and out the big window opposite. I glanced in the same direction. Oyster Bay and the open water of Puget Sound beyond were achingly blue. Clouds scudded across the summit of Mount Rainier.

"Well," Marion said, "I wish you'd thought a little straighter. I was getting used to having you around. And the *Echo* was a better newspaper when you were part of it."

She turned back toward me. "Besides," she said, "I could use some help."

Pain showed in the set of her mouth, the cast of her eyes.

"What's wrong, Marion? What's going on?"

"It's hard," she said. "All the layoffs. The ad linage is way off. Chesty's getting panicky, and he's talking about cutting the press run to sixteen pages. I'm having a hard time coming up with stories that aren't all doom and gloom. And I've got a conflict of interest on our main news story and don't have anybody to cover it."

She stood, crossed the aisle, and looked out the window toward the Sound, her arms crossed. I sensed that she had more to say.

"What's going on with Lars?" I asked.

She stood silently. Finally, she sighed deeply, turned back toward me, and lowered her arms. "He never sobers up anymore," she said. "He just disappears into himself and broods. And drinks. And broods some more."

She lowered her arms. "Dennis came over last night. I thought

229

maybe Lars would snap out of it some, with his little brother and all. Denny's always been his favorite."

I sat quietly, waiting.

"They ended up screaming at each other. They broke things. I went into the bedroom and locked the door, hoping he wouldn't try to get in."

"What did they argue about?"

"The business. The crew being out of work. And Lars not doing anything. Not bidding any sales."

I leaned forward and put my hands on my knees.

"And Hal's gun."

I stood up. "What gun?"

"Some gun Hal had," Marion said. "From the war, I guess. Anyway, it must have meant something to the boys. Denny and Lars flipped for it after the funeral. Lars won."

"A rifle?" I asked. "A shotgun?"

"No," Marion said. "A pistol. A big black pistol. 'The automatic,' they call it. Denny said, 'Where's Dad's automatic?' Lars told him to fuck off."

"I thought Lars won the toss."

"He did. But Dennis was all excited about it for some reason. He just kept at him. He wanted the automatic. I couldn't hear Lars saying anything, from there in the bedroom. Then the screaming started. And throwing things. And Dennis stormed out of the house."

*   *   *

Sandy Harper hauled on the halyard, and the mainsail climbed up the little sailboat's mast. The breeze caught the sail, I cranked the tiller, and the boat slid away from the Officers' Club dock. Sandy, barefoot and dressed in tight white shorts with a sleeveless striped top, cinched the halyard to its cleat and grabbed its counterpart on the jib. A couple of months earlier, my eyes would have been glued to Sandy's pert little bottom. But by then, I had begun to notice how she posed for me, constantly making sure she was the center of attention.

She finished the figure eight around the jib cleat and dropped into the cockpit. "I love this stuff," she said. "Whoever thought a girl from the Willamette Valley would turn out to be a sailor? A *real* sailor. On a sailboat, for God's sake!"

"Coming about," I said. "Hard a lee." The little Catalina daysailer wheeled upwind, and Sandy stooped under the boom as it swung across the cockpit. The sails filled, the Catalina heeled over, and I joined Sandy on the port gunwale, leaning out to counter the force pushing to starboard. Sandy giggled with exhilaration. "You're doing pretty well," she said, appraising the wake boiling out from behind the boat. "We're really moving."

The sun, the sails, the blue water and spray—the setting should have exhilarated me. So why was my mind everywhere but in the moment? I jumped from one fragmented thought to another and found nothing that held me for more than a second or two. The old structure of my mind had broken apart. Things were shifting around, bumping up against each other, and nothing seemed to fit with anything else.

I plotted a course for the narrow Angel Harbor entrance. If the Catalina was going to clear South Point and get into the open channel, we needed more sea room. "Comin' about," I said again, pushing the tiller to starboard. Sandy released the jib, and we ducked under the swinging mainsail boom just as the wind sagged and almost died. The turning bow slowed and then stopped entirely. A sudden gust caught the mainsail full on the beam, the Catalina heeled over, and the boom came swinging back the other way, catching me upside the head. I fell into the bottom of the boat, torn loose from the tiller, and the boat righted itself, swirling in the breeze with the sail flapping. Sandy jumped to the tiller and brought the boat back into a quartering wind. I sat on my butt, my hand to my aching head.

"Hey, sailor!" Sandy shouted over the hiss of water and wind. "Nicely done! You're some kinda yachtsman."

I deserved the sarcasm. Guys who grew up in the Skookum during my day learned powerboats, what real sailors call "stink pots." All I knew about sailboats was the little bit I'd learned at summer camp. Still, I resented the criticism.

I motioned Sandy aside and took the tiller again, drawing a bead straight for the harbor entrance with the wind directly astern. The bow hissed up the waves and made soggy impact in each trough, spray pulsing over the bow. Sandy slid off the gunwale and onto the bench ringing the cockpit. "What's up with Bellevue?"

"Interview next Tuesday."

"You're cutting it close," Sandy said, scooting closer. "I move at the end of October."

"You're assuming I'll get the job."

"You're a shoe-in. Since when does Bellevue get a reporter with your experience?"

"Or my baggage."

"Oh, Tom. Nobody fired you in L.A. You quit. And from what I hear, the *Journal-American* is a fine little paper. That won't count against you there."

"I blew an A-1 story. I embarrassed the *Times*. For all the *J-A* editor knows, I'm the kind of reporter who puts the blinders on when he's on the trail of something too good to be true. A reporter who can drag his paper into expensive libel suits and hassles with the government. What sane editor wants that?"

"A good one," Sandy said, reaching back and cupping her hand over my knee. "A brave one."

"How good is a guy who blows it at a paper with a circulation of more than a million and then manages to get himself fired at one with a circulation of three thousand."

Sandy didn't want to hear it. "Think about how much fun Seattle will be," she said, scooting even closer to me. "The restaurants. The clubs. Museums. Shows. We can go dancing. To concerts."

"Yeah," I said, "a lot more nightlife than the Spar, the Griz, and the O-Club, that's for sure. On the other hand, you don't just grab a fly rod and run off to the Tak. Or," I said, my eyes locking on hers, "pull off the road and throw a blanket on the ground."

The Catalina suddenly shuddered, and a scraping sound reverberated through the hull. Sandy whipped around, and I snapped my head up. South Point loomed overhead, the bluff only a hundred yards away. Waves broke over boulders not twenty yards ahead.

I pushed the tiller to starboard, and the boat heeled sharply to port. But it was too late—the centerboard bounced in its housing as it crunched along the rocky bottom. The boom lurched and threw us against the downwind gunwale just as the centerboard smacked sideways against a rock on the bottom. The wind pushed against the sail, our weight lowered the boat's port rail to the waterline, and the rock held the centerboard motionless. The Catalina heeled over, and we somersaulted into the water. The mast came over after us, carrying the mainsail with it. The hull came to rest on its side, half submerged. Cushions, the bailing pail, and the picnic basket bobbed in the water. We worked our way back toward the boat, grabbed the hull, and looked at each other, water streaming down our faces. My foot found the rock that had flipped us, and I pulled myself to a chest-deep standing position.

"Got to watch where you're going, bub," Sandy said, laughing.

I felt that flash of resentment again. "Neither one of us was paying attention," I growled.

Sandy dog-paddled around the boat, collecting debris. "Don't worry about it," she said. "The water's not so bad."

Not yet, I thought. But by the time we hauled the Catalina ashore, bailed it out, and gathered all the gear, we'd be cold and tired. And then we had to tack upwind all the way back to the club.

It was going to be a damned uncomfortable trip.

36

The clock radio read 10:30 when I pushed the door open, stepped into the dark room, and spotted the glowing red light on the message machine. Sandy again, I figured. "Aw shit," I grumped to the empty room. "What's she want now?"

I flopped onto the bed, activated the machine, and sat up with sudden surprise as Marion's breathless voice filled the room. "Tom," she said, her voice rising. "Tom! You've got to get out here. Quick."

* * *

A sheriff's office cruiser idled in the Mayfield driveway, the red light revolving on the roof and spinning a band of color around the wall of dark firs that circled the place. Light filled every window in the sprawling one-story house, and the front door stood open.

I walked into the hall and paused outside the parlor, which Hal Mayfield had long ago turned into the office where he kept his accounts and calculated his timber bids. A deputy stood at a rolltop desk, his back to me. He pulled scraps of paper from one of the pigeonholes in the back of the desk and examined them. "What's up?" I asked.

The deputy jumped and turned. Paper fluttered toward the floor, and his right hand hovered above his pistol. He recognized me and relaxed.

"Oh, it's you, Tom. How are ya?"

He cocked his head toward the back of the house. "Marion's in the dining room."

I turned and continued down the hall. Marion sat at the big May-field family table by herself, her hands cradling a glass filled with clear liquid. She looked up. "They arrested Lars. They read him his rights and led him out. In handcuffs. Sheriff Hasslebring himself did it."

She raised the glass and took three quick gulps. I sat down in the chair next to her, reached out, and covered her hand with mine.

"Tom," she said. "The sheriff . . . he said Lars was charged with murder."

The grandfather clock in the Mayfield entry hall read 2:20 by the time Marion downed her fourth vodka and ran out of things to say. Dottie Mayfield came to fetch her, taking her by the elbow, raising her from the dining-room chair, and leading her off down the hall toward the bedroom. "You'll be goin' now," Dottie said over her shoulder as she disappeared into the dark hallway.

At first, Marion had been shocked, disbelieving. "Eddie and Terry Dykes!" she said, elbow on the table, her eyes closed, and her forehead pressed against her fist. "That's what the sheriff said. 'Lars Mayfield, you're under arrest for the murder of Eddie and Terry Dykes, on or about Tuesday, August 4, 1981.'"

She raised her head and looked at me. "Tom, he was so formal. It was like he didn't even know Lars."

"Did Lars say anything?"

"Not a word. He just hung his head and let Walt lead him out of the house."

Marion asked me what would happen next. I filled her in on felony arrests, how Walt Hasslebring would press forward with an interrogation that night unless Lars refused to talk and demanded a lawyer, how an arraignment worked, the pleading options Lars faced under Washington State law.

"But Tom," Marion asked, "how can this be? Why would Lars do anything to the twins? He got along fine with those boys, hung out with them."

I explained links between the Dykes boys and the log-rustling scheme. And the links to Lars. "I don't know exactly what happened, Marion. A deal like that . . . lots of things can go bad."

Marion took it all in, punctuating her questions with slugs of vodka, processing the information and nodding, as though pieces of the puzzle that had been Lars were falling into place. I could see that she was gradually coming to accept the idea that Lars might indeed have been involved in the murder of the Dykes twins. She stared down at her glass, her brow furrowed, trying to take it all in.

"Marion, forgive me, but I have to ask you this. You know the gun that you mentioned when we were at my folks', in the motor home?"

She looked up again.

"Do you know what kind of gun it was?"

"The automatic? I told you that before. Denny and Lars, they just called it 'the automatic.'"

"Did you ever see it?"

"Sure. I even shot it once. Lars wanted me to. He set up some beer cans out back and showed me how to cock the thing. It was heavy, it made a huge noise, and it kicked back against my hand something awful. I hated it. And I never shot it again."

"How did you cock it?"

"You pulled back on the top of it. The slide, I think Lars called it. Then you let it go and it slammed forward, and that loaded the bullet."

She was, I realized, talking about a semiautomatic, not a revolver. But I asked another question, just to make sure: "And when you pulled the trigger, did you have to cock it again?"

"No. It just cocked itself. You just kept pulling the trigger until it was empty."

I told Marion about the gun Walt Hasslebring had shown me, the rusted slug of metal the state patrol divers had fished out of Scatter Creek. "That was the gun that killed Eddie and Terry, Marion. The state crime lab matched the bullets."

"And you think that was the automatic, the gun I fired?"

"There's no way to tell for sure that it was Lars's gun," I said, reaching out and taking her hand. She dropped her head again.

"But it was," she said, so softly I could barely hear her. "Wasn't it?"

* * *

I was still zonked the next morning, dreaming about an L.A. traffic jam, when I dimly realized that the honking I heard was coming from the parking lot in back of Benny's, and not the San Diego Freeway. I glanced at my clock radio—8 a.m.—groaned, rolled out of bed, and peered out the window. In the middle of the dusty gravel lot was Walt Hasslebring's big green Chevy cruiser. The sheriff himself stood just outside the open driver-side door. He spotted me in the window. "Git yerself down here," he hollered. "I ain't climbing those goddamn stairs."

I pulled on my jeans and descended, tender-footing it across the sharp gravel toward Hasslebring. "Don't you own no goddamn shoes?" he asked, hands on his hips while I slowly approached.

"You're up early," I said, "for a man who was up all night grilling Lars Mayfield."

"Ain't been to bed," Hasslebring said. Then he thought about my question and asked, "But what makes you think I been grillin' anybody?"

"That's what cops do, in my experience. Did Lars demand a lawyer? Or did you smooth talk him into spilling his guts?"

"Never you mind about that," the sheriff said. "You got more immediate concerns."

I stood there, trying to ignore the gravel gouging my feet and wishing I'd brought my Marlboros down the stairs with me.

"Just stopped at the Shell," Hasslebring continued. "Was kinda wondering what in the hell's happened to Arnie Dykes. Figured Hank mighta seen him."

"Yeah, had he?"

"You know goddamn well he had," Hasslebring said sharply. "But he ain't seen him since before you come in askin' about him, which kinda left me wondering what truck you got with Arnie Dykes anyhow."

"I suppose I might ask you the same question," I said, desperate, by then, for that Marlboro.

"I suppose you might," Hasslebring said. "And in good time, you might get an answer. But for now, you might want to be worrying about something else."

I cocked my head and looked at him silently.

"Old Hank Potash," Hasslebring continued," he told me somebody else was in askin' about Arnie. Couple a days after you."

"Yeah, anybody we know?"

"Nobody Hank knew. But old Hank, that boy's got a pretty good eye. I asked him to describe this fella, and he comes across with a description good enough for an FBI poster."

Hasslebring paused, reached into the pocket of his wrinkled uniform shirt, and pulled out a White Owl. He apparently planned to go through the whole ritual of clipping and lighting the thing before he told me what was going on.

"So what are you getting at, Sheriff? Did this description mean anything to you?"

Hasslebring paused, his cigar clipper in one hand and the White Owl in the other. "Oh yeah," he said. "I know the man, all right. Might actually be on an FBI poster for all I know. Oughta be, by all rights. Feller goes by the name of Roy Hammer. And I figure you probably come across his tracks with all the pokin' around you been doin'. That right?"

"Sure. Pretty hard to miss those tracks. But I can't help you find him, if that's what you're asking. Last I heard anything about him, he was in Tacoma, running a meth cook in the Hilltop."

"Well," the sheriff said, "he ain't in Tacoma no more, as is god-damned obvious. But more to the point, he's not just tryin' to run down Arnie Dykes."

"Oh?"

"That's why I hustled my butt on over here, instead of headin' right for bed where I oughta be," Hasslebring said. "Because Roy Hammer was also askin' Hank Potash about you. About why you wasn't at the *Echo* no more. About whether you had family in the Skookum. About where in the hell you lived. And I figured all that was something you oughta know about right away."

* * *

Benny Brill put both hands on his glass counter and leaned on them. Under the glass, on either side of him, a couple of dozen pistols stretched out on a shelf covered with red velvet. Rifles and shot-guns stood upright against the wall behind a locked chain running through their trigger guards. Next to the long guns, shelves held hundreds of cardboard boxes containing enough ammunition to kill every deer, elk, duck, and Canada goose in the Skookum.

"So what kind of .38 rounds you want?" Benny asked. "What kind of slug? What kind of load?"

"Geez, Benny. I don't know. My dad gave me his old revolver. I just thought I ought to get some practice with it. That's all."

Benny turned back to the shelves of ammunition. He came back with two boxes, put them on the counter next to his cash register, and said, "No use spending more for target practice." Then he bent over and reached down under the counter. When he rose, he had a sheaf of heavy paper targets in his hand, each the size of a small poster and carrying the stylized black silhouette of a man. "The targets are on the house," he said. "They're designed for twenty-five feet. Put six in the black at that distance, and you'll be shooting good enough." He plucked a small plastic bag off a display board standing next to the register and put it on top of the targets. "Wear these ear plugs, too. Get to be my age and you'll wish you'd done a better job of protecting your hearing when you were young."

I paid Benny and threaded my way back through the dense aisles lined with fishing rods, camp gear, paddles, anchors, and every other imaginable outdoor item. I went around back, climbed the stairs, and retrieved Dad's revolver. Twenty minutes later, I was in the county quarry out past Henry Logan's, hanging one of Benny's targets on a battered stump splintered by hundreds of earlier practice rounds. I stepped off ten paces, turned back toward the stump, and aimed. Dad had taken me out shooting a few times, and I knew I was supposed to squeeze, not jerk, the trigger. But the first round went at least six feet wide, pinging off the rocks and raising a little puff of dust. I flinched my way through a box of cartridges, eventually winging the edges of the target a few times.

When the box was nearly empty, I set up a new target and focused on my breathing as I tried to stay absolutely calm while I squeezed off the last six rounds. It was my best effort yet—I hit the target three times. But not one was in the black.

37

Marion's hair hung limply around her face, ragged strands askew. Her eyes looked sunken, dead. She slumped in her desk chair, leaning forward with her elbows on her knees, her hands clasped. Chesty stood next to her, his hand on her shoulder. "C'mon back," he said, gesturing to my old chair. I pushed through the swinging gate and sat. Chesty pulled his own chair over to face me and dropped into it.

"Marion and I have been talking," he said, his voice steady and hard. "This is one hell of a situation, and she's convinced me that there's only one way to handle it. But I'm not happy about it. And I want to make one thing perfectly clear. You were way out of line when you pulled that shenanigan with the *Times*, and I have never for one minute regretting canning your ass."

Chesty's eyes bored into me, implacable. I wanted to look away, but I did my best to keep my eyes fixed on his. "I understand," I said. "And I think you did the right thing."

Chesty's head twitched back a fraction of an inch, his eyes widened slightly, and his features softened a bit.

Marion raised her head and spoke, her voice raspy and tired. "Tom," she said, "we have a huge story on our hands. It's probably the biggest news in the history of the *Echo*. And I'm totally conflicted out on it. There's no way I can write a word about Lars, Hal, the twins . . . anything."

"I've got to admit that you know the story better than anyone," Chesty said. "No way we can get anybody else in here and up to speed in time to do anything with it.

"Besides," he said, tossing one hand in a gesture of concession, "no outsider is gonna get a handle on this thing. Our readers, they're only gonna take this from somebody who understands the Skookum like a native."

"Walt Hasslebring's called a press conference for this afternoon," Marion said. "We'd like you to cover it for us."

I looked back at Chesty. In the silence, the sound of the Regulator's slowly swinging pendulum filled the office. "Yeah," he finally said, his voice still heavy with reluctance and resignation. "I gotta admit that the *Echo* needs you. Marion needs you. Hell, *I* need you. So we want you back. Full-time. Just like before."

"Chesty," I said, "thank you. You won't be sorry."

Chesty grunted and looked away. I turned to Marion and asked her what time the sheriff's press conference started.

* * *

Reporters jammed Walt Hasslebring's office. The AP woman from Olympia sat dead center on the sheriff's old couch, flanked by the Shelton radio guy and the police-beat veteran from the *Olympian*. The Seattle reporters, both print and broadcast, were there, too, standing against the back wall and crowded around me in the wooden chairs ringing Hasslebring's conference table. A camera crew knelt in the corner, lights glaring and foam-swaddled microphone pointed at the sheriff.

Hasslebring seemed unaffected by the attention. "Here's the deal," he said, perched in his usual press-conference position on the edge of his old oak desk. The TV camera, an old film model, began to roll.

The sheriff scanned the packed room through half-lidded eyes and launched his spiel. "Last night, we arrested a suspect in the murder of Eddie and Terry Dykes," he said. "The accused is Lars Mayfield. He's thirty-six years old, has lived in Klahowya County all his life, and is president of the Mayfield Logging Company."

Hasslebring paused and looked around the roomful of faces. "But all that stuff—with spellings and such—is on the poop sheet. What I really want to point out is that this here concludes a three-month investigation by this office. Far as I know, it's the most extensive investigation in the history of Klahowya County. In all, we talked to more than a hundred potential witnesses, conducted multiple sustained searches for physical evidence, and consulted the experts at the criminal laboratory operated by the Washington State Patrol on three separate occasions.

"Klahowya County can be proud of the professional work done by the deputies employed by this office." He crossed his arms. "Any questions?"

Hands shot up, and several reporters spoke at once. Hasslebring nodded to the rumpled journalist from the *Olympian.* "Go ahead, Gus," he said, raising a hand to quiet the rest of the room.

"What we're all wondering," the gray-haired veteran said, "is why? What's the motive here anyway?"

The sheriff turned his head to a lean middle-aged man sitting in a wooden chair a few feet to his right. Hasslebring raised an eyebrow. The man, wearing a three-piece blue suit and highly polished wingtips, stood. He stuck his thumbs into the side pockets of his vest and spread his feet.

"Our theory," he said, "is that Lars Mayfield believed the Dykes brothers murdered his father, Hal Mayfield. And that Hal Mayfield's murder was proximate to an illegal conspiracy that involved both Lars Mayfield and the Dykes boys.

"The motive," the blue-suited man continued, "was revenge."

One of the Seattle reporters asked the speaker to identify himself. "Excuse me," Walt Hasslebring interjected. "This here is Spencer Morley, Klahowya County district attorney."

The Seattle reporter, an intense man in a baggy sports coat, stood and barked crisp questions at Morley. He clearly was a police-beat veteran, experienced in big-city crime.

"When's the arraignment?" the Seattle man asked.

"This afternoon," Morley said. "Before Judge Brinton."

"And what's the official charge?"

"Aggravated murder."

"Because there was more than one victim?"

"That's right," the district attorney said. "Last fall, the legislature mandated that any homicide with more than one victim constituted aggravated murder. So that's what we're charging Mr. Mayfield with."

"The death penalty, eh?"

"That's right, too. In view of the Supreme Court's ruling last year and the new legislation, the people are entitled to ask for the death penalty. And we will."

The room stirred, the print reporters bending over their notebooks, scribbling the DA's exact words. Copy desks might fiddle with the phrasing, but Morley had just written the headline that would run above every one of their stories.

The buzz died down, and the questions continued. But no, Morley wasn't about to reveal the details of the conspiracy that brought Lars

Mayfield and the Dykes boys together. And no, Sheriff Hasslebring had nothing to add about the physical evidence that had led him to his conclusions. And no, the reporters would hear nothing about why he thought Lars believed the Dykes brothers had killed his father.

"Let's just say," Morley concluded, "that we consider the murder case involving Hal Mayfield closed. You can draw your own conclusions from that, but you'll have to get the particulars at trial."

*   *   *

Marion sat at her desk, her eyes following me as I pushed through the swinging gate and settled into my chair. "Anything new?" she asked, her voice empty.

"Not much. Morley says he's going for the death penalty. But that's what we figured. What else could he do?"

She sat silently, staring out the window. She sucked in a deep breath and said, "We can't let my involvement in this whole horrible mess affect how we cover this. In any way. People here need to believe they're getting it all. And that they're getting it straight. You understand?

"You should do a sidebar on the family," she added. "A history. What the Mayfields have been to the county. The outfit. All the jobs. You should mention me, how I'm connected to the paper."

"Let it all hang out, you mean."

"Yes. Let it all hang out. Don't let anybody accuse the paper of holding anything back. And let's get it done tonight. We can still make tomorrow's press run if we gut it out. I've already told Harris to stay late."

She stood and took a couple of shaky steps toward the door. "I'm going home," she said. "I'll get cleaned up, I'll go see Lars, and then I'll get back here. I'll take care of all the inside stuff while you handle page one. I'll leave you an open page of jump space."

The screen door slammed after her. I leaned back and stared at the ceiling, thinking about my story.

Everybody already knew about the arrest, I figured. So maybe I should skip the "Klahowya County Sheriff's Office has announced" hard-news lead. Tell the whole thing as a story. Start with the bodies in Cutthroat Creek. The look and feel of the place. Follow the investigation. Fuzz up some of the physical evidence, like the tire tracks, that might screw up the DA's case but stick to the chronology and the scenes. The Dykes place. The storage yard the twins had hidden in the woods. Give readers an inside view they wouldn't get anywhere else.

I walked over to the counter and fired up the Mr. Coffee.

*   *   *

Mitch Martin stood in the first Thriftway checkout line, leaning against the cash register. "Hey, Tom," he said, looking uncharacteristically serious. "You got the only hot item in the whole damned store."

The other two cash registers were unmanned. Big gaps separated the canned and packaged goods on the shelves, and the store looked like a house in mid-move. I shifted the heavy bundle of newspapers to my other arm and paused. "A murder charge against Lars Mayfield isn't exactly the way I'd choose to sell newspapers. But it's sure moving 'em. We ran an extra eight hundred, and this is the last of them."

"At least," I added, "your ad's getting out there, too."

Mitch shrugged. "For all the good it'll do. I advertise beefsteak, and all anybody's got money for is macaroni and cheese."

I took another dozen steps to the publications shelves against the front wall. The *Echo* was down to three copies. I dropped the bundle on the floor, cut the strapping tape, and lifted the papers onto the pile. It was my third Thriftway run that morning.

Myrtle Johnson, brilliant in a flowered blouse and bright purple slacks, pushed a grocery cart out of a center aisle and spotted me. She left her cart standing on the linoleum and bustled over. I turned, and Myrtle reached out to take me by the shoulders. "Oh, Tom," she said. "How's poor Marion?"

"Shaken," I said. "But she's tough. She was in the next day, helping get the paper out."

"Imagine that. Her own husband arrested for a thing like this. And she's right back at it. She really cares about the *Echo*, doesn't she?"

"I guess she does. She thinks it's about the only thing holding this town together. And I suppose she's right."

"She is. She certainly is. Nobody around here knows how much we owe her."

244

"So what are they saying?" I asked. "What's the word in Angel Harbor?"

"Everybody's kind of in shock, I guess," Myrtle said. "Everybody knew Lars was a loose cannon. But nobody expected him to do anything like this."

"About Marion? What are they saying about Marion?"

"I don't guess anybody but feels sorry for the poor girl. People talk, sure. Especially around here. But I don't see how they could hold any of this against her. Or dare to tell me so."

"Thanks, Myrtle," I said, bending to pick the strapping tape off the floor. Myrtle patted my back and turned toward her cart. "Myrtle," I said, "what brings you here? Don't you usually shop in the Harbor?"

"Yes," she said, glancing back over her shoulder. "Yes, I do. But I reckoned Mitch could use the business.

"And," she added, "he has this terrific special on beefsteak."

38

September light streamed through the Palladian window in the courthouse stairwell and filled the space with the burnished glow of old-growth fir. I climbed to the third floor, headed down the hall, and stepped into the district attorney's office. Anna Morley, the DA's plump daughter, looked up from behind a clutter-free reception counter and put down a paperback book. "Tom Dawson!" my old classmate said, brushing a lock of limp auburn hair off her forehead.

"Mornin', Anna," I said with a courtesy smile. "Your dad in?"

"Sure," Anna said, bouncing awkwardly to her feet and gesturing to the door next to her. "Go on in."

Spencer Morley's wingtips protruded from the kneehole of his oak desk. He pushed aside a stack of pleadings and waved me into a chair. "Thanks for coming. This is really your story, and I thought I'd give you a little head start on the city papers."

I popped a ballpoint out of my shirt pocket and waited, pen poised, wordless. Morley would say what he was going to say without any prompting from me.

The DA pushed his gold wire-rims up his nose with a long, bony finger and spoke slowly, carefully. "We've cut a deal with Lars Mayfield. He's pleading guilty to murder one, two counts. We've agreed to ask the judge for a sentence of life with the possibility of parole after twenty years of good time."

I looked up from my notebook. At the press conference, Morley had blown smoke about the death penalty. And Lars, after all, had plugged the Dykes boys in the backs of their heads, them on their knees in the dirt. An execution, plain and simple. So what was with Morley? Did he lack the brass necessary to hammer a prominent local family? Was he afraid to spit in the eye of the Klahowya County sense of frontier justice? Or did he maybe have his reasons?

I stifled any hint of surprise in my voice, summoning up the tone of flat neutrality I'd learned by tagging along with the old investigative pros at the *Times*. "What made you decide to settle for twenty,

Mr. Morley?" I asked quietly. "Initially, you indicated this was a death-penalty offense."

Morley paused. He pushed back from the desk and scooted his wheeled chair around so that he could face me directly. "Let me say something for publication about that, okay?"

"Of course."

"And then I'll explain it off the record. Walt Hasslebring says I can trust you. And that's good enough for me."

"Go ahead," I said, embarrassed about feeling flattered by anything a public official said. "Let's just be clear about what's what when it comes to ground rules."

"Okay. Officially—meaning you can quote me on this word for word—the district attorney's office recognizes that state law allows the court to take 'extreme provocation' into account during the sentencing phase of trial. We further recognize that Lars Mayfield, thinking that Eddie and Terry Dykes were responsible for the death of Hal Mayfield, was emotionally disturbed in the extreme. Had the case gone to a jury, most local citizens probably would have recognized the impulse that moved Lars to do what he did. Which of us wouldn't want revenge on the men who killed our father?"

"But," I said, working to coax another on-the-record quote out of the DA, "Lars has confessed to first-degree murder. And murder is murder."

"Murder is murder," Morley said, looking down and pausing. "But the law recognizes that motives for murder may differ. Therefore, punishments for murder may differ. Lars Mayfield will serve a long time for his crime. But he won't die by the state's hand for it."

Morley pushed his chair back behind his desk, reclined, and relaxed. I leaned back, too. "Is this sort of like the temporary-insanity plea?" I asked. "Like what jealous Texas husbands use to beat the rap when they shoot their wives' lovers?"

Morley smiled. "Off the record?"

"Sure. Off the record."

"And what do you mean by that?" Morley asked. "When I say 'off the record,' I mean you can't use it. Period. I don't want this credited to some 'high county official' or some damned thing like that. Everybody in town will know who that is."

I smiled. "Nope. When I say 'off the record,' you'll never see it in print unless I get it from somebody else on the record. If I'm going to use it and attribute it to a high county official—or whatever—we'll agree on that in advance, and we'll agree on the job description I'll use. 'High county official' or 'person close to the investigation,' or whatever you say. That's the way I work."

"Fair enough," Morley said. "You'll get a lot out of this courthouse that way. And, yes—off the record—extreme provocation is pretty close to temporary insanity. A cuckold would use the same argument to save himself from the hangman's rope."

I stood. Closed my notebook. Walked to the door, reached out, grabbed the knob, and asked the Columbo question, the one the seedy television detective always used to produce results when the subject thought the interview was over and let his guard down.

"So what about all the death-penalty stuff at the press conference?"

"Still off the record?"

"Yeah, still off the record."

"You play poker?"

"Some."

"Stud poker?"

"Sure."

"Well, if you're gonna bluff a hand, you don't show the card that's gonna bust your straight first. You come on strong."

"Thanks, Mr. Morley. I kinda figured that at the time."

"Tom."

"Yes."

"Off the record, mind you."

"Yessir."

The door clicked shut, and I headed back down the hall, puzzling over the interview.

Morley, it appeared, had some brains and balls hovering above those wingtips. Not like the weasels filling county cubicles in L.A. All glances over the shoulder, those guys. All flicking lint off their cheap suits, hoping they didn't break any rules, didn't attract any attention, and didn't leave the office so late they got stuck in freeway traffic.

I paused on the stairwell landing and looked out the Palladian window. Sun sparkled on the Big Skookum. An old pickup rattled across the bridge. I shook my head. Morley and Hasslebring. How in the world had Klahowya County managed to elect those two?

I pushed through the heavy courthouse doors and headed up the street to the *Echo*. Marion heard the creak of the screen door when I walked in and looked up from her desk, a question in the tilt of her chin.

"He confessed."

"Why?"

"For twenty years. He can get out after twenty years."

Marion stood and walked to the counter. She leaned against it, facing me. "Then it's over," she said. "It's finally all over."

Chesty Arnold rose from his chair and stepped over to Marion. He put a hand on her shoulder. "Marion," he said, "get out of here. Go for a walk. Have a drink. Go home. Get some rest. Stay away as long as you have to. Tom and I will take care of things."

Marion turned and looked at him. Without saying a word, she walked over to her desk, grabbed her purse, turned around, and marched out the front door. "Nobody should have to go through what she's going through," Chesty said as her footsteps receded across the gravel, "least of all Marion."

I went to my desk and sat down, staring at the wall. "Tom," Chesty said, "there's something else you should know."

I swiveled around to face him.

"She's carrying plenty," he said. "I couldn't lay anything more on her. At least not now. But she'll learn soon enough."

"Learn what?"

"It's Mitch," Chesty said, his voice barely above a whisper. "Mitch says he just can't keep it going anymore. Can't pay his bills. Can't keep any stock in the store."

His voice thickened, and he looked down at the floor. "He's shuttin' down the Thriftway. Our last full-page advertiser is going goddamn bust."

"Aw," I said, "don't worry. We'll figure something out."

Chesty stared at me, his eyebrows raised. "Figure out what, Tom? How to print money? Don't you get it, boy? You can't publish a weekly newspaper without grocery ads."

He ran the palm of his hand up his forehead. "Ninety-two years," he said. "For ninety-two years, this paper's been coming out every Thursday. Never thought it would die on my watch."

* * *

I worried about Marion through the weekend. Finally, on Sunday afternoon, I picked up the phone and dialed her home number. Dottie Mayfield answered, recognized my voice, and turned surly. I asked for Marion, and the only sound I heard in return was the receiver thudding onto a hard surface.

When Marion came on the line, her voice sounded almost normal. "What's up?" she asked. "Do you need me at the paper?"

"No. Everything's fine. I was just worried about you. How are you doing?"

"I'm bouncing off the walls here. Dottie's in a foul mood, and the house is like a tomb filled with bad air. I'm thinking about going to the office, just to get a change of scene."

"You feel like talking? I could meet you."

"Sure. Thanks. That would be good. I'll be there in thirty minutes."

A half hour later, I walked past Marion's VW Bug and climbed the *Echo*'s front steps. The office door stood open in the warm September sun, and I walked through it to find Marion sitting at her desk, listlessly sifting through the Saturday mail. She heard me, looked up, and managed a weak smile. "Thanks for coming down," she said. "Dottie hasn't been much company. And I needed to break loose from everything that just kept going around and around in my head."

"No problem. You want to go somewhere? Get a drink at the Spar? Take a drive?"

"If we go to the Spar, everybody will want to talk. How about a walk?"

"Sure. Have anyplace in mind?"

"The beach. I want to smell some salt air."

We climbed into the Bug, drove through town, and parked at the first Oyster Bay turnout. The tide was low enough to expose some firm sand above the waterline, and we walked silently for a while, taking in the view. A bank of low clouds obscured the far shore, but the summit of Mount Rainier rose just above it.

Marion finally broke the silence. "I still can't wrap my mind around all this. You live with another human being. For years. You think you know him."

"Lars wasn't that easy to know."

"You're right about that, I guess. Maybe nobody ever really broke through to Lars. I guess I didn't. He was always off in the distance somewhere. I'd try, but I just couldn't get close enough to find the real man, to discover whatever was going on in there."

"Why did you stay with him?"

"I just don't know. Habit? Some warped sense of obligation? With no kids, it didn't make much sense, did it? What obligation?"

"Well," I said, "Bent Fir girls just got married. Maybe that's all there was to it."

"Maybe. I sure didn't think about it much when the baby was coming and Mom started making wedding plans. God, I wish I had."

We stopped and turned toward each other. "Women's lib took a long time to reach Bent Fir," I said. "You didn't have much in the way of role models for independent thinking."

"There were plenty of feminists at Lindley. I knew I had options. But, you know, sometimes little towns like this close in on you. You lose sight of everything else."

"No kidding. That's why I hightailed it out of here the first chance I got."

"It doesn't have to be that way. Only small-minded people make a small-minded town."

We resumed our stroll down the beach, climbing over a gravel bar that ran down across the sand.

"The newspaper makes a difference, I think," Marion said. "It can help people see the larger things."

"Like the Baptist bake sale? Wiener winks on the school lunch menu?"

Marion took my hand and pulled me to a stop. We turned and faced each other. She dropped her head an inch and looked at me with eyes angled up just a bit, mouth compressed in disapproval.

"Hey! I was just joking!"

"I know you were. I'm not that dense. But Tom, you wear your cynicism like armor. As long as you're skeptical and disapproving of everything, you'll never connect with anything. The town's in trouble. People are hurting. Everything that happens isn't just another news story, something that will give Tom Dawson's career a boost."

She grabbed my other hand and pulled me closer. Then she took a step forward and wrapped her arms around me. "What's the point," she said softly, "if you don't belong to some place?"

She rested her head on my shoulder.

"And to somebody."

* * *

I popped through the back-shop door first thing Monday morning to find Harris hunched over the Linotype, a cigarette dangling from his lips and his eyeshade casting a green light across his lined face. He read the pencil-edited copy that hung from a clip in front of him while his hands punched at the keys. The matrices clicked into position. Hot lead flowed into the forms. Slugs of fresh type dropped into the galley near his elbow. Eight lines a minute, steady as the journeyman he was.

I leaned against the windowsill next to the ancient machine, arms crossed. "You've worked at a lot of papers, Harris," I said. "What do you think of our chances?"

The old printer paused and looked up. "Whadda ya mean?"

"Our chances. Of keeping the *Echo* afloat. Since we lost the Thriftway account, I mean."

"Shit," Harris said. He snorted, taking his cigarette between his thumb and forefinger. "No groceries. No paper. Pretty simple, that."

"So what can we do about it?"

Harris turned back to his keyboard and typed a line. He paused again and looked back at me. "Not a damn thing, as far as I can see."

"So we're sunk?"

"I reckon."

"So what're you going to do?"

"Figure I'll be moving on."

"Where to?"

"Well," Harris said, turning on the Linotype stool, "ain't much call for a guy like me in these parts anymore. All the papers is goin' to computers and shit. These boys," he said, nodding toward the two Linotypes, "Christ—nobody running these old fellas anymore. They all been shipped south. Argentina. Brazil. Mexico."

"Yeah. So what are you gonna do?"

"This here," Harris said, "this is all I know. Reckon I'll go teach me some Mexicans how to run hot lead."

39

The expanse of fresh asphalt reeked of oil, but it was a welcome refuge. The Monday-morning traffic through Seattle and across the Lake Washington floating bridge had been a frantic swerves-and-nerves pavement panic straight out of L.A. I parked the Dodge and stretched up in the seat, peering into the mirror to tighten my tie. It felt awkwardly snug as I headed across the lot toward the Journal-American building, a suburban rectangle of steel and glass. Neckties and traffic, I conceded, were two urban irritants foreign to Klahowya County.

The newsroom lay up a set of open concrete stairs. A swinging metal door opened to the smell of stale coffee and cigarettes. A receptionist at a Steelcase desk pointed across the room to a windowed office along a far wall, and I walked past a half dozen cluttered cubicles to reach it. As I raised a hand to knock on the open door, a stocky, mustachioed man in shirtsleeves and a loosened tie looked up and grunted. "You must be Dawson. C'mon in."

The *Journal-American*'s managing editor had a good reputation around the Sound. Everybody I asked about him said he was a straight shooter, an aggressive newsman who'd kept the Seattle papers on the defensive while his little daily grew steadily with the booming eastside suburbs. The paper's circulation had climbed to more than thirty thousand, the local news staff had reached nearly three dozen, and the *Journal-American* was beginning to tackle ambitious projects that went way beyond routine daily news stories. Personality profiles. Feature takeouts. Even some investigative work.

The ME rummaged through the paper heaped on his desk, extracted the packet of clippings I'd sent him, and leaned back in his swivel chair, leafing through the collection of stories from the *Los Angeles Times* and the *Echo*.

"You've had quite a summer," he said. "Not many weekly reporters get a triple homicide, a major fire, and a mill closing, all in a few months. Not to mention the goat thing. Good little feature that."

Apparently, he hadn't heard the whole goat story. I breathed an inward sigh of relief and launched the interview bullshit—self-deprecating and self-aggrandizing all at the same time. "Well, it's a weekly. You get a little bit of everything. In L.A., I might have spent the whole summer doing legwork on a single story. Besides, we got lucky. Klahowya County had a boatload of news this summer."

"Yeah, well. I always figure a reporter makes his own luck."

Beyond him, through a dirty window, I could see one scraggly fir rising in the parking lot. The managing editor leaned forward, put his elbows on the desk, and rested his chin in his hands. "Now tell me," he said, "about this business in L.A."

I slowly exhaled, relaxed, and told the story in a voice as flat as I could make it. And I took full responsibility, admitting right out of the box that I'd been played for a sucker by an LAPD cop who knew how to play the game a lot better than I did. "No excuses," I said. "All I can say is that I learned a lesson. It won't happen again."

I stopped talking. A lone typewriter clacked away somewhere out in the newsroom. The ME steepled his fingers. "We all have to learn lessons like that," he finally said. "I don't know a reporter worth his salt who hasn't been snookered a time or two somewhere along the line.

"Besides," he added, "I'd just as soon have my reporters seasoned on somebody else's watch. A small daily like the *Journal-American*, we don't generally get young reporters with the kind of experience you've had."

"But that will change," he continued. "Things are going nuts over here, on this side of the lake. Growing like crazy. The *P-I* and the *Times*, the boat sailed without them. They've got strong little dailies on both sides of them, north and south, and us over here. They're bottled up downtown. Another ten years, we'll be kicking their asses. Circulation and advertising, too.

"We're gonna need guys like you. Guys who know how to dig. And how to write. Gonna be lots of good features here for a guy with good eyes and ears. Lotta interesting folks moving in here. Doing interesting things. A guy like you could make a splash here. A lot bigger splash than you can make at some podunk weekly."

I stiffened, surprised by my own reaction to the offhanded slur. I felt color rise in my cheeks and sat upright in my chair. "Look," the ME said, "I have to run all hiring through the editor, and he has to take any budget stuff to the publisher. Looks like we've got a little recession brewing here, and things are tightening down. But we've been hiring pretty steady. I'll get back to you in a week or so."

The ME stood, and so did I. We shook hands across the desk. "You'd be a good fit here," he said. I turned, silent, stepped out the door, and worked my way through the cubicles. They looked dark, cluttered, and cramped.

The smell of fresh asphalt filled my nostrils when I reached the parking lot. The image of Myrtle Johnson clutching her Angel Harbor dispatch at the *Echo*'s front counter suddenly filled my mind. Yep. Pretty podunk, all right. Pretty goddamn podunk.

* * *

"Geez," I said, stepping onto the rocky beach. "Will you look at this?"

The state Department of Fish and Wildlife agent, saying nothing, plodded ahead, his boots crunching on barnacles. I followed, my boots crunching, too. After Don Dykes ribbed me for my Hawaiian shirt, I'd dumped my entire California wardrobe—sandals and all— into the Salvation Army box outside the Thriftway.

My eyes darted back and forth, surveying the carnage.

"What are they?" I asked.

The F&W man stopped, turned, and disconsolately shoved his hands into his pockets. "Blackmouth," he said. "Chinook salmon that never leave Puget Sound. They're about six months old. Most of 'em probably came from the Minter Creek hatchery."

I stopped, pulled out my notebook, and turned slowly in a circle. Dead fish, each the size of a large herring, lay scattered across the rocks and gravel.

"It's a damned shame," the F&W man said. "We get 'em this far, the battle's about won. Nothing can touch 'em now except seals and killer whales. Maybe a big cutthroat. And fishermen, of course. It's gonna be a dry year in the South Sound."

"How many do you think there are?" I asked.

"We figure at least ten thousand," the Fish and Wildlife man said. "They school up down here in the late summer. Lots of bait fish collect here in the bay."

I walked on by myself, jotting in my notebook. Tuesday's storm had blown through, and Budd Inlet sparkled in the September sun, unsullied blue stretching to Olympia's industrial waterfront on the far shore. The dome of the state capitol rose in the distance.

I squatted to examine one of the fish. A beach crab the size of a dime skittered over the little chinook. The salmon was still relatively fresh, and its moist scales refracted the September sun in glittering rainbow colors. "What caused this?" I asked.

"Dunno for sure," the F&W man said. "Not disease, that's for sure. No disease kills ten thousand fish in one fell swoop."

"So some kind of poison then?"

"That's about right. Could be something from the mill in Shelton, I suppose. Those folks have pretty well done in the oysters. But my money's on sewage."

"Sewage?"

"Yeah, sewage," the F&W man said. He pointed across Budd Inlet. "One of Olympia's big storm-sewer outfall pipes runs into the bay right over there."

"But you can't just dump sewage in the Sound."

"Not straight out of the sewer system, you can't. But storm sewers dump the runoff straight into salt water. And for the most part, that's okay. Problem is, most cities have a combined system. A big rain, like yesterday's, exceeds capacity. Raw sewage floods into the storm sewers. And it ends up here."

"Geez," I said. "So this happens all the time?"

"Yeah, well . . . mostly in the winter. We don't often get a gully-washer like yesterday's in late September, when these guys school up down here.

"But it's getting worse," he added. "Tacoma, Seattle, Olympia"—his hand arced through the air toward the north—"hell . . . they're all growing like some kind of big fungus spreading along the east side of the Sound.

"And they're killing it."

* * *

The Selectric keyboard stared back at me. I'd opened with a scene-setter, describing the expanse of rotting chinook salmon on the Budd Inlet beach. That was the easy part—I just lifted the image that still burned in my mind and dropped it onto my copy paper. But deadline loomed, and the rest of the story was coming hard. I reached for a cigarette, and then restrained myself.

It was time to get serious about giving up the coffin nails.

The flunky I'd talked to at the Olympia Water Board had flatly denied that any sewage overflow had taken place, and I still wasn't entirely clear on how the city's sewage system worked and exactly where the outlets ran into the Sound. The public information officers at Fish and Wildlife hedged their bets, refusing to specifically blame anyone without hard proof. Nobody along the Olympia waterfront had much to offer, and nobody in the state environmental offices was returning my calls. Five o'clock had come and gone, and all the bureaucrats had left work.

I sat in the *Echo*'s little newsroom alone, pecking away. The old Hoe press turned in the morning. But before it could, Marion would have to edit what I produced, Harris would have to set the type, and we'd all have to reconfigure the front page and the jump page. And to turn up the heat just a little bit more, Sandy was expecting me for a drink at the Officers' Club.

The phone rang. The head water guy from the Washington Department of Ecology. He'd checked his messages, thank God, and was calling from home. Yeah, he knew all about the Olympia combined system, and the outfall in Budd Inlet. He'd cited the city multiple times for raw sanitary-sewage spills in the bay. How many? Wasn't sure.

"Is it okay to quote you on 'multiple'?"

"It's 'multiple,' all right," the DOE man said. "Just spell my name right."

Bingo!

Just after I closed out the phone conversation, the door pushed open and Marion stepped in.

"Sounds like a great story. You need some help?"

"Geez," I said. "Yeah. Thanks. Wasn't sure you got my message. Got a call in to Harris, too."

"So what do you have so far?"

I handed her my first take. Marion took the sheet of copy paper, stepped back, leaned against the counter, and began to read. I watched her face for a reaction.

She looked up. "This is great stuff. How's the art?"

"Dunno. Haven't even souped the film yet. I've been trying to get through to the Olympia water honcho."

"I'll take care of the film. We're going to need it if we're going to hold the center of page one with this."

"It's still in the Roly."

She pulled the Rolleiflex out of my camera bag and rewound the film as she walked toward the darkroom. She stopped, turned to look at me, and gave me the first real smile I'd seen on her face in nearly a month. "This newspaper isn't dying," she said. "We'll get through this. Because this"—she held up the camera—"is what we do."

She stepped into the darkroom, and I mulled over what she'd just said. Obviously, she knew about Mitch and the Thriftway. And, presumably, she knew that Chesty thought the prognosis was terminal. So why the big smile? But before I could get any further with that thought, the phone rang again. I grabbed the receiver and spoke. "Echo."

"This Tom Dawson?"

"Yup."

"This is Martin Milstein. Olympia Water Board. Got your message."

I told him what I'd seen, and what the man from the Department of Ecology had said.

"I'm not gonna deny it," Milstein said. "We've had an inch and a half of rain in the past thirty-six hours. We didn't check to make sure, but that almost guarantees sanitary sewage in the storm sewers."

"And that means raw sewage in the Budd Inlet outfall?"

"If it's in the storm sewers, it's in Budd Inlet."

"And the fish?"

"Don't know about the fish. That's F&W's business, not mine. They say we killed 'em, then we killed 'em."

Milstein continued: "But I do know this much. This damned jury-rigged system is way overloaded. We been saying that for years. Voters have rejected two bond measures aimed at doing something about it. They just want to flush it and forget it. So don't blame my guys. Blame them."

"Can I quote you on that?" I asked.

"Damned straight. You can quote me on anything. This system was built for half the people who are using it now. And it was built when nobody worried about what they dumped into the Sound. I'm tired of this crap—no pun intended."

"Thank you, Mr. Milstein. What's your official title again? And would you please spell your name for me?"

The front door pushed open again, and Harris stood there, his face expressionless. "You got something going?"

Marion stepped out of the darkroom, holding a fresh print. "Harris," she said. "Good to see you. We're remaking the whole front page. And we're holding the B&B feature on A8 to clear out some jump space."

Harris said nothing. But I thought I saw a faint smile as the old printer walked through the swinging gate, brushed by my desk, and stepped smartly toward the back shop. Marion handed him the print as he passed. "Get going on the halftone for this," she said. "Make it six by six. And warm up the Linotype. I'll have the first take of my copy to you by the time it's ready."

Harris turned at the back-shop door, the print fluttering in his hand. "Somebody maybe gonna give me a new page dummy?"

"Five minutes," Marion said. "Just get going on the halftone."

"Yes, ma'am," Harris said, with mock deference. "I guess this here must be one of them newspaper places I been hearin' about."

40

Sandy sat at her place at the counter that spanned the picture window, nursing a Jack Daniel's and gazing out past the overturned sailboat hulls stacked along the Officers' Club dock. I paused for three heartbeats in the middle of the bar and admired the glow of her blond hair against the twilight blue of the bay. Then I stepped forward and slid onto the stool next to her. She turned and smiled. "Hiya, Mr. Newspaperman. I was about to give up on you."

"Sorry," I said. "Turned out to be a pretty damned good story. But we had to tear up the whole paper to shoehorn it in." I signaled to the bartender, pointed to Sandy's drink, and held up a finger to show that I wanted one, too.

Four young lieutenants gathered around the Pong game in the back corner of the bar broke into laughter. The jukebox hummed, clicked, and launched a Moody Blues song. The bartender walked over with my drink. Sandy raised hers, we touched glasses, and we both sipped. "So," Sandy said, "have you heard from Bellevue?"

"Yeah," I said woodenly. "The managing editor called me this morning."

"And?"

"He offered me the job."

"That's terrific, honey," Sandy said. She raised her glass and held it out, expecting me to meet her in a toast. I didn't move, and Sandy looked at me quizzically. "Why aren't you happy? What's wrong?"

I put my drink on the counter, turned on the stool, and faced her directly. "Sandy, I turned him down. I'm not taking the job."

She pressed her lips together, shaking her head. "You're not taking the job? But, Tom, it's just what we wanted. What are you thinking? What will you do?"

I sat silently, looking out past the dock toward the bay. Mount Rainier still glowed faintly against the night sky.

"I was afraid of this," Sandy finally said. "You've changed, you know. You've gone off someplace where I can't quite reach you."

I took a stiff belt of my bourbon. She did the same.

"So what are you going to do here in Podunk, Washington?" she asked.

That word again. I felt the same unexpected rush of irritation I'd felt in the *Journal-American* newsroom. My cheeks flushed with color, and I practically barked at her. "I'm going to be a goddamn Podunk, Washington, newspaperman."

"Remember when you kept calling this a 'shit-hole excuse for a town'?"

"Yeah. I know," I said, settling down. "Nowheresville."

"Seattle's not so far," she said, looking down into her drink. "We could still see each other on the weekends."

"I'm not so sure that would be a good idea."

"Maybe not," she said. "But ending everything now doesn't seem right."

"Look, Sandy. It's me, not you. You're a terrific woman."

"Just not terrific enough for you?"

"Not that. But, Sandy, a lot's happened to me. Things that didn't make sense . . . well, now they do. Or at least they're starting to."

"We don't seem to want the same things anymore," she said.

"No," I said, "we don't."

"I got out of one small town. And I sure don't intend to end up as a housewife in another one. There's a whole world out there, and I mean to see it."

"And you should."

"Something sure happened to the guy I met last spring."

"I'm sorry," I said, "but I'm afraid something did."

I stood, turned, threaded my way through the officers who'd filled the bar, and walked out into the parking lot. The Dodge started on the first crank and powered smoothly up the hill. The Marine at the gate snapped a smart salute, and then I was out onto the Angel Harbor Highway, unwinding the big V-8 with all four windows rolled down and the night air rushing in.

* * *

Little Jim's Chevy pickup lurched into a deep rut, and I slammed against the metal door. "What if I bought the shocks?" I asked, my voice laced with sarcasm. "Then would you at least mount them on this piece of shit?"

261

"Putting shocks on the Lone Ranger here," Little Jim said, patting the rusted dash, "would be like putting a dress on Tough Tony Boren."

I laughed, imagining the notorious Northwest wrestler tricked out in a flouncy prom outfit. "He could work a tag team with Gorgeous George," I said, bracing myself as the Chevy skidded to a stop on fresh gravel. Two dozen cars and pickups were parked haphazardly around a large lot recently cleared from the fir and cedar. The Takamak flowed by beyond them, rolling languidly around a large bend with the unhurried pace of low autumn water.

I felt buoyant. Clearing the air with Sandy had given me a strange, unexpected sense of release. And the announcement we were about to hear was the first unadulterated good news the Skookum had produced all summer.

We climbed out of the pickup and headed toward the small crowd gathered at the river's edge. Freddie Bangs saw us coming, broke off his conversation with a Fish and Wildlife officer, and turned toward us, hands on hips and smiling broadly. "Big day," I said, pulling my notebook out of my hip pocket. "You've been working a long time on this."

Freddie eyed the notebook. "It's a big day for the Takamak Tribal Council," he said. "The elders showed great vision when they backed this project."

I smiled, whipped a ballpoint out of my shirt pocket, and dutifully jotted the pro forma pronouncement into my notebook: Bg dy 4 + Tk Tb Cncl.

"Yeah," said Little Jim, punching his cousin in the shoulder. "You can always count on a Tak to show up when there's a free fish in the neighborhood."

"How's this going to play in your paper?" Freddie asked.

"Page one. Above the fold. Best news we've had in quite a while. A new hatchery. A dozen jobs. Restoring an important fishery. The chance to bring in fishermen from the outside. And some outside money, too. Geez. That's the kind of news we need. You bet we'll put it on one."

The F&W officer who'd been talking with Freddie earlier stepped up, shook hands with me and Little Jim, and suggested it was time to get the proceedings under way. Freddie climbed to the top of a three-foot-high gravel bar, raised his arms, and asked for the crowd's attention. The conversation died, and the murmur of the river replaced it. Freddie, poised and practiced with the kind of Seattle gloss seldom seen in the Skookum, picked his way through a long thank-you list of local dignitaries. He pointed up the riverbank, and the crowd turned to look as he described the rearing ponds and adult holding pens that would be producing chinook salmon smolts and sea-run cutthroat trout by the following spring. Then he introduced Charlie Satlebanks, the eighty-two-year-old tribal chairman, who scrambled up on the gravel bar.

I usually let my pen rest during official speechifying. But I found myself writing down every word as Charlie spoke simply and beautifully about fish and the Takamak way of life. He recalled the first-salmon ceremonies of his childhood, when the Tak families gathered for the first spring chinook feast of the year. He compared the coming of the fish runs to a great clock that set the seasons and measured out the history of the tribe, generation by generation. And now, he said, the young men of the tribe would take the white man's science and produce the fish that would keep nature's great clock running forever.

When he finished, Freddie took his arm and helped him down off the pile of loose gravel. An F&W official climbed up onto the bar and made the obligatory comments about legislative committee chairmen, bureaucrats, and other political types. Then he thanked everybody for coming and declared the proceedings closed. I shut my notebook and scanned the crowd, looking for Little Jim.

A clatter caught my attention, and I turned back. Jimmy Winthrop's elbows pumped as he scrambled to the top of the bar, river rock cascading down behind him. He reached the top, spun around, and waved his arms above his head. "Hey, everybody!" he shouted. "Hey, everybody!"

The spreading crowd paused like a startled flock of mallards. Jimmy cupped his hands around his mouth. "We got a new marina on the way, too. Just got my check from the Hoodsport State Bank. New building. New floats. New everything. But I ain't waiting to start spending. Put in an order for twelve aluminum skiffs and twelve six-horse Evinrudes. Fishin' boats for the marina to rent. Catch all these fish this here hatchery's gonna produce. Tell all your friends."

He spread his hands wide, grinned a wide grin, and threw his head back. "The Big Skookum Marina's open for business."

* * *

I breezed past the Shasta daisies that had come in after the daffodils and banged through the *Echo*'s screen door. Chesty stood at the counter, leafing through the big bound volume of back issues and measuring ad linage with a pica pole. I pushed on through to the back shop, where Marion and Harris stood at the composing counter, arranging type in page forms. Harris spoke the ancient jargon of printers, and to him the marble-covered counter was a "stone." A page form was a "chase." The heavy table on rollers used to move a completed page form around the back shop was a "turtle." I'd learned some of the lingo when I'd worked at the *Echo* in high school. But Harris still sometimes sounded as if he were speaking a foreign language.

I picked up the galley that held the type for my press-conference story and started working my way through it, word by word. I'd never handled raw type before that summer, and the skill of reading upside down and backward came slowly to me. "You need a mirror?" Harris hooted. "Shit! What kinda newsman can't read type?"

"The kind who works at newspapers where union guys in the composing room take care of all that bullshit. You want my help or not?"

I held the galley out toward him in one hand, motioning as if I were about to toss it. Harris flinched. Dropping a galley and jumbling the type—compositors called it "pieing the type"—was a major back-shop faux pas.

"Don't need no help," Harris huffed. "Little Maid Marion and me have got things well in hand. At least we do unless you pie that type. You'll need a goddamn mirror then."

"What are you up to this morning?" Marion asked.

"Dunno. Figured I'd wade through the releases. See if anything's worth a look-see. Maybe drive out to Henry Logan's. Find out if there's anything new from the Navy."

I walked back to the newsroom and saw Chesty strolling down the front walk, headed out on his rounds. I fetched the news releases from the morning-mail basket and pawed through the pile. The Do-Se-Do-ers were headed to Spokane for a square-dance convention. A red tide had closed clamming in Totten Inlet. The Boy Scouts were collecting newspapers. Nothing that deserved anything beyond a listing in the Community Briefs. I grabbed the Rolleiflex and headed for the door.

Marion stepped into the newsroom. "When will you be back?"

"I'm just going to Logan's. Should be back by noon."

"Great. The sun's glorious. Maybe we can have a picnic."

41

Marion looked up and smiled as I bounded through the front entrance. Chesty's desk was empty, the door to the back shop closed.

"Well?" Marion asked.

"Ha! Old Henry's turned the tables. After the Navy legal eagles announced they weren't pressing charges, Henry saw a Shelton lawyer. Now he's demanding ten grand from the Navy. Harassment, slander, violation of his property rights—the lawyer threw everything he could think of into the demand letter."

"Henry Logan might have ended up in prison. He should count his lucky stars and leave well enough alone."

"It's a lot better story this way."

"I bought a couple of sandwiches at Thriftway," Marion said, rising from her desk. She wore a yellow summer dress that came to just below the knees. Bare legs, I noticed, nicely tanned.

"You can tell me all about Logan on the way to our picnic," she said.

"You were serious, eh? Where?"

"You decide," Marion said. She picked up a white paper bag off her desk, stepped to the open front door, adjusted the cardboard clock hanging in the window, and turned back to me, her head tilted toward the front porch. I shrugged, smiled, and walked out, glancing back at the clock as she pulled the door shut behind us. "We'll Be Back . . ." it said. And Marion had set the big plastic hands for two o'clock.

We drove east on Front, and I swerved into the parking lot behind Benny's. "We'll need a blanket."

I was up and down the back stairs in seconds, a ragged Pendleton clutched in one hand. I headed out the Angel Harbor Highway and turned right onto a narrow dirt track just before Cutthroat Creek. The car bounced along the rutted road, brush scraping against both sides. It broke out into a meadow that stretched to a low bluff overlooking the Sound. The water sparkled; Mount Rainier rose above a shrinking bank of clouds in the distance.

"Hmmmm," Marion murmured. "Pretty."

"An old homestead," I said. "We used to ride bikes out here when I was a kid." I extended my arm out the open window and pointed at three twisted trees along the meadow's edge. "You can still get good pie apples here in the fall. And you can still see what's left of the house and barn over there," I said, pointing to a pile of gray lumber lying flat in the grass.

We sat cross-legged on the Pendleton under one of the apple trees, munching the sandwiches. Marion stared at the mountain, lost somewhere in her thoughts. "It's been a rough month for you," I said. "But now things can start sorting themselves out."

The words finally penetrated to wherever her mind had drifted, and she slowly turned to look at me. Her eyes scanned the meadow, and a tentative smile crept onto her face. "You know," she said, "some couple spent a lifetime here. Maybe raised some kids."

She gestured across the whole spread of the place. The meadow. The expanse of sparkling water. The mountain rising against the horizon. "And it looks as though they were a couple of romantics, too."

"You'd have to be," I said, "to get through a winter's worth of cold rain out here. No real shelter from the Sound. Wind and wet every day."

"Good excuse for a warm fire on the hearth."

"And two or three cords of wood each winter to keep it going."

"Twice warmed.

"Tom," she said, "would you ever think about staying in someplace like this? Making a life?"

A two-masted sailboat emerged from behind a distant headland, both mains and twin jibs filled and a frothy bow wave leading the schooner south. I watched it silently, my whole body relaxing into the sweeping vista. I turned back and looked at Marion, sitting expectantly.

"What kind of life? The *Echo*'s about to go under, and the town's not far behind. This view's hard to beat, but you can't eat it."

Marion looked out toward the mountain, and her eyes seemed to fix on the schooner, which heeled over sharply once it cleared the headland and found fresh wind. "The recession will end," she said. "They always do."

"Sure it will. But the old growth's mostly gone, and before long there won't even be any left to steal. The second growth isn't far behind, and what's left is so far into the high country that it will cost a fortune to get out. There's cheaper timber up north. Canada. Alaska. The mill's never coming back the way it was."

"Look at this, "Marion said, her hand sweeping across the vista in front of us. "The Northwest's growing, Tom, and here we sit, right in the most beautiful corner of the most beautiful piece of the entire country. They'll want to come here, all the high-rollers who will come skating out the other end of this recession. And there will be plenty of them. Seattle builds airplanes, and the world needs airplanes. All those new computer companies are set to take off. And China, Japan, Indonesia—they're all growing, too. Think of what that means for the ports. My God, Seattle and Tacoma will be shipping enough wheat and coal to build empires. If a penny on the dollar rolls down-hill to Bent Fir, the *Echo* will run thirty-two pages every week."

I stared at her, stunned into silence by this sudden flood of grand vision. I'd never heard Marion say anything that reached much beyond the Bent Fir Garden Club agenda, or maybe the prospects for a new squadron at Cedar Springs.

And she wasn't finished. "Bent Fir can make it," she said, "but the town has to get its act together, get a plan. We need a dozen Jimmy Winthrops. People willing to take a chance, to get ready for when things start coming back. And to make that happen, we need the *Echo* pointing the way."

She looked beautiful sitting there, her eyes intense, color filling her cheeks. A breeze tossed her dark hair around her eyes. "I've filed for divorce," she said. "Whatever there ever was between Lars and me was gone a long time ago. Everything that's happened . . . it just forced me to recognize what was right in front of me."

She shifted on the blanket and looked back out toward the moun-tain. "I found a little place down on the Skookum," she said. "An old summer cottage, right on the water. It's tiny, but it's enough for me. And I'm moving next weekend. Thank God. I don't think I could stand another week alone in that house with Dottie Mayfield. It's time to start a new life."

She turned back to me, reached out, and grasped my hands. "I talked to Chesty," she said. "He just needs a little each month to live on. That's all he ever wanted to take out of the *Echo*.

"Tom, he'll sell us the paper on a contract. And we can hold on until the town starts coming back. We can set the type ourselves if we have to. We can sell the ads. The building's paid for, and it won't cost much to run the paper without Chesty or Harris."

"But Marion," I said, finally catching up enough to actually say something, "you heard Chesty. The *Echo*'s losing money. He had a little to fall back on. But what are you going to do? Sooner or later, the paper will clean you out, and you'll have nothing. Nobody wants to buy a money-losing weekly."

Looking sobered, she turned her eyes back out toward the Sound. The schooner had run clear across the open expanse in front of us and was about to disappear behind the southern headland, apparently bound for Olympia.

"I'll get some money out of the divorce," she said. "I hate to take anything, especially now that everybody's out of work. But I've been putting my salary into the Mayfield family pot for a long time. I should get a little bit back, enough to keep the *Echo* afloat until things turn around."

I had no idea what to say. So I just leaned over and kissed her full on the mouth.

*   *   *

Marion stepped out of the Dodge onto the dusty grass. Around us, several hundred cars filled the field, distributed in ragged rows that stretched from the log barrier along the edge of the fairgrounds to the neighboring stand of scraggly second-growth fir. A Ferris wheel lurched to a stop near the main entrance, the upper cars swaying wildly and the teenage girls in them screaming in unison.

I stepped up to the ticket booth. The woman behind the counter, a laid-off checker from the Thriftway, recognized Marion standing behind me, looked back at my face, and recognized me, too. "Go on through," she said, tossing her head toward the midway.

"We're not working," I said, pushing two five-dollar bills toward her.

She shrugged, ripped two numbered tickets off the large roll mounted on a peg at her side, and said, "Raffle's at four, main stage in the arena."

269

We stepped onto the sawdust that lined the midway. The smell of freshly cut fir mingled with grilling burgers, frying onions, and sickly sweet cotton candy. We paused at a booth and watched ham-handed loggers cock their arms behind their ears and flog darts viciously at pink and yellow balloons.

I ordered cotton candy, and an acne-scarred teenage boy spun the cardboard handle in front of the ejection machine, collecting a halo of pink fluff. Marion held the handle gingerly and gathered the candy with her lips and tongue as we resumed walking. She slipped her free hand into mine. "You think that's a good idea," I said, "out here in public and all?"

"Oh the hell with it. I really don't give a damn. The divorce papers went in this week, and we'll have to run the notice in the courthouse agate this Thursday. Not that everybody in town won't know it by then anyway."

We stopped and turned to face each other, there in the middle of the midway. "Spencer Morley called me this morning," I said. "I was gonna tell you, but I didn't want to just spring it on you. The papers came through on Lars. He's out of the jail tomorrow morning. They drive him over to Walla Walla, to the penitentiary, to start serving his term. If you want to see him, you have to get there between seven and eight."

"I don't think so," Marion said, turning back down the midway and pulling at my hand. "That's done, too."

We walked on, past the last of the booths and into the shadow of the wooden arena in the center of the fairgrounds. Following the undulating whine of chain saws, we turned into one of the cavernous square openings in the weathered facade. The dark interior smelled earthy, and as our eyes adjusted, rows of produce displays emerged from the gloom, banked along the wall and carefully arranged in abstract patterns. Carrots, onions, and turnips crafted into landscapes. Pint boxes of berries arranged in complex geometric shapes. "Look at that," Marion said, pulling me along and pointing to one display after another. "This is my favorite part of the fair. So oldtimey. Close to the earth. Something the pioneers must have done."

We stepped into the arena, blinking against the blinding light and deafening noise. Four burly men crouched before sawhorses holding short lengths of log, bucking furiously with identical McCullough chain saws. The loggers pushed and pulled. The saw bars rose and fell. Cascades of sawdust poured onto their boots. And in seconds, rounds the size of serving platters fell from the ends of the logs, one an instant ahead of the others. The victor thrust his saw above his head, and the announcer's voice boomed over the public-address system. "Hey!" I said. "It's Stubby Lancaster!"

The old Mayfield logger climbed the steps to the awards platform, his McCullough still gripped in one hand. Marion and I made our way up into the stands and took seats on the wooden benches. "He's the one who roped up and went down the gulch to Hal's truck," I said. The announcer stepped out from his enclosure behind the rail, shook Stubby's hand, and presented him with a check. "Great!" I said. "Stubby can use the money. Those boys have been out of work for weeks now."

The announcer returned to his microphone. "Next up," he bellowed, "the toppers."

"This is *my* favorite part of the fair," I said. "These guys are the real bulls of the woods as far as I'm concerned."

The competitors walked to the center of the arena, where four sixty-foot fir spars stood ten feet apart. Each logger wore the caulked boots of his trade and staged pants roughly shorn off above ankle level so that no cuffs could ever get tangled and trip him. Each carried a long climbing strap hooked on one side of his belt. Each picked a spar and looked up, eyeing the top as though he were, in fact, working a real job in the woods. There, he'd climb to dizzying heights with a chain saw strapped to his belt and cut the top out off a tree so that it could carry rigging as a spar. The main trunk could snap back as the top broke free, hammering the topper grievously or even fatally. And big firs swayed wildly as the top cracked and fell, threatening to pitch the topper off. It was one of the most dangerous jobs in a trade made up of dangerous jobs.

"On your marks," the announcer shouted. Each topper stepped into place, looped his climbing strap around the spar in front of him and snapped it to the other side of his belt. "Get set," he continued. The toppers squatted and held their straps out in front of them, their wrists cocked. "Go!" The toppers looped the straps high up the opposite side of the spars and planted the climbing spurs they wore on their boots. Then they pulled themselves upward in one fluid motion. They lifted their knees, sank their spurs into the wood, straightened their legs, released the straps, and repeated the process in a synchronized motion that sent them almost running upward. In seconds, the first man reached the top, grabbed his saw, brought it roaring to life with a vicious tug on the starter cord, ripped through the top of the spar with a couple of bites that sent a round of wood flying off into space, and then started dropping toward the ground in long, arcing leaps that made just enough contact with the splintering wood to prevent total free fall.

The winner hit the ground. The crowd roared. The three other toppers thudded to earth one after the other like the beat of a bass drum. The winner unsnapped his climbing strap, whipped it free of the fir spar, and strutted through the arena, swinging it above his head.

I felt a sudden wave of sadness wash over me. I put my arm around Marion. "I'm afraid," I said, "that all this is done, too."

* * *

I walked along the woodsy path that led from Benny's to the *Echo*, stepped into the parking lot, and saw that Harris had backed his battered old Ford up to the back-shop door, where it sat with the trunk open. The wizened printer stepped out of the building, blinking in the morning sun, and shuffled toward the car, bent over a large cardboard box and squinting against the smoke curling up from the cigarette dangling from his mouth. I felt a familiar urge and reached into my shirt pocket for a smoke of my own. One Marlboro left. I crumpled the pack and stuck it in my pocket.

I lit the cigarette and walked up to the Ford just as Harris dropped the box into the trunk with a groan of relief. One of the steel pica poles the printer used for measuring columns of type stuck out of the box at an angle. A jumble of ink-stained aprons, green eyeshades, ashtrays, and other back-shop detritus filled the rest of the box. Harris straightened, one hand on his lower back. "I'm getting too old for this shit."

"Geez, Harris. I hate to see you go. Sure you won't hang around a while? We're gonna be in a helluva jam without you."

"Look, kid," Harris said, spitting onto the parking-lot gravel, "you and Maid Marion wanna piss into the wind, that's your business. The rain's comin'. I'm headed for sunny Meh-hee-co."

"Well," I said, "at least you picked a good day for it."

"How so?"

"Columbus Day. What better time to discover a new world?"

I walked back into the relative dark of the back shop. In the far corner, where dust motes swirled in shafts of sunlight streaming through the big room's little windows, I heard the hiss and click of a Linotype. A figure hunched over the keyboard.

I walked up behind Marion and watched for a silent moment as she punched awkwardly at the keys. They had a long throw, much longer than a typewriter's. The rhythm was different, too, slower and more broken. And operating a Linotype took forearm strength. The morning was cool, but sweat had beaded on Marion's forehead, matting curls of hair to her temples. She was pitched forward on the stool, jaw clenched and shoulders tight, intensely focused. The matrices clicked into place. The hot lead flowed slowly into the slugs.

She sensed somebody behind her, turned, saw me, and broke into a broad, moist smile. "Oh, Tom," she said. "I think I'm catching on. Three lines a minute."

I turned and walked out back just in time to see Harris drive out of the lot. After a deep drag, I flicked the Marlboro far out onto the gravel.

It was the last cigarette I ever smoked.

42

I shifted my eyes from my typewriter keyboard to the Regulator, ticktocking on the wall in front of me—10 a.m. With Marion and Chesty out making rounds, midmorning on a Tuesday was about as quiet as the *Echo* ever got.

I swiveled my chair toward the sound of the front door opening. Maxy Stewart stepped in and stood in front of the counter, his hair neatly combed and his cheeks glowing with healthy color.

"You're looking good, Maxy."

He grinned. "Feeling pretty good, too. Home cooking. Lots of sleep."

"I'm glad you've been able to kick, Maxy. Things weren't looking so good there for a while."

"Yeah, I know. Funny how you never think that'll happen to you, isn't it? But it's easy. Could happen to anybody, given the right situation. And it'd be easy to slip right back into that shit."

"Do me a favor and don't let that happen."

Maxy smiled again and scratched the top of his head with the shy absentmindedness I remembered from high school days. "Hey," he said brightly. "I'm just taking things one day at a time."

I nodded, and Maxy put both hands on the counter, leaning forward. "Anyway," he said, "I didn't want to leave without stopping by to thank you. You've been a friend. I haven't had that many of those around this burg."

"Leave? Where you headed?"

"Big Sur, I think, like I said. The pickup's all loaded outside. I'm heading down the road now—this is the last thing I'll be doing in Bent Fir. Guess I'll know where I want to be when I get there."

If I'd listened to my response, it would have told me something about the way I was headed myself. But at the time, it was just an automatic reply, something you say without thinking when somebody's moving on. "I'm sorry to see you going, Maxy," I said. "Be sure to look me up when you get back this way."

"Listen," Maxy said, ignoring the invitation, "there's something else."

I sat expectantly. Maxy looked down at the floor for a minute, exhaled, and then looked me in the eyes. "I want you to be careful," he said. "Roy Hammer's around, and he's in a mean mood. He found me at my folks' house Sunday. Got me outside and gave me a raft of shit. Wanted to know where he could find Arnie. He had a cold look in his eyes."

Maxy paused and looked up at the ceiling. "Jesus," he said. "I can't get that look out of my mind."

"You tell him anything?"

"Nah. I don't really know where Arnie is anyway, although I have some ideas. But Roy wasn't about to beat those out of me with my dad just inside, peeking out the window. Besides, Roy knows how Arnie comes and goes. He probably believed me."

"What do you think he'll do if he finds Arnie?"

"I don't want to think about it. But Arnie's got a lot of dumb luck, and he usually skates when everybody else is breaking through the ice."

"I don't have much use for Arnie Dykes. But I hope you're right about that."

"Tom, I'm more worried about you. Arnie's just a dumb fuck. The Hammer knows that. I suppose he has to deliver a beating or something, if he can. You know, just to send a message. But he knows you're not a dumb fuck. And he was asking lots of questions about you."

"What kind of questions?"

"You know. Where you live. Where you hang out. What folks you have in town."

"So what did you tell him?"

"Not much. I don't know where you live, and that's the God's truth. I told him you didn't have any folks around here, and I think he bought that. Why not? As far as Roy knows, you're from Bumfuck, Nebraska. Of course, he could ask somebody else who knows better. And if he does, he'll be more pissed at me, too. All the more reason for me to be moving down the road."

Maxy stepped back from the counter, gave a little wave, and turned for the door. When he reached it, he turned back.

"I don't have to tell you this," he said, "but Roy Hammer already knows you work here. It's what you do here that got him pissed off in the first place. So watch your goddamned back."

* * *

The next morning, I had a leisurely breakfast at the Spar before ambling up the street toward the *Echo*. I passed the vacant Thriftway, its windows covered with sheets of plywood, and stepped into Front Street to cross. A gray Navy sedan pulled out of the *Echo*'s lot, and the driver gave me an expressionless glance through her closed window as she slowly rolled by me.

What, I wondered, was Sandy Harper doing at the *Echo*? Looking for me? Guess not—she just drove right by me. Laying some trip on Marion? What would be the point of that? Sandy and I were finished. And what could she say that Marion didn't already know, in broad outline anyway?

I continued across the street, headed up the steps, and cautiously pushed the screen door open. "Tom," Marion said, "Lieutenant Harper just left."

I must have looked anxious. In any event, Marion smiled and shook her head. "Don't worry," she said. "This wasn't about you."

"Oh?"

"The lieutenant and I," Marion said, "had some business to discuss." She smiled enigmatically.

"Business?"

"The Navy," she said, sounding triumphant, "has decided to hire an outside printer for the air-station newspaper. Lieutenant Harper was thinking we'd be a logical choice."

"The *Echo*?"

Marion looked a little offended. "Why not? We have the equipment, we're close, and we're cheap."

I stood there wondering why Sandy would want to throw a bone to the *Echo*. Why help keep the joint afloat when the *Echo* was, in a sense, the jealous mistress who'd taken me away from her?

Marion jumped into the silence. "Lieutenant Harper seemed to think we were perfect," she said. "She's sending a sailor down with the official paperwork.

"They have to put every contract up to bid," she continued, "but we can beat anybody on price. Oh, Tommy! It's only eight pages,

276

2,500 copies a week. It's a piece of cake to run. And we'll clear more than Chesty ever did from Mitch's Thriftway ad."

She threw her arms around me and squealed.

*　　*　　*

The horn honked insistently in the *Echo*'s parking lot. I pushed out through the swinging door and stepped onto the porch. Walt Hasslebring leaned out the window of his big Chevy cruiser and motioned for me to join him, then he clenched his fist and pumped his arm up and down. "Double time!" he said sharply.

I turned back into the office, grabbed a notebook, shouted good-bye to Marion through the back-shop door, and ran out to jump in the passenger seat. The sheriff flipped on the cruiser's flashers, gave the siren one quick burst, and gunned the Chevy onto Front, spraying gravel. Tires squealed as he hit the pavement, and the Chevy's V-8 roared as he headed up the Longmont Grade.

"What's up, for God's sake? And please don't tell me 'All in good time.'"

"Well, seein' as how you're legit again, working at the *Echo* and all, and seein' as how this seems to be something to do with your story, I figured you might as well be going along."

"Going where? What in the hell's up anyway?"

"Goin' to the Dykes place. Sounds like old Don got himself all messed up again, and this time 'tweren't Maybell swinging a beer pitcher."

When we hit the main highway, Hasslebring floored it, and we must have been pushing a hundred when we caught up with the ambulance, its siren screaming and lights flashing. The sheriff slowed a bit, and we followed the medical crew as the ambulance turned onto Cutthroat Creek Road and into the dirt lane that led to the Dykes homestead.

Maybell and Moochie were kneeling over Don Dykes, who lay on his back in the dirt at the bottom of the front steps. Maybell held his head up. Moochie pressed a blood-soaked towel to his face. The sheriff and I hurried up and bent over Dykes, surveying the damage. His scalp had been laid open in three places. One blackened eye had already swollen shut. His upper lip was shredded, and he'd lost several teeth.

The emergency techs arrived with the gurney, but Hasslebring put his hand up, palm out, to stop them. "Just a minute, boys," he said calmly. He leaned a little closer to Dykes, putting a hand on Maybell's shoulder. "What happened, Don? Who did this to you?"

Dykes rolled his eyes up to look at Hasslebring, trying to focus. He finally spoke in a weak growl, sputtering spit and blood. "Big sumbitch," Don Dykes said. "Took a fuckin' ax handle to me. Just whaled on my fuckin' ass."

The sheriff leaned even closer. "What big son of a bitch? What's his name?"

"Dunno. Never seen the bastard before."

"What'd he want?"

"Wanted Arnie. That's what he wanted. Wanted my boy."

Hasslebring started to rise, but Don Dykes wasn't finished. "But never told him nuthin'," he said. "I never told him nuthin'."

* * *

I hadn't had a real talk with Walt Hasslebring since I'd lost my job at the *Echo*. I'd never been big on sharing information with cops, but the sheriff and I had been developing a decent working relationship when everything hit the fan. He didn't tell me everything. I didn't tell him everything. But when one of us absolutely needed to know something to avoid heading down the wrong path or embarrassing ourselves, we shared. So it was high time I brought him up to speed on everything I'd turned up working on my own.

Don Dykes had forced the issue in any event. What had just happened made it clear that Roy Hammer was a guided missile zeroing in on Arnie Dykes. And the Hammer wasn't the only thing pointing toward Arnie. Whenever I started digging around, Arnie seemed to pop up. So I could hardly hold back on my visit to the Johnson cabin and my little run-in with Arnie there.

"He confessed to trashing your place and fired a goddamn shotgun and you didn't come to me!" Hasslebring said sternly. "What in the hell did you plan to do? Wait until that psycho meth freak stuck a twelve-gauge right up your ass? Think you might pick up the goddamn phone and call me then?"

"Look," I said. "You've hardly been a Boy Scout when it comes to being straight with me. God knows how much time I wasted running down Rush Creek leads when you knew perfectly well that when somebody tampered with the Mayfield truck, Maxy and his buddies were either in Colville or cooling their heels in your little county hotel."

We both sat without speaking for two or three minutes while the Chevy barreled back down Cutthroat Creek Road. Hasslebring broke the silence. "The Johnson cabin, eh? Ain't that perched on the ridge above the federal highway, just north of here?"

We were there in minutes. The sheriff slowed to a crawl as soon as we emerged from the trees and could see the pretty old log lodge across the meadow. Warm October sun beating down. Tall grass and poppies waving in the light breeze. Not a vehicle in sight. The scene was utterly peaceful.

Hasslebring cruised around the circular drive and pulled off onto a spur so that he could see behind the building. No vehicles there either. He backed up, cranked the wheel, and drove forward to the front of the porch. Then he yanked the short-barreled twelve-gauge that stood upright against the dash out of its clip, stepped out of the cruiser, and pumped a round into the chamber. The door to the Johnson place stood open. Not a sound came from inside.

I hunched by the fender while the sheriff climbed the steps and then stood with his back to the doorjamb. One of the things I learned about Walt Hasslebring that summer, one of the things that helps keep my memory of him so warm, is that he always went in first . . . by himself.

The sheriff turned his head into the open doorway and shouted, "Police! Anybody home?"

Not a sound.

The sheriff disappeared through the doorway, and I followed, coming up behind him as he stood surveying the living room. Empty beer bottles and frozen-food cartons littered the area around the broken-down couch. Cigarette butts were ground out all over the wide fir planks of the floor. The room smelled of smoke and urine.

I walked over to the fireplace and held a hand close to the grate. Faint heat rose from a mound of ash. "Somebody was here last night," I said. "But nobody stoked this fire this morning."

Hasslebring turned without saying anything, walked back into the front hall, and moved on into the dining room, disappearing into the kitchen. When he came back out, he shook his head and started up the stairs, me following. The rest of the place was empty, too.

"Well," the sheriff said as we stood on the porch, looking back over the meadow, "looks like something spooked our boy. Or maybe he just had an itch and decided to move along. You never know with Arnie Dykes."

We stepped off the porch, and I motioned to the sheriff, pointing down. Remember these?" I asked as Hasslebring stepped up beside me. He bent over the tracks Arnie's pickup had left in the dirt.

The sheriff squatted for a closer look. "Ain't those the LT235 tracks we saw up on the Mayfield landing?" he asked. "Are you telling me these was left by that old beater truck Arnie Dykes drives?"

43

A summer's worth of growth almost obscured the rutted track through the woods, and the brush threatened to scrape paint off the Dodge as it lurched slowly along. Marion grabbed the dashboard with both hands and held on as the sedan broke free of the salal and Oregon grape, emerging into the sunlit meadow. The three apple trees standing beyond the ruins of the old homestead already showed fall color. Beyond the open expanse of Puget Sound, Mount Rainier rose in clear October air. The summer had stripped it of snow, leaving only rock and streaks of glacial ice.

I put my arm around Marion, and we sat, taking in the scene. A freighter appeared beyond the headland opposite and churned southwest, its orange hull clashing with the blues and greens that filled the rest of the scene. "Plenty of traffic down the channel toward Olympia," I said. "You'd never get bored sitting by a picture window and rocking your old age away here."

I grabbed the blanket, jumped out of the car, and went around to the passenger side. I opened Marion's door, took her outstretched hand, and lifted her to her feet. She rose straight into my kiss. My hands went to her hips and then slipped around her, pulling rhythmically and kneading the thin cotton of her dress.

When we finally broke the kiss, she stood back a step and smiled. "Old age?" she asked, playfully. "Who's thinking about old age?"

I took her hand and hurried through the tall grass toward the bluff. She grabbed one side of the blanket and helped me spread it, both of us dropping to our knees and flattening it against the grass. We fell onto the plaid wool and pressed against each other, hips thrusting, quivering, and rushing with shaking hands to pull clothes off and roll back and forth, first me on top, then her. We finished with her astride me, hands on my chest and head thrown back, jerking with a moan as she felt each of my spasms. The tension drained from our muscles, and we collapsed next to each other,

We lay in the October sun, languid in utterly relaxed afterglow, until I finally rose on one elbow. "You're gorgeous," I said, looking her up and down. "This is the first time I've ever seen you this way, and you're gorgeous."

She was more womanly than Sandy, a little shorter, with more curves and pillowy softness. Her breasts, rounder and fuller, swayed a little when she moved. Her eyes were bigger and more liquid, the hair between her legs darker and bushier.

She propped herself up on an elbow, too, facing me but looking down, and then up again. "You're gorgeous, too," she said. "I've thought that since the first day I saw you, after you came back to the paper. But being here, like this . . ." She let the thought trail off.

"I remember that day in the darkroom," I said. "Your perfume. Your touch. The warmth of you so close to me. I felt something then, but I had to put a lid on it."

"Me, too. I think I loved you from the first. But I couldn't admit it to myself."

"Well, you can admit it now. And so can I."

*   *   *

The Regulator ticked comfortably. The minute hand clicked into the vertical position, and the old clock gonged three times with the resonance of Big Ben. On cue, the front door opened, and Marion stepped in. I let my hands drop from my Selectric keyboard and looked to where she stood in a halo of luminous autumn sunlight, trying to push the door closed with her hip while she struggled with a heavy cardboard file box. I rushed forward to grab the box. "What's this? And where in God's name have you been?"

It had been four days since that Monday afternoon at the old homestead, and we'd been scrambling almost every minute. On Thursday, only our second production day without Harris, we'd worked sixteen hours straight, somehow managing to get the paper laid out, the type cast, and the cranky old Hoe press running well enough to turn out the entire press run of 3,500 copies.

I took the box from her and eased it onto the front counter. "And what in the hell is this?" I asked.

"Those are the directions," she said. "And you'd better start reading."

"Directions to what?"

"Directions to the new press."

I dropped the box on the counter. "The *what*?"

"The new press." Her hands were on her hips. Her eyes sparkled. "We have a big new printing contract, so we need a new press. Hot type is so yesterday."

I backed through the swinging gate and sat down in my chair. "You're serious, aren't you? What kind of press? Where did you get it?"

Marion stepped to the counter, opened the cardboard file box, and plucked a three-ring binder out of it. She flipped it open to the title page and held it up, facing me. I squinted at the type. "The Goss Suburbanite," it said.

"I've been in Oak Harbor, is where I've been," she said, smirking. "If you'd read that boring old Washington Newspaper Publishers Association bulletin, you would have known that the *News-Times* was upgrading to a Metroliner. That meant this little ol' Suburbanite was on the market. Cheap."

"Cheap is relative. How in God's name are you going to pay for an offset press?"

"A Navy contract is pretty damn good collateral for the Washington Mutual Savings Bank Small-Business Loan Department."

"But Marion, you don't even own the *Echo*. How can you get a loan? And Chesty's sure not in the market for a new press."

"No, he isn't," she said, walking to her desk. She pulled open the top center drawer and grabbed a hefty sheaf of paper. "But Chesty likes the idea of retiring with a steady income. And the Navy contract convinced him that the *Echo* could supply that. So we closed the deal." She dropped the stack of paperwork onto my desk, where it landed with a substantial *thwack*.

I leafed through the first few pages. It dawned on me that I was looking at a real-estate contract, an agreement between Chesty Arnold and some kind of private corporation. "What's this?" I asked.

"The deal. I gave Chesty $10,000 down and agreed to pay him $1,500 a month on the balance. With his Social Security, he'll be fine. In fact, he's thrilled."

Numbers rolled around in my head. The Navy contract would cover Chesty's piece of the action and maybe some of the payment on the press. But salaries? For Marion? For me? Maintenance on the building? Property taxes? All the other expenses that come with running a small business? My God! All that would have to come out of advertising and subscriptions. And unless the town bounced back in a big way, we'd never have the income to cover it. Marion was betting big on the come.

"What did you have to pay for this loan?" I asked.

"Money's not cheap," she said. "Small-business loans are going for nearly 8 percent. But we can refinance as soon as the recession's over and the rates drop."

She was *really* betting on the come. Who knew if interest rates would ever fall again?

My head was swimming. I stood, took the few steps between me and the counter, and flipped through the glossy pages in the three-ring binder.

"Jesus," I said. "You own a newspaper. And you're offset. You've got a goddamn offset press! But Harris is gone—you don't even have a printer. Who's gonna run the damned thing?"

"No, honey," Marion said. "*We've* got a goddamn offset press. And"—she ran her thumbnail up the file folder like Jerry Lee Lewis working a keyboard—"these are the directions. *We're* gonna run the damned thing."

* * *

The ring echoed down the hall. I dashed into the first room, found no telephone, and moved on to the next. That was empty, too. And so was the next, and the next. Still the phone rang. Loud. Insistent. Close. But I couldn't find it.

I rose to an elbow, blinking and shaking off the dream. I reached out, plucked the receiver off the nightstand, and Walt Hasslebring's gravelly voice boomed into my ear. "Tom," he said. "Better get yourself down here to the station house."

My sluggish brain stumbled through an inventory of the reasons the sheriff might be calling me in the middle of the night. "Why?" I rasped. "What's this all about?"

Hasslebring was nothing if not predictable. "All in good time," he said.

I hung up, flipped on the reading light, and flopped on my back. The clock radio read 3:03 a.m.

Front Street was deserted, lit only by the harsh light cascading down from the big sodium-vapor lamps on the utility poles. In the sheriff's office, a deputy looked up from his magazine, pulled his feet off the reception desk, and nodded toward the hall. "They're in the back. The interrogation room. Go on in."

Hasslebring sat across the table, facing the door, his hands cupping a mug of coffee. Another deputy sat to his right, a legal pad in front of him and a ballpoint pen in hand. The woman across the table from the sheriff sat with her back to me. Dirty brown hair hung below the bloody bandage wrapped around her head.

I paused in the doorway. "This little lady's awfully anxious to see you," Hasslebring said to me, raising his mug in the direction of the woman across from him. "Been asking for you for quite some time now."

Moochie Dykes twisted in her seat and looked up at me. A huge purple bruise surrounded one eye. Three deep scratches, crusted with blood, ran across a cheek.

"Got into quite a fracas over at the Grizzly Tavern," Hasslebring said. "Took a pool cue to Missy Lancaster and 'bout killed her. Won't say why."

I slid into the seat next to Moochie, who dropped her head, wobbled, and steadied herself by grabbing the back of her chair. She smelled of beer and vomit.

"Stubby and Missy were playing a game of eight ball," the sheriff said. "Moochie here was pounding 'em back at the bar, by herself. Guess Missy said something. Anyways, Moochie came after her. Whupped her a couple of times with a pool cue before Stubby could pull her off."

Moochie raised her head and looked me in the eyes. "She said, 'There's one of 'em left. Ain't nobody in this town safe long as there's one of 'em left.'"

She slumped in her chair, sobbing. Then she sucked in air and looked back up at me. "Missy Lancaster," she said, "she's from that damn Mayfield crowd. Lars Mayfield—he killed Eddie and Terry.

"And that's what I told her," she said, growing stronger. "'Your Lars killed the twins. Your Lars just gunned 'em down for no reason.'

"Then that Stubby Lancaster, you know what he says? He says, 'No reason! Them fuckers killed the best man in the whole fuckin' county. Them fuckers killed Hal Mayfield.'"

I glanced at Walt Hasslebring. The sheriff was signaling to the deputy, making a scribbling motion with his hand. He silently mouthed the word "write."

Moochie leaned forward and put both hands on my knees. "You put this in your newspaper, Tommy," she said. "You tell everybody."

And then she told me something that burned itself in my brain, incinerating every trace of the arrogant certitude that a young investigative reporter brought to the Big Skookum in the spring of 1981. For more than thirty years, I've reminded myself of that moment every time I found myself believing anything absolutely, anytime I thought I really understood how this world works. That was the moment I learned the value a little humility can bring to journalism, or anything else.

"Eddie and Terry never hurt nobody," Moochie said. "Was Arnie that was the crazy one. Always was. Was Arnie who started the fire, just trying to hide what Eddie and Terry was doing with Lars, stealing them logs up there on the creek. That was all Arnie. Crazy Arnie. Near to burnt the whole Skookum down, Daddy's house and everything."

Hasslebring and I looked away from Moochie and stared hard at each other, the shared realization of what she'd just said sinking in. Arnie Dykes had started the Scatter Creek fire? My God! Hundreds of firefighters. Millions in firefighting costs. Tens of millions in lost timber.

Moochie's blade had made a good bite, but she wasn't quite through her cut. She needed another stroke or two to topple the whole damned tree.

"Was Arnie that messed with Hal's rig," she said. "Just thought he was helpin' his brothers, that's all. The twins, they was mad as hell when they found out. Wasn't them.

"Stupid Lars Mayfield. He killed the wrong Dykes."

44

After the deputy led Moochie from the interrogation room, Hasslebring and I had sat silently for two or three minutes, absorbing the enormity of Arnie Dykes's crimes. Hasslebring was the first to speak. "All of a sudden, that little son of a bitch is not just a tweaked-out twerp with a hot-tempered meth cook on his tail," he said gravely. "Ten minutes ago I didn't give a rat's ass about Arnie Dykes. Didn't care whether Roy Hammer found him and used his ax handle to drive him right into the ground. But Little Miss Moochie has shined a whole new light on the runt of her fucked-up family."

He raised an eyebrow and let a half smile creep onto his face. "My," he said, "you do have a way of getting that young lady to talk. You want to share the secrets of your persuasive powers?"

I started to say something and realized he was pulling my chain. But he was serious in what he said next. "So Arnie Dykes is suddenly our number one priority. Got any ideas about where we might find him?"

The possibilities were limited. Either Roy Hammer had spooked Arnie badly enough to run him right out of Klahowya County or he was still somewhere in the Skookum. If he was gone, we wouldn't find him until he was inevitably, somehow and somewhere, booked into somebody else's jail. If he was still around the Skookum, he was at Rush Creek, his dad's house, or somewhere we didn't know about.

"We only got two options we can check out," the sheriff said. "And both of them is out the federal highway."

The sun, rising behind Mount Rainier, cast an enormous triangular shadow that reached out across the foothills, across Puget Sound, and into the parking lot next to city hall, pointing right at Walt Hasslebring and me as we climbed into his cruiser. The Big Skookum shimmered in the pink light as we raced along a deserted Front Street and up the Longmont Grade. Two patrol cars, each carrying two deputies, followed us.

"Reckon we might as well try the Johnson cabin first," Hasslebring said. "Arnie knows that Hammer knows how to find his way back to both there and the Dykes place. So it's six of one, a half dozen of the other."

We spotted Arnie's old pickup when we broke out of the trees and onto the Johnson meadow. A wisp of smoke curled out of the lodge chimney. The front door, as before, stood open. Hasslebring picked up his radio microphone and instructed the deputies behind us.

The sheriff slowed to walking speed as he drove around the circular drive, his head turning both directions and his eyes flitting across the early morning landscape. Once more, he pulled the cruiser alongside the building to check the rear. When he saw nothing there, he backed out, just as before, but this time he continued in reverse a hundred feet back the way we'd come, right to where the two patrol cars had stopped. The sheriff pulled the twelve-gauge out of its clip, opened his door, and turned to me before he climbed out. "This time," he said, his voice low, even, and intense, "stay in the goddamned car."

I did as I was told, sitting anxiously as the sheriff motioned his deputies forward and deployed them around the house. Then, with one deputy at his side, he repeated his routine at the front door. He apparently got no response this time either, and after a wait of only seconds he stepped into the entry hall. The deputy followed.

Two or three anxious minutes passed before Hasslebring reappeared, alone, in the doorway. He raised his cupped hand to his mouth and shouted, "All clear. Y'all can come on in."

Arnie Dykes lay on the living-room floor, sprawled face up in front of the big stone fireplace. His pump-action shotgun lay next to him. A red stain the size of a basketball filled the front of his T-shirt, and drying streams of blood ran in several directions across the uneven floor. His eyes had turned completely up into his head, showing only white.

"He went down fightin'," the sheriff said, pointing at the three empty shotgun cartridges lying on the floor to Arnie's right. Then he pointed to a trail of blood that ran between Arnie's feet and the front door and said, "It looks like he gave a pretty good account of hisself, too."

* * *

The sun was high in the sky, shining straight up Front Street from due south, when the sheriff finally turned into the lot behind Benny's and dropped me at the bottom of my steps. "You sure you don't want me to send a deputy over?" he asked. "We got one crazy in the bag, but we still got a hothead on the loose."

"I'll be all right," I said. "I just want a beer and a nap, and I don't need one of your guys standing here watching while I do that. Besides, you're practically across the street."

"You got any protection?"

I nodded.

"Keep it close," the sheriff said, and motioned for me to get on my way. "And lock the goddamn door," he shouted after me. I wearily climbed the steps, did as I was told with the door, and went straight to the refrigerator to grab a Heidelberg. Then I slumped at the kitchen table and spotted the red message light on my answering machine. I rewound the tape, punched "play," and heard Marion's voice. Where was I? she asked. She was worried about me.

I dialed her new number at the cabin she'd rented. I could hear the relief in her voice when she heard me . . . and the growing concern as I told her where I'd been and what I'd seen. "I'm coming right over," she said.

"Thanks, babe," I said. "I want to see you right away. But I'm wasted. And I stink. Let me grab a shower and a couple of hours in the sack. Then I'll come straight to your place."

She protested, but gave in. The minute I toweled off from the shower, I fell into bed. I must have been asleep in seconds.

The sound of the door smashing open brought me bolt upright. Midafternoon sunlight streamed in past the shattered jamb, and standing there, with face and arms bloodied by a blast of birdshot, stood Roy Hammer.

* * *

His arms hung at his sides. And in his right fist was a large, black semiautomatic pistol. Hammer took three steps forward, raised the gun, and pointed it at the center of my chest, his hand steady as an old-growth stump. "You and Arnie Dykes," he said evenly, "have managed to turn this quiet little corner of creation into one major mess. Everybody was doing just fine until the two of you started raising a ruckus." He spoke quietly, evenly, with none of the rough edges that colored most speech in the Skookum. He sounded like just what he was, somebody raised in a blue-collar neighborhood who received a fine education and tried to hide his origins by enunciating every syllable. Like me.

"I've just been reporting the news."

"If that were true, I wouldn't be here. Most hick newspapermen would just be reporting the news, and that wouldn't have been a problem. You've been digging like Woodward and Bernstein. And that *is* a problem."

He took another step forward. "Now the question is," he said, "whether I can trust you to go back to reporting the news and stay off my case"—he paused for obvious effect—"or whether I need to make sure you never write another word."

The instant became an eternity. I pictured Arnie Dykes lying on his back, coals smoldering in the fireplace behind him. I pictured Don Dykes, his head pulped and his teeth lying in the dirt next to him. I thought of the sheriff offering to lend me a deputy.

Footsteps clattered on the stairs outside. Hammer turned slowly toward the door, the semiautomatic still leveled at chest height. Whoever was coming had to climb two full flights of old wooden steps. Hammer had enough time to land a trout.

The footfalls skipped a beat on the landing, then pounded up the last flight. Walt Hasslebring lunged onto the porch, his revolver drawn, turned into the doorway, saw Hammer's pistol pointed at him, and froze.

Why Roy Hammer didn't shoot in that instant I'll never know, but he and the sheriff stood there in tableau while I reached under the apple crate next to the bed. I pulled out my father's .38, pointed it at the center of Hammer's back, and cocked it. Hammer heard the click and started to turn. The sheriff's eyes shifted from Hammer's pistol to mine, and he dropped to the floor. Before Hammer had moved more than an inch or two, I put three .38 slugs between his shoulder blades. At that range, every round was in the black.

The meth cook dropped like a fir falling to a logger's saw, the only sound the thump of his big body hitting the linoleum. The sheriff lay motionless on his elbows, his revolver thrust out in front of him in a two-handed grip held a foot from Roy Hammer's ear. He held the pose for a couple of seconds, saw that the man in front of him would never move again, and pulled himself up onto his knees. I dropped the .38 to my side. The sheriff struggled to his feet.

"Guess I owe you another one," he said.

"Guess I owe you more. How in the hell did you know he was here?"

"Now you don't think I'd leave you up here snoozing all alone with an asshole like this"—he waved his revolver at the corpse in front of him—"on the loose, do you? Hell, I had Clancy Howard watching the street out front from the time I left you alone here."

I felt the adrenaline then. The revolver in my hand shook. My knees felt weak. "Then what in the hell took you so long?" I demanded.

"Ah shit," the sheriff said. "I underestimated this son of a bitch. He parked all the way up by the mill, cut around behind the *Echo*, and came through the woods. Clancy didn't spot him until he stepped out into your parkin' lot."

"I'm not sure he was going to do anything," I said, hearing the shakiness in my own voice. "He might have just made his threats and left it at that. Maybe nothing would have happened."

"Yeah," the sheriff said, "maybe not. But one thing's for sure. Nuthin's gonna happen now."

45

I stood shin deep in the Takamak, leaning back against a big cedar log, resting my lower back. We'd been fishing most of the day, starting far up into the headwaters of the river and working our way back here to the Cable Hole. But Mark still showed no signs of slowing. He crouched low and worked the big riffle at the head of the hole intently with a sidearm cast that sent his fly low along the water and dropped it lightly into the foam just below the rapids. He'd already taken three big rainbows from the hole, and I figured the ruckus had spooked whatever remained. "C'mon, diehard," I shouted over the sound of tumbling water. "These fish are down. Me, too. Buy you a beer."

"Couple more casts," Mark countered, his eyes fixed on the upper pool. "Gonna be the last of the year."

His graphite rod arced deeply, and the line looped back thirty feet and then forward, three times, in a series of perfect false casts, before the elk-hair caddis settled gently onto the foam and twisted down into the pool. A big rainbow darted straight up from the bottom, engulfed it, and headed back down. Mark simply raised the rod, and the fish set the hook itself. Then it quickly resurfaced, bouncing down the pool in a series of acrobatic leaps, rolls, and somersaults. Mark backed down onto the gravel bar and brought the rainbow to him in ankle-deep water. He bent down, grabbed the hook, and released the fish without touching it, a move calculated to help the trout survive.

"You're quite a sportsman for a redneck," I hollered, pushing off the cedar and slogging through the water toward Mark. We splashed along the gravel bar together and clambered up the bank into the clearing.

"Rednecks understand more about fish than college boys ever will," Mark said with a smirk. "So don't bust my balls about technique.

"Now what was that about a beer?"

We sat on the tailgate of Mark's pickup, pulling off our waders, breaking down our rods. "Season's over," Mark said. "Trout are done. Ain't nothing keeping me here now."

"You don't have to leave. At least not yet."

"We'll see. Southland might start looking pretty good once the rain starts and the state checks quit comin'."

"Either way, you have time for a brewski before you go. How about that new lodge that opened down on the canal? Hear it's quite the joint. I can scope it out, ask a few questions, and get what I need for a little feature."

"Jesus, Tommy! Can't we go anywhere without you workin'? We have the damned day off. We're fishin'."

"We *were* fishing. Now we're drinking. And you might as well be drinking with the swells, sitting at a table on the deck, looking out at Hood Canal. C'mon. It's just a couple of miles up the highway."

We stowed our gear, climbed into the pickup, and headed down the Takamak River road. Scraggly third-growth fir and meadows dotted with river-smoothed boulders streamed past my open window. My calves and thighs ached pleasantly after the hours of climbing, stumbling, and fighting the current. I propped my elbow in the window and rested my head against my palm, utterly relaxed. Nowhere to go. Nothing to do. I couldn't remember feeling so content.

"Awful quiet over there," Mark said.

"Nothing to say."

"That's a good thing. And I notice that when you do have sumthin' to say these days, you say it nice and relaxed like. Christ. When you first come home, you sounded like a goddamn city boy for sure. Rat-a-tat-tat. Words pourin' out like BBs outta the box. Drove me crazy."

We reached U.S. 101 and turned north along Hood Canal. The new resort nestled on the lower side of the highway, stretched along the beach, all low-slung buildings in natural wood and cedar-shake roofs. Mark pulled into a winding driveway and parked the pickup in a landscaped lot by the main lodge entrance. "Looks pretty good," he said. "Guess they left their Taco Time designers back home in California."

"C'mon," I said, climbing out of the truck. "The bar's gotta be on the canal side." We pushed through carved wooden doors with leaping cedar salmon for handles, walked past the sheaves of corn, cutouts of black cats, and jack-o-lanterns that cluttered the lobby, and strolled out onto a deck that ran the width of the building. A few couples, Seattleites by the look of the epaulettes on the men's sports shirts and the extra-short shorts on the women, sat at tables taking in the view of the canal and sipping white wine. Mark and I grabbed a table along the railing and ordered Heidelbergs from the teenaged blonde who hurried up to us. No Heidelberg, she said, with a superior air, only imports. Oh, I said, is Mexican good enough? She looked confused. I ordered two Coronas.

"You suppose any of these knuckleheads think it really is a canal?" Mark asked.

"Can't imagine anybody would think anything this wide, with a shoreline like this, is a real canal," I said. "Besides, most folks have seen pictures of a fjord. And most folks know this is glacier country. Glaciers. Fjords. Who wouldn't figure it out?"

"Dumb-shit tourists," Mark said, waving his hand at the couples scattered around the deck. "Look pretty clueless to me." The blonde arrived with our Coronas. Mark waved off the glasses, and we tipped the clear-glass bottles back. A shrimp boat chugged by a hundred yards offshore, headed north toward Hoodsport.

"Don't knock the tourists," I said. "You see any loggers here, spending money? This here's our future, if we have a future. This place will draw a few thousand bodies a year out this way. They'll have plenty of company, too—more and more folks from the cities, wanting to get out here, to the Olympics, to Hood Canal. Lots of 'em will drive up and down 101, and some might stop in Bent Fir."

"Yeah," Mark said, "maybe Jimmy can rent his boats." He laughed and raised his beer.

"And," I said, raising mine, "maybe you can find a job."

We emptied our Coronas and ordered another round. More tables filled. Some couples ordered dinner. Behind us, the sun dropped behind the Olympics, and the autumn light reddened on the canal. Beyond the deck rail, a thick patch of salal rattled, and I turned my head. An old man stepped out of the shrubbery, holding a rake. He scanned the deck lazily, spotted me, and shuffled up. I stood and leaned over the railing. "Henry!" I said. "Henry Logan! Great to see you. What are you doing here?"

"Got me a little job," Logan said. "Come on up here three days a week. Pull some weeds. Rake a little. Sweep a little. Get me some beer money."

"Yeah," I said. "Good for you. Living off the tourist economy."

"And my guvmint check. And that nice little chunk of cash the Navy give me. But I like workin'. Gets me out of the house. Gets a little lonely down there. Up here, all kinda interesting folk coming through.

"Besides," he said, "the girls . . . they like it here." He looked back at the shrubbery and made a clucking noise.

I looked at the salal. Four hens came strolling out of the shadows, pecking at the bark ground cover, and cackled their way toward Logan.

*   *   *

The sound of tires on gravel filled the open front door, and I looked up from my keyboard. The big motor home rolled to a stop, taking up half the parking lot. Marion followed me onto the *Echo*'s porch. Dad sat at the PacWest's wheel, beaming. He pulled the driver-side window back and leaned out. "Well," he said, "you youngsters enjoy the rain. We old farts are off to Arizona."

The passenger-side door popped open, and Mom stepped around the front of the big rig. She marched up, threw her arms around me, and said, "Oh, Tommy, the summer flew by. We're going to miss you so." She pulled back, her arms extended to my shoulders, and looked at Marion. "You take good care of my boy, you hear. Make sure he gets a decent meal now and then. And make sure he takes care of my house."

Marion laughed. "I can't cook like you, Mrs. Dawson," she said. "But I'll make sure he keeps an eye on the house."

I stepped close to the motor home, reached up, and grasped my father's hand. "I'll miss you, Dad," I said. "Especially when the fall chinook run."

"Yeah, well," my father said, reaching down to my shoulder with his left hand, "catch a few for me. And take care of the boat. Don't forget to put oil in the damned gas, will ya?"

"You call," I said. "Keep us posted on where you are and stuff." My mother climbed back into the PacWest; her head appeared behind Dad's, and she waved. Dad put the motor home in drive. Marion and I waved as the big vehicle cruised up Front Street toward the Longmont Grade.

We'd just turned back toward the porch when I noticed the little man standing in the shadow of the firs that flanked the parking-lot entrance. Clean-shaven, balding, slightly built, wearing a short-sleeved blue work shirt and jeans. He held a small suitcase in one hand. No car was in sight.

The little man smiled. "Help you?" I asked.

"Name's Oscar," the man said, stepping forward and extending a hand. "Oscar Bowman."

"What can we do for you, Oscar?" Marion asked.

"Hear you just bought an old Suburbanite."

"Yeah," I said, a little suspiciously. "That's so."

"Well," Oscar said, reaching into his pocket, pulling out his wallet, and extracting a ragged blue card, "here's my union card. Expired now. Don't need no union wages no more. Can work for whatever you can pay. But I'm a printer all right. Yes I am. Good one, too. An offset man. And I know Suburbanites. Yes I do. Been working on 'em ever since Goss hatched the damn things."

* * *

"Let's peek in the Thriftway and see what they're up to," Marion said. She grabbed my hand and pulled me across Front Street. We strolled down the new sidewalk and stepped up onto the fresh lumber that had replaced the porch decking across the facade of the old store. The plywood was down off the windows, and we peered inside.

"Myrtle Johnson says the new owner's from Seattle," Marion said. "A Boeing guy. Some big shot who's tired of the rat race and wants his own business."

"Oh," I said, scanning the store's gutted interior. "Well, running a store isn't exactly my idea of avoiding the rat race."

"Myrtle actually met the man on the ferry. He thinks Bent Fir's going to start growing like Belfair. He's going to give this place a real rustic look. Old-timey Northwest. Touristy."

"We'd better find the guy and get a story before the men in the white coats come for him," I said, pulling Marion along the porch and back toward the sidewalk. "C'mon. I'm thirsty."

"I think he's right," Marion said. "Look at a map. The Navy's beefing up Bangor. The new resort's open on the canal. Traffic's up on 101. The eastside cities are growing. Even Olympia. We're surrounded by activity. Once the recession ends, things will really take off."

We ambled down Front, soaking in the view of the Big Skookum in the gap between the old Thriftway building and the Grizzly. Already, at six thirty, autumn twilight had darkened the water, and a damp chill hung in the air. Low ocean clouds streamed overhead from the southwest, the classic winter weather pattern, and the season's first wood smoke drifted up from the shacks along the water. "That smells good," Marion said. "It's been a long, hot summer. I'm ready for a little cozy Northwest hunkering down."

"You'll get plenty," I said, pulling open the door to the Spar and stepping into the warm buzz of a Saturday-night crowd. Orange and black paper chains hung from the ceiling, each table held a small pumpkin, and three manikins dressed in ghost outfits stood on the corner bandstand holding toy guitars. We greeted Henry Anderson, polishing glasses behind the bar, and headed for the window booth.

Jimmy Winthrop—decked out in a red devil costume, complete with horns—scooted across the bench to make room for us. "Happy Halloween!" he said with a cheerful slur that suggested he was a few beers ahead of us. Benny Brill, Marvin Dervish, and Chesty Arnold wore no costumes, but they enthusiastically raised their glasses.

"How's the new printer working out?" Chesty asked.

"Great," Marion said. "He knows that Suburbanite like he was born in one. We're already up and running."

"Glad it's you," Chesty said. "I've done my time worrying about presses and deadlines and this damned town."

Henry arrived at the table with beers for Marion and me. "Well, lookee here," he said. "The Front Street mafia. Guess we got ourselves a Chamber of Commerce."

"Marion says the town's on the upswing," I said, raising my Rainier. "New store. Tourists coming."

"And my marina," Jimmy Winthrop said. "New boats should be here in a month or two. Plenty of time for spring chinook."

"Yep," Benny said. "All we gotta do is get folks off the highway, down the hill, and into town. I'll sell 'em the fishin' gear, Jimmy here will find 'em the fish, and Henry will help 'em celebrate."

"And I'll part-out their cars when they wreck 'em after that," Marvin said, raising a laugh around the table.

"Well," I said, "We've already got a pretty good Fourth of July celebration. Maybe we should chip in for some fireworks and stage a funky little parade."

* * *

Marion propped herself on one elbow, watching from the old Pendleton blanket at the edge of the bank as I picked my way through the barnacles along the shoreline. The first of November, and that year's skookum run of autumn sun still held. I marveled that we'd spent our lunch hour on a picnic blanket instead of listening to rain beating down on a roof.

The tide had ebbed, exposing the life that crept and dug, usually unseen, along almost every Puget Sound beach. Anemones swayed in the gentle waves. Starfish crept across the bottom with the imperceptible pace of an hour hand, feeling their way toward some hapless oyster or cockle. The necks of geoducks protruded from the gravel, only to suck back into their deep holes as the giant clams sensed my footfalls.

I spotted a sun star at the edge of the water and picked it up, its multitude of legs radiating around a deep-purple body like a child's drawing of its namesake in the sky. I turned toward Marion and held it up, dripping, in two hands over my head. "My sun shines for you," I shouted.

Marion stirred from the lingering languor of our lovemaking and sat up. She cupped her hands around her mouth and shouted back. "The sun's about done with shining, birthday boy. The weatherman says the rain starts tomorrow."

"And once it starts, it'll keep up for eight months."

"C'mon back. I have a birthday present for you."

"I already got my present," I hollered with a self-satisfied smirk. "Besides," I added, "I'm too old to climb up the bank." Then I lowered the sun star, flipped it backhanded into the water like a Frisbee, and crunched my way through the barnacles toward her.

I reached the six-foot bank, grabbed a drooping limb from one of the old apple trees, and pulled myself upward, scrambling for footholds. A blackberry vine snagged my bare ankle and stripped a ribbon of skin off it. "Damn," I said. "You're such a goddamn romantic. We're out here in the stickers when we could be in my bed. Or yours."

She laughed, stood, and extended a hand down to me. "C'mon. Just because you're thirty doesn't mean you have to turn into a fuddy-duddy. It's beautiful here today. And this is our place."

I grabbed her hand, she pulled, and I stepped up into the meadow. The autumn-gold grass, full length after a summer of growth, almost obscured the heap of weathered lumber that marked the site of the old homestead. Apples, puny, worm-eaten, and rotting, littered the ground, yellow jackets buzzing between them. Marion dropped down on the blanket, cross-legged, and I did the same, facing her. "I really do have a present," she said as she leaned forward and gave me a peck on the lips. She reached into the cloth beach bag at her side, pulled out an envelope wrapped in a red ribbon, handed it to me, and settled back expectantly.

I pulled the ribbon off, tore the envelope open, and shook out a sheaf of papers. I looked up at her. "What's this?"

"It's my gift," Marion said.

"But what is it?"

"It's a contract."

"What kind of contract?"

"A partnership agreement."

"What do you mean, a partnership?"

"A business partnership, dummy. It makes you my partner. It makes you half owner of the *Echo*."

I sat silent, looking past her at the bay, Mount Rainier rising against the horizon. Then I handed her the paperwork.

"My God, Marion. I can't take this. I haven't done anything to earn it. What kind of partnership is that? It's your money in the *Echo*, not mine. Nothing that one-sided could ever work."

"Nothing one-sided about it. You're the journalist. Look at what you've done this summer. One terrific story after another. You're the one who kept this newspaper afloat. You're the one who's going to keep this town afloat. Nope"—she handed the partnership agreement back—"you earned everything in this.

"Besides," she added, "I don't have much money in the *Echo*. Mostly what I have is debt." She broke into a broad smile. "And you're more than welcome to half of that."

"Look," I said slowly, "if I do this, I've got to pay you back. At least pay you back for the equity you've got in the place."

"Oh, you will. I have that all figured out." She grinned and leaned forward.

"Oh yeah?" I said, smiling in spite of myself. "How so?"

She swept one hand in a slow, broad circle around her head, taking in the scene around us—the encircling firs, the meadow, the ruined homestead, the old apple trees, the broad view of the bay, far shores, and mountain.

"This," she said. "You're going to buy us this. And build us a house here."

And I did, of course. The house we still live in, forty years on. The house we leave each weekday morning, headed to work at our newspaper.